THE BRASS AGE

Slobodan Šnajder

THE BRASS AGE

Translated from the Croatian by
Celia Hawkesworth

First published in Zagreb, Croatia as *Doba Mjedi* in 2015
by TIM Press

First published in the English language in 2024 by
Mountain Leopard Press
An imprint of HEADLINE PUBLISHING GROUP

1

Cataloguing in Publication Data is available from the British Library

ISBN (HB) 978-1-914495-22-9
ISBN (eBook) 978-1-914495-23-6

Typeset in Sabon LT by CC Book Production

Printed and bound in Great Britain by Clays Ltd, Elcograf S.p.A.

Headline's policy is to use papers that are natural, renewable and recyclable
products and made from wood grown in well-managed forests and other
controlled sources. The logging and manufacturing processes are expected
to conform to the environmental regulations of the country of origin.

This book was published with the financial support of
the Ministry of Culture and Media of the Republic of Croatia.

HEADLINE PUBLISHING GROUP
An Hachette UK Company
Carmelite House
50 Victoria Embankment
London EC4Y 0DZ

www.headline.co.uk
www.hachette.co.uk

For my Father and Mother

And the Lord sent fiery serpents among the people . . .
and much people of Israel died. Therefore the people
came to Moses and said: We have sinned, for we have
spoken against the Lord and against thee; pray unto
the Lord that he take away the serpents from us. And
Moses prayed for the people. And the Lord said unto
Moses, Make thee a fiery serpent, and set it upon a
pole . . . And Moses made a serpent of brass and put
it on a pole, and it came to pass, that if a serpent had
bitten any man, when he beheld the serpent of brass,
he lived.

Numbers, Chapter 21, 6–9

I have plucked nothing out of the air.

Władysław Stanisław *Reymont*

A civilisation brought up on punishment and obedi-
ence gave us the First World War, and in the Second
the blind following of those obsessed with belief in the
rat-catcher leader.

Czesław Miłosz

I

Transylvania

The Pied Piper of Hamelin

A hungry year in Germany.

Heavy rains, everything rotted. The potato had not yet been recognised as a friend of the poor, some grew it for its attractive flowers. The wheat had been battered by storms. And wars had played their part. A soldier doesn't sow, he eats. The barns gaped empty, there was no livestock to be heard, but the houses whimpered with hunger. The poor have no friends.

In the autumn evenings, the men sat by an oil-lamp, silent, smoking pipes, the women cut up cabbage. Cabbage was all there was and everyone was heartily sick of it.

On one of those evenings, into the circle of feeble light stepped a stranger. No-one could remember afterwards who had let him into the house, or even heard any knocking. He was of medium height or rather less than that. When he removed his hat and bowed deeply, his forehead gleamed. His face was muzzle-like: he had a snout rather than a nose, and whiskers too. It could have been a human face, of rather long profile. But everyone vouched for the snout. People will always vilify a stranger. In that village, since the end of the war, they had not seen anyone who had not been born there. Whether it was a muzzle or a human face with a protruding nose remained undecided; but there was complete agreement that something about the stranger's appearance made them recoil, not knowing why. But there was also a kind of thrill because he was not ordinary.

Starvation was tedious. The stranger brought something disturbing into this house. Boding well?

One of the more prominent figures in the village, certainly one of the burlier villagers, seized an axe from behind the stove, another grabbed his hand.

"Can't you see this gentleman wants to tell us something?"

The stranger bowed deeply to his defender, drew himself up (to the end of their days some of those present persisted in their assertion that he folded his tail and pushed it into his trousers) and then began to speak:

"Good people! Allow me to address you in the name of my master, whose faithful servant I am. I would do anything for him, so were my master to say: 'Go to the stream and submerge yourself,' I'd do it at once. My master is well acquainted with your distress, I have come on his instruction to offer you salvation."

The women clambered over the mountains of uncut cabbage to get closer and sat on the floor.

The stranger bowed again.

"Look around you: nothing but misery and suffering. No grain in the stores, the barns are empty, what livestock there was has been slaughtered, plague has come to the village from over the hills. The potatoes are black, the gruel poisonous.

"I know that others have come here before me on the same business. I know there are those who journey through the German lands stealing children and the Gypsies are blamed. Everyone throughout the German lands knows about the pied piper who slyly deceived the townsfolk of Hamelin in Lower Saxony and stole all their children, who vanished, quite simply vanished, in the mountains . . . Ah, what a weighty slander is that!"

. . . here the stranger waved his hand in one of his ceremonial gestures . . .

"Good people! Whoever heard of a mountain gaping open like a wolf's jaws?"

"Whoever heard of a rat talking!" interrupted the oldest peasant who on his deathbed still affirmed that the stranger was a rat, albeit very large, something like a super-rat.

"Someone has to speak up. You're all just suffering silently. If there was a real man among you, he would understand what I am trying to tell you. You need a Leader!"

"We know that, in Hamelin, near Hanover, a travelling charlatan promised to rid them of rats, and then he lured their children away with his playing and they were never heard of again. He should have been cut down with an axe."

"It's a sad story," the stranger said. "Every story has two endings: one is told at the end of a hardworking day ploughing and digging. The other is told on God's day."

"Tell us the first ending."

"Death, of course, but you can die anywhere."

"And the Sunday ending?"

"Transylvania."

None of those present had ever heard of that land.

There was a silence in the room, which spread under the other roofs as well. The whole village was listening.

"I ask you to listen, good people, not to interrupt, for I will lose my thread, and if I lose my thread, you too will be lost."

The one who had at first wanted to leap at him seized the axe again.

"Good people," the stranger bowed, "listen to what I have to say, and then attack me if you are intent upon killing a stranger.

That's always easy. But why, when I'm bringing you good news, a new gospel?"

"There are legions of such folk. At market you can buy good news for a trifle from a hare or a bearded lady."

"But you know nothing, so you don't know where fortune awaits you. Beyond the seven hills, of which you have some knowledge, there are many more you don't know. Between them flows a great river along which, with a little luck, it is possible to sail at no great cost. When it leaves the mountains behind, the river flows through a valley: the soil is black and so potent that a week after casting seed, you can harvest it. It's on the other side of the great forests that belong to no-one and where no-one will have you birched for an armful of firewood. There, far away, lies Transylvania. There is the life for you. Here there is no life, you will all perish, as will all the rats with you, you don't need a pied piper of Hamelin to steal your youth; you'll perish from hunger or be battered to death by drunks in uniform."

There was silence. All that could be heard was the rain, which, yet again that hungry year, was sheeting down.

"If this land is so good, why does no-one cultivate it?"

"You hardly need a plough there."

It was quiet under the roof, as though the rain too was stilled.

"If the land is so good, it can't be that it belongs to no-one."

The stranger nodded. "Of course. All good things in this world have an owner."

"If you ask me," someone said, "this fellow is raising an army. It would be best," he whispered, "to take him out and give him a good hiding."

Although this was whispered, the stranger heard the whispering.

"At least let me tell you everything to the end. My master has many estates in Transylvania. There's no hunger there, no cold."

"But if the earth is so productive, why doesn't your master himself work those fields?"

At that point some of the villagers decided there might be something in what this man was saying.

Two parties formed under this roof. Some were in favour of beating up the stranger behind the house, others of giving him a chance. The more prominent men withdrew into the next room to decide what to do.

When they returned from behind the wall of cabbages, the stranger said: "Good people! I can see that you are at odds. That is why such great misfortune has come upon you, why your stomachs are protesting. You need a leader. Even one you would kill on the spot would be better than none. I can't serve you for that purpose, for I am myself led. But you will find no-one better than my master, I guarantee, for I have not found one myself. May I now take my leave?"

That was approved because the voting had been inconclusive.

"Get ready. When the time comes, you will know more. Then, not before, I will be back!"

The stranger vanished, but, they all swore, not through the door. It seemed he had disappeared through a hole in the wall no-one had ever spotted before. One might have thought that he was like an idea from the past. It did not occur to anyone that this stranger could have come from the future. Ideas, even the most terrible ones, know no impediments. They usually do not show their true colours, they pass through walls, they travel fast. "I will be back!" – the words with which the stranger had departed went on ringing in the villagers' ears. They could not decide whether that was a threat or a promise of good fortune.

Transylvania? A land beyond seven mountains? On the other side of the forests?

In the judgment of the sharpest minds present, that must be a long way away, somewhere at the very edge of the Earth. From that edge it would not be difficult to leap into nothingness, but then where was good fortune? That would be like – drowning.

The way all the rats of Hamelin drowned. Admittedly, only for the unwelcome visitors to appear the next day in a different town, so the whole sham could begin again. That piper of Hamelin was a villain, smeared with all possible greases, painted all possible colours. But the young are gullible and no-one can ever be taught.

The saga of the stranger, perhaps a rat that spoke with a human voice, spread at once through the German lands at the speed thoughts travel. But it vanished as soon as the young sap in the fruit trees began to rise, as soon as the new corn began to sprout.

The Imperial Envoy

A new hungry year – 1769 – since the birth of the Saviour. The Kempf family too were hungry, including the young Georg Kempf, born into its bosom. He was agile and handsome, with skilful hands. He had worked for a while as an apprentice to a wheelwright, but then returned to his father's house because hands were needed on the land. This meant he had half-learned his craft. It was time for him to be married, but that autumn there had been no wedding feasts: what could be put on the table for the guests?

Nevertheless, the Kempfs decided to send marriage brokers to one of the village girls. She was not among the ugliest and had a dowry of sorts. But something was drawing young Kempf into the larger world. He got it into his head that he was born for something better.

It was raining heavily when a stranger knocked at the door. Had it not been raining, they would not have let him in at this hour, though their dogs were quiet. Besides, he was very polite; and he had the additional recommendation of the uniform of an imperial official.

The stranger bowed and introduced himself:

"I have been sent from Vienna! I come by order of her Imperial Majesty, bearing papers from the Vienna Chancellery."

They brought out what they had to offer, which was almost

nothing. They were not afraid because many houses in the neighbourhood had recently had similar visits.

The man declined the plate offered him, saying he was not hungry, but they clearly were, terribly hungry, he said, that was obvious.

"There is misery and pain under this roof. How much land do you have?"

"Little," replied old Kempf. "And whatever we sow is trampled by the masters of the village when they go hunting hares."

"Don't you be hares. Be foxes and wolves. Do something with your lives. It's high time."

"Why? Has the plague come over the mountains again? Are they preparing for war at court? We will survive."

"Perhaps you will survive, but why should you not live? Why rot away here, suffering shortages and the wilfulness of your masters ... Do they molest your women?"

"No," old Kempf frowned, "not now."

"The count can't be up to it anymore."

"He's on his last legs. But then his sons will come from Paris and it will all start again."

The villagers were silent.

"And a new war is on its way, that's true."

"Anything but that!" cried old Kempf.

"But here's good news for you, a new gospel: Her Majesty Empress Maria Theresa wishes to settle her frontier lands. She knows of your troubles."

"That she knows the peasants' troubles is not something we would dare believe. How is the Empress?"

"The Empress is sorrowful."

"Whoever heard of an empress being sorrowful?"

"How would you feel if you had to look at fields filled with weeds, empty barns, burnt ruins where houses once stood . . ."

"That would be sad to see."

"Well, that's why she's sorrowful."

"You say that the earth there is good, that it is easily ploughed and fertile. So why is no-one cultivating it?"

"At last one of you shows some sense. It was cultivated until yesterday by the Turks."

"And they no longer wish to?"

"They would, but they have been driven out. And now no-one is there. It is a while since the great commander Eugen of Saxony celebrated his victories there. The fields are overgrown, the roofs collapsed. Even the graveyards are disappearing. Those lands are now the possessions of the Empress. Be her colonisers!"

"How could I, a sack of old bones?" said old Kempf.

"Let the youngsters go. Once things go well for them, when they have feathered their nest, they will summon you."

"If the count's servants could hear what's being said under this roof, they would beat the life out of us."

"The Empress will watch over you. She is the wisest ruler the world has ever seen. You will journey down the great river called the Danube, and that can be done at little cost. We will pay for your transport."

"Where is that land?" the young Kempf finally asked, already half-decided to let himself be led by the envoy.

"Beyond seven mountains, on the other side of the great forests: Transylvania."

"Do milk and honey flow there, is that the land of Canaan? The Promised Land?"

"I do not promise you milk and honey, and countries are called by whatever names they have. But I vow to you, as I stand here in the trappings of the Empress' loyal servant, that where I am taking you anyone who works honestly in the sweat of his brow, and who lives a decent life, will live well and in relative plenty. Vienna is giving every coloniser land for a house, an individual household plot, a field, a plough and a cow . . . as I've said, she will settle the cost of the raft . . . A priest will be appointed to every village."

"She'll give us land, a plough and a cow?" exclaimed the young Kempf. They had eaten their own cow a month before. "And a priest?" A cow was far more important than a priest, he thought.

"And what land! You spit into it, and in a week, you'll be scything and harvesting. The court will turn a blind eye to tithes for the first five years, until the colonisers have found their feet. In other words, you will not pay tax."

"Who could believe such miracles!" old Kempf protested. "One needs strength for belief, my good sir."

The imperial envoy stood up.

"Where are you going, sir, in this rain?"

"To your neighbours. There is nothing better than a neighbour settling next to his old neighbour."

"We've said nothing as yet," said old Kempf.

"Look around you. Consider what awaits you here. And how things could be over there. When the time comes, you will know more."

"Things could not be worse," said young Kempf, and the imperial servant looked at him as his acquisition. His earnings were counted in souls.

Two weeks after the imperial envoy's visit, the Kempfs were sitting round their oak table after the evening meal, if what they had eaten could be called that. The men were smoking pipes, the women cleaning cabbage, the children, those tousle-haired little monkeys, hunting lice under the table.

Young Kempf was the most lost in thought.

The evening was passing in almost complete silence. Mice could be heard scratching in the wall, and also the rat running wild in the larder, where there was virtually nothing stored. It was in fact beginning to lose faith in humans, a fatal condition for any rat. It had been raining relentlessly for five days, a black cloud had settled on the gable of the house like a saddle, and every time the cloud shifted new ramrods of torrential rain would beat down on the house.

The young Kempf had spent the previous day at the cemetery beside the church, where the Kempfs had been buried for hundreds of years, talking with the priest but saying nothing about the imperial envoy. The conversation had turned to the soul, and whether it was a terrible sin to leave the home of one's birth and set off into uncertainty. To his surprise, the old priest had replied: "God will be with you everywhere."

Apart from the old priest, Kempf had no-one to talk to. The gravestones washed by time had nothing to say to him, neither "yes" nor "no". Kempf tried to remember whether there had ever been a conversation around the table about where the Kempfs had come from. No, that had never come up. He concluded that they had sprung up here, around the house, like maize or peas. But that had been in the golden age, when God had walked the earth, and there were not only people multiplying as though sprouting over the fields, but for all who sprang up there was abundant maize and peas. There was no excess of mouths to feed. But the golden age passed, for some time people lived reasonably well in the silver age, then wars started up over the length and breadth of the earth, with people slaughtering one another on every threshold, sowing the furrows with hatred instead of seed. Iron ploughs were better than wooden ones, and the swords cut more precisely than bronze ones, while in the contest between ploughs and swords, man was the loser. For man is, of all creation, the creature always on the losing side, and progress is, it seems, nothing other than his steady loss. That is what was going through Kempf-the-younger's mind, as he splashed through the puddles: a new Hesiod had appeared in Germany, but left no trace. This book is the first and only mention of him.

It was still pouring, but there was a hint in the air that the shackles of winter were being loosened. True enough it was still not the weather for a stroll, but he had wanted to take advantage of his last opportunity to visit the graves of his forebears. New thoughts kept overtaking one another in his head, each new one stumbling on the one before. Kempf returned home, and everything on him was soaked. He spent the rest of the day brooding on the stove. Who would there be to walk behind the plough when his place on the stove was empty?

Everyone in the household understood that something was happening to him, no-one dared disturb him in his half-sleep.

Shortly before midnight, Kempf-the-younger got down from the stove, thumped his hand hard on the table and shouted: "I'm off to Transylvania!"

Old Kempf, unexpectedly, did not oppose him. He even said that it had been clear to him for days that Georg would leave. He gave him his blessing and his old pistol, from the days when these parts rumbled with the sound of that great war of evil memory, during which Catholics and Lutherans pursued one another, inflicting on each other cruelties unimaginable until then.

"Wherever you go, know that God is one," said his father, and Georg kissed his hand. "Be true, beware of wicked people and crazy women. Stay well, honour God, don't steal, and don't forget us."

His mother withdrew to get her son ready for his journey, it was already past midnight, the hours were now breathlessly chasing each other. She didn't rightly know what to prepare for her son for such a lengthy journey. What should he take to Transylvania? The catapult his father had carved for him when he was a child? The pipe he had made for himself? A rod and hook?

They were fleeing in the night while the count's servants were sleeping because an encounter with them and the count's dogs could have been fatal.

The rain had stopped, the sky was bright, and the Milky Way more luxuriant than ever. Crickets could be heard, for the first time that year.

In the small hours a column of young men set out, some of them still children, with sacks on their backs, trunks and bags of bread. They were led by the imperial herald, and now for the first time it was obvious that he was a little lame. After three miles of marching towards the east as the sun was rising, they were met by a cart the imperial envoy had hired for them. The shared aim of the procession, in which Kempf felt lonely because he knew no-one, was Ulm, where a raft belonging to the good Empress was waiting for them. For the next two to three weeks the raft was to be Kempf's home on the water.

As soon as he had slipped out of the house, Kempf realised that he was the only one from his village who had made the decision. Whether it was for good or ill remained to be seen.

Kempf-the-Ancestor Floats to Transylvania

Kempf's home on the water was as colourful as a tent at a church fête; in that tent were displayed various exemplars of the human race as well as other elements that populate the Earth in the name of wonder. Admittedly there were no bearded ladies or two-headed calves and no-one was loudly promoting his miraculous lotion. But there was a Turk, a merchant travelling from afar, from Hamburg indeed, where he had a carpet warehouse; a Hasidic Jew from Poland; there were Lutherans, whose anxiety was rising as they drew near the border . . . behind a wooden barricade pigs were squealing. What a varied world, thought Kempf.

The Turk had wide trousers of bright red homespun cloth, a long kaftan with a broad belt shot through with gold threads, and a turban, white with a violet top. The captain of the raft, experienced as he was, knew that the Turk was a Sunni and a merchant. If in no other way, then because of his turban. Green was the colour reserved for the Holy Porte. The Turks set great store by colour and form.

The Turk's servants were travelling with him. They ministered to him constantly, particularly when he didn't need anything, they were forever on their feet, following his every move. Sometimes he dispersed them as if they were flies. The Turk was travelling on this terrible raft to a place called Wolkowar, where he intended to join a caravan. His ultimate destination was Sarajevo. He was surprised that Kempf had not heard of Sarajevan moccasins, which he thrust right into his face. The man used a language the well-disposed might have acknowledged was a kind of German dialect. Finally, he had a warehouse in Hamburg, he was prosperous and well travelled. As soon as they left Ulm, the Turk got busy having the pigs moved to the other end of the raft, as their stench and grunting would not let him rest.

The Jew wore a black coat and black boots. But the most striking thing about him was on his head: his hat – *shtreimel* was what his people in Galicia called it – the Hasidic Jew never took it off. It must be expensive, thought Kempf. Of course it was: it was made of seven sable tails. Kempf had learned this in his native village because it was not unusual to meet travelling merchants who were Jews. However, in the case of this Jew, it was impossible to count the number of sable tails, and Kempf did not feel it appropriate to ask. The Jew sat scowling on his barrel, entirely lost in his own world.

Counting his tails – that would be like counting his fleas. No, it wouldn't have been right.

The captain's forehead was furrowed with deep lines, he had a prominent nose. That could have made one think of a leper. But since a leper was prohibited from approaching a healthy person by less than a lance's length, no-one would have entrusted the raft to him. Kempf plucked up the courage to ask one of the crew members about those furrows and mentioned the captain's large nose as well. The answer was that the captain had been born crumpled, as though his forehead was a handkerchief, and his nose was the result of boozing. The captain treated the staff roughly, and all but assaulted the passengers. The vessel moved as though of its own accord along the great river which played with it from time to time as with a toy. Oars, one of which was used to steer the raft from a raised board in its centre, were the only way of avoiding a fatal whirlpool or some other disaster, such as crashing into a rock. The raft, enormous logs bound together with thick rope, floated at the mercy of the river towards its distant mouth. From time to time one saw nags hauling a raft upriver and that was a painful sight. Most of them pitied the suffering of those innocent animals. The captain said that every creature lived its own destiny. "They too are God's creatures," muttered some. "It's not good to mistreat beasts of burden."

At one point, judging by the actions of the crew and the captain's suddenly serious expression, Kempf realised they were heading towards danger.

The nightmare for all those sailing downstream from Ulm on the Danube in the eighteenth century was called the Dipstein Crags, in those days a two-day journey from the small town of Engelhartzelle; the name was spoken in a half-whisper among rafters on the Danube. But people still travelled because they had to.

A source states: "The oars were berthed and the crew asked the travellers to start saying the Lord's Prayer or something similar, each in his own language."

Notably, in this place a terrible whirlpool summons travellers into an underwater castle where the Emperor of the Danube reigns, while the dark-grey reefs threaten the raft in their own way. On the river bottom gleams a glass palace, in the middle of which is an enormous table at which sit the emperor, in the guise of a huge catfish, and his subjects, while great glistening fish cast the brilliance of their scales over the feast; on the table are glass jars, like those in which preserved fruit is stored; these jars contain the souls of the drowned.

The Turk immediately spread out his prayer mat and started

praying; the Jew sent an urgent message to his God; the Christians said the Paternoster out loud.

Jahve Gott Allah

were called on and each of those zealous prayers on the raft knew that he was

ONE.

Only the Christian God was divisible by three.

With the arrival of the whirlpool, all trace of courage vanished, they had no strength even for a whisper . . .

Allahu ekber . . . Almighty . . . Only Father . . . *Allahu ekber* . . . Supreme . . . All-powerful . . . Our Father who art . . .

Like sterling silver – a weave of gold or silver thread – on the cloth of water that was here dark, almost black, the floating Babel inscribed its messages in a mixture of Arabic, South-German, Hebrew, Polish . . . The raft had suddenly shrunk, seemingly a helpless splinter controlled by a terrible force . . . However small, this raft was now turning in the whirlpool like a devotee under the sign of a cross, like a synagogue, like a mosque.

It seemed that this Babel jumble would not trouble the One and Only. These people would not be building a tower of Babel in order to scratch the Almighty's feet, but at the end of the journey, wherever that might be, they would scatter like dande-lion seeds. What is more, the travellers did not converse with one another but addressed their God on high directly. Why muddle their languages?

God would grant their prayers, and those of the captain and crew, who were no longer praying but holding firmly to the pieces of wood, barrels, chests in which they put their trust, rather than in God the Father, if the whirlpool were to take hold of the raft or the current hurled them against the crags. They knew full well that their prospects were in the balance. On the other hand, the travellers on the raft were all People of the Book, there were three such peoples, and three books, although there was just one Book. For them it was the first time.

Everyone on the raft was thinking contritely about the ultimate, about the first and last things. Even the better dressed among them now behaved like penitents in hair shirts. The travellers, not to mention the crew, were aware of the risks. The agents in Ulm had of course reassured them, but they all knew that every second raft was wrecked, and nothing more was ever heard of many who had sailed this way. Their raft too, the raft of Kempf-the-ancestor, was now in God's hands. Their fate was in the balance.

The travellers grasped the railing firmly, if a few stakes hammered into the logs could be called a railing, and endeavoured to calculate how many seconds remained before the main impact: until the moment when the raft would again spin in the maw of the largest whirlpool and then perhaps break up against the cliff. Each prayed to his Father the way he had been taught, the Jew with the long beard chanted a psalm, the Muslim kept falling prostrate on his prayer mat . . .

The raft got through.

The raft got through, for had it broken up I would not have been born and this book would not exist, which might not have been such a great shame.

It's not clear which prayer did the trick. It's possible that God appreciated the fact that there were so many. Or the water level of the Danube was sufficiently high after the spring snow melt? Or else it was low enough that the whirlpool was calmed? That is to say, I don't believe that God on High had a particular interest in my birth: he was father to so many.

The Dipstein Crags had drowned many a hope. At one moment or another God cannot have found in the assortment of languages one that he could understand without a dictionary. It's possible that it was not God's day. Although God is a polyglot, he had in his time lamented greatly over Babel: no-one likes thick dictionaries. The captain had also taken the risk that a sinner had crept onto his raft, one who could not, in the eyes of God, be saved. He excluded himself, a murderer and pickpocket. Besides, he, the captain, was also an entrepreneur, that is the patron of several rafts, and now he was carrying a colourful collection of mostly poor people, imperial colonisers, who had sold everything they owned in order to embark on the raft, in order to take the risk at all. They were carrying all they still possessed that could be carried. So, for example, Kempf, a youngster who had several years of apprenticeship behind him, was now looking for people to whom he could sell his skill, however incomplete. There were soldiers, mercenaries, drunks who were also seeking someone to palm off their skill onto, or who were returning from distant battlegrounds, often with wounds attacked by swarms of flies. Men who had fought each other mercilessly in war frequently found themselves travelling together. One could also presume a number of women would not add significantly to the weight of the raft. Such were the captain's clients, with the addition of a priest who accompanied his small flock. On Kempf-the-ancestor's raft there were no women, which later turned out to be a problem. And the priests, too, came later.

The officials of the Monarchy, not yet a Dual Monarchy at that stage, travelled in a different, less risky way. The year under consideration – 1770 – as we are following the dramatic and, it turned out, successful passage of rafts on the Danube at the Dipstein Crags was the year James Watt had presented his steam engine: this marks the beginning of the Industrial Revolution, which elected to start in England rather than Germany. Trains were nevertheless nowhere in sight, people travelled through Europe by horsepower. Civil servants, the upper classes, the nobility, regardless of the language in which they recited the Lord's Prayer, did not travel by raft on the Danube. The Lutheran nobility did not travel in the territories under the rule of the powerful Empress. The Habsburg and Catholic nobility had no need to travel, except in wartime. And no traveller of means in the eighteenth century would be inclined to risk an encounter with the Dipstein Crags.

So, the captain had before him people escaping from one kind of privation into another, but nevertheless with the hope of salvation. Those escaping were on the whole from the southern German regions or Schwabenland. It seems that these last were in the majority, which was why the local inhabitants referred to all the colonisers as Švabe.

As noted, the year 1769 had been a "hungry year" in Germany. Perhaps there were no widespread deaths, as there had been that year in Bengal: ten million souls. The greatest natural catastrophe of all time. But, so as not to die, it was advisable to leave Germany.

The direction of this hunger was the exact opposite of the direction of the nineteenth century when hundreds of thousands fled for their lives towards Germany, often from the regions colonised in the eighteenth century by German peasants and craftsmen under Maria Theresa's reforms.

Once the danger was behind them, everything reverted to the way it had been. It was important for the captain to spread out the whole net of languages in which God's mercy could be included. That the clientele of the raft was so varied was considered to be advantageous. Had a Chinese merchant happened to embark, he would have thought it a good sign, whether he was a Buddhist or a follower of what he himself called Tao. The captain did not mind that the Hasidic Jew had embarked in his own year: the Jews counted 1770 as the year that came between 5530 and 5531. So they all calculated and reasoned in their own way, all their rosaries ascended in a flock to the Heavens, while the reefs came ever closer, the green vortex ever more wild and powerful. Fish awaited, as did the Danubian nymphs, and the tsar-catfish in his glass palace, in the depths. Above the Empress reigned; down below, at the entrances to the underwater empire, there were other, different customs officers. As for the Danubian nymphs, seductive and irresistible, it was dangerous even to mention them.

But, all of that would now be *vorbei*, already becoming a vanishing past. The captain was again scowling and unapproachable. At one point Kempf asked him: "Where exactly is Transylvania?" He brushed him aside so rudely that Kempf thought he was mocking him, on top of everything. What reasonable person travels such a long way, not knowing where he is going?

Wolkowar, Transylvania

When they embarked at Ulm, the imperial envoy said goodbye to the young men he had recruited, wished them good fortune and once again indicated that their destination was Transylvania, adding they would receive further instructions when the time came, but that would not be before they reached Vienna. In the city where Her Majesty the Empress had her court, they would be met by other imperial officials and informed of details which had to remain withheld for the time being. The cost of transport was covered, the captain had a contract with the Vienna Chancellery, and it was in his interest that everything should go smoothly.

As the winter had finally given up, the nights were warmer, but even so Kempf slept badly on the raft. He would wrap himself in a blanket and examine the vault of the sky as he had enjoyed doing in his native village, where he used to stretch out on the meadow and watch the stars.

At night the raft was still. The crew members took it in turns to snore, they were all armed and all kept watch. But they did so casually. Kempf was often the only person awake on the raft. He would then clasp the pistol his father had given him, alert to every rustle among the water lilies. Everything appeared hostile. It was different during the day. The inhabitants of the villages and small towns along the Danube would wave cordially from the bank, offering to sell them supplies, some thumbed their noses at them, but that was a joke compared to the nameless dread of the silent nights. He once had a bad fright, thinking that they were going to be attacked by a pack of wolves, but it was a roebuck that had come to drink its fill of the Danube water and the animal was not aware of the raft, lying there silent as though dead.

Kempf now had many hours to be tormented by increasing numbers of questions, which oppressed him at night even more than in daylight.

Transylvania?

In the imperial Chamber in Vienna, the officials had a map on the wall, a coloured copperplate by Alexis Jaillot from 1696. There was a fairly ordinary greenish "rag" attached to the map, looking as though it had been hung on a line to dry in the wind: on it was written *Transylvanie*. It was surrounded by *Valaqui que d'autres nomment Moldavie*, that is to say, "Wallachia, otherwise known as Moldavia", then *Russian Land*; to the west was *Hongrie*, a little lower down . . . *Sclavonie,* still further down *Bosnie e Tourquie* . . .

Within the bounds of "Sclavonie", *Wolkowar* and *Illok* were also written.

He had heard the Turk mention Wolkowar as his final destination. And that was all. Kempf had no conception even of Vienna, let alone Transylvania. Until now he had not moved out of his village. He turned over in his mind everything the imperial envoy had said. He had no notion that Transylvania was a land in which demented noblemen craved young women's blood, that wolves as big as oxen howled constantly, and at full moon that howl became unbearable to the human ear.

For him, Transylvania was something far worse: like those nights on the Danube, a nameless threat, worse than the vampires that so willingly leave their graves, while the others, the dead, are tranquil. Kempf now had many wakeful hours for uninterrupted observation of the sky. He knew, from home, the names of many stars. He easily found the Pleiades, which would soon be reminding his people that it was time for ploughing and which he would discover were called Vlašići in the regions south of Transylvania. He had no idea that the previous year, 1769, so fateful for the Kempf family and many others now travelling in search of a better life, the Pleiades, the luxuriant Seven Sisters cluster in the belly of Taurus, had been included in Messier's prestigious catalogue of the stars. Kempf watched them for hours, sitting on a barrel wrapped in his blanket, unaware that their promotion had occurred only recently.

The Turk, the carpet merchant, would have been surprised as well . . . He carried with him catalogues with samples of silver and sketches of his carpets. The idea that someone would cram stars into catalogues seemed nonsensical to him, worthy of an idle Gallic astronomer. Meanwhile the Hasidic Jew, following the ancient Cabala, believed that stars were the divine sparks of beings as yet unborn. Hence the fantastic success of the Seven Sisters from the sky went unnoticed on this raft.

The Dipstein Crags were forgotten. A new excitement on the raft: they were approaching the frontier of the empire of the ruler in Vienna.

At the entrance to the empire, imperial customs officers took away the Lutheran Bible. A German colonist could bring in his cat, dog or cow, and no-one asked him for money. The imperial officials supplied him with the necessary papers, provisions and a small amount of money, precisely calculated as expenses for the journey. The customs officers knew that a poor German colonist would not be carrying so much foreign currency that it could threaten the imperial coinage. The officials knew that the colonists were bringing into the Empire only themselves, their bare physical and reproductive strength. But what they could carry in their heads did have to be assessed, and, if possible, aired and cleansed. The Lutheran translation of the Bible, the origin of the modern German idiom, was not tolerated in the colonists' luggage. The travellers handed it over voluntarily, even if they were Lutherans, even if they had been settled in the imperial lands as a punishment. Who knows how many Bibles, fertilised by the godless seed of Lutheranism, ended up at the bottom of the Danube.

Differences, welcome on a raft sweeping towards ordeals it may or may not overcome, now became suspect. Having been united in the face of deadly danger, now mistrust and suspicion dominated as the travellers began to emerge as individuals. They discovered that their aims were different, even if the names of those settlements meant nothing to them.

Transylvania was the name for everything beyond the German forests. They discovered that they were each travelling with a different "why?"

The Jew disappeared in Vienna and some others abandoned the raft. The company was suddenly reduced, though the end of the journey was still a long way off.

They were told it was wise to look after the raft. At the landing stage in Vienna scavengers of all kinds sniffed around, testing the logs, measuring it, you could see their mouths watering. They wanted to buy it, and, if that didn't work, to steal it. The imperial customs officers reminded them once again of such regrettable circumstances. The captain nodded, he knew where he had tied his raft and he knew everything that a major city like Vienna concealed in it. For example, large numbers of inns with Gypsies, which were as a rule also brothels. The captain and crew went off in pursuit of their various pleasures, maintaining they were entitled after such a long journey. Essentially, they would have liked to have a rest in Vienna, a proper sleep, to eat their fill and satisfy other needs. They didn't feel like going further. It would be good if middlemen bought the raft, either to travel upriver, when it would become an instrument of torture for the poor nags that pulled it, or for firewood. Journeying downriver meant sailing into ever greater misery and poverty, along with ever greater risks of attack by bandits. Plenty of them even in Vienna.

Knowing who they were dealing with, the imperial customs officers sent two soldiers to the raft. They stayed on the raft overnight as well, taking it in turns to sleep. The remaining passengers decided they would also keep watch, afraid one pair of eyes was too few. And so Kempf, who in any case could not sleep, spent his first Vienna nights sitting on a barrel, wrapped in his blanket, clutching his pistol. The Turk's servants also kept watch, following an established timetable, while their master snored in his enclosure.

The little pig that he had once driven into a corner near the prow of the raft no longer bothered him; the crew had long since roasted it on a spit. The people stank because the water was still too cold for anyone to dare to bathe. But in the eighteenth century, that was more easily borne. For the greater part of his history, Man has largely reeked.

Sitting on the prow, Kempf listened to the night life of the Empress' capital; he watched the city of Vienna glistening as though illuminated by the scales of fish in imperial service at the bottom of the river; he listened to girls shrieking, stringed instruments lamenting, men yelling, shots from pistols; here and there a fire would flare. Vienna nightlife was full of dangers.

What is Wolkowar, Kempf wondered. For the imperial officers here in Vienna had finally disclosed to him the ultimate destination of his odyssey. The Turk was not displeased that they were to stay together until the end of the journey on the Danube.

Kempf-the-Ancestor Sets Foot
on the Soil of Slavonia

Are these regions safe from Turks? Did Prince Eugene of Saxony defeat them conclusively? Does the local population speak German? What is their religion? What do they eat? Do they produce children? Did the Mohammedans rape far and wide? Even old women, mares too? Above all: what is the soil like? Is it really as black and fertile as in the tales woven by those who lured us onto this raft with the sounds of their flutes, intended essentially for rats and children?

Even while Kempf was weighing up whether to ask the grouch in the guise of the captain about Transylvania – just that one time – the captain had pointed to a passenger secreted in a woollen blanket who everyone on the raft thought was ill since he was forever dozing or muttering in his half-sleep. "Let him tell you. He's been there, he went back to Ulm, no-one knew, because no-one ever goes back. He informed me that he's carrying a message, but what kind or to whom, he didn't say."

But nothing could be prised out of the fellow. He did understand German, you could tell by the movement of his eyes, yet he would turn aside in mid-conversation and sink into silence again.

They all thought the passenger touched by the sun had justifiably withdrawn into the exalted peace of a veteran, who would not in any case have been able to explain what awaited them. And when no cunning ploy, no bottles of wine, no bacon, succeeded in extracting even the least information from him, the colonists gave up. No-one looked at the silent figure anymore or asked any questions.

He made use of that. At night, when everyone had fallen asleep, when the moon turned the whole expanse of the Danube to silver, the stranger would retrieve his message from where he kept it close to his chest. The captain who watched him surreptitiously had discovered his secret but was indifferent to it.

Reverently, the way a nation honours its false gods, the silent traveller held up to the moon's face three potato tubers as if making an offering.

Kempf too had caught him in the act. He himself had no rest on the raft.

The man was carrying those tubers to Transylvania and hiding them like the greatest treasure. The Kempfs had once tried to grow potatoes, which they were told had attractive flowers. They had not been thrilled with the result. The enlightened ruler in Vienna knew better, she expected a lot from the potato, just as the Prussian king did. So her colonists carried potatoes with them.

Kempf had been on the raft for less than two weeks, but he had seen all kinds of wonders. What a world it was!

Wolkowar, for instance, where was that?

Kempf whispered this question to himself, as the raft slid calmly along the Danube, in the spring of 1770, on its way to Sclavonia. It was generally held to be a land of wolves. Had Baedeker guides existed in those days, they would have mentioned them. But another one hundred and fifty years would have to pass before the first guides were published.

The silent stranger told them nothing, which may have been

all to the good, because the thing with the wolves could have turned out to be a lie. Like the tales of malaria.

One day, and according to Kempf's calculations the end of the journey must have been approaching, the captain opened a bottle of wine and they all toasted the arrival of the raft in – Sclavonia. Later, in honour of that significant event, they all urinated together from the raft into the river.

Kempf was exhausted when the raft finally tied up in Wolkowar. There was almost nothing and no-one at the landing stage, let alone fireworks. So Kempf-the-ancestor did not feel any need to roll out a flag and stick it in the ground. Besides, that ground had already been conquered. The enlightened Empress had laid her hand on it.

He spent his first night in his new homeland in a shack, not much bigger than the raft, after he had ceremoniously parted from the Turk and his retinue. They had sworn to meet again one day. Three more days passed before an imperial official showed him a piece of land where he could build a dwelling. What is more – wonder of wonders – that dwelling was sketched on a piece of paper. Later some people whose language he did not understand, and who were not friendly, brought some boards and other building materials, evidently because they had been paid to. But there were also people who understood his language and were prepared to offer him every assistance without recompense.

So, some cast spiteful glances in his direction, others approached him as though they were acquaintances, asking for news from the German lands. Some were also subjects of the wise Empress.

"Do not require any undue level of culture and enlightenment from people whose destiny it is to remain in the lower classes.

Do not strain their intellects for that will encourage in them awareness of their station, and then they will carry out with bitterness tasks that by necessity and according to their station have to be undertaken."

Also sprach die Kaiserin – thus spoke the Empress.

Kempf-the-Ancestress on the Horizon

So, the lads set about constructing dwellings according to the sketches from Vienna. They even succeeded in planting kitchen gardens, following the instructions of the Pleiades, that is the Vlašići. The ploughs had not yet arrived, nor the oxen. Under various pretexts, the established settlers did not want to lend them their ploughs. In their first year the colonists would harvest virtually nothing. They had to buy from the local population at sky-high prices.

What was the basic problem with the people already there, who knows since when but in their view forever? Had they all sprung out of the neighbouring fields like wheat, like beans?

The main problem was that the Vienna Chancellery envisaged ever more cleared land. The fields intended for the German colonists were still forested: and what forests they were! In winter wolves surely reigned there.

In fact, what was being reincarnated here was the age-old conflict recorded as far back as the Bible, between herders living a nomadic life, wanting free pasture and freedom of movement, and farmers, who want fields untrodden by the hooves of anyone's herds. The former wanted meadows, which they were ready to defend with weapons, like ancient nomadic tribes. The latter built houses, they wanted arable fields, kitchen gardens, vineyards, where they were permanently settled. In the end, Cain slew Abel, and then founded a town.

Just one week after Kempf disembarked in Wolkowar, the first murder took place. Abel took his revenge on Cain. The colonists sought and obtained weapons from the Vienna Chancellery. Since his first night in "Transylvania", Kempf slept with his pistol under his pillow.

Things did not settle down until a regiment arrived in Wolkowar, armed to the teeth.

Kempf had not yet seen any wolves, he would probably have to wait till winter. All in all, the first winter would likely be as hungry as those in Germany. True enough, there were no longer any Turks; in their wake were drinking fountains and burnt mosques. And indeed many villages were completely abandoned.

Kempf-the-ancestor had told the imperial envoy the day before the flight to Ulm that he did not on any account wish to move into a house someone else had lived in. He was looking forward to a fresh start and it was because of that fresh start that he had responded to the all-powerful Empress' invitation. The imperial official promised that the Vienna Chancellery would take note of his wish, although it was most unusual. In this part of the world it was the custom for abandoned villages to be settled by those who tagged along in the wake of conquering armies.

"Your request is based on pure superstition!" the envoy said. But he did pass on the request to Vienna, not wishing for any reason, let alone a superstition, to lose a single soul.

To be on the safe side, the colonists' dwellings were built like fortresses. A person gets used to that. Even so, it is better to make an accommodation with the devil himself, if one intends to live here forever, rather than constantly fear for one's life and property. People can't constantly wage wars. Farmers are fundamentally peaceable folk. There was so much fallow land here, it was not worth artificially enflaming conflicts, even with those locals, Vlahs, who had in their time associated with the Turks; even with those who had served the Turks as soldiers, *martolos*.

Kempf took long walks through his surroundings, although he was advised not to. Indeed he took pleasure in these lowlands, and he saw many good roads raised on the embankments of old Roman highways. But there were also swamps generating fumes Kempf believed could be deadly.

He watched a stork raise its beak high in the air so the frog it had caught could more easily slip into its stomach. He had not seen drinking fountains or mosques in Germany, but innumerable storks. And it looked as though the bird that was now stepping along the edge of the marsh was an egret. There were no wolves, no lions, no vampires.

But there were herons. What a show-off!*

Apart from the traces of Turkish occupation, everything here was like Bavaria, except that the plain was flatter and probably more fertile. But he began to be aware of a lack that was worse than hunger.

There were virtually no free women here. It is possible to deal with hunger, something will always be found in a village. But

---

* "Ardea: Capite laevi, fronte & collo supra, infraque sordide albo, testaceo, nigroque longitudinaliter litturato, e pennis ex sordide albo in dilute testaceum vergentibus, nigro marginates." (Heron: Smooth head, brow and neck a dirty white, reddish and black alternating along its length, out of feathers moving from dirty white to a diluted brick red, black on the edges.) From the account of a journey through Slavonia in 1782.

In truth, Kempf was not at all interested in ornithology. I am including this description only because of the beauty of a dead language describing life. As such, it is quite superfluous. The letter he would soon send to his native village does not mention herons.

But even our ancestor Noah was not interested in details. He was only concerned that embarkation should happen in pairs.

where to find a woman? You can pick a leftover apple to stave off the pangs of hunger. But there are usually no forgotten women on the branches!

Send women! That was the message the colonists, including Kempf, sent to the German lands via the Vienna Chancellery. The office expressed understanding of the men's needs. They couldn't manage without women, any more than they could manage without livestock.

Horses would come, some time, but women? We don't know how the Greek colonisers solved the same shortage, whether they coupled with the local women, was that not perhaps the materialistic key to explaining the phenomenon of the centaur?

Where there are settlements and taverns, there are harlots. The tail end of the regiment brought several because they always hang around an army. But harlots are not counted in the equation of scarcity, which therefore includes a major unknown: wives and mothers. The erotic imagination of her Majesty the Empress – Maria Theresa Walburga Amalia Christina of the house of Habsburg – and the reality of life in Slavonia had nothing in common, they were two entirely different kinds of deprivation, the former could be called playful, while the latter must be considered existential. The former would be lived out in the Empress' boudoir jockeying with someone answering to the name of Trenck, while the latter scarcity was a matter of the survival of the future colonies, and indeed the colonists themselves.

Hence the need to solve the unknown quantity of the said equation at any cost. And it had to be solved in the same way as the equation of hunger – by holding up three potato tubers to the divinity of the moon. But Luna is a female deity, and she would look more gladly on a cheerfully singing crowd of girls from the South German regions whose brightly coloured skirts would cover the whole "deck" of logs that made up the raft.

Grammar was not the strongest aspect of Kempf-the-ancestor's letter to Germany. He did not beat about the bush in that letter, he expressed himself clearly, and because of its brevity it did not contain many mistakes. Essentially, it amounted to a cry: send *Frauen*! And because nothing else occurred to him – and since it seemed stupid to inform his relatives so far away about the weather in these parts – Kempf-the-ancestor sketched the figure of a woman according to his own imagining.

And so there we are: Germany did indeed send a contingent of marriageable girls, who in Slavonia, where they were hurrying to, would be called *snaše*, and which by the second generation would be their only name. That was to be a more cheerful journey and a far more cheerful raft than the one on which Kempf-the-ancestor arrived. On this raft there was accordion music, along with girls' laughter, which cheered the crew and even the captain, all men smeared with every possible grease. But this captain was far more talkative than the one who had brought Kempf; he was a man of his word and the Chancellery knew whom to put in charge of this treasure for it to remain untouched.

The Dipstein Crags once again required respect and silence, the songs were interrupted, the accordion closed; the oars were drawn in, as well as something that swelled under the sailors' and the captain's heavy, sodden clothing. The girls too prayed, as prayers are addressed to the Virgin Mary in Catholic houses of God; psalms were sung, as they are sung in cathedrals. There were no harlots on this journey, because the person who had organised it had taken enormous pains over the morals of his cargo: potentially infectious exemplars had to be excluded. Naturally, there were no Jewish or Turkish women. The rafts' agent had guaranteed that the girls would be delivered in the state in which they were at the beginning of the journey, and, under no circumstances whatever, in any other. The Dipstein Crags were a relatively minor danger compared to those that threatened the women's honour on such a long journey, in the middle of the eighteenth century. Hence the rafts' agent, at the expense of the colonists who had already taken refuge in Slavonia, would pay also for supervision, in the form of three sturdy young men who had sworn that, for a specific price, they would guard that honour from any possible attack, even from the crew themselves; the last was the most difficult, given the sanitary and other conditions on the raft. In a word, the singing girls had three bodyguards, who protected the honour of their flower, while in return they protected them from the charms of the Danubian sirens as from the nymphs who had lured many a Faun to the bottom of the river. Man dreams, God decides, or rather the child who shoots his arrow blindfolded does: all three lads found the woman of their life on the raft, and without knowing it all three of them were travelling downstream on the Danube for the first and last time. Their task was to guarantee them protection from seducers, but not from love, about which nothing had been said in their contract with the agent. Let us take that as a triumph of *force majeure*.

After various tribulations and hazards, the raft with the marriageable girls was on the point of reaching Wolkowar.

"They're coming, they're coming!" shouted children when they saw the boat at a previous bend in the river, and now they were running along parallel with it, exclaiming: "They're coming, the Švabice are coming!"

This time the regimental band was playing at the landing stage, and the lads, farmhands and tradesmen had brought all the best things they had. The priest supervised the scene from a rise. The wise Empress had decreed that there should be a priest and a doctor for every three villages. As far as the last is concerned, these were better conditions than nowadays.

The raft tied up, a narrow bridge was lowered onto the river-bank, the band played a fanfare. An excited individual fired a pistol, the band played the fanfare again, followed by frenzied drumming. The girls crossed the little bridge, they were coming . . .

The lads watched from the bank, some had fieldglasses, now at a great premium, but they were not for loan.

Among them was my ancestor, called Kempf, and now for the first time, through the eyepiece of his binoculars, he saw my ancestress, sighing with relief that she was not the girl from his village for whom marriage brokers had been sent long ago.

Fräulein Theresia, with a slight blush, and a wide skirt that could have easily borne her upwards like a balloon, stepped uncertainly along the narrow bridge between yesterday and tomorrow. She had to lift her skirt a little, with a multitude of petticoats beneath it – and my ancestor Kempf spotted through his eyepiece a white garter on her red stocking. That was too much: he surrendered.

Charmingly, like a water beetle from lily pad to lily pad, my ancestress hopped onto the bank. The wedding was arranged that same evening.

The Kempfs had the custom, as did other families, of passing a name from grandfather to son. So Theresia's name was also passed from generation to generation. But still it took a hundred years for Theresia to become Tereza, and another fifty for it to become Reza, Rezika . . . It took even longer for the name Georg to become Đuro, then Đuka, as my father was called: Đuka Kempf.

The Kempfs survived and remained in their new homeland. In the 1930s they became Volksdeutsche, ethnic Germans outside the Reich. That was no guarantee of good fortune.

In the graveyard at Pećuh, not far from Vukovar, which was at the time of the Kempfs' arrival in Slavonia part of the same world, there is a German inscription to this day:

To the first death, To the second need, To the third bread.

That's how life was rhymed: *Tod* (death), *Not* (need), *Brot* (bread). Kempf-the-ancestor did have a bit of luck.

II
Volksdeutscher Kempf

Louse

A son was born to the Kempfs, an only child, in July 1919. It was the greatest joy.

In truth, the Great War was not yet forgotten, the "Green Corps" of military deserters were still rife in the forests, the imperial and royal currency was exchanged for the Serbian king's dinar at a rate that provoked anger, but in the end you had to have money acknowledged by your own state in the house. Besides, Austria had collapsed, like no state in history up to then, and many had collapsed.

Their little son was greeted by the Kempfs as a sign of more stable conditions, above all in trade. But a peasant could also be more confident that he would be able to reap what he had sown, that no-one would requisition his stock, at least until his house and fields came under the hammer.

Few of the descendants of the German colonists in the little town of Nuštar took any interest in the situation in Germany. They were barely aware of Hitler's putsch. That there was hunger in Germany was, they felt, only to be expected. It wasn't a bed of roses here either. They cared nothing for Versailles.

Now and again there was news of a returnee from Russia. And a certain Haberle also came back. He was the son of a civil servant, who had come from Graz at the beginning of the century and worked as a surveyor. His father had been a good and honest surveyor, a rare thing in that line of work. Land registries, roads, canals and schools – in this region all of these had been bequeathed by Austro-Hungary. Not for philanthropic reasons, but as evidence of tax investment. It had built schools because the Austrian civil service was unable to cover all needs; and that was where people learned about hygiene and measures to suppress epidemics. Finally, a modern industry needed a work force that was better educated than country bumpkins. People also learned how to protect tubers from the potato beetle – the potato having become fully established.

At the Jew's Tavern Haberle talked about what was going on in Russia: that the peasants and workers had taken things into their own hands. He spoke increasingly zealously, and the peasants bought him drinks, one after another, nodding and puffing on their pipes. At the Tavern he drank on trust, with just a wave of the hand. Was it here, in this tavern, that some heads came up with the notion that the Jews had a connection with the Soviets?

Police came for Haberle and took him into custody. He was not heard of again.

Life, quiet as it was when it had to be, continued in the rhythm – winter tranquillity, sowing, harvesting. In those years the plums cropped abundantly.

When Hitler clambered into power, one of the Germans, a distant relative of Đuka's father, came out in front of his porch, but still behind his own gate, and fired his rifle.

A few Germans gathered there. Those who hadn't known were then informed that Adolf Hitler had become the German Chancellor. They smoked their pipes and went home to their wives.

And then, for a long time, nothing.

The newspapers began to carry items stating that Germany had betrayed the Treaty of Versailles. None of the Germans in the little town of Nuštar would have been able to say exactly what was in that treaty, but they all now knew that it was a disgrace for Germany.

Then news trickled in that there was no unemployment in Germany and that hard roads were being built the length and breadth of the entire country. Also that bad Germans were being "protected" from good Germans, by being separated from them and surrounded by barbed wire. Only that was unclear.

But who could be against hard roads being built and everyone being able to make a living? That was what that man Haberle had said as well, some recalled.

Latest news had it that the largest countries were arming themselves, Germany most of all. Was a new war on the way? On land, on sea, in the air?

On the contrary, everyone everywhere was talking about peace. Hitler called on all nations to cooperate and claimed that he would defend peace at all costs. Stalin said that the U.S.S.R. did not want war. But France was building its Maginot Line, separating itself with a belt of concrete bunkers, where it concealed heavy guns aimed towards Italy, Belgium, Switzerland . . . In Italy Il Duce proclaimed socialism, which was the least clear of all. National Socialism sounded far better: something like that ill-fated communism about which Haberle had spoken, and which was finally acquiring a basis and meaning.

But few people cared about a basis or meaning. Kempf-the-father's business was going well, he was able at last to put a bit of money aside. A lot of brandy was brewed.

At that time emissaries from the former homeland began to arrive in the little town of Nuštar. Unlike Haberle, who seemed to have vanished into thin air, they didn't want to campaign among the Jews. The local Germans were a bit surprised at that: many of them, including Kempf's father, dealt with Jews in their work. But many peasants were in debt to Jews, as were the innkeeper and the moneylender. Some had taken out credit from them that was hard to repay. Hence the emissaries from Germany, campaigning in an inn belonging to a Hungarian, had a better reception among the peasants, the old settlers.

"There's a lot of butter in Germany!" observed one.

"So what," muttered one of the local German employers, "we make tons of butter here too."

"There's full employment in Germany . . ."

"No-one's lazing around here either."

"Germany has to lead the nations in the battle against Bolshevism . . ."

"Alright. But we don't have any Bolsheviks here and none of us has ever seen one."

"You're all pulling in different directions here. There are as many flags as there are houses! What you need is a leader. Someone needs to take you back to where you belong."

But the Reich's envoys' invitations to return, with their families and all they had acquired here, to their one and only homeland, fell on deaf ears.

"How do I carry my soil with me?" Johannes Kempf, Đuka's father's brother, was heard grumbling. "I'm not a Jew to carry it in a little bag round my neck."

The emissaries kept coming for two years, then stopped. German affairs here, among the Danubian Swabians, should be taken in hand by the local Germans.

In 1938, people everywhere were talking about war. As never before, the politicians talked about peace. But the people weren't convinced. Each just looked to his own, not wanting to see further than the end of his nose.

In the little town of Nuštar almost everyone thought the threats of war were so much hot air. And even if it did come to conflict between the great powers, the Kingdom of Yugoslavia would remain neutral. It seemed that the King favoured the English, not a bad move; if you had to have a master, it was best that he was as far as possible from your borders. This may have been an age-old reflex in remembering hard times, passed down from generation to generation: Kempf-the-ancestor had fled Germany to escape the greed and cravings of his masters.

The local Germans mocked the Croatian–Serbian quarrel, endeavouring not to take sides.

"Trade doesn't like borders," Kempf-the-father maintained, "it doesn't acknowledge nations or bow down to their false gods. Trade recognises only the power of money and the laws of the market."

Until the moment the war flared up, old Kempf was a man of very modern views.

But no-one really believed that it would come to war. Until the following occurred:

On the land of a friend, in fact a partner of Kempf's father, lived Juliška, a Hungarian woman, whose age could only be guessed at, but almost everyone believed that she had passed her first hundred. Juliška was half-blind, but clear-headed even if her body was frail. She served the German family, she was the mother of a Hungarian who had disappeared in the Galician mud, but had never married. Her son Đula had been despatched into that war, already an old man, called up three times by then, so people could only imagine how old she was. She had seen it all, experienced it all. Processions of girls and women went to the house where the old woman lived. Juliška was forever dozing by the stove, or in summer she sat outside in the shade of a walnut tree. They asked her about women's things, children's ailments, they asked her to cast a spell on one young man or another, or on one rival or another . . . they asked her questions about God they did not dare ask their priest. They asked her about the beginning of the world, about the soul, whether it was immortal and what happened after death; where was Heaven, where was Hell, was what people said about hot pitch true . . . was it a sin if a boy touched a girl's breast in passing . . . and if that did happen, should marriage brokers be sent immediately; was it true that old Grga had become a vampire . . . and if not, why had the soil on his grave risen up as it did?

And so one day they came to her with the news that almost all the children in the school were infected with lice . . . that they were having their heads shaved and rubbed with paraffin at school. One of the anxious mothers had brought a squashed louse in a handkerchief as proof.

Everyone was surprised to see just how agitated Juliška was at the sight of the louse. There had always been lice in the country, just as there were constant battles with fleas, wasps, hornets . . . rats so large and fierce they chased cats . . . Mice on the other hand were considered domestic animals that nourished cats, so they didn't need to be fed, unlike the eternally hungry dogs.

But this time the lice were an epidemic, a plague on a large scale. For kilometres around the little town of Nuštar, there was not a single child that did not drag itself to school shaved like a soldier or convict . . . The lice had made nests on the small heads equally of those who never bathed and of those who washed every Saturday. They were all shaved to the roots of the hair: little Croats, Serbs, Germans, Hungarians, Jews . . . Each of these groups was outraged by this injustice because they kept themselves clean, while all the others were mucky scruffs with a feline aversion to water. The most vocal were the Germans who had always considered themselves the avant-garde of hygiene.

At that time no-one yet made clothing for submariners from human hair. No-one could grasp the sense of this misfortune. It contributed nothing to settling political issues: lice are indifferent to racial matters and fairly apolitical.

So, a group of mothers had gathered around Juliška, each with the same tale. Several more exemplars were brought to the light of a flickering lamp for inspection.

"There will be war!" Juliška said.

And, as soon as the news of what Juliška had said spread through Nuštar, everyone, both men and women, knew there would be war.

What she had said stuck in the women's memory so forcefully that they didn't hear what came next from her lips.

What she said was: "God in Heaven grant that my eyes will no longer see it."

The following day, Juliška passed away in her sleep. Those who were the first to see her in the morning thought that she was smiling, and that smile lay frozen on her face until they tucked her chin in. The hundred-year-old woman laughed like a child who had played a trick on someone and got away with it by vanishing.

On the eve of the German attack on Poland, a stranger appeared in Nuštar, a chance traveller who stayed at the inn belonging to the Hungarian. He was dressed in a dark suit, which was strange because it was already hot, June. Odder still was that he had come from a long way off but had no luggage. Up to then emissaries had always come with suitcases of leaflets and books.

"He'll be some sort of gangster," was people's first reaction. Some noted he had unusually long arms in relation to his height, and so likely long fingers as well.

He used only new banknotes to pay his bills, he didn't drink alcohol, and he often went for long walks outside the town. Word went around that he might be a surveyor sent from Belgrade to take new measurements, and that was never good. Others maintained that he was a spy, but no-one could say on whose behalf or why he had come by horse-drawn carriage all the way from Vinkovci to their little town. Others again swore that he was an agent of the Comintern who had come to Nuštar to light the flame of world revolution, but the police dismissed the idea: Hitler and Stalin were now thick as thieves. In this new constellation, Haberle would have been released from royal prison, had he not been buried long ago.

End of story.

But a child chanced to see the stranger while walking some distance from her home. The child was picking cherries, she had filled her whole apron, and was now hiding in the bushes, eating them and spitting out the pips.

The stranger climbed onto a rise which had a fine view and stayed there for a long time.

When he came down, he stood beside a puddle left over from the downpour of the previous night and leaned over it.

"It's time. I'm beginning to look like myself. I need to work."

That's what the stranger said, seeing in the water a snout and shining eyes.

Had the child amusing herself with cherries been able to hear that, she would not have understood it, and the image from the puddle vanished along with the stranger.

Before she fell asleep, the child told her father and mother what she had seen: a stranger dressed in city clothes talking out loud to himself, using incomprehensible words, as though casting a spell. The child said the man frightened her although she couldn't say why.

Her mother thought that only Juliška would be able to provide an explanation, but her husband reminded her that Juliška was now far away, like Haberle.

The very next day processions of young men, some still children, began to move around the little town of Nuštar, with drums providing a steady rhythm. They headed in this direction, or that, back or forth, to the east, to the west – the drums always beat loudly, as though the direction was entirely clear and unambiguous. These young men came from German families, Germans living outside the Reich, Volksdeutsche. Some stayed in their houses, some were shut up in the storeroom by their mothers, but as time went on more and more of them followed the drumming. The drummers, it turned out, had an unusual love of fire, and bonfires were lit on the edges of plantations, in outdoor camps new comradeship was cemented. Suddenly they were all *Kameraden*, even those who had previously laid into each other in true Slavonian fashion at village fairs. The rhythm of drums is so intoxicating, sitting round a fire so enticing.

The drummers taught them various songs. Some had been sung to them by their parents, others were new.

And so, together and from the heart, they sang about the village king Florian Geyer and the black troops that thronged after him.*

---

* Florian Geyer (1490–1525), leader of the failed German peasant war of 1524. A song about him became one of the hymns of the S.S. It sings of a red cockerel crowing from a church roof, which matched the anti-Christian sentiments of the S.S., for whom God, particularly the Christian God, was a rival.

Corso, 1941

In the house of the widow Marija, it had always been hard to make ends meet. She received only half of her husband's pension, he had worked on the railways. He had returned from the war that was not then known as the first, as a second was not anticipated, with a trophy rifle and syphilis. He died, leaving Marija with two small children. The savings she had after the war were devoured by the conversion into royal dinars. Politically, her husband had allied himself to Stjepan Radić and the Croatian Peasant Party. Hence Marija too favoured political "peasants".

The managers of the railways disputed the widow's right to a pension. She appealed, but since she had no money to pay the lawyer, she agreed that if he won the case he would take half the pension owed her for life. The lawyer won the case, the pension arrived at the house halved, and in any case modest.

Marija got by as best she could. She sewed dresses for the town ladies, and had a real gift for it.

Whenever she had not collapsed from fatigue, Marija read. Mostly the great Russian writers. For her times, she was educated. By nuns of course.

There were always student lodgers in the house. Some came from the countryside, some were the sons of civil servants, they came from all over. Some were arrogant, some reasonable. Many were almost as poor as their landlady and her children. They could have good conversations with them. There was no need to avoid any topic. And they dared to show them their banned books.

Marija's children were inclined to the left.

What else could they do? Their chances in future life were non-existent if nothing in their country or in the world changed. Indeed, if everything did not change.

As the conflicts in the country became more acute with intimations of war, Marija's children grew radicalised. Marija admired the Russians, but not the Soviets. Her children put all their hope in the Soviet star that was rising. They saw almost nothing else in the sky, while Marija saw a great deal, including the Lord God as a just king, who moreover spoke Tolstoy's Russian. The children thought that this God was called Josif Visarionovich and that he would liberate all the captives on Earth, and especially those who had to share their meagre plate with students from the ever more remote provinces.

Marija avoided political discussions with them. She thought they would see sense one day and prayed to God this would happen in time. And that is what her children thought about her: that she would finally realise where justice lay and how to reach it. It wasn't possible to pray for it in a church, thought the children. Were that to be at all possible, it would have already happened.

When, towards the end of their final years in high school, the children began increasingly to leave home at night, Marija was not concerned for their morals but their lives. Only once did she say: "Take care who might hear what you're saying." That told them she knew where they had signed up. In those days Tolstoy's Christianity would not have landed anyone in prison, but connections with the banned Party were dangerous.

The children, too young for the Party, were greatly drawn

to the communists. They met them at secret meetings, where they would be overwhelmed by the almost voluptuous thrill of conspiracy. They considered themselves superior to their contemporaries, who kicked balls around or smooched at fairs. Her children, Marija observed one day, were too serious for their age.

Whether that was good or bad, she could not judge.

Then showdowns with political opponents began. More than once her son came home in the small hours, bruised and bloody. When a policeman arrived the next day to take a statement, she explained that her son would sometimes come home well-oiled and crash onto the doorstep. The policeman downed a glass of plum brandy and left. She had known him for years. He had been a friend of her late husband's and that was a bit of luck.

These conflicts became increasingly frequent as the war approached.

The Molotov–Ribbentrop Pact brought a moment of confusion into young heads filled with the schematic version of Marxism that circulated, condensed in small leaflets, among the enlightened. Stalin and Hitler had come to an agreement at the expense of the Anglo-Saxons and their imperialism, their older comrades told them. But both Vera and her brother guessed that this could not be quite the case. There were all kinds of agreements.

The directive was that preparations for war should be halted.

But certain signs led the children to conclude that the Party was having none of it.

Everyone was preparing for war, and when it broke out, the weapons that had been stolen from the royal army's depot were few and inadequate. They were preparing for war in their heads, thought the children. In truth they believed in the power of the idea that would unite all the poor of the world, then bring about revolution; ideas dwelled in the head and not in a dark pit, where the king's stolen field gun was rotting.

As soon as war knocked on the door, the comrades disappeared, either plunged into the illegal movement or imprisoned. Police actions were increasingly comprehensive, increasingly brutal. Some thought that the pact between Stalin and Hitler would enable them to enjoy the light of day, to go out into the street and say what they thought and felt. Quite the opposite happened: more and more people took refuge in the Underground. In the end, it seemed that no-one believed in the validity of the agreement signed by Molotov and Ribbentrop; apart perhaps from Stalin, whose pictures started smirking from walls in the small towns in the annexed parts of Poland. They say that, on the day the armoured divisions of the Wehrmacht began to crush the agreement, Josif Visarionovich was enraged by Hitler's betrayal. They say, too, that throughout the Fatherland war he had kept Hitler's photograph on his desk. Whenever he was in the room alone, he would gaze at that picture, trying to understand who that man really was. They sat like that, Hitler on the desk, Stalin at the desk, moustache to moustache, so to speak. It is likely that Hitler's burnt jawbone, which the Red Army soldiers dug out of the ash, ended up on that same desk of Stalin's, with the aim of completing the picture and resolving a Sphinxian riddle. Stalin had not discerned the Sphinx, probably because of too great a similarity. He was left with no alternative but to smash it to pieces, like a mirror that held the truth.

At the end of March 1941, almost everyone could see that the war was on the verge of reaching them. The young people, it is true, still trod the corso in Vinkovci in front of the old grammar school: back and forth, back and forth, because, as always, it was important to see and be seen. One of those on the corso was Đuka

Kempf who had done his time on the school benches in Vinkovci and was now there as a medical student, on his semester break. Of course, Marija's children were also there, when they were not conspiring. Glances to the side, jokes, little passing flirtations, the young Jewish girls' pony-tails, the brazen self-confidence of the sons of landowners and merchants, the furious expressions of the subjugated, the superior expressions of the aspiring intellectuals – young people filled with expectations, yearning for the spring in which everything awakens, but also afraid . . . this was the corso in 1941.

The policeman sat in the bar, twisting his moustache and observing the situation over a flask of brandy. Fights could break out at any moment. There had been trouble again the night before at the Sokol building and a prosperous member of the Croatian True Rights Party had been badly beaten up on his way home.

That was why a lot of informers had infiltrated the young people, listening to what was being talked about in case a seed of rebellion could be detected in their youthful exuberance.

The young men and women signed up to the far left were serious and always a bit outside the mainstream. But they too joined in the corso because one had to.

The far left, that is, because at that time the extremes were growing increasingly far apart so they could attack one another to extinction. From the point of view of the Rights Party, as from that of the enlightened, it was clear that this time they intended to go all the way.

There were no Jews among the Rights Party members of course, although their leader was a Jew, and some could be found among the communists as well. As with everyone, some Jews were rich and had a lot to lose; others were poor as church mice with only their lives to lose. Now both groups were afraid. The rich calculated that they would be able to buy themselves out somehow; the young suspected that they would be left completely isolated and exposed.

The Serbian peasants and merchants took themselves to one side and chatted with their priest. They kept offering him brandy, he stroked his beard, evidently calming them down. That some of them were intending to move to their relatives, nearer Belgrade, or even further south, the priest did not like because it would diminish his flock. His church was, admittedly, somewhat fuller than a year before, but his colleague, the Catholic priest, said the same thing. He had also said that it would be best for all of them to convert to the Catholic faith and for the priest to shave off his beard. This was said half in jest, but with such people you never knew what was concealed in the other half, whether that other half would devour the first, joking half which would make it serious, in fact bad.

The Volksdeutsche were a group apart; indeed, they seemed to have formed several groups, but, again, the outside world experienced them as a unit. All believed, and some feared, that their time had come. Some swaggered, throwing their weight around, glaring at Jews, hurling insults at them, even at girls. Others were more measured, distancing themselves from the rabble-rousers, standing to one side, sensing a kind of duplicity in those who did approach them, and the only people who really respected them were adherents of the Rights Party. The cleverer Germans began to feel like foreigners. It was only recently that they had discovered their German identity, they were unsure whom to join, how to align themselves. People today would all like to grow into some kind of loyalty, and so possibly conceal themselves, or maybe win.

Win, for sure, thought one group of young Germans who qualified for military service.

They were just waiting to be called up. In spring 1941 the German prospects were bright. France was crushed, the English had been driven back to their island, Poland had been dismembered and returned to Germans like themselves, Volksdeutsche.

Đuka Kempf stood in one of those groups, calmly smoking and enjoying the spring sunshine, watching the people walking back and forth on the corso. The Jewish girls are the prettiest, he thought.

Why war? Kempf-the-son could not come to terms with it, he quarrelled with his father, who became a passionate German and a Hitler supporter. Things were going well for the Kempfs, couldn't be better. Today every merchant wanted to become a wholesaler at all costs. You feign a new allegiance and horizons open up, long live trade. The Kempfs were not exactly poor in any case. Đuka Kempf had been bilingual all his life, but that was roughly where his Germanness stopped. His uncle Johannes mocked these "new Germans", who had suddenly discovered the call of the homeland, where they would have perished of hunger had they not heeded Maria Theresa and left. Johannes Kempf would not exchange his garden for any kind of "Reich" in the world. He did a wonderful imitation of the Führer at family gatherings; everyone laughed, even those who didn't approve of such clowning. It was just that the Führer lent himself to such parody. But when once at the table Johannes said that Hitler had been a squad leader in the Great War, that at one time he had been blinded by gas and still couldn't see, there was a terrible quarrel and an end to all jokes.

After that Uncle Johannes had only conversed with pumpkins and string beans in his garden. The children would overhear him. Johannes did not address the vegetables in German. The children knew it because they could understand his muttering:

Uncle Johannes gabbled to his beans like a Slavonian peasant.

But, for heaven's sake, why get rich, Kempf-the-son thought. In the end, you could eat all you could eat and not a crumb more! It was nice to travel, to enjoy the wide world, but that was already accessible to him, Kempf. He was studying to be a doctor, that was a good life, people were getting sicker by the day, whole nations were dying. But that business with the Jews . . . Why, all his Belgrade professors, all the authorities in medicine, to a man, were Jews. Sometimes "nation" is an incurable illness, thought Kempf. It seemed to him that the German people had succumbed to a serious illness. And no nation could be cured, only an individual could be, even when he was opposed to everyone else.

War itself was insane killing. Why, in Slavonia people don't slaughter for no reason! His father sells pig fat, that will always be needed, which means it will always be possible to sell it for more than one paid for it. Why go to war?

Franja too, his best friend, also a Volksdeutscher, was of much the same opinion. The two of them were interested in girls, whom they dreamed of taking for a tumble in the fields and vineyards. Both were avid readers. Đuka had already started scribbling . . . His most severe critic was in fact his friend Franja who thought his poems feeble, though he considered Đuka a devotee of the Muses with a future, and perhaps one day he'd prove himself a poet.

Some Volksdeutsche had joined up with the German army with the first summons; Kempf knew them, slightly, but was impervious to all their coaxing to join them.

Those young men went off with the Gauleiter and his drums and now they were preparing in Germany to attack the Bolsheviks. It seemed that the unfortunate Transylvania, where the pied piper and recruiting agent had brought his rat-children, could spring up anywhere on the globe. Until now it had always been somewhere south, but now it had settled in the west, tomorrow who knows?

A number of other Volksdeutsche, including some from his own street, were rejected by the S.S. doctor because they were not tall enough or else poor-sighted, which made Kempf say mockingly: "Of course, whoever heard of a Superman with glasses?" He laughed at them, but deep down, it was beginning to feel dangerous to spread jokes, because even among the Volksdeutsche there were people who'd inform for a glass of brandy. In a cinema news bulletin he saw Heinrich Himmler fuming against repulsive Jews who were trying to suck our German blood. "For sure, a not particularly clever Superman! He would certainly have had all the mirrors in his castle smashed!" thought Kempf, munching sweets he had bought on his way to the cinema – from the Jewish corner shop. Needless to say, the owner of the cinema was also a Jew, who sold his goods, even Himmler on the screen. It was stupid to kill Jews, Kempf went on thinking. His father traded with them, and they with him. Many of them were very able. They would bargain over every small coin, but were accurate in payments, as a rule they did not cheat. There had to be trade, people would always trade. It was stupid to kill the Israelites. They took care of the flow of money, they were like the veins of humanity.

Kempf-the-son had overheard innumerable conversations his father had held, sitting behind his counter, with Jewish traders, and had frequently heard something along the lines of "Let's go for trust! A man is tied by his word, an ox by its horns!"

Nevertheless, a few days earlier his father had confessed that since the beginning of the year he had stopped trading with the Jews. Because they were all Bolsheviks.

But at least he hadn't mentioned German blood.

The Party considered that the majority of "our" Germans were for Hitler. While it was common knowledge that among them there were different trends and strands, the Party still considered most of them written off, enemies therefore. What is more, to Vera and her brother Đuka Kempf was a toff. Maybe they had brushed in passing on the corso, but they didn't know each other. They lived in separate worlds.

The corso went on for hours, every day, especially on Sundays.

Vera stopped for a moment with a group of young Jewish girls, some of whom were beauties. It was impossible to overlook their lovely plaits. It was impossible not to hear their slightly forced laughter.

"What's going to happen to us?" they asked.

"Come to the meeting."

"But you're already being arrested, crushed, so what will it be like when the Germans get here? You can't help us. Everyone's out to protect his own life. What's going to happen to us, Vera?"

That question ran through the group of young Jewish women, bouncing from one to the other like a ball in a cruel game, a ball no-one wanted to have land on their chest. "What's going to happen to us?"

A friend from grammar school, Jewish, told Vera that she had gone to the station the day before and laid her head on the rails, listening to the distant rumble of trains on their way.

Horrified, Vera pictured that lovely head with its heavy black plait lying on the railway track. The young Jewish girl had firmly resolved to escape forever from her fear by throwing herself under a train. But then she had not done it, she had just listened to the rumble, convinced that it made no difference as a train would very soon take them all away on a journey of no return.

"Trains can be blown up at will!" Vera said, after she had

ensured that the informer she knew slightly had moved away to spy on another group of Jews. "What a career choice, damn him," ran through Vera's mind.

An outsider observing the swaying of the corso might have registered a multitude of tiny gestures, but most of them, although wrapped in frivolity, geniality and youthful mischief, intimated a final reckoning.

"Will you come to say goodbye to me when they get us all together at the station?" asked Vera's friend.

She promised she would. Of course, no matter what. "But you're not going anywhere."

"If it was in your hands . . . But nothing will be in your hands."

"Everything will be or the whole world will be gone."

"The whole world won't be gone. Only we Jews will be."

"Come and see me, we'll talk. I have some books that might interest you."

"My father would thump me. We adhere to the old faith, and you don't believe in God."

"God's not the problem. It's the priests!" Vera said defiantly.

A year and a half after this conversation on the corso, the local Jews, all those who could be found, but most of them had signed up of their own accord, were shoved into cattle trucks which then stood for half a day in the extreme heat.

Vera was not able to say goodbye. She too faced arrest, avoiding it at the time only by sleeping in a different house every night. To go to the station and say goodbye to a Jewish friend was a risk that her contacts would not have forgiven. She lived in a kind of grey zone of the semi-Underground, feeling that she would soon be swallowed up by total darkness.

Who Am I?

Jakub Šalamun lived in one of four apartments in a large house on the dark side of the street. As a would-be doctor, it had not escaped Kempf-the-son's notice that in that row of rented buildings, which let the rain in on all four sides at the whim of the winds, more people died than elsewhere. Tuberculosis was rife. People said that hearses drew up on that side of the road twice as often to collect the dead than on the other side that was warmed by the sun. It once seemed to him that on the notice declaring: "I'm on guard here", instead of a picture of a dog there was a skull. There was nowhere better in this town to study the Manichean division between darkness and light, between *having* and *perishing*.

Kempf heard that his friend Branimir, Šalamun's son, was in trouble: the Rights Party people had abducted him in broad daylight, on the corso, thrown him into a cart and taken him off to a farmstead, completely abandoned for fifty years, on the other side of the Bosut river. Branko Šalamun was a year younger than Kempf and wanted to follow in his footsteps, that is to study medicine. He wanted passionately to cure people, he was especially interested in tuberculosis, he subscribed to professional journals, cutting out everything to do with the disease. Like many Jews, he read and spoke German.

But what kind of Jews were these Šalamuns? Certainly not

orthodox. Not once in the many times that Kempf had been to that apartment had he seen any of the requisites that orthodox adherents to the Jewish faith hold sacred; no kosher customs connected with food . . . The Šalamuns ate like all impoverished people and could not be fastidious. Jakub Šalamun had worked at the Bata shoe company in Borovo practically since the factory was established, in the early 1930s. For almost a decade, Šalamun had been sticking soles onto shoes, sitting in the dust and stench of leather, complaining of nothing. His mother was a Slavonian (Catholic), she held up the four corners of this apartment in which at every downpour they opened every umbrella they could find, and where the walls were green with mould. They had christened their son in a country church where God had been represented, for as long as anyone could remember, by a somewhat warped priest, a distant relative of Šalamun's consort, and they chose the name of the old Croatian Prince Branimir. If anyone in this little town wanted to be "like everyone else", it was the Šalamuns.

Was it possible that they had come for Branko, of all people, and why, for heaven's sake?

The boys had been together the previous day in the yard behind the grammar school; Kempf had handed him a bunch of cigarettes, knowing he didn't have any and was a passionate smoker. Their conversation had gone roughly like this:

"So, Branko, what's new?"

"Nothing, as yet, thank God."

"What do you mean, as yet?"

"The Jews are meeting at each other's houses."

"Well, that's nothing new."

"They sit round the table and say nothing."

They finished their cigarettes and parted. Branko struck him as frightened. For a moment he thought it would be good to invite him to stay with him for a few nights. He meant to say to come and spend the night with the Germans, but he had second thoughts.

Kempf waited outside the door for a long time, he knew that the Šalamuns were there, that his father had come straight home from the factory when he heard the news. He knew this because someone had met his father hurrying home and that person had passed the news on to Kempf; and he could hear through the door the sounds of stirring, those produced by muffled footsteps over a rotten floor.

"Open the door, it's me, Ðuka," Kempf said quietly. He could clearly hear breathing on the other side of the door, which was finally opened. Mrs Šalamun looked him up and down, fearfully. He even thought that she didn't want to let him in. That astounded him.

Kempf was used to coming and going through this door as though it was his second home. Young Šalamun and he had been friends forever. He had only one other friend as close as this: Franja. Since Franja had disappeared and no-one knew what had become of him, Branimir Šalamun was his only remaining friend . . . as Ðuka himself liked to say: a top-notch friend; all the others were just acquaintances.

Branko was sitting on the couch, leaning against a faded tapestry, which could, to a well-intentioned judge, resemble the Venetian lagoon. He was gazing blankly in front of him, his arms crossed on his chest as though intending to defend himself from blows. His face was almost completely blue. It looked to Kempf like a mask; eye sockets surrounded by black, like a pumpkin in which someone had cut the usual four holes for a face. Branimir didn't say hello, only the family dog wagged its tail, recognising Kempf's smell in its file of the few visitors who ever came here, and began to wind round his legs.

Branko moved onto the edge of the couch, put his head in his hands and fell onto his knees. He didn't want to see anyone, or he didn't want anyone to see him. He seemed to have sunk into his own thoughts; in truth as though he was far from this room, but where could that be? Mrs Šalamun came in with a bowl of water from which steam was rising; she wanted to sponge her son's face, but he declined.

"What in God's name has he done?" his mother wailed. "Why did they pick on him? What harm has he done anyone?"

Kempf wanted to say something comforting, but he couldn't think of anything. Her questions were so absurd that there was no answer. Of course the Šalamuns had never harmed anyone. Kempf knew that now almost all non-Jews had the patriotic duty of spitting at Jews. There was one Jew who owned a mill and cheated over the flour; another was a loan shark, so a bloodsucker to the core; it wasn't right that a Jew should have a mill, it wasn't right that a Jew should have anything, but that would be sorted out by the new times. The debts the loathsome usurer recorded in his books would disappear, the books would disappear, and soon all the Jews would disappear ... The most loathsome among them were the Jews who rented taverns; they were past masters at exploiting human weaknesses. It was a public duty to spit at the very mention of them. Taverns were national institutions and they should be owned and run by true locals.

A lot of that would change and soon. Those who did not understand this would end up like Branimir Šalamun ... What had happened to Branimir Šalamun at that abandoned farm was just another warning sign. A far more serious rounding up of the Jews would soon begin.

Kempf sat at the table, refusing anything offered him and gazing helplessly at his friend. "Who did this?"

His friend didn't reply. It was a stupid question. Who today would not have done it?

Only the communists. And where had they hidden? Deep underground, they were printing their leaflets. They were collecting medical supplies and ammunition; they stole from the royal army. It was rumoured that they had even stolen and buried a field gun. Above all, they were waiting. Everyone was waiting for radical events and everyone hoped that they would favour their side. The communists were convinced that everything would be the way it was written in their books. Some of which the worker Šalamun had read. The others didn't believe in books, firmly convinced that everything would turn out as determined by life and God on high, in whose name men had been thundering from the pulpit against the chosen people.

In the eyes of the local Slavonians, Branimir was seen as a somewhat tender plant. He wore glasses that shattered as soon as they threw him into the cart. Since then everything had been just a fog for him, adding to the impression that he was mentally absent. As a doctor in training, Kempf wondered whether the wounds one couldn't see, inflicted by the beating, were not worse than the visible bruises. What about his kidneys, for instance? Might not the worst yet show up in blood in his urine?

Branko was timid and intelligent. He was among the best students at the Vinkovci grammar school. At the end of every semester, his success would be rewarded with the prize of a book. Kempf now recognised those titles on the shelf above the couch. He was surprised that he had never noticed the books before. It was the kind of reading matter that the Rights Party people would have considered patriotic: a beautiful edition of the poet Silvije Strahimir Kranjčević: "*Eli, eli, lama azamtani . . . Lord, Lord, why hast thou forsaken me . . .?*" Then the writings of the Father of the Homeland, Ante Starčević . . . the very father of whom the Party of Rights had declared themselves the sons. Since when did books matter to people? Poetry especially.

"We'll lie in wait for them somewhere! They won't get away with this!" Kempf said as he was leaving.

At the door Branko's father whispered: "Don't tell anyone about this. Our misfortune is our misfortune. Take no action!"

But it was only later – in Poland – that Kempf grasped the terrible isolation of "our" Jews.

Outside, the sun was shining on the other side of the road. Kempf encountered a hearse: horses with black trappings and blinkers, with yellow tassels on the cover. Need it be said that the owner of the funeral company in this little town was a Jew? This was viewed by the townspeople and neighbouring peasants with particular suspicion, grumbling something along the lines of "what more can we give them, what else will they take? The Israelites have even bought up our graveyards . . . They collect interest even on our death . . ."

Kempf was fearful that this was a sign, although he had just seen the Šalamuns alive; he was fearful that the hearse would stop in front of the house where they lived. But that didn't happen, the hearse rolled on over the cobbles . . . Little changed here in fact, Kempf observed. This cobbled road was built by the Ottomans at the time when beys and agas ruled here.

Kempf left the Šalamuns with the idea of getting together a few lads who weren't averse to village fights, on the contrary, they took pride in them. In this part of the world no village fair could pass without bloody noses.

Walking between the chestnut trees, Kempf ran through several names. There were many he drank too much with, some he had fought alongside, when they were attacked by lads from another village. It's a well-known fact that nothing strengthens friendships more, even superficially, than a good fight. But one by one all those names were discounted. Most of the notorious drinkers and merrymakers were members of the Rights Party. Some even openly antisemitic. Two or three were left-wing. But it was hard to imagine they would let themselves be led by a German. Moreover, as far as those on the left were concerned, he had simply not been included. Besides, none of those who had signed up had ever made even the slightest effort to let him into their secrets. To be honest, he had never been interested in the books secretly read by members of the communist youth wing. Was there a revolutionary movement anywhere in the world that needed poets? Kempf doubted it. He knew that the left-inclined considered him a useless aesthete who came, to cap it all, from an indecently rich family. That was unforgivable. It's true that he could drink, he wasn't arrogant, he'd kick a ball around with the apprentices, he didn't stick his German nose in the air, he virtually never went to church. But nonetheless, in their eyes he was a bourgeois, a toff, a dandy. In his great universal pain, refined and, oh, so profound, he could not see the misery of those summoned by a siren every morning to the factory. He could not see the suffering of those on the side of the street that was always in shadow. That was unjust, but to whom could Kempf apologise and what would that accomplish? He knew there were people on all sides who could not be persuaded of anything if it conflicted with what they believed. If he was only a Calvinist, like many Germans and Hungarians, there would then be at least some seed of rebellion . . . but he wasn't even that, and he didn't stay away from church out of some inner revolt, but because it was an inconvenience. He didn't want to be bothered by triviality, for him a visit to the priest with a basket of eggs at Easter was as meaningless as world revolution. He didn't get out of bed before noon for just anything.

But even all that, taken together, might have been O.K., had he not been German, and they, like everyone else, were now fleeing to their flock. Kempf had just once, in a chance conversation in a tavern which he should not have witnessed, heard two or three youngsters maintain that the Hitler–Stalin pact was a brilliant trick played on the General Secretary and that the Germans and Soviets would sooner or later come to blows and then feathers would fly as never before.

He spent the afternoon in his room, bad-tempered and brooding. He went over the details of his visit to his battered friend. Apart from the dog, no-one there seemed to have wanted to see him. As though the air in that apartment – people really ought not to live in such apartments – was filled not only with damp, but with a kind of reproach directed at him. As though it had occurred to them that day for the first time that he was German.

What kind of German am I? Everything in Kempf rebelled. When all this antagonism that had come over people, settling in them like a kind of illness, finally passed, the three of them, Franja, Branko and he, Đuka Kempf, would once again hang around together in the lanes and vineyards, as far as Ilok, as far as Sremska Kamenica . . . And they'd go to Venice, definitely, one day. And to Tuscany, as they'd be in Italy already.

His afternoon dragged on in this unhealthy, listless frame of mind, and at dusk, he finally went out to the corso, which was already thinning out. Just a few strollers passed, up and down, in the same senseless movement, as though commanded by a squad leader: "Left, right, about turn!" Just like this little river, the Asser Savus in the language of ancient Rome, and today named Bosut, a word probably of Illyrian origin, which always, at the same time of year would suddenly alter direction and start to flow upstream, almost entirely choked with rushes and water lilies, so too, at the end of the corso, this procession of walkers turned and began walking – upstream. The Asser Savus mocked the very concept of a riverbed and current, and did so unusually persistently, that is every year: it was the only river Kempf had ever heard of that flowed away from its river mouth. It was a shame he wasn't interested in puzzles: it would have been a good question for a crossword.

Was there some message in this? In the opposite direction from its mouth, that must mean: it flowed towards its spring, towards its origin.

What kind of German am I, Kempf wondered probably for the first time in his life, before lying down fully clothed under his sheet, too lazy to get undressed. Some people around him quivered with a special elation at the theme of *Germanness*; he was himself yet to feel any such twinge.

Before he fell asleep, he remembered what he had overheard, on the corso, like a secret called over the shoulder to someone who didn't in fact deserve to be let into it. Someone, that is an unknown number of people, had that afternoon beaten senseless a group of four Rights Party members in a barn somewhere. They used fence posts, hoes and, apparently, knives. The victims' lives were saved at the last moment by the police.

"I must warn Branko not to go out on the street anymore!" That was his concluding thought before falling asleep. But a vain hope. That night the God of sleep had a list of far too many frightened people who needed to be soothed to sleep but were kept awake by deadly terror. On that long night, Morpheus found no time for Kempf. But he had nothing to fear. Whether he liked it or not, Germanness watched over him. What it would bring him, he would soon find out.

One way or another, this business with the Jews would not end well, he concluded. It was dangerous these days to own anything and to be a Jew. But, Kempf remembered, the Jews who had worked with him at the brickworks were all poor. It seemed that it was dangerous just to be a Jew. To be simply a person had become impossible.

What to Take to War?

"You don't need anything," said his father, who, freshly shaved, was running his magnifying glass over the newspaper. "You'll be given everything. Pack a razor and a small bottle of cologne. Let's hope all this won't last much longer."

To start with, Kempf-the-elder had been proud of his son's drunkenness. But when Georg was brought home often completely incapacitated, the old man began to frown.

"Everyone knows what a German carnival is like. Everyone here knows that we Germans have our days. And when we have our days, everyone else stays at home, watching the street from behind the curtains. But with you now every day's a carnival. No German does that."

And lately this last had become a kind of catchphrase: *No German does that; he doesn't do this*, or, simply, *we Germans . . .*

This "we Germans" was something new. Georg couldn't remember anyone in their house ever saying something like "we Germans" before the Führer clambered to power. Not even anything like "we". If used at all, that "we" referred to the wider Kempf clan, but those relationships were remote, even if they were blood ties. The memory of 1770 survived in the family saga. The year before that had been a hungry year in Germany, when many Germans tore themselves away from the German "we" and set off down the Danube, under the skirts of the Empress, to the south of the empire . . . and, along with their pots, pans, bed linen (hardly anything more than that), they carried their blood. But that blood, *Blut*, had now acquired a new tone, far stronger and more resonant. Kempf-the-son had previously heard: So-and-so is "my blood"! There were proud fathers and mothers. But none of them had emphasised the little word "blood" so proudly and forcefully as old Adalbert Grumm, who was known as the local "Gauleiter", and who used at "ethnic German" gatherings to shout about "German blood", how precious it was, but how honourable it was also to spill it when the Führer put that on the agenda. As though there were infinite supplies of that blood.

And this was also new: the community of those connected by blood had suddenly become immeasurably broader than the one encompassing the Kempf family. Đuka tried to remember when that had occurred, but the 1930s were the years of his boyhood, filled with quite different interests and enthusiasms. It was only later he realised that the German children with whom he associated did not on the whole belong to that new burgeoning "we". And it was, so to speak, yesterday that he had suddenly grasped that among those with whom he had kicked a football around, there were also the children of Jews. Who had sprung from which egg had been of no account, just whether it had been a good kick, to left or right.

"A German soldier is an orderly soldier," concluded Kempf-the-elder as he left. But he said it in a quite un-German, half-hearted way, believing that a father had to say something along those lines to his son as he went off to war. "You don't need anything, you'll get everything from the army."

But the son had underestimated the father. Kempf-the-elder knew how to read between the lines. He had himself realised that the German military machine had got bogged down, with the Stalingrad catastrophe Hitler had lost his famous strategic initiative. In addition, he had turned against some of the local Germans who were now making such a song and dance because he knew too much about them. They all lived in a small world where everything was known. Above all, the old man was furious that he had not managed to buy his son off.

He didn't himself wish to show any of this. In that respect Old Kempf was a true German: he knew how to conceal his emotions.

For a while the recruit was left alone with his mother, who was wiping her eyes with the edge of her apron. Now that her husband had gone out for his obligatory couple of glasses, her tears could flow more freely.

His father had given him a rucksack, which he had brought back from the war. The war? The war that was not yet called the first, as only now was this war in the process of involving the world. And then it would mean that the 1914 war became the first world war. Into that rucksack, Kempf now put his shaving gear and woollen socks . . .

Did he even then anticipate the east and the terrible Russian winter? The season now approaching was summer, but his mother had clear memories of images from newspapers; soldiers with forced smiles, unable to conceal the fact that they were not equipped for the Russian winter.

Next to go into his rucksack was a little notebook of poems, his own. Only a few chosen people had been permitted access to that treasure trove . . . In effect, just two.

Franja, who had vanished for the time being, and Sofija – who knew what had become of her . . . ?

Looking through his papers and books, Kempf-the-younger came upon his atlas and opened it on the table: the Union of Soviet Socialist Republics, Poland, still whole, before it was dismembered by the Soviets and Nazis. Austria, still independent. The world of yesterday. How arbitrary frontiers are, he thought. Today a frontier is here, tomorrow one hundred kilometres to the north or south; states move about, whole, like Prussia, probably seven times. And now it was in a completely different place, stronger than ever. Then Poland, as if pulsating, alternately bigger and smaller, and all drenched in blood, but it was Polish blood . . . Where are "we"? What do the Polish "we" have to say about it all? Now that Poland is no more?

Kempf embarked on a little thought-perception experiment: he decided for a moment to erase all the frontiers, those of yesterday, and those relevant today . . . What was left? An enormous expanse in the centre of which Europe and Asia collide.

In truth, it was so enormous that even the Reich in its current expansionary mode was still small. That space simply swallowed the army raised by Napoleon, digested it and spat out the remains along with all their human fluids – near Paris.

Frankly speaking, he had no idea what to take with him to war.

All at once, drums. And singing from many throats, which was meant to sound strong and masculine, but childish voices predominated.

Đuka peered from behind the curtain. "German carnival," he thought, and withdrew into the room.

Even a brief look had let him recognise the man marching at the head of the procession, briskly, one might say, and more so than one could have expected at his considerable age. Old Grumm, the "Gauleiter". Some twenty lads of an age still tender, with their first stubble and pimples, accompanied him; right behind him marched a rather older fellow banging with all his might on a drum so big it knocked against his legs . . . They were all still wearing shorts, but also carrying at least some trace of a uniform. An army coming into being, thought Kempf.

Out of the yards of the houses, lined along the street, as in all Slavonian villages and small towns, little children emerged and ran after the column, trying to catch its rhythm ... Most started singing straight away, while old Grumm, the only true Nazi Georg knew personally, set the beat. It seemed to Đuka that several village dogs that had joined the procession, were endeavouring to harmonise their four legs to the same beat ... the cats were more cautious. From a barn a cow lowed sorrowfully.

She hasn't been milked, thought Georg, her udder must be full to overflowing. And she hasn't been milked because the lad who takes care of her has hopped into the procession ...

Where is it heading, that procession? There are ever more of them. Kempf would never have imagined that there were so many children in those yards. Where were the girls? There they are, they too have joined the procession, waving their headscarves ... Mr Grumm the Nazi is stepping out ever more decisively, turning round from time to time, as though counting, he's obviously pleased. The results of his campaigning are probably paying dividends.

They're all following him. Where to, in God's name? To Transylvania? To Russia? To Wallachia? Where the piper lured all the youngsters? The tune from his pipe was still swirling. What remained now was the rhythm. Nazis love drums. And, probably, fire. The local paper writes of "the Nazis' curious love of fire". Torchlight processions were common in these parts too.

He was roused by a banging on the door, at first timid then increasingly loud.

His mother went to open it, but Georg stopped her and glanced behind the curtain: in front of the door stood a lad he didn't know, in shorts and a white shirt that was probably white so his armband with its swastika could be more clearly seen.

Kempf opened the door and asked him what he wanted.

"A gathering on the square has been ordered, Mr Kempf."

"Who ordered it?"

The boy was confused. It was clear that he couldn't understand how Mr Kempf didn't know.

"I can't go," Đuka said. "I'm ill."

The boy's eyes widened. The man in the doorway didn't seem remotely ill to him.

Đuka began enumerating:

"Neuralgic pain in the perineum. Weak Achilles reflex. Haemorrhoids hanging down to my heels."

It looked as if the boy was about to say goodbye because the column had already moved into the street that turned right by the Holy Trinity Church.

Suddenly Kempf, noticing the disappointment on his face, decided not to leave him entirely empty-handed.

"I've been called up. Into the S.S."

Only then did the boy look at him, as though measuring his height. "Stalingrad."

And here the child, full of wonder, gave him the Hitler salute and scurried after his people; after the "Gauleiter", into whose wake little boys continued to emerge from a great many houses.

Here, in Slavonia, there are no mountains that could swallow up those children on the way to Transylvania, thought Kempf. But there are plenty elsewhere.

Kempf closed his atlas and put it back in the drawer. No-one would ever open it again.

He hadn't lied to the boy. He was getting ready to go to war.

He heard his mother rummaging through cupboards, sighing all the while. His father had not yet returned.

Perhaps he too was marching behind the "Gauleiter"? He couldn't see him through the window. He was simply too old for war, even for marching. His father's heart was not in the best shape, it reminded him too frequently of its existence. A healthy heart does its job peacefully.

Kempf-the-son lay down on the couch with an almost obsessive thought: perhaps these were the last moments of peace in his life?

A film ran through his head, entitled *The recruitment of Georg Kempf, future soldier of the Waffen-S.S. Wochenschau.*

First a thunderous title, announcing: *The Imperial Eagle*, then the news. Kempf's old school.

He knew it well. By the third year of war nothing much had changed, it was merely even more dilapidated. What is more the recruitment medical took place in his own classroom, looking onto the garden and orchard. Both the garden and the orchard had been dug, weeded, manured and harvested by the pupils, many of whom Kempf remembered. The desks were still where they had always been, and Đuka easily found the one with the initials Đ. K. cut into it. Then a heart with one letter placed in its centre: S, standing for Sofija.

Out of habit, Đuka sat down at his old desk. He had liked sitting by the window and always chose that spot when they were permitted to choose. That was why in school hours his gaze would wander over the garden and orchard. What was taught here was on the whole outside his interests. He read abundantly and passionately, but largely what was not on the syllabus. On the contrary, some of the titles he chose were banned. He read books that were "not for his age"; he devoured Krafft-Ebing, for instance, at one sitting and survived, unlike the writer who was killed by the things he discovered.

To his right sat Franja Lauber, a Volksdeutscher (as it was written in more recent times, German nouns being written with a capital) like himself. Franz – that's how his name was written in school papers, just as his was written Georg. But no-one in the class called them Franz and Georg.

Franja derived from Franz, while Đuka, via Juraj, from Georg. Until a few years previously, the Kempfs had barely known that they were Volksdeutsche, a kind of "sub-species" of Germans, nor did they consider themselves special in any way. But in that class, consisting predominantly of little Slavonians, there were other kinds of Volksdeutsche: those who had always known they were Germans, who knew also what "Nibelung loyalty", *deustsche Treue*, was and were only awaiting "the call of the homeland". There were two of them. Out of fifteen Germans. No-one had taken their Germanness seriously until it all flared up.

On the contrary, when the call came, the majority had not responded with any fervour. Those who had always burned with a German flame had left Nuštar in the first year of the war. Little had been heard of them since.

Nor had Franja been heard from for two months now, thought Đuka, waiting at his desk for the commission. Franja had been called up to the Waffen-S.S., like many Volksdeutsche from the town. His war journey took him east. Georg thought that anything would have been better than that, even Africa. Franz Lauber had been given his military number long ago, and already at this stage of the war, March 1943, the achievements of the German postal system had become legendary: letters had been delivered in unbelievable circumstances, in spite of all difficulties; some had been thrown from the air to besieged armies . . .

Besieged armies? In March 1943 very few in Germany knew that Paulus had surrendered at Stalingrad and that the 6th Army had been annihilated; so given that, how could anyone in Nuštar have known anything about that well-concealed catastrophe? The last letter Đuka had received from Franja was sent from a position some sixty kilometres south of that town of ill-fated name. And as Franja had stopped writing, Đuka had easily concluded that his unit had moved forward . . . And that it had been vaporised somewhere in the Stalingrad cauldron. Kempf-the-son had a premonition. He asked at the post office every day, the postman was a friend, they played football together . . . The postman shook his head and shrugged, as though he was to blame . . .

Đuka had been friends with virtually everyone in the class. Franja played the mandolin, Đuka could play a bit of guitar; no further than the circle of fifths, but they could manage duets and so, instead of Pan pipes, the Slavonian vineyards rang with songs sung by boys, Slavonians of distant German origin . . . The songs were gentle, sentimental, as though sung with the foreboding of imminent partings.

The postman was called Lacika, he was of distant Hungarian origin. But he didn't speak Hungarian. The Germans were different: most could at least stumble their way through a bit of German, learned at home. It wasn't the German of Goethe or Schiller, and few "real" Germans would have been able to understand them, as became obvious very soon in the war into which they had been dragged.

Dragged, yes. Few really went off voluntarily, particularly in 1943. *Freiwillige Gezwungene* – that's what they called them at that time: *forced volunteers*! That may have been an exact translation of the ironic German phrase. Among the people there was a more practical expression: *forceteers*.

Language may enjoy such nonsense, at least no-one complained about it. The people enjoyed it less, even if they were in fact "Volksdeutsche", a sub-species of German not born in the Reich.

On the desk behind which Đuka's teachers had once taught, leaning on a vase full of chrysanthemums, was a photograph of the Führer, taken some years earlier. On the wall above the blackboard, where the King had once hung, there was a rectangle, lighter than the wall around it: the King was absent. The new Leader was present, but he didn't seem particularly belligerent, a little melancholy, perhaps. Had the year 1943 made its way into the picture? Or had he perhaps heard something about the Paulus debacle, that is the total annihilation of the 6th Army at Stalingrad?

There were several men in the Recruitment Medical Commission, and two of them were people Đuka would never have dreamed were German. What was their problem, he wondered. They're summoned from all over the place and they emerge from their holes, like rodents.

The Kempfs had been "born into" wealth, almost from the start. The hard work of generations had annulled the terrible poverty of Maria Theresa's colonists. The Germans had increased their properties, developed their trades, right up until the beginnings of proper industry . . . The war was an opportunity for new acquisitions, the black market flourished, everywhere food had become far more expensive. Pig fat became lucrative. All armies needed pig fat, the top lubricant in wartime.

But Đuka, soon to be Georg, knew that Dr Schlauss was incorruptible. Or maybe not? Everyone has his price. The said Schlauss was now sitting beside Hitler's picture, tapping his pencil on the edge of Georg's file, and Georg realised that everything hung in the balance. He had been in the same class as little Schlauss, as there weren't many classes in Nuštar . . . Hans Schlauss always conducted himself like a German, he bore his Germanness in an obvious way, from his short trousers with *hosenträger* braces. In brief, a true son of his father and a true son of his original German homeland. Dr Adalbert Schlauss had likewise always been a doctor in the town, and, of course, he had always been a German . . . even when the "local Germans" supported the King, in the hope that this would better protect their interests in his multinational, turbulent kingdom. Schlauss was the first, after the Austrian Anschluss, to put a swastika in his window, and when that ill-fated swastika leaped, like a huge bug, onto the doctor's sleeve, it swelled still more, becoming the heart of the Third Reich's flag, which was first seen in Nuštar fluttering on his two-storey house. The Führer's birthdays were celebrated in Nuštar long before the arrival of the Wehrmacht in the April war in 1941. On the day of France's capitulation, Dr Schlauss declared his house open "to all neighbours of good will" and placed barrels of brandy in front of his house, for everyone . . . "not to take home, but to drink as much as they could . . ."

His son, Hans Schlauss, quite handy with a ball, and in possession of a pleasant and confident tenor voice (his rendering of German songs could send shivers down the spine of listeners even if they weren't German), had barely made it through school. He went off to the war, which he was firmly convinced was his own, as early as 1941. At the moment when Georg Kempf came before the commission, in March 1943, Schlauss junior had been elevated to the lowest rank in the military hierarchy of the Waffen-S.S.: he had become a Sturmmann, which in the old army would have been a squad leader. His father was not pleased. It is not at all clear how something like that could have spread like news beyond the family circle. But Dr Schlauss succeeded, until the end of the war, in concealing the fact that his son never was at the real front; he was a guard in one of the collection camps in the occupied remains of Poland. And it was hard to advance there. The Jews did not resist their annihilation, or at least not in a way that their resistance would have been an opportunity for real military merit . . . But still, Hans saw a lot. And, as always, he drank. He is now fading out of this novel, deservedly so.

Well, Đuka liked the occasional drink. Recently he had had several bouts of drunkenness that left him insensible. A few days earlier he had almost frozen in a vineyard; he was woken by the rising sun, drenched with dew. As the recruitment came closer, he drank nearly every day.

He didn't want to go to war.

Đuka sat in his former classroom, trying to remember where everyone had sat. Franja here beside him, at the same desk, throughout their schooling. The third would have been the Jew Šalamun, but he was a year younger.

They used to meet up with him at break, in the school playground.

Branimir Šalamun was short-sighted, he didn't join in the ball games, he didn't join in anything. He was brilliant at maths, but the spiteful put that down to his specific Jewish brain. Šalamun would stand in a corner of the playground, waiting for someone to talk to him. Usually either Đuka Kempf or Franja Lauber.

Once, before morning classes had begun, Đuka noticed through the fence boys stalking the Jewish boy and trying to trip him up. He knew that they abused him whenever they could, but this time Đuka was incensed.

At break, Franja and Đuka asked all the boys for their attention. "Anyone who touches Šalamun from now on will have to answer to us!"

For various, in fact contradictory, reasons, that sounded convincing. First, Franja, although of medium build, was an amateur boxer and spent at least an hour every day beating a punchbag. Đuka didn't have a similar reputation, but it was known that he never ran away from a fight. The fact that he used to write little verses in girls' autograph books was at that time of secondary importance.

But there was something in this threat of Franja's that was even more convincing: both were Germans, and that carried some weight. Increasingly so, in fact. It couldn't have been said that most of the pupils were antisemitic. Their games never went further than popular humour on the theme of Jews. But with his small stature and great success as a student, Šalamun's very existence provoked anger and aggression.

However, after their initial surprise, there were some louts who didn't like Franja's little speech.

Some began again to try some of their "games" with Šalamun. When it came to a skirmish, there was a split lip and a couple of bruises. A scandal broke out at the school; Dr Schlauss, whose son had been given a bloody nose, was exceedingly "alarmed". He demanded that those "Jewish sycophants, Jewish servants" be thrown out of school immediately, with no right to register anywhere in the kingdom. Nothing came of that. Need one say that Dr Schlauss had a primordial dislike of Jews? If they were to disappear, all ailments would be Schlauss' own.

The war was approaching, brawls between young men were becoming increasingly frequent and increasingly serious. Both Kempf and Lauber realised that they could no longer protect Šalamun.

Possibly only through the system – a bruise for a bruise, an eye for an eye . . . But, in any case, Šalamun would always be the target. He disappeared in the first days of the new state. Where was he now?

As Kempf sat at his desk, memories came flooding back.

There was that Professor Neurath, for instance, who had come straight from the Reich. When he came into the classroom, he would always go to the window and open it wide, even if it was pouring. He evidently thought that the air inside was contaminated.

The first time he came into the classroom, Professor Neurath asked that the three blue-eyed boys sit apart, with a space between them and the rest of the class.

After that, someone tried to draw his attention to the fact that there were other Germans in the class.

Neurath leafed through the register. There were as many as ten Germans. But only three had fair hair.

Then one of the three said that he wasn't German. "So what are you, lad?" asked Neurath.

"A Kurd," the boy replied.

And that was the end of that.

We didn't know what Kurds were, Kempf remembered. Our Kurd told us that he had come across the name in a crossword. He was in fact Romany. But, exceptionally, fair-haired. That Kurd's fine "Aryan" head would be smashed in the concentration camp at Jasenovac.

Neurath stopped lining us up and dividing us. But he went on opening the window. That was all a long time ago.

Then a more recent memory came to him: of Ferdo Ferk, a lively, inquisitive but somehow always melancholy boy who sat in the middle row, level with Franja Lauber. Ferdo seemed always to be gazing into a misty future. On one occasion, he had astonished Đuka by announcing: "Has it ever occurred to you, my friend, that the entire world could disappear in the blink of an eye? No-one actually knows what's holding the world together. It isn't at all far-fetched that the world could come to an end at any moment, and then start again. Everything's so uncertain."

Much later Kempf recalled that this had been a kind of introduction. They happened to be in the Ferks' house, on some occasion he no longer remembered. Kempf and Ferdo were alone, on the first floor of the house belonging to Ferdo's father, a sought-after waggon-maker.

For no obvious reason, Ferdo Ferk went up to the wall and, to Đuka's astonishment, removed a brick from it.

"Look, my friend. Maybe one day you'll need this hole . . . should you ever want to hide something of great value to you . . ."

"Why would I want to hide anything?"

"Your little ditties, perhaps?"

"They're of no interest to anyone."

"My old man's smart. And prescient. At some point, the two of us will be picked up. You, Đuka, are too clever to let yourself be killed just like that, but who knows? That is, no-one knows what it is that holds this world of ours together and it's not impossible that in a few years' time our world will completely disappear."

Ferdo Ferk was right in one thing: he was "picked up" a year ago.

Where is Ferdo Ferk now? Does he write home, does he receive letters? Or has he vanished like Franja?

Half the class had disappeared, some had run away to the other side. And there was no word of their having perished.

And where was he now, Georg Kempf?

Now Georg Kempf, his hands hiding his genitals, pathetically wizened because of his evil forebodings, was standing in front of Dr Schlauss, the man who had wanted to drive him out of school and now considered him an enemy of the German cause, an immoral coward, who would do anything he could to get out of it. He, Dr Schlauss, on the other hand, would do all he could to engage him in the "German cause", as commanded by the Führer, God and the Reich.

There were another four of them, in addition to Kempf, at the medical examination, but the others didn't interest Dr Schlauss half as much as Kempf did. On the doctor's side of the table sat two others, one of whom was in uniform, with the S.S. insignia, a true German, it seemed. The other, keeping the register, was from Osijek, an older man who did not appear to be all that interested and kept chewing on his pencil. Georg knew him superficially, he used to see him at Schwabian events before the war. In a word, in the middle of Slavonia, the medical examination was a one hundred per cent "German affair". Although between their "German roots" and the Volksdeutsche of today almost two hundred "Slavonian" years had passed, and many dark-haired Dinarics had jumped into Schwabian women's beds, but now that was unimportant, erased in fact. Hitler, with his almost sorrowful expression, leaning on the vase of chrysanthemums (flowers for the dead?), had summoned all Germans, including those who had long forgotten their Germanness, to his banner. At that moment, in March 1943, Georg could not have known that the lowest height for soldiers suitable for the S.S. had been brought down to below the 170 centimetres that had prevailed at the start of the war, that is at the time when the S.S. was being transformed into a parallel army, growing in competition with the Wehrmacht. The criteria, in other words, had been somewhat reduced.

And had he known, how would that have helped him? He measured 176 centimetres. He didn't know that from now on an S.S. soldier could wear glasses.

He wore them, for reading. In other words, that wasn't worth mentioning.

He read a great deal. He drank and read. In war there would be no time for such bizarre activities. Virtually everything he had done as he waited for a change in his circumstances, at times completely immobilised by the uncertainties threatening to wreck his life, was now, at this table, being erased and written anew. He waited, therefore, in trepidation, for the change he gradually realised he would not be able to avoid.

And it came.

He no longer knew how he could have believed that Dr Schlauss would be withdrawn to Osijek, where many young Germans, perhaps as many as a thousand, were waiting for his verdict. When Georg saw him entering the classroom of his old school and sitting down, bursting with his own importance, he understood everything.

With a bitter taste in his mouth, at the end of the examination, Georg Kempf turned, with that brisk *About turn!* movement he had learned in the army of the kingdom of Yugoslavia, where he had done his military service, wishing only to leave the classroom as soon as permitted. Did it seem to him that a muscle on the Führer's cheek had quivered? Presumably as a sign of Hitler's approval and encouragement.

The Great War: Sturmmann Hitler! In the armed wing of the S.S., that was merely a squad leader.

Look at me, said the picture by the chrysanthemums, and you will be immune to the Bolshevik poisonous snakes. Then Kempf recalled a passage in the Old Testament: God had ordered Moses to cast a serpent of brass and place it on a pedestal so that all those of faint belief would come and look at it and all their doubts would vanish. In a way, the serpent acted in God's absence. The

Führer was unconvinced. He had ascended the pedestal on his own. Look at me and you will be cured of all doubt. Just as in a village tavern the innkeeper announces: I am your God and you owe me!

On his way out, Kempf managed to overhear Dr Schlauss concluding the consultation on his case with this gnomic conclusion: "My dear gentlemen, respected colleagues, please! Why, what is this compared to Stalingrad?"

Letter to Franja Lauber in the East

Franja, my dear friend,
I've never felt such heartache
as in this sunny early spring.
Iron fingers claw at my nerves.
Birds in the treetops, have they
been shot at? Is that a chirrup?
There, a blackbird has landed
on top of a post and is
addressing his invisible flock.
He's more angry than afraid.
Is that a love call? No, it isn't.
The blackbird is announcing
that what is below him, as far
as the eye can see, belongs to
him. And he will not tolerate
interlopers. He will pluck
out their feathers ... Is that
love? Here and there someone
responds. Applauding, I think.
Potential interlopers can't be
heard. There, that's what a
wartime spring looks like in

We gather in places where the
souls of the unborn dwell and
observe events. I cannot tell
you more about myself so do not
enquire. We cannot influence
events. Hence the anxiety that
will fill the margins of some of
the following pages.

Although, should I be born,
I shall not be a Jew, I rejoice
that marginal notes like this
will resemble the Babylonian
Talmud interpreted through
the commentaries of learned
rabbis.

We the unborn tremble for
there is no greater terror than
the terror of not being born.
With our first breath, all that
we have known before our birth
vanishes. As soon as He casts
us out of a woman's womb, God
will seal our nostrils and all our
knowledge will disappear as
though it never was. Those who
maintain that it is impossible

your orchard. No-one any longer believes that cockerels woo their hens. They take them. Birds are no longer to be trusted. Nature is mobilising.

A group of schoolchildren just passed, giggling. Children! The sun is rolling down the avenue, like a football. An ordinary spring afternoon. And signs everywhere.

I think about the day when we waited for Švagelj, and then heard that he had been snatched from his doorstep and taken straight to Stockerau. Why, he hardly knew that he was German. And what kind of Germans are we, the two of us? Germans say: *Man ist was man spricht!* A man is what he speaks. And in what language am I sending this letter? Even if it had occurred to me to write it in German, I would have had to have a dictionary beside me. But that would certainly have made life easier for the military censors.

It was market day when they took Švagelj away, who

to know anything of God may shrug their shoulders. As for us, we are so anxious that we have no time for theological speculations.

My chances are slim.

The man who is meant to be my father is sitting in a room belonging to a friend who has already vanished in the East, writing him a letter that will not be sent. That man has recently discovered that he is a Volksdeutscher. He is not overjoyed. This is an age when people roll down the streets wrapped in flags, borne by a rhythm set by menacing drums. Among the souls of the unborn there is none that would not be appalled by the mention of Stalingrad. We have already bidden farewell to hundreds and thousands of unborn Germans and Russians because those who were to become their parents fell near the city of that ominous name.

One might think: there are many people in the world, they could all be mothers and fathers.

Should a father fall in the East, another will take his place.

That would be a false calculation. We all have only ONE father and ONE mother.

knows where. In recent times they have despatched all newcomers off to the East.

The East? By now you must know what that word means. I don't, but I can guess.

Nothing can be learned from the newspapers. I won't write about what can nevertheless be read between the lines – my old man is probably the last man in Nuštar who still buys a paper. But whether I write it or not, you will know. However, there hasn't been a peep out of you for ages.

We don't even know if you're still alive. And so maybe I'm writing a letter to someone deceased, in these days of my greatest distress, fear, anxiety. And seeking comfort.

It was market day, the carts generated a lot of dust in which at dawn the houses almost disappeared . . . As though thinking their own thoughts.

And this is what I'm thinking: once this is all finally over, let's lie on our backs in the vineyards and watch the clouds chasing each other . . . in those vineyards it would be so good to disentangle the threads of our lives which now, knotted, could be easily broken . . . There, where you kissed, before all of this, the fair-haired girl who told you as you parted that she intended to enter a nunnery . . . And if we were able to kiss like that, after it all, if, that is, everything yet to come was already past and behind us . . . where you kissed and she gave herself to you entirely, saying that it was the last time. Women often see what is invisible to us.

I'm sitting at your desk. There's a book on it that you didn't finish reading. It's not in German either. Will you ever read this letter? Your mother's busy in the kitchen, occasionally I hear a quiet sob; she bustles about to forget. Easter is later than usual this year, but it's unlikely we'll see you before Easter. You know what people say: "Expect me when you see me."

We did after all have some inkling that last summer was to be our last and that something mysterious, terrible was coming. Perhaps too human for a person to bear.

Here's your little brother by the desk. He's asking me to draw him a picture of a revolver.

Forgive me for writing so disjointedly. That's how I'm living, from one day to the next, so that it even seems that call-up papers would be a kind of relief. A man condemned to death, having reached the day of his execution, thinks: The worst is behind me!

I've become intolerable to those around me. I've taken to drink. Self-destruction.

A couple of days ago I wrote a few lines of verse. If they do mobilise me, I'll leave them in a tree hollow. Let the squirrels read them. They live in the tops of trees, while we're now compacted into the earth. As if crushed underfoot by some pre-Flood monster. You wrote to me long ago about the T-34, Stalin's tank. It was the first you'd seen of the Russians. You said these tanks emerged out of the earth and that no-one believed that Stalin could have so many. So much of it all was unbelievable and yet it happened. As a rule what happens is exactly what no-one would have thought could happen.

I'm sending you a couple of lines:

In the breezy murmur of daybreak Mornings reveal the
*   earth*
(. . .)
I kneel among the plum trees And pray to God to kill my
*   father.*

Unfinished, disjointed.

I don't agree with my old man. But I can't tell you why in this letter.

I'll leave the lines to the trees, the way children often leave their handkerchiefs in the treetops. Oh to be a child! To have been born in some other time. But who ever asked us anything?

P.S. On the 12th of this month I went for another medical. Diagnosis: neuralgic pains in the forefront of the peroneus. Achilles reflex reduced, paraesthesia not present.

Do you know who was in the commission? Old Schlauss. The father of that hooligan Schlauss who used to bully Šalamun with a bunch of other hooligans, and you once gave him a bloody lip. Nothing is known about him either, except that he too is in the East. I hadn't split his lip, but I had, so to say, held his hands. And I held his hands to stop him punching the Jew. Now they've brought old Schlauss out of retirement, he's got an office in Vinkovci. He travels around and gives expert opinions to the S.S. He also travels with the court martial, but in that capacity he confirms a death. In this other role, on loan to the S.S., he sends us volunteers to war.

The diagnosis does not hold out much hope. And since I was examined by Dr Schlauss, it would not have helped me even if I had been at death's door with some ailment. I hear he sends off T.B. sufferers with open cavities. As though we healthy Germans were in short supply.

People are saying they're drafting Muslims as well. So there will soon be an S.S. division made up entirely of Bosnian Muslims. Himmler, where are you? They will be allowed to wear a fez and to pray. If I do have to go to war, I'd be glad to go with them, at least I could eat my fill of the pork they won't touch.

Forgive me for this inappropriate attempt at humour. I'm not up to it anymore.

Laughter's dried up.

In short, I'm expecting a summons from the Waffen-S.S. between 15th and 24th March.

After that come Stockerau, drilling and the front. Where that will be, who knows? If someone does know, I certainly don't.

The medical was held in our classroom. The desks were where they'd always been, and the stove. Even the chest for wood and coal. But the building is in a bad way, it's not used as a school anymore, the army has taken it over. Soldiers are usually bad landlords. The fruit trees outside have grown a bit, and a branch of the apricot had bent down to the window; you could reach the fruit with your hand.

I didn't notice that at the medical, I just remember it now, as I'm writing you this letter. At the medical I was only trying not to meet Dr Schlauss' eye, which is full of hate, and that effort took all my attention.

Do you know what that creep said as I was leaving? "What's this compared to Stalingrad?"

He meant my various diagnoses.

But even if a more normal doctor had been sitting there, in his place on the board, those diagnoses would not have got me off. The army doesn't count your diagnoses, you have to rely on just one of them. It bothers me that he was able to triumph so easily and that my body behaved so treacherously. As though it wanted to go to war. Maybe it thinks war is good exercise.

Still, I didn't want to cut off my finger as some people have done. One of those was put up against a wall, as a saboteur and deserter, because he had scorned the flag and the swastika by cutting off his finger. Court martial, Dr Schlauss!

If by any chance you get this letter, don't reply straight away. You know how long it takes to get a number.

Greetings, Đuka

The letter was not sent, that's how it was preserved. Had it been sent, it would certainly not have been delivered to Franja. Kempf's assumptions about military censorship at that time were still fairly romantic.

With the Dead

Georg checked once again whether there was anyone in the street, but the small town appeared deserted; people had withdrawn, if they could, into the back rooms of their houses, or, if they were Volksdeutsche, had set off to the town square. No dog even dared walk down the street. Flags with swastikas fluttered from most of the houses. Even from the one concealed by an enormous mulberry tree, planted before a single house was built here. The tree was older than old age, thought Georg. But even that house displayed a flag, to his astonishment. He was astonished because the house belonged to Oskar Frojnd and he was Jewish. The world has turned upside down, Georg thought, setting off rapidly towards the end of the street where the fields and meadows began.

How often had he walked along this road!

His heart beat harder when a uniformed figure sped past him on a bicycle. Why, in fact, where did his unease at a possible encounter come from? He had just registered with the masters, his call-up paper crumpled in his pocket, the next day or the day after he too would slip into a uniform; one of those tight ones, sharply tailored, which some girls had recently described as chic. But his Sofija had long ago said that this uniform filled her with fear and anxiety because it was worn by murderers and looters. If she were to see him in that uniform, would she be afraid of him?

Absurd idea! Under a uniform, of any kind, a human heart beats; under a uniform, of any kind, people think their own thoughts. And he would carry on thinking his own thoughts, even if he had not yet thought up anything meaningful. In the territory of his thoughts, he would remain sovereign. That's what the Stoics once called the freedom of slaves in chains.

The previous week several tanks had found their way into their small town. That was a rare sight in the third year of the war in the Balkans. They were more urgently needed in the East.

The soldiers had taken off their boots and begun to play football on the soft grass. Barefoot like that, they seemed boyish and vulnerable. The tanks, abandoned, appeared to have fallen asleep. Then local youths appeared, a whole band of them, with their chief, and in a moment there were two teams, then suddenly spectators . . . Was that war? An international contest!

Yes, but the tales coming from far away . . . what could be read in newspapers between the lines . . .

On several occasions, Georg had toyed with the idea of making a swift getaway. Who of the bright young romantics had not done so? Such a person would never make a poet. Kempf counted up the people who would regret his departure and cursed those who would be glad. The vast majority would be indifferent. In his twenty-fourth year, of course he could no longer be a child; unless he had to be. Unless he acted a child. Or forgot himself . . . But whom had he really antagonised? It's true that he had clashed with two or three guys, but that was men's business. He hadn't stolen anything, he hadn't seriously hurt, let alone killed, anyone. Not even blind drunk.

And if I were to hang myself right now, considered Kempf. What would change in the history of the world, or on the battlefields if there was one soldier fewer, and of his own volition?

By now Georg was in the depths of the countryside. He had reached a point where the well-trodden path divided: left towards a stream with the biggest chub in the world, or right to the graveyard.

Kempf set off towards the dead.

The graveyard was barely hedged: wild dog rose, blackberry bushes, the remains of a fence. Pigs could wander in freely, thought Georg, with a hint of bitterness that surprised him. Because it was a largely German graveyard. He knew the majority of those laid to rest here by name. As with many villages and small towns in the vicinity, founded in the eighteenth century, the first person to be buried here dated from then. His surname was Kempf. This is where the Kempfs were laid to rest.

Here too were the forebears of other German families. Could they hear the drums of the "Gauleiter" Grumm and the hissing of Dr Schlauss? It was quiet here. The graveyard was at least a half-hour's brisk walk from the little town. Here there wasn't a sound. The dead did groan, one could hear it. That was the branch of an oak which had held onto the tree until this moment but had now broken off. Heavy, wet snow that had blanketed Nuštar in the last onslaught of winter had brought down a lot of trees. A flock of crows started cawing unpleasantly.

I'm becoming carrion, thought Georg, and now they're angry that I can still move ... Hey, dear birds, here you are, help yourselves. He opened his shirt. Astounded, the crows arranged themselves along the ridge of the hut on the edge of the graveyard. He was sure they were weighing him up.

He felt another branch on the same oak: would it be able to hold him? He had put on weight recently, probably from anxiety. He was one of those people inclined to eat their fear, or drink it.

Like a true young genius, Kempf gave himself up to imagining his own funeral.

All the women I've had anything to do with would come! That's good, let them meet and exchange experiences. My old man would be sad, my mother's heart would break.

Franja would be there, he's not one to abandon a friend.

All in all, there aren't many at my send-off. But those who have come know why they've come, just as those who haven't come know why they're not here. It's alright, it's up to me now. In any event I won't die in my bed, once they send me where they're sending me.

In the oldest part of the graveyard, he easily identified the mound of his forebear Georg Kempf's grave. It was right beside the fence, shaded from the other side of the fence by part of a tree canopy that now, in March, was filling with young sap. Time had wiped out the names of most of the Germans resting here.

He grimaced to himself: this could be his own grave. It would have the same words on it: *Georg Kempf.* But the Catholic faith that the local Germans subscribed to would not permit suicides to be buried in this place. Once, long ago, a fellow pupil had hanged himself, someone Kempf knew only slightly, as one of the hundred faces in the school corridor. He was older than Kempf, and at this moment he couldn't remember why he had hanged himself.

Kempf recalled that he had not been to the graveyard for at least three years, since the beginning of the war.

Not even at All Saints.

For the last half-year, Kempf had been working. As his uncle Johann joked, he was playing the proletarian, in the sweat of his brow. His father had found him a job at the brickworks. Although old Kempf considered himself a good German, he would not have been pleased about the Waffen-S.S. taking his son. Young

Kempf had overlooked the fact that his father, for all his faults, was nevertheless too intelligent to be a convinced Nazi.

Old Kempf thought that employment at the brickworks might delay his recruitment because bricks were strategic material. But that calculation proved flawed. A waste of time, Kempf thought now.

"You'll learn how the common people live," his father said. Fat chance. Kempf hadn't seen any common people, just men and women obliged by privation, cheating in petty ways and stealing when they could, and more fearful of the boss than of their God.

The gravestones were simply carved; they were barely distinguishable from the stone blocks scattered on the riverbanks over the millennia. And the inscriptions were simple too: Theresia Kempf, hardly legible, Georg read, filling in the missing letters. His great-great-great-grandmother, the one who had floated here on the raft from Ulm; on the raft of marriageable women accompanied by hired protectors so they should sail intact over almost all of what they knew of the world on their journey to – Transylvania. Georg remembered the stories the children had listened to in winter, when night came early and there was nothing to do but talk and listen to stories . . . About the way the Empress' officials had enticed them in every conceivable way to set off to "Transylvania", the country beyond the seven mountains, on the other side of the forests, that ran with milk and honey, where there was land in abundance, dark soil that brought forth in a week or two whatever you threw into it, even an old coffee mill . . . It became a big mill, the impoverished colonist became a miller, a rich peasant, craftsman, a factory owner, today one would say – an industrialist . . . And then one day his Kempf forebear, a man at the peak of his strength, embittered by constant poverty, the landowners' tithes and no prospect of improvement, gathered his family round the table, stood up when the last plate had been collected and announced simply, banging his fist on the table: "I'm going to Transylvania!"

The landowners looked on this with great hostility, they had their informers, there were beatings, incarcerations. But Kempf and other young men, all in fine fettle, stole away along secret pathways and on silent, dove's feet, reached a spring where the eloquent persuader awaited them . . . When day broke, they were already far away. *The e s Ke f*, Georg spelled out. The girl who his forebear had seen through his binoculars hopping off the raft.

"Dear Granny Theresia," whispered Georg, "I know why you all came, but did you regret it? I don't know where I'm going now or whether I'll regret it. Granny Theresia, be with me and watch over me in the darkness . . . No-one knows what will happen."

"Dear forebear Kempf . . ."

That was the way little Đuka had murmured in the dark, asking his mother to watch over him from her bed while he, in the middle of the night, urinated into his potty. He only felt safe embraced by her gaze. Her confirmation had to come in the form of a murmur: "I'm watching you, I see you . . . Pee into the potty, not beside it!"

Although it was easily cleaned up. In their house the floors were wooden, not compacted earth.

What now remained of those Germans here in the rich Slavonian soil? Bones, skeletons? The first ancestor Kempf had been of average build. Theresia was tiny; Georg knew that from the story of her hopping, like a flea, from the board thrown to the raft as it docked . . . he knew, because they all knew it, that the first Kempf had liked the fact that she was tiny, fragile and – refined. All the other lads looking through their binoculars at the raft as it slid towards the landing stage were seeking fuller-bodied women. And then, the white garter round the leg of fluttering great-granny Theresia had played its part.

Theresia had brought five books from Germany, Georg never knew which. They were burned in a house fire. Did he write verses now because there was something in him of the woman who was lying here, with nothing remaining of her but her incomplete name on a stone barely touched by the chisel?

What was Georg looking for in the graveyard? He had left the house with no aim or plan. His father had announced that he wouldn't be coming home to eat as he had business that couldn't be postponed. That business was a game of cards.

The boy (Georg) was going to war, he had long since ceased to be a child, he knew how to swear, he knew what a woman was, he knew how to stand up for himself, opposing even his own father – so let him see that coarse side of life just as he, an honourable trader in pig fat, had experienced it in Bukovina . . . War was war, as the French said. That's what his old man would have thought on getting up that morning.

But, by evening, his mood would have changed: It would really be too stupid for some Russian to put a bullet through the boy's head! Now we must wait, and tremble! All in all, Georg didn't get on with his father, but there was no open enmity between them.

Politics were of secondary significance. The son was so stubbornly uninterested in politics that he was unable to name the parties that used to trash each other at elections. One of his father's friends maintained doggedly: "If we Germans don't get things sorted, these Balkan tribes will massacre each other down to the last man."

The Germans are here now, thought Kempf, but nothing has changed.

"We Germans brought progress of all kinds to these parts," said another. "From potato tubers to threshing machines."

Fine, thought young Kempf. It could have stopped there.

Uncle Johannes, with his impersonation of the Führer, was closer to young Kempf. At family gatherings, the aunts still fell about laughing as soon as Uncle Johannes stood up and started pulling faces. But since April 1941, that humour had dried up. All that remained was his truly three-pronged, scurrilous curse: *Doner-veter-parapli!!!* Thunder-weather-umbrella. The son, however, underestimated his father. Because he had virtually written his father off, Kempf had not noticed that changes had taken place in the older man. He was well able to read between the lines; he was unsurpassed in "reading" news items that were persistently "skipped over". The older Kempf had realised that there had been a disaster at Stalingrad. Things had begun to arrange themselves differently in his head. To be sent today to the East, towards Stalingrad, was almost tantamount to murder.

Only one evil was greater: to be, as a forced volunteer, "remitted" to the S.S. division, composed locally of Danubian Schwabians. They'd be wreaking all kinds of havoc, thought the older Kempf. The Russians and local "Reds" would annihilate them to the last man. The woods were crawling with Partisans. In the east it was hideous, but not entirely hopeless. Besides, it seemed that the eastern fronts would soon be penetrated. If you have to end up a prisoner, then it's better to be captured by a foreigner than your own people. Here there was a lot to be avenged, there you are a foreigner. And there must surely be some rules of war.

The secret success of his mission to Dr Schlauss amounted briefly to this: Kempf-the-son would definitely be "remitted" to the eastern front. The Waffen-S.S., overseeing everything from

Berlin, had sifted carefully through the "military material" and what they needed above all were doctors; even unqualified, even students. In the spring of 1943, that is, the Waffen-S.S. was already bleeding heavily.

So, the son was mistaken and there was nothing to be done about it, and it didn't even matter. Now they were on bad terms, without either of them remembering why. There, the old man had gone to play cards, while his son was, literally, packing for war.

That was why the son couldn't think of the slightest reason to hurry home. He could eat alone, just as, since Franja had been picked up, he largely drank alone. And he went to bed alone. Sofija had not been seen for three months now.

There was a sudden clap of thunder nearby, with no warning. Georg sheltered under the oak, knowing that it could be dangerous. If even the sky is against me now . . .

What's that, compared to Stalingrad?

He began to head home when it was already getting dark. The Kempfs lying there said neither "yes" nor "no". The crows on the trees around him said more, as they warily watched his departure.

Second letter to Franja Lauber in the East

Dear friend, here I am hounding you.

First, about my journey. My ticket and identification document were inspected by a local man, but not a Swabian. He has a son in the Wermacht, he said, in France now, I don't remember the place. I asked him how it was possible that he was taken into the German army when he wasn't German. He's a volunteer, said the conductor, very proudly. Well, we're "volunteers" as well, I thought. As though he had sensed something, the conductor added: "My son really volunteered."

Idiot, I thought, but of course didn't say so. When he saw my papers he seemed

The collection of Kempf's unsent letters is growing. In this letter he will inform his friend about the way he took the oath to the Führer. I, the Unborn, deduced from his expression that he was, as far as the oath was concerned, insincere. He put on a mask of dedication, but I know that his thoughts were far away.

On the other hand, other young men around him would be genuinely elated, affected by the spirit of a troop in the process of being created. Kempf's new address is: Waffen-S.S. Galicia division. But he doesn't yet know where that is, presumably in Poland.

Nor does he know that he's writing to a dead man.

The little town of Stockerau would be appealing were it not for so many soldiers there. Here they "drilled" the man who to draw himself up. He all but kissed my hand. Idiot, I thought for a second time. Of course I said nothing.

Then a lout came into the compartment, we were already near Novska, and took off his shoes. The entire compartment stank so I had to go into the corridor to count telegraph poles.

At Zagreb I fell asleep, but not before I had got off onto the platform to have a long drink of water. Yes, water, would you believe?

I arrived in Stockerau, rested but with black thoughts.

I presume you know the little town, so I won't write about it. Baroque like our own. In the atlas at home I had read that there were some 15,000 inhabitants. Catholics, by and large, you can tell from the churches. What else could they be? On the main square, I found a pleasant pastry shop, Hungarian. I ate Linzer biscuits. It's called *Mignon*, you must remember it. I know you,

was meant to be my father. In the Waffen-S.S. Galicia division he's one of the few who understands German. He even speaks it, albeit in a long-since forgotten dialect. For a soldier it's more important to understand than to speak. And for the time being Kempf on the whole says nothing.

In his letter Kempf will inform his friend about how he experienced the little town of Stockerau.

I see him sitting in the church, in the second row, participating in a prayer as he has been taught. I know that Kempf is a token believer. He thinks of God so little that he doesn't feel it important to deny His existence.

Should I ever be born, and my prospects are diminishing by the day, I will be born into a civilisation defined by Christianity. If there was any way I could choose, who knows what I would choose?

We the unborn know well each of the holy books of mankind. Those books are the medium of our existence.

From one fat holy book, I derived the lesson that the act of being born would make me at once a debtor. I shall be obliged to the son of an honourable you've got a sweet tooth too. When officers shout at you all day long, in German, it's pleasant to hear a hubbub of language, Hungarian, which is impossible to learn, but by contrast with soldiers' curses it sounds like a love serenade. So, I too have just got through a week of drilling, and I'm writing this just before the evening summons, when we'll be told where we're each assigned. The war is everywhere, in front of us, behind us, only in this little town you don't see any of it. Outside the circle of the barracks complex, the contented citizens go on living their lives. I spotted a couple of good-looking girls, but they're not like ours. They're all short-legged.

Other than that, my balls ache from all the marching. We're drilled by an S.S. colonel, a true Prussian. We strut in our boots, new, unbroken in, round the cavalry barracks; I developed blisters that the surgeon had to treat. I march

Galilean carpenter who made a fantastic career by means of the brilliant notion of a universal loan that all those born Christians will have to repay. I too will be obliged as I must redeem my guilt. That guilt is a debt under the name of original sin. I did not commit that sin as there is nothing in the world more innocent than an unborn baby. The sin was committed by my ancestors. The generations mentioned in the Bible lived far longer than today's generations, and it always surprised me that they had not managed to settle that debt to the suffering Christ. To be fair, by a strange omission that debt was not revealed until the coming of the Son of God. I truly do not like the idea that someone has to suffer on my behalf. It would be a million times more agreeable to start one's life without obligations . . . as innocently as existence itself is innocent.

Tonight Kempf and his comrades are setting off for Poland, a land of misery and misfortune, forever engulfed in a history which it never had. He is going to Poland not because his father bribed the S.S. doctor, but because the Waffen-S.S. has such enormous losses there and he is almost in military fashion endlessly, in the same place as you; so, I was not assigned to the Prinz Eugen barracks, which I take as a good sign for myself; I don't know at this point what to wish for. The East, Africa? As if this was an agency for foreign travel, and you get to choose! But the name Prinz

a doctor. The fact that he did not want to be a doctor in this war is a choice of his that I do not endorse as I feel it would be safer for him not to go straight into the fire.

But whoever listened to their child, especially one not yet born?

Eugen makes me apprehensive, because I wouldn't want to stay in the Balkans and do who knows what. You ended up in the East, and it all began right here in this barracks surrounded by stables. I know that the chances of me surviving in the East are lower than anywhere else, but then, since I have to go to war, if I have to kill, it's better that I fight, and possibly kill, people I know nothing about. Maybe it's stupid, maybe I'm just a sentimental old cow, but, there, that's what I think.

We too sleep in the old Uhlan barracks. The rooms are orderly. Each one has a famous name inscribed over the door. I sleep in a room called "Ante Starčević". I don't believe the Prussian colonels have heard of him. The old man looks sternly at me from his portrait, conveying: "This is all you need!" Jacobin Starčević has his own perverse views of the freedom of the individual. There's a dormitory named after Boroević, a general in the imperial army. It just gets better and better.

There are men among us from all over, but mostly Ukrainians. For the most part they are not Volksdeutsche at all and don't understand German. They understand me better than they do the German officers. They are Ukrainian nationalists and above all they hate the Soviet government. Is that enough to make them good soldiers? I don't know. They can certainly drink! I would say, like all Russians, but I'd better hold my tongue: they really hate Russians. I'll have to practise keeping mum. There are increasing numbers of questions that it's best to keep to oneself. They say the Gestapo are everywhere, but that may be an exaggeration. Fear and uncertainty are definitely all around, as is hatred. I don't know what will emerge from this human mush into which I too have fallen.

As far as the training goes, you know it all. You know that, except when I'm on a binge, I take regular physical exercise, and that for years I've washed exclusively in cold water. I didn't at all regret doing military service. You know how it all was: at first I wanted to study, then the experiment with medicine in Belgrade – Belgrade because it was geographically closer. Then a circular letter came to all of us saying that if we Volksdeutsche were joining the army, we should sabotage it in all possible ways, stealing weapons and hiding them in holes. I thought it was funny; the army like a game of hide-and-seek. I couldn't grasp why we should steal from the army of an allied country. But there are always those who know everything that ordinary mortals don't. Such visionaries have a crystal ball in which they can make out what's coming. They do it so assiduously that the ball eventually shatters under their penetrating gaze.

Do you know why I'm writing this to you?

It's because I feel that this letter won't be sent either. Nevertheless, I believe that through the thoughts I'm putting on paper, we are communicating at a distance. After all, you too have been through all of this, every step of the way.

Regarding that circular letter, here's a spooky event for you: at some point, in 1940, I met a man, young in appearance, who I suspected was inclined to Bolshevism. And that man told me – I don't know how I came to gain his trust (maybe over a glass, we were standing at the bar of the inn on the corso) – that he had given the emperor what was his, that he had recently shed the King's uniform, and that, on the order of I no longer know who, he had buried a field gun in the forest above his village.

Imagine, he buried a field gun.

Now one can really see how much has been buried in our country, and how much more will still be buried, and how many more of us will be buried, now that everyone is at war against everyone else.

I still have no news of Sofija. She comes to me in my dreams, I see her crushed, humiliated, I don't dare describe all I see and all I fear is being done to her. The Germans would do well to take over the camps at Jasenovac, Gradiška and other places, about which there are all kinds of rumours. German camps must be different, at least they'd be orderly.

There's the call for assembly. I'll get back to you.

P.S. The assembly's over. On Monday, at 3 a.m. my unit will leave by train for the General Government. That used to be Poland.

I've been issued with an assault rifle. They've also hung two hand grenades on me, so I look like a Christmas tree. I have just become a "grenadier" (that reminds me of the *Grenadiermarsch*, dumplings with onions, that my mother so often put in front of me). As far as I understand, my division will be called Galicia. I'm speaking in the future tense because it's only just being formed.

So, I'm going to the front, armed to the teeth. The Waffen-S.S. had other plans for me: imagine, because of my Belgrade flirtation with medicine they wanted to send me to the medical corps. I wouldn't allow it. In the course of this week of training, I've learned a bit about the S.S. There is only one way to change a decision these gentlemen have in mind: to be a greater Papist than the Pope. And so I acted a more committed Nazi than they are: I couldn't wait to confront the reds through my sights. Imagine that, dear friend: me a Nazi writ large.

I'd do worse things just to avoid being shoved into the medical corps. You and I read a few things about the Great War, about the massacres at Verdun, at Ypres . . . My flirtation with medicine enabled me to visualise a hospital in wartime. And could one begin to imagine that the red cross on its roof would be respected these days?

When I was studying medicine, I bore heroically all the anatomy lessons, after fainting at the first one. In the end I was able calmly to hold a leg that had been cut off. So, that's not it. Quite simply I didn't want to join the medical corps. If there's a war on, let's go to war!

And Poland could not have been further from my mind.

And now that unfortunate Poland can't manage without me. How can I explain to that country that I could certainly have managed without it? Why does Poland think that I'm now all she needs?

I haven't yet got a number for the Feldpost. I'll send it.

Sturmmann Georg Kempf, Waffen-S.S.

Polonia

Polonia? Polska? Poland?

What did Georg Kempf know about Poland? Little. From a few books.

Sienkiewicz, of course. Why, Kempf too had now signed up with the crusaders. *Quo vadis?* – he'd like to know too. The sensitive Pan Tadeusz; Mickiewicz, who was a good Pole, although born in Lithuania. "Poland is not yet lost . . ." Everyone in Croatia knew that this anthem had been stolen, from us, of course. Was that all? Although he had drunk a lot in his life, including dubious concoctions, Georg had not tried Polish vodka. Nor a Polish girl.

All his knowledge was from books. He could not now recall, as the train carried him through Austria, whether he had ever in his life met a Pole. That Piłsudski was a mystery to him. Tyrant or father of the nation? They can be the same thing, you have to judge case by case. He knew that Poland had been divided as the spoils among all those who could get their hands on it. He supposed that the Polish language was lovely, that it harked back to chivalric times, but in fact he had never heard anyone speaking it. With the best will in the world he couldn't recall a single object that could have been associated with Poland. He remembered only that in September '39 all (almost all) the Volksdeutsche had reproached and cursed the Poles for attacking a German radio station . . . and that Poles, somewhere in Poland, launched a pogrom, not of Jews, but of Germans . . . those Germans who had arrived in Poland at the time of Germany's hungry years when his ancestor, whose name he bore, had stood up, banged his fist on the table and shouted: "I'm going to Transylvania!"

He was sceptical about the story of the radio station, and it was quite incomprehensible that Poland, which had barely managed to gather itself together in 1918 within its borders, would have dared to provoke the mighty Reich in such a way. And any kind of pogrom against the German minority, for instance in Slavonia, was way beyond his powers of imagination. People did remember murders of colonists during the reign of the powerful Empress, Kempf knew that there had been quarrels with the indigenous folk over woods, fields, grazing . . . Herders and tillers had never got on, anywhere. But that was long ago. The drunken brawls in the taverns had nothing to do with race. In 1939, Kempf had thought it wasn't his problem if the Poles really had offended the always angry Reich, or else it had all been set up. It was no skin off his nose. That was the year, a good, profitable one for his father and his wholesale pig fat business, when he had come back from his first semesters studying medicine in Belgrade and decided to see "something of the world". Franja and he had intended to go to Venice. He couldn't now say why Venice in particular, but then there had been a game of barefoot football, the ground was still cold and Kempf, who although German was no *Übermensch* like Hitler's artillerymen, developed a bad bout of pneumonia and the Venice trip came to nothing.

But what should an individual do if he wants to see something of the wide world about which he has no clue? He must prepare. Once he reaches that wide world, he won't have time. He has to know what he's looking at, get his bearings. That's why, in that now so distant year of 1939, Georg had bought the Baedeker guide to Venice.

And now, in the little Austrian town of Stockerau the brand new Sturmmann Georg Kempf had the previous day purchased the Baedeker guide to the General Government, that is the left-over part of Poland that was under the rule of the Reich. He was destined to get to know in a different way the part broken off by the Soviets.

Venice remained a dream: the needlework in Franja's mother's kitchen showing the lagoon, a gondola and a crescent moon over St Mark's.

So it was that at this moment the very name – Poland, Polonia – sounded unreal to him. It was getting dark, the landscape was hilly, a full moon was gliding over a clear sky.

He hadn't come to terms with the other soldiers about light in the compartment, so he went into the corridor, not to count the telegraph poles, but to have a look at the Baedeker that promised to reveal to him the secrets of the General Government, and prepare him for the experience. That's why Kempf considered that book (not exactly thin, nearly three hundred pages) with the purple cover he had spotted in the shop window at the station in Stockerau a lucky find and bought it, as soon as he had changed Pavelić's kunas into Reichsmarks.

So here he was now, standing in the corridor, catching the blinking light, leafing through Baedeker, his instructor. Year of publication: 1943. Fresh, thought Georg, sniffing the smell of the printer's ink: three maps, plans of six Polish towns. Not including Warsaw, because it was now in the Reich. The capital city of a non-existent country.

But there was Kraków, the main city of the General Government.

First Dzieditz (unpronounceable, and not even Hungarian): a

railway hub! Kempf read with approval about the little town of Dzieditz. Like Vinkovci. And the little town of Nuštar, where he came into the world, was not that far from Vinkovci where one went to buy everything that was not food grown in the garden or the fields. Mostly from Jews. Jews ran almost all the commerce. Apart from the pig fat trade, probably.

In Dzieditz there was a small lignite mine. That's where the similarities ended. As a foreigner approaching an unfamiliar territory, Kempf was more interested in differences.

"The train to Kraków goes north-east through Auschwitz, a small industrial town of some 12,000 inhabitants (roughly like Stockerau), the former centre of the Piastowski Voivodeship of Auschwitz and Zator (the Zator Hotel in Auschwitz is recommended) . . . It is possible also to take a local train, Kraków–Auschwitz, 69 kilometres . . ."

There is everything the chance traveller needs here. Where to stay, where to eat well. Exchange rate, Reichsmark to złoty. Average temperatures by the month. City maps. A welcome from Hans Frank, the head of the General Government . . . A cordial greeting, come and visit us, get to know the beautiful country in the meeting place of West and East, with the characteristics of both; come and visit us, to see what a charming corner of the Earth has fallen to us as General Governors . . .

Come to us, stay here, die here . . .

From Vinkovci to Jasenovac is roughly the same distance as from Kraków to Auschwitz, reflected Kempf. And try as he might, he could not remember the name of the hotel on the Vinkovci corso.

Absorbed in his book, he missed the moment the train entered the General Government. There was no border control, it was a military train carrying an armed unit of the S.S. to the East.

Who would ever venture to inspect that? Why, they were crawling through the depths of Hitler's empire.

Nothing could be made out through the darkness. Kempf sat down on the floor in the corridor, the smell in the compartment was terrible. He had slept by an open window all his life, even at minus ten Celsius.

Trees glided past as the train sped through a cutting. It seemed to Kempf that the branches of the trees on the hillsides had opened their arms – some praying, the rest cursing . . . as though the trees were crucifixes. From time to time he seemed to see a bear standing on its hind legs.

Creaking, the squeal of brakes, light in the darkness, shouting . . .

The train stopped.

Hurrying footsteps, curses. In these German curses the emperor and king are shit:

Scheisse, Scheisse . . .

He remembered his uncle and his curse: *Doner-veter-parapli* . . .

Thunder-weather-umbrella . . . Poor thing, he must have racked his brains dreaming that up. The Germans have a limited range of curses. In our language dogs are called on to attack the wombs of mothers. Our curses sound like mass rape.

But now on both sides of the train, crap was flowing from the mouths of the S.S. officers.

"Who's the most senior here?" With that cry an S.S. petty officer, an Unterscharführer judging by his insignia, leaped into their carriage. He shone his torch on the soldiers, who were rubbing their eyes, and you could see from their confused faces that some of them had no idea where they were, they were still half-asleep. "Sturmmann Kempf, get your men up. We've been attacked!"

There was no need for Sturmmann Kempf to rouse his men.

They were all now fully awake and pulling weapons out of their rucksacks.

"*Was ist los?*"

Kempf was too late with his question. The petty officer had run off to waken the other carriages.

A fine parade, thought Kempf. With fireworks.

In fact, there was no shooting. It turned out that about a dozen metres of track had been blown up. Someone – *on that side* – may have miscalculated. It occurred to Kempf that their train had stopped in a siding along the way for two, possibly three hours, without anyone knowing why. The engine did take on water, it's true. But water and coal had been added in Stockerau. That delay had saved the train from being blown sky high along with the track . . . And with some of the S.S. Galicia division, which was still in the process of formation. How despicable!

This was the first time Kempf heard the phrase "blue police". These were Polish police, loyal to the German authorities. The diversion had been caused by *bandits*. That word, in the context of the war raging everywhere, was not new to him. In Slavonia, those whose role was to hunt down and destroy the enemies of the Reich had been called bandits. Kempf sat on the steps of the carriage, smoking. So, he thinks, there are two kinds of Pole: blue Poles and Polish Poles. Blue Poles saved their train: one of them waved a torch at the place where the track was destroyed. Polish Poles had wanted to blow their train up. It seemed that people had to consider that risk: on both sides of the embankment where the railway ran, everything had been cut back; nothing taller than a dandelion grew. That was presumably as high as the Polish Poles dared rise above the ground if they didn't want to become bandits.

If only the business with the blue Poles and those others were that simple. As simple as it is to clear any terrain. Because if it were, Georg Kempf, with the experience he had so far accumulated in his life, would have been able to understand "Poland": traitors and those others. Superhuman and subhuman. Jews and everyone else. Aryans and Semites.

Nationalists and internationalists. "Authorised representatives of the state and nation" and "bandits". The regular army and "men of the woods". Polished boots and "the barefoot". Gods and idols. New Europe and Europe as an outworn whore. So simple. Either one or the other.

But everything here was even more confused than in Croatia. Here in Poland everything had knotted into a bloody ball and after a very short time Kempf understood that it could not be disentangled except at an unimaginably high cost: with the ball being annihilated almost without trace. With the contradictions being mutually destroyed: the total triumph of nihilism.

Dostoevsky, of course, not Sienkiewicz; the latter's book, which Kempf had "devoured" in two days as a boy, was called *In Desert and Wilderness* and wasn't set in Poland at all.

He had read so few Polish writers. There wasn't a single Polish book on his father's shelves. In the Vinkovci public library the translations of Polish writers could be counted on the fingers of one hand. Long ago Kempf had read something by Reymont, he even remembered some of it.

The Poles came off badly in Dostoevsky's works: petty landowners, petty gestures, petty cunning; those were all just character masks, not living Poles. What did Dostoevsky have against Poles? It's unclear. It seems he had some bad experiences with them in Siberia, but their real dilemmas were worthy of his pen.

Dostoevsky's Poles weren't real Poles, though. Kempf was now eager to meet "real Poles". It didn't at that moment occur to him that he was entering this country armed to the teeth and under oath to their new master.

For the last few days Kempf had been muttering increasingly frequently to himself: *Das bin ich nicht* ... This isn't who I am ...

The Poles in Dostoevsky were treated in roughly the same way as the Jews in Reymont. With the difference that the Polish Nobel Prize winner attributed to some of his Jewish characters demonic qualities. Dostoevsky saved demonism for characters he really considered important. That's not what Poles were, that's not what Jews were ...

That's not who I am.

The business with the oath of allegiance on the *Appelplatz* of the old Uhlan barracks had been a comical performance. As the Ukrainians barely understood German, they were ordered just to open their mouths; "real" Volksdeutsche were placed among them and it was their task to repeat in a loud shout the words of the oath after the Prussian colonel who had been drilling them for days:

Ich schwöre dem Führer, als obersten Befehlshaber ...
Treue und Tapferkeit ...
Ich gelobe dem Führer und den von Ihm bestimmten Vorgesetzten Gehorsam bis den Tod.
... I swear allegiance to the Leader ... unto death, etc, etc ...

In fact it was the oath, a little altered, that the Wehrmacht recruits had to swear. It seemed that the talents of Himmler, the real master of the Waffen-S.S., did not lie in the realm of the lyrical. If they had, he would presumably have composed a different oath. This one mentioned loyalty to God, but the S.S. was in conflict with God. In this Waffen-S.S. division, rolling by train towards the East, that conflict was a problem. The Ukrainian nationalists were, of course, believers. That was why the Galicia division had been permitted a few chaplains and Orthodox priests. In 1943, the Waffen-S.S. had to give way in some areas.

The scene on the *Appelplatz*, after marching in a circle in the rhythm of the "Präsentiermarsch" (that jaunty little piece had been composed by none other than King Friedrich Wilhelm III), when the units had been finally drawn up at attention and when the oath had begun, was eerie: rigid mummies opening their mouths with no sound emerging. Indeed, it was forbidden.

That moment was meant to be the apex of their lives.

Kempf bellowed along with the other Germans. He couldn't be dumb here!* In his village he had kept on saying: "That's not me, that's not me . . ." But he bellowed and so he was sworn in. Fortunately, he was not superstitious. The magic of words meant something quite different to him – poetry.

It turned out that the technical platoon that was going to repair the track was on its way, but it would take time. If it too was not blown sky-high, it would arrive in a couple of hours. The train would not move on before dawn. As Polish communist and various other bandits (!) were operative in this area, the Scharführer ordered that guards be posted on all four sides of the train.

This made Georg Kempf think that they were surrounded. In a country ruled by the Germans, with their governor in

---

* The word *nijem* (dumb) in the original is the word from which the word for German, "Nijemac", is derived, denoting the original Slavs' first impression of the foreign tribes' command of language. [Translator's note]

Kraków, sixty-nine kilometres (if the track was not blown up) from Auschwitz, where one was most warmly recommended to stay in the elite Zator hotel, sections of their S.S. division in formation were surrounded. "But what's that compared to Stalingrad?" At least they were not freezing and not yet gnawing at each other's skulls.

As a non-commissioned officer, Kempf did not have to keep guard. But he offered to take a shift because he wanted to be in the open air. Those who had not been assigned to guard duty were forbidden to leave the carriages, unless they needed to relieve themselves.

One could urinate in the completely shitty train toilets, but it was nicer outside. It was nicer to urinate on the earth, looking at the starry sky, as far as the full moon allowed us to see, above us (Immanuel Kant).

Kempf had been allocated the late shift: from 3 to 5 a.m. Until his turn came, he sat, bored, in the compartment, which had now been aired.

The Romanian, a bright spark, always the first to speak, the first to fart, the first to snigger, altogether the one responsible for humour and jokes, a type found in every male collective, took a piece of paper out of his rucksack: it was folded in half, on one side was a drawing of a vulva overgrown with a thick dark little bush; on the other side was a penis, and the drawings had been so arranged that the deft movement of one part of the paper demonstrated the complete "act": the cock entered the vagina, at whatever speed you liked. Everyone in the compartment, and the whole carriage, wanted to see this incredible phenomenon of the penis entering a slit in the little bush.

The movements of the soldiers who went out into the darkness round the train after that suggested to Kempf that the lads were to a man subscribing to Onan's sinful brotherhood. How long had they already been away from their homes, far from their wives and girlfriends? Perhaps a month altogether. What would it be like later on?

It seemed to him that he could hear male seed falling over Poland the way rain can be heard dropping onto fallen leaves.

What would sprout from all of this? What was written in the stars that the full moon barely enabled one to see?

At 3 a.m, at the beginning of his shift, the train had fallen asleep; all that could be heard was someone occasionally groaning or farting. Everything had calmed down. At this time of night even vampires return to their beds under the gravestones.

Kempf, armed with an assault rifle, with grenades on his belt, stood by the embankment, staring into the dark. There were a few trees in front of him, beyond which stretched an endless plain. Poland looked as flat as Slavonia. What was the land like here?

In such circumstances, every rustle induces panic. Kempf strained all his senses, clutching his rifle. Judging by the stars, he concluded that he had been allocated the eastern side of the train. He had always been good at stars. There were the Pleiades, which would soon tell the farmer it was time to plough. *Ex oriente lux*? From the east came danger, not light . . . Black darkness, Bolshevism, was what came. Without the "blue police", their train would have been blown to bits and who knows, maybe for Kempf the war would have been over before it began. Now they were waiting for the rail inspection car to test the safety of the track and newly laid sleepers.

That was a rustle, his senses weren't deceiving him: there was someone, something in the darkness, in the undergrowth beside the embankment.

Kempf was drenched in sweat from his head to his toes. Should he shoot? Give the alarm signal? Were they bandits?

Another moment and he would have shot.

But it was only a roebuck looking at Kempf, at least as alarmed and surprised as he was.

Kempf stamped his feet to send it away. He had had many such encounters in the forests around Nuštar or Vinkovci. Coming across a buck or a doe, finding a lost fawn, climbing a tree in mortal terror in the face of an enraged boar – those were Đuka's childhood experiences. But here, for the buck, this place beside the embankment where the stopped train was groaning was neither good nor safe.

"*Was ist los?*" Kempf heard the voice of the officer walking along the train waving his torch.

He waved his hand. The buck vanished into the darkness, with some cracking of twigs that the officer could no longer hear. Nor would Sturmmann Kempf let him hear.

Although that little word "Sturmmann", which Kempf wore in the form of a badge with the S.S. insignia on the lapel of his uniform, meant storm trooper, attacker, one couldn't imagine that the buck knew that. But it did.

That was his first encounter with a living creature that ate Polish grass and inhaled Polish air; it had been conceived in Poland and it would be shot in Poland. Kempf had not had a chance to explain that he had no intention of attacking it.

His first encounter with a Polish creature was in fact a success because it didn't happen.

Trial by Fire and Water

The woods were swarming with enemies but they were invisible. Kempf's unit had yet to experience its baptism. Here and there they would shoot at shadows that ran from tree to tree – deer perhaps?

Who were the enemies?

The officers talked about bandits who had rejected German law and order. They said that Soviet commissars followed the renegades, forcing them with rifles into battle. Did that mean that the bandits didn't want to fight? So why had they rejected our law and order? The officers told them they were dealing with the actions of a lower rank of law-keeper and that the real war was ahead of them, where the Russians were pushing from the East: the people of the steppe wanted to trample underfoot all that was sacred to the West. In effect it was precisely detachments of "reserve police", in other words German law-keepers, who were carrying out the greatest atrocities against the Jews in Poland, but the officers glossed over that; it was a "police", "law-keeping" aspect of this war. Kempf's unit had still to see a real Russian; or even an armed Pole, apart from the blue police. The episode with the train was an underhand, cowardly act. It was well beneath the level of military honour fostered by Himmler's divisions, those that had already "distinguished" themselves, and those that were in the process of formation, like this one, the S.S. Galicia division.

In the early summer of 1943 there was already a competitive hatred raging between the Wehrmacht and the Waffen-S.S. The Wehrmacht officers maintained that the best equipment was going to the S.S., which was gradually subjugating the regular German army. As the army of the ruling party, the Waffen-S.S. enjoyed the favour of the Party. Himmler would have dismissed such accusations: the Waffen-S.S. fought well. The Waffen-S.S. was the best army the world had ever seen. The Waffen-S.S. was defending German honour and was pre-eminent in the East. And then the angry commanders of both armies began competing over numbers of earned medals, losses, numbers of the fallen, wounded and disappeared ... In these terrible statistics, the Waffen-S.S. came out on top. Some S.S. divisions had not merely been decimated, they had completely disappeared.

At the front, some 200 to 250 kilometres ahead of them, it must have been hell. At present they were still searching for the main body of their division in order to join it and set off into the real war.

"You are the Waffen-S.S.," their Scharführer told them every evening before the sunset bugle call. "Never forget that. Nor will you ever be forgotten. You are the flower of the German nation and the main bulwark against Bolshevism. Your motto is *Honour and Loyalty*!"

Blood was not mentioned here. Logically, given that Ukrainians predominated in the battalion. Blood, it turns out, is on the one hand something acquired at birth. But blood is also something that can be ... earned. But the division and its battalion had yet to prove themselves.

In addition to the Ukrainians, there were also "real" Germans in the battalion, then there were "real" Volksdeutsche, that is "real unreal Germans", Romanians, Hungarians.

However, many "real unreal Germans" had returned to the Reich at the end of the 1930s "by agreement" as it was then defined, under the German–Soviet pact. Kempf's situation was specific, he came from Croatia, a loyal ally of the Reich. The Gestapo certainly knew that Georg Kempf was not related in any way to Werner Kempf, the renowned general of the armoured divisions right here, in the east, the Kempf, therefore, about whom the army spoke with respect – that he was a bear of a man, almost god-like. He would never have surrendered to the Reds, as Paulus had ... That real German was a walking memorial even in his lifetime. With a little (bad) luck, Georg might have met him, say near Kursk.

N.C.O. Georg did not dare ask the Scharführer how many Ukrainians were fighting on the other side, i.e. how many there were in the Red Army. He suspected that there would be many, hundreds of thousands.* Fratricidal war, otherwise a Balkan speciality.

They sat around the fire, smoking, staring into it. Reflections of the flames flickered over the Scharführer's face. If only he didn't start getting emotional. He had said what he had to say, they had heard it before. Some believed, some didn't, but that was how it had always been. There are those who are born into honourable families, but do not believe in anything. Something simply snaps in them, at that time of life when formative experiences are being accumulated, and from then on they no longer believe in anything. I am one of them, thought Kempf. These lads seemed to him too indifferent.

They weren't like his presumptions about the S.S., which

---

* There were at least seven million Ukrainians in the Red Army, 1941–5. [Author's note]

had come from German sources. This army really was a new Internationale. The Waffen-S.S. had gathered under its banners representatives of almost all the European nations. It was more European than the Crusaders' army Pope Gregory X sent to demolish the holy city of Jerusalem, plunging it into blood that the chronicles state was knee-deep.

I believe only in what I see, thought Kempf, warming himself at the fire. Someone passed a bottle of brandy round. Sitting shoulder-to-shoulder in the agreeable warmth of burning beech logs, sipping alcohol from the same flask, were they becoming a collective? Anything was possible. Or nothing. When would the *troop spirit* come into being?

It was too soon for any conclusions. I, a *forceteer*, can't be bought off so easily, I can always say, that's not who I am . . .

Kempf had no idea what the fighting value of his unit was, nor did the officers. From a purely racial standpoint, these "crusaders" were a strange gathering. The Volksdeutsche were all, more or less, *forceteers*, more or less drafted "volunteers". It was certain that there were no Jews among them. Many Ukrainians loathed the Bolsheviks, particularly when those Bolsheviks were Ukrainian. But they hardly cared about anything else. They had their own concerns in this war. As it had been decreed in Berlin for all Slavs, after the final extermination of the Jews, it would be the turn of the Poles, Russians, Ukrainians and all the others. They would live in labour camps, they would be permitted to reproduce within limits, they would learn to count up to ten. They would not be taught to read and write, except to be able to sign their name. So Hitler and Himmler had radicalised the Empress Maria Theresa's old programme of enlightenment. As soon as this generation of Poles died out, no-one would be able to read Mickiewicz, Słovacki, Krasinski, and what need would there be for that? A nation of prisoners and labourers would be allowed to sing their primitive ditties in their huts, but who would still remember Chopin? So a nation robbed of its culture would be suitable for being kept in slavery. But better such controlled "enlightened" slavery than the kind dreamed up by the red pharaoh in the Kremlin.

These men had not yet seen a real Bolshevik, let alone a commissar. The Scharführer seemed to be preparing them for this in his daily "sermons".

"Russians fight like tigers!" he warned them. "Nothing is sacred to them. Russians have no preconception of honour, they will steal their mother's wedding ring out of her coffin. Moreover, they're prepared to cut that finger off. Even eat it. It's well known that Russian prisoners devour each other.* Russians don't take prisoners, bear that in mind. Don't leave your men surrounded. Because the Russians will have no mercy. According to the Führer's orders: every captured Red commissar has to be shot, on the spot, with no trial."

Here Kempf wanted to ask something along the lines of: "But that commissar is a prisoner of war as well, is he not, does that mean that we don't take prisoners either?"

But he held his tongue, he didn't ask anything, instead he spat out, with a little piece of tobacco that had stuck to his tongue, his need for logic.

After the "sermon", the shadows of his fellow fighters crept silently away, each towards his own tent. There were heavy guards on all sides. Around them was forest and Poland. Some sort of Poland.

---

* However, there are also recorded cases of cannibalism among the besieged Germans at Stalingrad. [Author's note]

Kempf slept fitfully, and in the morning he announced that he would go to fetch water. He wanted to be alone at least for a moment.

In this part of the world there wasn't a single well that hadn't been poisoned. And so a cistern had been parked, some eight hundred metres from the camp. Kempf was in no hurry.

It was on that walk that he first saw a Soviet star from close to. He came upon the wreck of an Ilyushin. Their officers had told them about that plane. They called it a flying tank. You could see that it was armour-plated, so it couldn't fly particularly fast. But its dive-bombing was considered dangerous. They had been warned about a new Soviet tactic: as they dived, the Ilyushins showered the Germans with a rain of small calibre shells. The Germans mocked this small monster, made of wood, but they remembered it from their bad encounters with it, especially in this phase of the war.

The Ilyushin II-2 really was in part made of wood. But the front was armed like a real knight. Its tail guarded a machine-gun nest.

Beside the plane were two graves, with no markings.

That the Ilyushin was a threat was immediately clear. On the other side of the forest path there was the blackened wreck of a tank. Beside it were five graves. That conformed with what Kempf had learned about the tank known as the Tiger: it had a five-member crew. On the crosses of those who lay here hung steel helmets bearing S.S. insignia.

These graves, unlike the Soviet ones, were not nameless. There had been a collision of epic proportions here; a tournament between heavily armed knights. All the knights had remained in the Polish earth, where they had perished. For the rest of his life, Kempf would remember this discovery of his as the battle of

Kursk in miniature. In truth, the Ilyushins had exacted a terrible toll there among the armoured vehicles.

Here, on Polish land, Germans and Russians were fighting each other. In truth, no kind of Polish resistance had even been mentioned at any of the troop meetings. But from conversations with the ordinary soldiers, Kempf had concluded that at this moment the Russians were far away – the Asian steppes were always mentioned – but Polish partisans were all around. Two months before Kempf got there, Poles had killed six Germans, including a major in the Waffen-S.S., at Smolensk. They must have been some kind of "national guard".*

At dawn the following day, finally, a baptism of fire. Kempf immediately understood what his fellow fighters meant when they said that the forests were crawling with all kinds of riff-raff. But they had known nothing about the real divisions between the Poles; to them all renegade Poles were bandits.

The bandits in the forest started shooting. Kempf's unit formed an exemplary skirmish line, furious firing began. It was only a few hundred metres from their camp, they had come upon the enemy while carrying out reconnaissance duties.

It seemed that the enemy was retreating. The signal for attack was given. A stream, dark green, stretched before them. The Bosut ran through Kempf's mind. How often had he swum in

---

* The Gwardia Ludowa, which grew into the Armia Ludowa (the National Army), was another branch of the Polish resistance. Towards the end of the war it was in increasingly bitter contest with the Armia Krajowa, the Home Army. The communist partisans considered the Home Army to be nationalistic, while they saw the partisans as servants of the Soviet occupier. The division between the Poles was tragic. But it could not, however, be compared to the only apparently similar divisions in Yugoslavia, because there both "armies" fought courageously against German might. [Author's note]

it, along with otters . . . They stepped into the water, the stream was deeper than they had thought.

In the middle, the water was up to their waists. Did all these men know how to swim? An absurd idea struck him: if some were illiterate, maybe they were also non-swimmers?

The shooting did not last long, no casualties on their side. When the Scharführer, with the main body of troops, in just as exemplary a skirmish line, broke through the scrub behind them, it was already over. The bandits had retreated deep into the forest. There was no need for those who had arrived with the officer to set foot in the dark-green water.

The forest now loomed in front of them, just coming into leaf, a young forest of birch and oak. Not too thick.

Shall we pursue them? They conversed across the stream with the rest of the unit.

Was that enough for today? Was it sufficient for them to have lost their bachelor innocence? Were they now fighters, warriors, victors?

For a while, considering, the officer left the decision in the air.

The forest stretched into the distance. Who knew how far it was to the first communications.

It was as if the Scharführer was attempting to assess the depth of the forest with an invisible plumbline.

It was his job to think. His was the greater responsibility.

The night before he had told them that he was more than a father to them.

Another, thought Kempf. I have my own, and we didn't get on all that well. It occurred to him then that he had not yet written to his family, and by now he could have hoped for a reply because he had a number.

The order was given to return to camp.

The S.S. dragged with them two corpses as booty. A man and a woman, astonishingly young, almost children. Both blond. Unlike the Reichsführer Heinrich Himmler, a short-sighted gardener, both the dead were textbook examples of Nazi race teachings. Or they had been.

If they were Bolsheviks, thought Kempf, then Bolshevism is a youthful affair! Were they Poles?

The examination of the bodies revealed nothing. No documents of any kind. The boy had a handgun, cobbled together from who knows what. No familiar make, neither German nor Russian. It was more like the kind of weapon sometimes used in Croatia at carnival time. Museum material, perhaps from the Hundred Years War. Corpses don't usually speak. There was no way of knowing whether they were Poles or Russians. The former was far more likely.

The Russians had better equipment. Besides, they were supposed to be at least two hundred kilometres further east. The real clashes were yet to come. The Germans must finally end this war while their tanks could still move. When the autumn downpours began, the war must stop. That had already happened twice, and the Germans were so close to final victory.

The officer who alone had some experience of waging war in this territory maintained that they were not Bolsheviks. He thought they were bandits supported by the underground Polish state. But they were just as callously merciless as the communists. Their mutual relations were entirely unclear, they attacked, retreated, sometimes collaborated, overall they hated or despised each other. Unfortunately, they were all against us.

Kempf learned later that these formations were called the Home Army. We have two armies opposing us, he thought. And those are only the Poles. Where are the Reds?

"These bandits," the officer went on, "aren't clear about what to do with the Jews. We have data about them persecuting Jews as well, but not with the requisite determination. For us these Poles are an inferior race, which is, naturally, not thrilled with its fate."

Then came praise. The commander expressed his satisfaction that the unit had acquitted itself so well.

"Today you have defended the honour of German arms and you rose to the demands of the occasion in the way that the Leader and the German nation expect. Warmest congratulations! You will be a good military formation, borne by the spirit of your troop!"

Sturmmann Kempf was also praised – for conducting himself well in the face of a fanatical enemy.

"Today marks the beginning of your war journey, I wish you all many more similar heroic actions about which, in the warmth of your homes, you will tell your wives and children once you return to Germany, or" – here the officer paused as though he had difficulty with a badly remembered phrase – "to a free Ukraine."

The spirit of the troop? To Germany? Kempf gaped, as if he had seen a real spirit in front of him. Why, I want to return to Slavonia! But it too would probably be Germany by then. Will the lads I played football with be driven into labour camps? That rich soil on which his ancestor had once long ago knelt as soon as he had leaped from the raft that had brought him safely from Ulm, and in his rapture kissed it, warm and moist – that was how he had dreamed of it, all that soft, yielding soil into which you could throw a coffee mill and in a week or two it would grow into a flour mill as big as the tower of Babel – would that all be his, theirs, German? And would he belong to the master race?

That idea did not appeal to Georg Kempf. He would prefer

for this all to pass as fast as possible and for everything to be as it was before.

And call those heroic actions, thought Kempf, but then bit his lip. Again he suppressed his too hasty idea. We were attacked by a bunch of kids with weapons that could be found in a local museum, displayed alongside a stone axe brought into the light of day by a plough.

Nevertheless, while they were all washing from the waist up, splashing each other and laughing, evidently pleased with their baptism of fire, Kempf, to his great surprise, realised that he too felt a kind of pride. Something like after a win at football, a sporting, male brotherhood . . . Which certainly, if this notion does not go too far, has a physical, bodily component.

They clapped one another, embraced, offered each other cigarettes and brandy . . . clapped again and their brotherhood was sealed. They helped each other, they wrung out their shirts with one holding one end and someone else the other . . . they sought out sunny places around the roots of the oaks where the still weak sun penetrated to dry the wrung-out shirts . . .

The spirit of the troop giggled and no-one glanced at the two bodies, covered with a tent flap.

Well, alright, Kempf concluded that day, before falling asleep: we couldn't have known that what we were confronting was such a weak, inexperienced and barely armed enemy. We assumed that it was Ivan (that's what the German soldiers called all Russians), from whose snouts blood ran, and that behind him still more bloodthirsty commissars were waving revolvers. And then behind Ivan and the commissar prodding him on thundered Stalin's monstrous T-34 tank, crushing everything in front of it, especially honour and confidence and loyalty, everything in which the West believed.

This unit of mine – they're decent, worthy lads. We've proved ourselves.

He did not volunteer for the burial of the two Poles because he felt drained, so immediately surrendered to sleep. But first he managed to overhear a conversation in front of his tent in which the troop chaplain was arguing that he ought to go with the gravediggers.

"Because the deceased are Poles and, as such, definitely Catholic."

The chaplain was an Evangelist, but that was not relevant in this instance. God is one.

That Jewish Old Testament angry God, Jehovah. People agree about God. The problems start with the Son.

That was the last thought with which the consciousness of Sturmmann Georg Kempf from the little town of Nuštar was extinguished for the night. The second to last. Kempf remembered again that he had still not written to his father and mother. I must do it tomorrow, he thought.

But he didn't.

A soldier's letter home – why, under such conditions, that was like dictating to someone very inquisitive. Someone just lying in wait.

Stara Gradiška . . .

Into the house of Maks' butchers* came Vera, virtually still a child, in the splendour of the blossoming orchards, she fluttered in the sun's rays filled with awakened insects, with a guard of honour of butterflies of every hue . . . And it seemed to her that nature too had conspired against her. They brought her in a black police car and left her at the gate. She looked around for the last time as a free person. A soldier waved cheerfully to her from his wooden nest – it looked like those watchtowers that rise up on the edge of woods

I first saw my future mother (I hope!) as a thirteen-year-old child bursting out of her house crying loudly. She had been offended by someone's poisonous observation that her eyes were as black as coal. I see her at the fountain (known as the Turkish fountain) soaping her eyes, rubbing them, in an attempt to wash the coal out of them.

When she grew up, she joined up with those who wanted to change the world. There are many such people and they persecute one another from one end of the Earth to the other. I would have been happier if my prospective mother had remained within the bounds of her original world at least until this terrible war was over. We unborn measure everything according to our own expectations. Through her choice of one side in a terrible dispute

---

* This refers to Maks Luburić, master of life and death in the Jasenovac camp, of which Stara Gradiška was an annex. [Author's note]

to monitor the movements of game. There were many such wooden watchtowers around the camp, with black, oiled gun barrels poking out.

She had hardly managed to look round before she found herself surrounded by guards in black uniforms. The gate opened before her, the camp swallowed her.

For less than half an hour she walked in a column of women endeavouring to cope like her with the wooden clogs she had been given "in exchange" for her little black lacquered shoes. The days that followed were like a hallucination. At first she thought she was dreaming and that, if she could only wake up, everything she had witnessed would disperse like a nightmare she would forever drive out of her memory. She had been woken at dawn by the sound of a siren, but all else had been like the day before. She had even asked the women in the hut whether she was

this woman is reducing my chances. She is guided by her own will, she has made a different decision.

Her name is Vera.*

Her beliefs took her off to the transit camp at Stara Gradiška. That's a kind of subsidiary of the concentration camp at Jasenovac, where all the same things are done to people as at Jasenovac.

What is happening to Vera now is a consequence of her decisions. By contrast, all that is happening to the man called Kempf is a consequence of those with power over him. He is not the master of his destiny. Vera, although she is in a camp, is. Both my father and my future mother are endangered and I have to fear for their lives. I now think it is more likely that I will not be born than that I will.

I see Vera with other women, surrounded by guards and barbed wire, digging a cabbage bed. Beside the field, on the other side of the wire, a procession of women passes, some very young, some holding babies. I know where they are

---

* Vera means faith, belief. [Translator's note]

hallucinating. As they didn't understand her questions, she concluded eventually that it must be a collective hallucination.

Vera, daughter of Mijo, of Roman Catholic faith, was registered in the camp's books under the number 1742. To start with she thought that, since apart from a tin plate and a rusty spoon, a pair of clogs and striped "pyjamas", she possessed nothing, now at least she had that number as something that was her own. But those who had been guests in the house of Maks' butchers longer knew that this number had been allocated once before and that its previous owner had been killed three months earlier "attempting to escape".

being taken and many souls must now be fearful.

Tonight there will be great sorrow among us.

Among the women being led away is Sofija, my potential father's great love, daughter of a textile merchant, a friend and associate of Kempf's father. What can be said about that? Only that my future mother is not in that procession.

But she has been captured, my potential father has been mobilised. The good thing about it is that at this moment they could not meet. I can only hope that they will meet at some point and that, as a consequence of the colours they bear on their uniforms or in their hearts, they will not be obliged to kill one another.

Vera is very beautiful and I love her very much.

In fact, she had moved a little way from the column because she had a bladder infection. It had remained as the theme of many jokes among the guards. Since then not one of them had gone to urinate without calling to someone: "Don't shoot me in the back, I've got a bladder infection!"

After the war there was a lot of disagreement about the number of people murdered in the camps. Some maintained that the impounded camp documents could give accurate information.

But Vera emerged from the war knowing this was not the case. Her own number had been allocated twice and who could know, in the spring of 1943, how many more times it would be assigned?

When she had begun to look around a bit and caught a glance that could be seen as encouraging, when one of the camp inmates said something in passing that was meaningful and suggested organisation and resistance, she decided that it was essential to keep her own audit of killings . . . But it already existed. The reality of the camp was beginning to reveal itself to her, now she could tell who was who.

She quickly realised that the camp was merely a temporary stopping place and that all those herded into the Tower, a menacing brick building from the days of Turkish rule in Slavonia, were liquidated within twenty-four hours. They weren't allocated numbers, the camp books didn't mention them. Hence it was impossible to establish the real number of those killed on the basis of the "evidence" that, who knows why, the murderers themselves kept.

As a Croat, Vera dared hope that she would not be killed at once, that she might even survive, if her bladder held out. The Croatian women's huts were in a somewhat better state, the guards, in principle, didn't rape them, they "flirted" with them. But many were forced to "participate". Admittedly, when the guards were thoroughly tanked-up with brandy, differences of race and creed played a minor role. The libido can be just as blind as hatred.

From the other side of the river Sava here and there, but increasingly often in 1943, came the rumbling of heavy guns from the direction of Bosnia, like an approaching storm. She noticed that this rumbling put the guards in a particularly bad mood. When it came so close that it seemed the guns were on the opposite bank, they would drink themselves blind. Vera was ever more certain that the guards drank out of fear. That is why, like all the other inmates, she listened attentively: widening her nostrils like a doe, she wanted to catch the stench of gunpowder on the breeze. One of the inmates whispered to her: "Those are Tito's guns!" and moved swiftly away.

Her brother had once mentioned that name – Tito – when they were leafing through banned books in the barn behind the house.

Where was he now, her brother? She knew he was being sought on all sides, in all corners of their state.

The guards were most frequently so plastered that they couldn't reach the women's huts walking upright. They crawled for as long as they were able and then crumpled into the mud. In the morning the more sober ones would collect them from the ditches and haul them off, "pickled", as they put it. She was convinced that even a small group of armed people would be able to liberate the camp, drenched as it was in brandy. In the forests – so dense that a squirrel would be able to pass from one end of Bosnia to the other without touching the ground – those with arms had different ideas, unfortunately.

What did those women dream about, many of them barely out of childhood, like Vera herself, daughter of Mijo, number 1742? What do numbers dream about?

In the warm spring air, Vera smelled fire. Perhaps a house was on fire nearby, or perhaps it was chimney smoke, or dinner was being prepared, over there, beyond the wire? She thought she heard the sound of cow bells, while the dogs that were now barking were sheepdogs, rounding up livestock, not people.

The women sat down in front of the hut as the evening seemed calmer than usual. The guns weren't booming, the guards weren't boozing. And then the younger ones began to sing:

I'd have my dinner
Rather than lie with you . . .

It was hardest at dawn, as asleep, at night, other images ran through their heads. And it was hard at the evening summons, when the officers' dogs would bark, creatures that in the camp hierarchy ranked higher than any inmate. From time to time, unpredictably, the officers would organise a hunt with live bullets, firing at anything that moved, or even stood quietly at the summons. Then it was important, as soon as they had been dismissed, to hurry to their huts, to their provisional security. The officers' dogs would lick the tufts of grass soaked in blood.

The women's huts were wooden, but in the centre of the camp were a few yellow-painted buildings, some of which had cellars. Every night people were beaten and killed in those cellars.

For a time, a family – father, mother and child of about five – lived in one of these cellars. The guards told Vera that they had been caught escaping, that the father was found with a gun, so he was a bandit. From time to time the inmates, the women especially, threw them something to eat through the bars of the cellar. The camp connected with them in a way, cared for them.

From her hut Vera was able to see everything that was happening in front of the building in which the family was held.

One clear, beautiful night, when it seemed that the silver moonlight had ennobled everything, that all ghosts had retreated to their lairs and God himself walked the earth, Vera watched soldiers dragging a naked female body out and tossing it onto a cart pulled by an old nag, then the body of a man also without trousers.

And she saw a soldier jumping over the steps that led to the cellar, holding a child under his arm like a suckling pig.

In the morning a murmur went round the camp: "Last night they slaughtered the little partisan."

All my mother told me of it was:

"We picked cabbages and cleaned them, it was late autumn, we were standing in mud up to our ankles, tossing the cabbages into a cart.

"About eleven o'clock a column of women, surrounded by guards, passed us, singing. They were singing to us, by way of farewell. We didn't know them, they had been brought in the day before and herded into the Tower. Many clutched infants to their chests.

"We all knew where they were being taken."

Those cabbages, like balls or heads, then the column of women clutching infants to their chests, that was all Vera ever said out loud about her experience in the house of Maks' butchers.

She never mentioned the little boy/suckling pig.

After those women had passed on their way to the Sava river, the prisoners went on digging cabbages. The singing had long since died down, nothing more was heard.

They all knew that none of those women was registered in the camp books, nor had been assigned a number.

When, on her way to the summons, Vera had to pass the Tower, she suddenly felt weak and sick.

In the evening, cleaning red cabbages and tossing them onto a sheet in the middle of the room, she thought of human heads. She had to go out of the hut to throw up.

After she had several times avoided the bullets of the officers' hunt, escaped from the pursuit of their dogs, and as the small privileges of her status were not removed, with time she developed the conviction that a powerful hand was watching over her, protecting her from harm. And that powerful hand remained hidden; that is – underground.

She concluded that this invisible hand smoothing her fate must have something to do with her brother. Of course, she continued to look after herself as well, she kept her eyes wide open as she looked around her, endeavouring to anticipate danger. She learned to distinguish between the guards, who had at first all seemed the same to her, all equally black, not only because of their uniforms. She came to realise that there were those among them who feared for their fate "once all this was finally over" . . . There were even some, although they were a small minority, who felt that what was being done to these people was not O.K., even if they were Jews, let alone if they weren't. Such men sometimes sought to buy "redemption for their sins" by small services, a cigarette, a shot of brandy . . . To be remembered afterwards.

But even with them experience demanded the greatest caution.

Caution, forethought, open eyes and ears . . . and a very great deal of luck.

But everyone there was cautious – a camp is a good school – and nevertheless some disappeared.

So, Vera concluded, there must be some higher force in my destiny, some kind of invisible hand leading me, watching over me, taking care of me.

After a year in the camp, this intimation was suddenly confirmed.

Sofija

What happened to Sofija, to whose white pupils Kempf had composed a sonnet? Sofija, his Slavonian pastoral idyll? Sofija, of the white pupils and silken skin?

No-one knows the complete answer. This fact should probably be attributed to the proverbial silence of fish.

A few hours after Vera and other women imprisoned at Stara Gradiška had seen a column being marched towards the riverbank, those women, some of whom were clutching tiny babies to their chests, singing their song of farewell, Sofija was floating in the Sava. Her lovely head with its white pupils remained as it had always been, but on her neck yawned a cut, red

We the unborn have the melancholy privilege of not being able to say: We didn't see, we didn't know.

This is what became of Sofija.

She was, first and foremost, the woman whom Kempf loved above all others and perhaps still does. Admittedly other women would come into his life, Kempf has done well with women in general. Sofija's name remained to denote that first, fateful glance when love comes into being, and, if it turns out to be impossible, is transformed into an enduring disquiet. Essentially, Kempf wanted to be a poet (!), and poetry is nourished by such disquiet.

But this was no time for poetry.

Now, when he doesn't know where she is, he loves her more than ever; more than when line, and a whiplash crossed her breast.

The catfish and sterlets respected her beauty. Untouched, Sofija floated down the Sava, which at Kalemegdan (known to Kempf as Kališ in his Belgrade student days) merged with the Danube. That was not the end of the journey. There is no such thing as the end of the journey, all that changes is the name of the river or the sea.

For days Sofija floated, startling the fish. At night her white skin shone bright. But on the banks no-one paid any attention to yet another floating body. In those days, there was a great deal of traffic on these waterways. It was not unusual for a corpse to be found in a fishing net. Of those who lived beside the river and from the river and cast their nets into it, it only occurred to a few that they could be chewing on their neighbours. There had never been bigger catfish, never fatter sterlets.

entering her room at midnight like a thief, he slipped into her bed, and they abandoned themselves to newly discovered raptures. For them Slavonia was Arcadia, and they truly revelled in their pastoral idyll.

Sofija was blonde, she looked more like a city girl than a peasant.

Her father was a fairly shrewd textile merchant called Radojica. Many had found employment with him. Kempf's father hoped that their propitious marriage would enhance both their businesses. Both were merchants, even comparatively honest.

His daughter was already on the truck when Radojica's neighbour brought every policeman a little flask of plum brandy and his wife served them black coffee.

I grieved for the lovely Sofija, in the name of her prominent father.

We the unborn live on pure regret. That is our bread and water, it's the ether we breathe and our only sustenance. In that respect we resemble God, only He is omnipotent while we can do nothing. We only ask Him: Why do you allow all this to happen, which always puts

Sofija did not find her own net until she reached the Aegean. Having floated as far as the Black Sea, the currents and winds carried her south, and it is not impossible that she came across the floating head of Orpheus. Her water-borne journey finally came to an end on a Greek shore. A fisherman reported to the Allies that he had caught a mermaid. And that mermaid was more fish than woman. In fact, she was a fish, because everything below her navel, all that is of importance to a woman, was fish-like. The fisherman had left her in his net under his boat, believing that the mermaid, should he drag her onto dry land, would suffocate. The local priest – the person whose advice was always sought in connection with natural phenomena, but particularly with supernatural ones – was informed about the discovery of the mermaid. The priest was annoyed to be interrupted at his lunch. To the best of his knowledge, no-one had seen a mermaid in this part of the world for at least two thousand years. The best proof of this was that St Peter, who had travelled in these parts and sent angry letters to the churches whose disorder he had inspected, had never mentioned nymphs, mermaids or similar phenomena of the pagan imagination; all of them had left Hellas as fast as they could after the arrival of Jesus Christ. They were the first displaced persons.

Finally a jeep arrived, containing Allies, British. It was August 1944, they had just disembarked. There had never been so many British men in Greece. Lord Byron had liberated Greece almost single-handed. Now, although they were many, affairs in Greece were still not settled. Yalta was a long way off, a lot of things here

> Him in a bad mood. Because we don't understand anything. Maybe it's better that way. We can only grieve, fear, wish. The born would add "pray". My mother's rival was tossed into the Sava.

were still in a raw state. So the officers took with them several soldiers armed to the teeth.

The moment had come to drag the net containing the mermaid out from under the boat.

The priest raised his hand in a gesture of triumph, while the British officers turned their heads away in great disgust, thinking what a good thing it was that they hadn't yet consumed their pudding.

"For God's sake! What is this?"

"Why don't you listen to me?" hissed the priest. "The last mermaid was seen in this geographical area two thousand years ago."

The sight backed up his statement. The "mermaid" in the net did not resemble a human being in any way, and it would have been hard for it to pass as a fish. It was "something" dark red, the colour of stale blood in other words, "something" crumpled, streaked with white that, with a bit of imagination, could suggest human skin.

That is to say: the Aegean fish, without a shred of respect for a foreigner, had virtually devoured Sofija as soon as she had been caught in the net.

The British commanding officer made a few circles with his finger at the height of his forehead, alluding to the mental capacity of the Greek fisherman. The officers were offered mastic liqueur in the fisherman's hut, after which they were served large, very tasty fish with the tenderest white flesh, which is to say with white pupils, expertly cooked.

There was nothing to be recorded in the notebook.

In the jeep winding up the serpentine bends above the village, one of the officers declared: "The war as a whole is not doing the Greek fishermen any good. Even if it's nothing to do with Markos' Partisans."

"Especially then," responded the driver, who as usual knew everything. "But the fish was excellent."

"All honours to the fish!"

The fisherman continued to maintain, until his dying day, that he had caught a mermaid. Everyone mocked him and when he died and was buried, many, passing his grave, would murmur: "There lies the man who slept with a mermaid and lost his mind."

Kempf would never know any of this.

Sofija floated for nearly a year through many waters, without disintegrating.

The Greek was right: she was a siren. In the column of women being driven towards the Sava, she was the one who sang most beautifully.

There is no further proof that Sofija was a mermaid, nor is any necessary.

The Blessing of Potatoes

What did Kempf know, in May 1943, about the mass killings of Jews? At the beginning of his "war journey" with the Waffen-S.S., which he later called his "little Polish war", in the territory where his unit was operating, there were hardly any Jews left. On the subject of the Jews, the older soldiers, especially the officers, stayed "buttoned up".

He had behind him several operations in which, as it was recorded officially in his file, he had "proved himself". He knew how to conceal himself, he knew where his place was when the unit spread out to fire, he knew how to shoot. He took exemplary care of his rifle, he was, whenever possible, shaven, etc. The height of

My prospective father had fallen on hard times. He was in conflict with the uniform he wore, and in particular with its insignia – S.S.

He was contemplating doing something rash and thereby once again threatening my future. He didn't want to join the firing squad that was to liquidate Polish hostages that afternoon. Kempf didn't know them and had never seen them. So there was no question of a sentimental attachment. Why was it suddenly so important for him to get out from under the steel crush of a group of murderers? There were hundreds of thousands of them. Hundreds of thousands of them fell every day, on both sides.

What could his philanthropy achieve at such a time?

The Waffen-S.S. is no kindergarten playground in a city park. I know that he didn't sign soldierly virtues. He patiently endured long marches, nocturnal frosts and the fact that their meals were increasingly meagre.

That he had rather less zeal than the Waffen-S.S. expected of such a young German, a volunteer, was noticed, but not recorded in his file. The senior officers all shared a conviction that war itself was a good school of fanaticism. Everything would change when the unit thinned out, that is when the list of its dead and disappeared grew. Then the natural human craving for revenge would do its work. Besides, once the Waffen-S.S. Galicia division had reached its full strength, it would go into operations on a bigger scale. Up till now there had only been skirmishes; but enough to see who was fighting material and of what kind. As was the case with other divisions destined to fight in the East, they had to reckon with

up voluntarily, but that's of no consequence now.

When you're with wolves, howl like them. Therefore, slay, so that you are not slain. How come Kempf suddenly doesn't understand that simple truth? Why, the pack organises history by disorganising it.

Didn't he know that? Until now he hadn't seemed to me an individual whose ill-considered, undigested philanthropy could threaten my existence. Was he beginning to doubt the very concept of power that is all that counts?

Admittedly, on the horizon it was becoming possible to discern that the Russians would prevail and the Germans would lose the war. The material superiority of the Generalissimus, residing in Moscow, would be decisive in the end. But who knew when that would be?

Thousands more hostages would be shot. They were rounded up on the highways, in the woods, in the streets. If Kempf were now to get out of it and not participate in this execution, what would it change? My prospective father had chosen a bad moment to play with his concept of honour and civilisation. That was a card he should have left for later. Every heavy losses. But the survivors, in the name of those who had fallen, would not flinch from anything. Storm Trooper Kempf, although he had smelled gunpowder in an assault charge, was still green and inexperienced.

Kempf had gone with his unit to dig trenches east of the camp, but the major part of the battalion had surrounded the little town of B, where they had been brought by transporters. The previous night a soldier had been wounded in a routine patrol. That insolence had to be punished. After a

opportunistic act is justified if it serves life, even if it means killing. That's what we the unborn think, and it's how the majority of you the living think as well.

Kempf was a cog in a large machine, and for the machine to function it was not necessary for the cog to understand it. Kempf could end up in court. Nowadays, courts make quick judgments.

I see him sneaking towards the kitchen, planning to fill up on raw potatoes. Then the great warrior would vomit into the latrine, declaring himself seriously ill and incapable of fighting people with blindfolds over their eyes.

short time, a group of Ukrainians, led by German officers, returned with five civilians, three men and two women. It was their well-tried custom to collect civilians in the street according to the "random sample" principle.

Kempf went to look at them when they had been unloaded into the barn.

The five of them were sitting on the floor, evidently not understanding what was happening. They were not dressed for an excursion into the countryside, they may have been on their way to visit someone, or to do some shopping. Perhaps they had just chosen the wrong moment to go out for a walk. None of them could yet believe that it could be fatal. Perhaps they had planned to visit the graveyard, where their bodies would be dumped in just a few hours.

Execution with the aim of reprisal, that was the order of the commanders of the S.S. division of which Kempf's unit was a part. It was considered a "mild" reprisal. Had an S.S. soldier been killed, the settlement would have been a hundred hostages. In recent times, the head of the General Government, based in Kraków, the notorious Hans Frank, had favoured a milder approach and better treatment of Poles if they were not communists. And there were few communists among the Poles.

That was why instead of twenty for one injured soldier, only five were to be shot as a reprisal for the Romanian "German from outside the Reich", wounded in the leg on his patrol.

But a rumour was spreading through the battalion that this was a self-inflicted wound, as some days before they had been told of decisive battles with the Red Army. The Russians, east of their camp, had begun to assemble vast equipment with the aim of surrounding the territory overseen by their division, and may the best man win.

Kempf saw that the hostages could not remotely grasp what was in store for them. That their lives would be abruptly curtailed because of an incident they knew nothing about. They sat on the straw, saying nothing. Except that a couple of them were playing cards. To while away the time.

It had fallen to his firing squad to carry out the execution.

His commander ordered him to inform the lads that they had to be ready at five in the afternoon, which Kempf did immediately, by mechanical reflex of obedience to an order. But Kempf thought that at that moment the heavens would open and crash onto his head.

He crept to the kitchen tent where there was no-one and

grabbed a few potatoes. There, that's why military service had been useful. It's worth knowing what a potato can do when eaten raw. Kempf chewed it and went to report to the medical corps.

When his turn came, he had a fever. He said he kept needing to vomit, and vomited, having gone out to vomit against a wall. He was diagnosed: poisoning, cause unknown.

Exemption.

Kempf ran to his commander who was surprisingly calm, he shrugged like a man who was bored and didn't care, saying only: "There have to be ten of you. A volunteer will be found, Storm Trooper Kempf. You can change places with him."

No problem. A decilitre of brandy and half a sausage on top of his rations, that bought participation in an execution. If Kempf didn't want to do it, there were dozens who did and they were already coming forward.

The place of execution was not far enough away for him not to hear the cries for help of the people who only now understood what was to follow.

No judge. No doctor. The division doctors had other business. Confirming death from a bullet fired at close range was a pure waste of time.

When supper was served, Kempf stood in line, as usual, with his tin plate. Suddenly, a soldier, a Ukrainian, whom he didn't know by name, leaped up to him and tied a white apron round his waist. Kempf turned round and punched him on the chin.

"Girlie Kempf!" shouted the soldier, spitting up some blood.

"Fräulein Kempf!" Some soldiers began to bang on their plates. "Come suck me!"

The officers prevented further incidents. He seemed to have restored a fragment of respect by knocking out the soldier taunting him.

He took his food and looked for a place far from everyone, intensely aware that mocking glances were sticking to him.

That night in his tent he considered the possible consequences. He'd easily sort these louts out on his own. Kempf had been fighting at village fairs ever since he was old enough for such things, he was capable of teaching any fool manners. But some disgrace would probably follow. What would they do to punish him?

The civilians were killed in any case. Kempf tried to remember their faces, their frightened eyes. Now they would already be growing cold.

What would likely happen would be degradation. His rank, already the lowest in the hierarchy of the armed forces of the S.S., had been rickety from the outset. A Sturmmann, storm trooper, not born in Germany, who had not therefore fought communists and social democrats in the streets of German cities. He had not trashed Jewish shops. He had not participated in torchlight rallies and book-burning. He had not done any of the things that make a good member of the S.S. before joining the armed wing of Himmler's chivalric order. For that was how the S.S. saw itself, though in a modern form. Nor had Kempf served time in the National Socialist German Workers' Party. In the Uhlan barracks in the little town of Stockerau, someone had liked the look of his face, and the fact that he had been a student, therefore literate, played its part, as had his military service in the Yugoslav army. He had been quite a good shot in training. It seemed that he enjoyed shooting.

That was all over now. He would no doubt be disgraced in front of the whole unit. Had these knights carried sabres, his would have been broken in front of the entire company, which is what happened to Dreyfus, the French Jew accused in a mock trial of spying.

But in this case, Kempf had clearly fallen short. The civilians had been shot by orders from the top of the division. Kempf had refused to carry out the order.

He hardly slept. Not because of the humiliation he would have to expect, but because of the dead civilians. Who were they, how had they lived, who had they left behind? What bad luck! They had been picked up on the street the way dog-catchers hunt dogs.

Meanwhile, the unit officers were discussing the documents of Storm Trooper Georg Kempf. These stated that at training he had professed to be a Nazi who hated Bolsheviks. Something didn't fit. He had refused the medical corps for love of guns and bombs. But now he had failed like the worst fraud.

Admittedly, in 1943, the Waffen-S.S. had to be a bit more lenient than in the days when things were going well for the Germans.

In the morning, as he was shaving over a bucket of water, his commanding officer tapped him lightly on the shoulder. "We all have moments of weakness. Some take it better than others."

A few days passed. He realised that the news of the incident had never reached the division headquarters. Only the routine report was sent that five Poles had been shot according to the order of action to be taken in the case of injury to an armed unit of the Waffen-S.S. in the General Government.

Life and fighting continued in a routine military manner.

Thinking it all over one night, Kempf realised that nothing at all had happened to him. He had not been disgraced, he had not been publicly humiliated, he had not been punished in any way. Even his fellow-soldiers' taunts had stopped, the very next day after the executions.

What would happen if half the unit had rebelled as he had done and refused to fire at civilians or prisoners of war? If for no other reason than because of the Almighty's Fifth Commandment that followed immediately after Honour thy father and thy mother, stating simply: Thou shalt not kill!

Kempf could not have known how unrealistic his assumption was that large numbers of soldiers could have refused to obey. It rarely happened that anyone declined to fire at helpless people. That was not a problem for the Waffen-S.S.

What in fact was going on in the heads of these young men under the black helmets designed à la S.S., what kind of hearts beat under their tight uniforms, he could not fathom. But most of them killed not only when ordered to, but whenever they were able. "The black hordes of Florian Geyer",* the German peasant king, subject of the song adopted by the Waffen-S.S. as their anthem, were not exactly a bunch of children on an excursion.

That was the way his commanding officer approached him in a new attempt at getting closer to him.

"Storm Trooper Kempf, you came to us as a volunteer. Germany expects more fervour from you."

And then: "Do you think the Reds, if you fall into their clutches, will spare you? Do you imagine that the Bolsheviks have any scruples? This is war, my boy! *À la guerre comme à la guerre!*"

So, some expectations had been placed upon him, in some unspecified place, in some people's heads, in some headquarters, and for the time being he was not fulfilling them. What was going on? Every day the officers described the enemy, naming them: Bolsheviks. It occurred to Kempf that in the whole of his former life he had not spent so much as five minutes wondering

---

* The anthem of the S.S., "Wir sind des Geyers Schwarzer Haufen". [Author's note]

about the question: who are they? Was that the problem with his motivation? How do you fight with someone if you haven't a clue who he is? How do you hate him enough?

In those important places where decisions were made about him, Kempf, did people know the kind of things that were said in the villages of Slavonia about S.S. recruitment and forced mobilisation? It was true that some went off singing, but not him. What was it all about? He was a forced volunteer. But it was better not to advertise such a thing.

The troop consisted mainly of Ukrainians. He fully understood their hatred of the Soviets. But here they thought of Kempf as German. And as a person to whom at the mention of Bolshevism, despite the greatest effort, nothing came to mind, and maybe that was the source of his rather feeble military morale. He hadn't heard anything about that phenomenon at school, he had not been hardened with his generation in the countryside like young men in Germany, so as to inscribe himself in the Master Race once they came into conflict with Bolsheviks, nor had it been a topic during his military service in the Yugoslav Royal Army. He plucked up the courage to ask his fellow fighters, Ukrainians, how it had been to live under the Soviets. They would have felt obliged to spit before saying anything. At first Kempf thought that this was about hatred of Russians. But then it turned out that there were Ukrainians who were communists, Bolsheviks in other words, which put paid to his first simplistic account of their quarrel. After a while, Kempf gave up such topics.

There were a couple of Germans in the troop, who, before being recruited, had lived in that same Ukraine, or Povolzhye, which was nearby. They were the descendants of German colonists, like him.

So one fine day Kempf decided to ask one of them to tell him something about Bolshevism. He was called Fritz, could that be more ordinary? He came from a village whose name Kempf had forgotten. Fritz immediately took the initiative, explaining that at a time of great poverty, the year that the Führer came to power in Germany, he had been fourteen. Kempf instantly did the sums: the two of them were contemporaries.

"Stalin crushed the Ukrainian peasants who didn't want to join a kolkhoz. You don't know what kolkhozes are? You're lucky. The Russians imposed impossibly high tariffs on us.

"The Holodomor* we called it. Millions died because the commissars would take their last grain. Children were dying in large numbers. I remember half-dead children with swollen bellies, lying in the streets. Some would be eaten by dogs. I shall never forget that the ears of those children were transparent."

"Did the Bolsheviks do that?"

The Ukrainian German was surprised that he didn't know.

"And that, my friend, is why I signed up as a volunteer in the German army. Since I'd survived the Holodomor, at least I could somehow pay back those who hadn't, and they included all my brothers and all my sisters. People ate mice, rats and then the dead. Hitler knew what was happening in Ukraine and Polvozhye where there were a lot of us Germans. Germany sent aid packages. The commissars forced us to send them back to Germany."

Kempf bit his tongue. For he too was a forced volunteer. He resisted any discussion along the lines of "Who was to blame? Stalin, the Russians, the Ukrainian Bolsheviks ...?" He had

---

* In Ukrainian, "hunger" is *holod*; the coinage would therefore mean "hunger-mare". According to conservative estimates, Stalin's repressive measures against farmers in Ukraine and Polvozhye cost the lives of three million people, in reality probably a lot more. [Author's note]

before him a German born outside the Reich who had genuinely volunteered for the Waffen-S.S.

We are different kinds of German, thought Kempf, tossing and turning on his bunk. Just as there are different Russians, different Ukrainians. In any case, it is always the weakest who come off worst. Now it's the Jews, and the Russian prisoners in camps whom we torture with hunger. In the troop there are tales of the phenomenon of cannibalism among the Reds.

Before he managed to construct an answer to the question: "Who compensates whom here?", he turned over into sleep, without dreams, to be on the safe side.

The first morning news he heard as he was shaving was this: the Romanian, whose wound the court martial had proved was self-inflicted, had also been shot. The fellow fighters from his unit had fired at him, the same ones who had executed the five Polish civilians. *À la guerre comme à la guerre.*

Dvoguba Forest

In truth, in their sector, it had been entirely peaceful for a month, but nonetheless the army combed the forest every day. Today, Kempf's platoon was allocated the forest on the very edge of the area their unit was monitoring. That unit was no longer complete, some men had gone deep into Soviet territory, towards Kursk, where the Germans were now concentrating the vast fire power of the armoured divisions of the Waffen-S.S. and the accompanying infantry.

There follows a charming little picture of the soldier's life. A modern fairy tale of sorts. Kempf, who again has effusions of humanism, will like it a lot. As usual, he will think about it a lot and hardly sleep. It could make a little poem.

In reality, it pierced living flesh, the jugular, and the fact that it was not decisive was just a matter of chance. I leave you, my father Kempf, to your allegories. You are consoled by the thought that all that you are experiencing has already been lived through by someone else.

Unexpectedly, the patrol was joined by Oberscharführer (a senior lieutenant) Hans Blumenträger from Altona near Hamburg. Now plunged into the reality of the German language, Kempf had stopped translating in his head from German into Croatian whatever he heard. To begin with he had done this automatically, but then, equally automatically, he had stopped doing so. But, when he was alone, his thoughts still flowed in the rivers, meanders and streams of the Croatian language.

Not knowing why, he now translated for himself the officer's name: He-who-carries-flowers. To a cemetery, for instance. But it was hard to connect that person, his bulky frame, sharp profile, piercing gaze – as though he had stepped down from the screen of the German *Wochenschau*, the weekly review – with a bunch of chrysanthemums.

Hans Flower-Bearer told them he wanted to show them something in the forest that they were due to comb today in their hunt for bandits of the underground army.

The forest was darker, denser than the surrounding woods they had already patrolled, consisting for the most part of young birches. This immediately reminded Kempf of the Slavonian forests, where the oak was king; in the autumn farmers would drive huge herds of pigs into those forests to fill up on acorns that would be transformed into fat by the time they were slaughtered. And then his father would buy huge quantities of fat to sell on to the hungry towns. The economic benefit to Kempf's Volksdeutsche family rested on the acorn and pigs' appetite for that produce.

But in this sector at that time, it was peaceful, the bandits had either been eliminated or forced to withdraw still deeper into the forest. Perhaps those where Polish bison still roamed, that prehistoric remnant, which Kempf had not as yet seen.

As they entered the forest, Kempf proposed that they form a skirmish line; he didn't have the nerve to give the order, given the presence of an officer of higher rank, just a proposal. But the officer nodded and they all obeyed Kempf, and here they were, entering the forest, as cautiously as ever, guns at the ready. Every sound seemed magnified, and whenever a large bird fluttered off a branch, they nearly threw themselves to the ground.

But there evidently were no bandits in this forest.

In the middle of the forest was an open space, apparently of long standing as there were no stumps and no evidence of clearing. But there were some enormous pieces of rock, a city of Cyclops or the like.

Hans Blumenträger halted them in this clearing: there were four crosses with black steel helmets hanging on them. A soldiers' graveyard like so many already scattered across Poland, Ukraine and Russia; white gravel between the graves. The dates showed that they had all fallen on the same day.

But on one of the graves, under the helmet was a pierced solder's cap with a red five-pointed star pinned to it. It was strange to see S.S. insignia and a red star so close together.

They removed their helmets and stood at ease for a while in front of the graves which could have been their own. One of them could certainly have been Franja's grave. How little time Kempf had to think about his friend!

The Scharführer invited them to sit on the grass, he wanted to tell them something.

They all realised at once that this was to do with the unusual grave marked by a cross, a German helmet and a star.

Blumenträger had no talent as a story-teller. He had always been a soldier and joined the S.S. as a professional. So his story was dry, but perhaps it was better that way. The poor translation of a Ukrainian Volksdeutscher from German to Ukrainian further drained the tale of life. In the end it made little impression on anyone.

"Last winter we provoked a heavy engagement with the Russians in this forest. The Waffen-S.S. surrounded a substantial unit of Soviet parachutists who had succeeded in making contact and digging themselves into this forest. They even managed to dig trenches you can still see today and, if needed, lie in. They made a good job of them. I tell you: don't underestimate the Russian soldier. Many have regretted doing so.

"It was deep winter. It can be minus thirty degrees here, gentlemen.

"The exchange of fire lasted all day. We calculated that sooner or later the Russians would run out of ammunition; they'd fallen from the sky, they couldn't have carried more than a couple of clips each. But these guys had evidently succeeded in dropping a few crates as well.

"Hauptscharführer Bernd wanted at all costs to be done with these Russians that same day: it was his birthday and he had arranged a party that evening for the officers.

"And when there was no longer any sign of life from the Russian side, we got out our bayonets and knives and set off towards their position.

"The red devils really didn't have so much as a bullet, our calculation had been correct. But they had bayonets. We fought chest to chest. For anyone who has not been through it, it will be sooner or later an unforgettable experience.

"The Russians were completely exhausted, but they fought to the last man. There were at least five times more of us. That was last winter, I recall. The times when the Russians surrendered to us in their thousands were long gone, when it had seemed that they didn't intend to fight; that's how it went, really smoothly, right up to Moscow when our advance was stopped so we weren't able to get our hands on Stalin and his clique as early as '41. And that was a great misfortune. For if we had, you would all by now be warming yourselves in your wives' beds.

"Important lesson: that Russians don't fight, that they don't know how to wage war, is not true. It's a good thing someone like me can tell you that in good time.

"By nightfall we had finished the job in the forest and returned, singing, in a column, to camp. We had four dead; we had counted twenty-two dead Russians, which would look good in our report.

"Later that evening, we were notified of the disappearance of another comrade. There was no moon, we had no dogs, we were tired and hungry, and, moreover, invited to the birthday celebration, we put off the search till morning.

"We all drank, as was right and proper, but then, in the morning, there we were, formed into a skirmish line, patrolling that same forest.

"We easily found the soldier who had not returned to camp, and we could see why.

"Notably, a Russian was lying on top of him. Our man's hand was holding a knife stuck into the Russian's throat; the Russian had thrust his bayonet into our man's back up to the hilt. The Russian's throat and our man's back were red with frozen blood.

"We tried to separate them, but realised it was impossible; they were frozen, stiff as wood, we could only have parted them with axes or a saw, but even that was debatable. So we buried them together, in that embrace, in this place."

That's where Hans Blumenträger from Hamburg concluded his part of the report. As always, the people had taken on themselves the poeticisation of such an event. What follows, the Flower-Bearer had heard only in part.

The Polish peasants who had been brought the next day to bury the fallen threw them, if they were Russians, into one single pit that the Germans had blown out with dynamite as that was the only way at minus thirty degrees Celsius. For their own, the Germans had gouged out single graves, and placed in one of them the two-headed being, red with frozen blood, as I said; the god Janus whose two heads look in opposite directions, thought Kempf. "They look as though they've been bathed in raspberry juice," an officer remarked.

The Polish peasants told the Germans that they were now in the Witches' Clearing, in the middle of a forest called Dvoguba. And it was called that because a two-headed knight once ruled over this forest. This was where he had his fortified town, the stones could still be seen under the tall grasses. He always slept on one side so as not to crush one of his heads; only one head ever slept, the other kept watch so he did not need a night watchman. He was invincible. When he got tired of living, he managed to put both heads to sleep and never woke again. The nicest death, in one's sleep. He had been a good knight and master to the serfs. Then another knight came. He had fifty guards and the peasants had to feed all of them. Here people still mourn the passing of the two-headed master.

The officer told them that they had also laid the Russian and our own soldier on their sides, out of some sort of piety so that they would be more comfortable lying in the earth.

When one day, in peacetime, the graves in Dvoguba forest are dug up, two tightly embracing skeletons will be found in one of them.

In the remote future, no-one will rightly know whether this was a loving embrace or the throes of death.

Herr Blumenträger had not intended to tell us a fairy tale but to bequeath us an instruction important for survival: "Do not underestimate an inferior race on the battlefield!" But Kempf kept remembering images from an event in 1939, which seemed to have been a forewarning of the horrors to come. Its site was by chance an inn in Sremska Kamenica. A few of Kempf's friends had found themselves there "on a national basis". Someone had knocked over a fiercely burning stove and a flame had got hold of the floor and blocked the exit ... The rest could have been narrated by this officer. The images kept recurring to Kempf ... but more than his friends who had perished, he thought about a Hungarian girl who had been bobbing on top of him while his friends were burning.

He received letters from his father and mother in the same envelope. Those letters kept him awake.

His mother wrote that there was a rumour in Nuštar that "your Sofija has died of acute pneumonia". She didn't say where. Sensibly. She didn't mention the camp. She greatly mourned the loss of her lovely daughter-in-law to be. Even the greatest despicable censor would understand that. Even in war people died. They weren't all killed.

His father wrote that everything was alright at home, Uncle Johannes still joking, although less than usual. His father too mourned the death of Sofija. He asked his son to bear it like a man and a soldier. He said he had wanted to express his condolences to her father "on behalf of all of us", but couldn't find him anywhere. It was strange that he had not come to tell us himself of such a great family loss, he must have gone to a "clinic somewhere".

How intelligent my parents are, thought Kempf. This was an allusion to the claim in the local *Croatian People* newspaper that Jasenovac was "not a convalescent home, but nor was it a torture chamber". It's a shame, wrote his father, if the two of you had married, we could have merged our businesses and everything east of the Danube would have been our patch. And he concluded: "Man dreams, God decrees. R.I.P ..." And in a postscript, his old man wrote: "Don't do anything where you are now that would make it impossible for you to return under your parental roof. Don't do anything that could impair German honour."

His father wrote in German, his mother in Croatian. She had been schooled by nuns, she had nice handwriting. Unlike Uncle Johannes who behaved and conducted himself like a Slavonian peasant and had never wanted to be anything else, his father had wanted to be what he was, namely German; he read and wrote in German. That was the same Johannes the joker who imperson-ated Hitler, who had seemed in those performances like a puppet at a fair that people threw rag balls at while it rose and fell.

That last part of his father's letter – about German honour – struck Kempf as strange. Naturally in his three letters home he had not written a single line about what he was living through here. He had been warned by his fellow fighters, by Germans, but also Ukrainians that the military censors scrutinised every line and that if he wanted his letter despatched from the front, he must take great care over what to entrust to it. What was his father alluding to? What could he know of his "war journey" with the S.S., there in Nuštar, which he had barely ever left? Given the circumstances of war – the treacherous murders of Volksdeutsche were increasingly frequent – his father's decision to stop travelling altogether even at the price of lost business was sensible.

On his camp bed, Storm Trooper Kempf fought against sleep with all his might: he was now the one who did not want to surrender. He knew well that the night could bring him some temporary relief, but that his first morning thought would be of Sofija.

Patrol

Good news: the building which they had taken to be a school, observing it from their position, was indeed that. Admittedly, it was a long time since that school had seen any children, that was clear. The little town appeared almost deserted. Here and there a feeble candle flame could be seen flickering in an occasional window. Starving dogs dragged themselves along the main road: rabies could be an issue.

But in the school there was still a milky aroma, an aroma of warmth. It smelled of children. On the blackboard, written in chalk, the letters of the Polish alphabet rustled; soft, silky. The geographical map on the wall showed Poland as it had been before September 1939. On one of the desks, a heart pierced by an arrow was inscribed for all time with the name Halinka. Someone had loved Halinka. All the children in the class had known the Polish letters, and also the shape of their country, which looked a bit like a pumpkin. Not all that small.

Where were those children now? Where was that Poland now?

On the teacher's dais, Kempf spotted a large wooden set square, with a compass. He tried, in vain, to remember the Pythagoras theorem.

Second cheerful piece of news: on the ground floor they found something that could have been a gymnastics hall. One door led into a large bathroom. In an instant they had the most natural thought in the world: washing in hot water. After they had suffered for weeks from a shortage of water and got used to shaving with a few inches and then using the same water to wash socks, squeezing mud out of them, it seemed unreal that water should gush incomprehensibly abundantly out of the taps in the school bathroom. Were there still in the world taps out of which water ran? Yes, there were such taps, yes, there was such water which delighted in running out of a narrow pipe into the freedom of a sink. But they barely remembered that.

The air already smelled of snow. It wasn't yet as cold, the older soldiers reminded them, as it would be. But they had to heat the water.

"Cast iron," muttered an officer, tapping on the boiler. "Not too badly made! We just need a good fire."

Frenzied activity ran through all the limbs of the soldiers' collective. One group set off to a copse with saws. More experienced men shouted that damp beech would not burn well and went with axes to break down the doors and windows of half-collapsed houses. In the end both solutions found themselves in flames. The logs whined, but they burned, and the windows that had seen a lot flared up silently.

The soldiers felt confident. There had been no resistance in the small town. They had entered it like friends on an outing and now that's exactly how they were behaving: a school excursion to an unknown country in which, in that mutilated pumpkin they found on the map, Polish lesser beings lived. What was the point of school? You could learn to count to ten without a set square or a compass. It sufficed to have hands, and hands – labourers', workers', slaves' – were the only kind the Reich needed.

They got undressed in the gym, soon they would be standing under the showers. The fire under the boiler was burning well.

Water would soon be running out of the showers, which was not always the case in this part of the world. In this part of the world what can come out of showers is death.

Kempf observed his fellow soldiers. He saw that the Germans from the Reich were better developed and more firmly built than the young Ukrainians. Open-air camping, gymnastics and other sports, *Kraft durch Freude* (Strength through joy), all the methods used by the Nazis to cultivate, or breed, a master race had an effect. But they did not all conform to those high racial criteria. There were asthenic bodies, there were some quite short soldiers, who would not have been accepted into the Waffen-S.S. at the beginning of the war; some evidently had poor sight, helpless now without their glasses they felt in the half-dark for the taps . . . On some of the supermen swung a member that did not measure up to the dimensions prescribed for the German race. How would it be if Heinrich Himmler, a trained gardener, or Adolf Hitler himself, a house painter, were now to stroll through this hall?

Himmler was a short-sighted dumpling. Hitler bathed in his own aura that had little connection to his physical figure. A statue of Hitler naked would not have convinced anyone. It was the brush under his nose that reinforced the severity of his expression.

Kempf knew already that he would never forget the moment the warm water began to thaw out his stiff hands. He watched his fingers emerge from the layers of soil, wheel grease, excrement, goodness knows what else. It wasn't easy to bury a 110 mm gun (military mark KI8), their field gun; in order to defend their position properly, they had dug down to roughly the height of a superman. In addition, they had dug out two positions for heavy MG42 machine guns. From these positions they could easily monitor the whole small town, but it seemed that barely anyone lived in it anymore; and if anyone did, such a person would have hardly considered resisting a field gun and two machine guns armed by supermen.

Hence their guard duties were more or less formal. They had left the gun crew up above the town; here in front of the school one soldier patrolled, more by way of punishment, for particularly serious drunkenness it would seem. In fact, they were all constantly tipsy; they were merry now too because the commanders had increased their daily ration of schnapps as a reward for their successful capture of the town, some fifty kilometres from Kraków, which had not offered any resistance. Kempf had no objection to that reward. On the contrary, the Germans were amazed at his prowess in that field, while the Ukrainians even suspected that he must be of Russian origin. There were a lot of stories going around of Russians charging onto bayonets, blind drunk. But on all sides, along with petroleum and diesel, alcohol was in fact the main fuel.

It was cheerful in the changing room, the lads thumped each other on the shoulders (as after a football goal), teasing one victim or another: they could be found in all school classrooms and all military units in the world; some pretended to have a boxing match, some wrestled in a friendly way, a piece of soap appeared from somewhere, water flowed from the taps, and the young men's bodies began to dissolve in a cloud of steam, just water steam ... Then the obligatory hitting of buttocks with towels as though they were in a sauna. Even in war one can sometimes live well.

And there was joy also in the fact that they were alive at all; that they still had two arms and two legs. For the time being they were defying the statistics that the central command of the Waffen-S.S. in Berlin kept for their secret needs.

When the showering was over, the lads stood in front of the mirror, battered but whole. Accustomed to small soldiers' mirrors, now they were all at once surprised by themselves, making faces and giving each other horns behind their backs. That's exactly what the children who had left their milky aroma here would have done; yes, the school had its aroma, and for these men, in the midst of the unbearable stench produced by war, that was the aroma of normality in a war that was in every way its opposite. Where those children were now, no-one asked. Besides, they were here. Kempf felt that. But then, they weren't, who knew where they were or whether they were alive?

It was an indescribable pleasure for him to stand with that warm, then hot, water from a tap running over his hands that had almost ceased to feel anything. It seemed to him that, from beneath layers, almost geologically ancient, some other hands were emerging, peacetime hands, made for quite other tasks than burying a gun in frozen earth. Scribbling verses under an oil-lamp at a farm, for instance.

The giggling in the deserted school continued. There was an atmosphere of general gaiety. The punished soldier peered angrily through the school window, then carried on walking in regulation fashion round the building. Would there be water for him or would he have to see out his punishment for his stupid drunkenness to the end? Because he had tanked up alone, and that wasn't good.

The lads looked as though they were preparing for an outing in town. They were like all soldiers all over the world: behaving like excited puppies let out of their cage. For most of them nothing would come of it. But there was no difficulty putting a patrol together, there were more than enough volunteers.

The space filled with the smell of cheap perfume. Really,

perfume. Supplies couldn't furnish them with clean underwear, but such clean bodies as these had not walked the Earth for a long time.

It was beginning to get dark outside. Still no sign of snow. Just its intimation, in the south wind.

Kempf's platoon picked up their black helmets and rifles and set off light-heartedly into the town in which there appeared to be no-one.

For a time they wandered through empty streets. There wasn't a single undamaged building. The south wind banged doors that were hardly held by their doorposts; they stepped over broken glass; windows with no panes gaped like the eye sockets of Cyclops' corpses. Dogs growled everywhere; that was their only greeting. They imagined that the town had been overtaken by rats. Headquarters had told them that the town was held by the Polish Underground so they should be careful. That must have been a specific military sense of humour nurtured by the headquarters of German armies. Because of course rats were the masters of the underground and perhaps the ultimate victors in the war to the death between the superior and inferior races. Ants, which wage their wars independently of humans, and rats, those supreme artists of survival – they would remain as the two species of totalitarian communities. Those that did not organise along totalitarian lines would vanish from the face of the Earth.

In truth, apart from the dogs and evidently feral cats, the occasional scuffling in the ruins suggested only rats.

Where were the humans, even subhumans?

Where were the subhumans who would emerge from the sewers, as their superiors had assured them, meaning the soldiers of the Home Army. Where were the Reds? Where, finally, were the Jews, who, despite being driven into mouse holes, were still dreaming of world domination and the final liquidation of the Aryan race (which was, namely, the "final solution" of the universal riddle posed by the sages of Zion).

Really, where were the Soviets?

After the disintegration of the front at Kursk, they hadn't set eyes on Ivan, at least not alive. Individuals who knew more about these things, the born strategic geniuses who existed in every military collective, guessed that, somewhere in the depths of the Asian steppes, the Russians were preparing for a final attack. They guessed that the terrible collision of the flowing lava of German fanaticism and the rigid ice of Bolshevism had neither frozen the lava nor melted the icefloes . . . that Kursk, from the German perspective, had in the end been indecisive. But at the same time, it had meant a major defeat and that German strategy was finished, kaput. And it was precisely now that the Bolshevik hordes were emerging from all their holes into the light of day with an unbelievable number of newly produced tanks, those cursed monsters known officially as T-34, which crushed all before them, vanquishing by sheer numerical superiority. How had the Russians come by so much iron, so many machines, so many hands to shift so many tanks? No-one, maybe not even the Russians, had reckoned with that. German High Command certainly had not, and it should have been the first to know. Something was very wrong here.

Suddenly, he thought he heard a piano. A real, actual piano in this desert. Kempf checked with his colleagues, afraid that he was having aural hallucinations: but yes, it was true. In the depths of this black sea someone was hitting piano keys, and it seemed they knew how to play.

A normal army wouldn't fire at a piano. In a normal war.

But this was something else.

In a normal war, a piano wouldn't fire at an army.

But this was something else.

Kempf recalled that, in some long-ago war in Warsaw, Russians (they were always the occupiers! They were the mythic enemy of the Poles and Poland) had thrown Chopin's piano onto the street.

One way or another, therefore, pianos participated in the wars waged here.

Kempf directed his platoon towards the sound. Amazingly, the wind stopped, because if it had not it might have taken the chords in the opposite direction.

And this was typically German, mused Kempf: if a German soldier set off in a particular direction, he would continue in that direction even if it was completely wrong. He would go to his own destruction convinced that a mistaken order was simply not a possibility. And he would march, despite snows and winds, in that completely wrong, diametrically opposite direction because that had been the order; until, after many, many years, circling the earth like Magellan who sailed round it, he reached his starting point, where there were now only ruins. This conjecture could explain a lot of things in this terrible war, at the very least all the events since Paulus' 6th Army's surrender at Stalingrad, if not since the failed attack on Moscow in the first winter of the eastern war.

At last they stopped outside a door above which was a sign with the inscription:

Zimmerman's Tavern – traditional Polish cuisine for gentlefolk.

They decided to behave decently. Why, they're dolled up, scented like Slavonian fast livers on a night out, thought Kempf. Not a fight out.

They opened the door.

In the room, not large, with maybe ten tables, everything stopped. Everything except for the strange phenomenon of a thin man in black tails, with grey hair falling to his shoulders . . . in ringlets – yes, ringlets – who carried on hitting the keys, pressing the pedals with his feet, bouncing on his stool . . . hitting them, crazily . . . he and the piano were one being . . . then he leaped into the air . . . carried on playing a strong rhythm . . . a mazurka, a czardas . . . something intoxicating . . .

Like Franz Liszt, it occurred to Kempf . . . he'd seen him in a magazine. A Polish local child wonder of at least seventy-five . . . Who didn't see anyone, who heard nothing other than his piano with which he merged in a deafening marvel.

Then a small man in an apron approached "Liszt" and began to gesticulate, trying to reach his ear . . . That was out of the question, his ear could hear only the piano . . . Then the small man in the apron pointed to the Germans by the door.

At that moment "Liszt" paused with his hand in the air.

The small man in the apron bowed. Had he been allowed, he would have kissed the Germans' hands; after all, those soldiers' hands were now clean. Clean hands, fragrant. For a good night, not a fight.

Another Pole who seemed to have emerged from a Dostoevsky novel, the man with the apron, who it turned out, was the new happy owner of the Zimmerman tavern.

Isaac Zimmerman, with his numerous family, had first been despatched to a nearby ghetto; not a large one, but effective, next to the small town where the German gentlemen were on patrol, and had now come to the tavern that as yet had no name but would be getting a new, Polish, not Jewish, national name soon.

For the time being, let it remain Zimmerman's Tavern – traditional Polish cuisine for gentlefolk! Because that was a business worth preserving. This was where the local intelligentsia gathered for a game of cards. The little man introduced a teacher; Kempf guessed that he had worked in the school where they had just washed in warm water. There were no children. No-one was able to answer the question of where they had gone.

Maybe they had been swallowed by a mountain? Whose pipe had those children followed? What pied piper had led them away? How many such ratcatchers were there in the world, those pipers of Hamelin who kept coming back, adapting the melody of their pipes to the spirit of the times? And if that was the case, how come there were so many rats in the town, had the piper of Hamelin not drowned them in the river?

"There's no sanitation!" the new innkeeper complained. "No-one cares about anything anymore. I'm barely keeping the business going. It's all gone to pot, from the front line to everything else. There's no honour in work!"

The overweight hostess, at least twice as bulky as her husband, brought schnapps and vodka.

They were offered venison stew. Most of Kempf's soldiers ordered the stew with enthusiasm. Why, war wasn't that bad. You shower, you smell good, and you are served game stew. The Poles barely drank wine, these people didn't know what good wine was. The Germans had foreseen this and one of them pulled a bottle of French red out from under his greatcoat, who knows how he'd come by it. The new innkeeper smiled and brought a bottle of Hungarian wine out of the cellar. How had he come by it?

Perhaps because of the deer that had greeted him on his arrival in Poland, Kempf ordered ordinary beef stew.

More calmly than before, after shaking hands with each of the Germans in turn, "Liszt" sat back down at the piano and everything fell silent.

But he no longer played with the enthusiasm that had, a moment before, so completely cut him off from everything at the inn.

What he played was undoubtedly a mazurka.

It was only then that the Germans noticed what every sexually starved soldier would have noticed at once: that there were a few women in the room of an age that could be of interest. The fact that they had not noticed them as soon as they came in proved the quite exceptional nature of the situation. Or had they appeared just now as a vision? The hungry could imagine all sorts of things.

One of the women climbed onto a table.

It was incredible in this war to see such silk stockings; a dress lifted up a bit (the woman was artful and she knew what to do on a table) . . . beside the table a Pole kneeled, with a cravat round his neck (Lord, a cravat), in a decent jacket over a white shirt. While "Liszt", not observing what was going on at the table, played the chords of his mazurka, the woman permitted the man to take off one of her shoes . . . The new innkeeper poured a small jug of vodka into the shoe. The woman placed her foot on the head, completely bald, of the man kneeling beside her . . . he drank the vodka from her shoe in a single swallow, and the woman, standing on one leg and resting the other on the skull of the man in the cravat, kept her balance, it seemed without difficulty . . . and that cravat of his was the colour of a tongue . . . Then "Liszt" stopped playing the piano, not even glancing towards the table. The drinking of the vodka was accompanied by complete silence, such as accompanies manifestations of high culture, attended by connoisseurs, citizens always well informed about everything.

Their strange coordination, not guided by any eye contact – "Liszt" had lowered his eyes to the keys – suggested to Kempf that this "number" had been practised and was regularly performed. The silence while the woman maintained her balance, her foot pressing on the head of the man kneeling by the table, was funereal.

Then, like gunfire, applause broke out, loud and heartfelt, in which the Germans joined. It was the kind of loud approval with which an audience endeavours to emerge from a state of elation with something uplifting.

"Perhaps the German gentlemen would like to take a look at our ghetto?"

That invitation was issued by the new owner of the Zimmerman tavern, accompanied by servile gestures, as he bowed to the floor.

Ghetto

One by one the soldiers trickled out of the inn; no-one felt like going out into the night that smelled of snow. The smoke-filled dive, where Mlle Katarzyna danced in black silk stockings on a table, struck them as torn out of reality. And set apart like that, it conjured a better reality. The imagination could dream up such a thing, but in this place no effort of the imagination had been required. The woman, the piano, the maestro – it had all been there, as if real.

It took a while for the patrol to be complete, but Kempf did not reproach his soldiers for that.

Black clouds were chasing each other above the small

We who are not yet born are now extremely agitated. In such states, we cling to each other, in an effort to alleviate our foreboding of impending misfortunes.

In the ghetto many fires are burning. It seems that its liquidation is under way. In German slang, that's called *Aktion*, action.

We all know that on the third floor of an old house there is a little family that until now has consisted of a father, mother and a boy of four. He was supposed to be the older brother of one of us. Tongues of flame lick the first two floors, a unit of S.S. soldiers stands on the pavement with rifles.

Bets are laid, will they jump, or won't they . . . the stake is half a litre of brandy.

We crowd around the unborn sister, hoping that our combined dread will put out town. Here and there the moon peered through them, and it was hard not to succumb to the optical illusion that the clouds were static while the moon was moving, as though going from window to window of some enormous building, appearing now at one, now at another and looking in, who knows at what or whom.

Sturmmann Kempf wanted the patrol to shake off the uninvited Polish civilians, but didn't succeed. Besides, how would they find the ghetto on their own? The new owner of the Zimmerman tavern promised he would take them to the gate. That is to the

the fire. Vain hope. It brings us some transient relief, but in the real world our collective prayer cannot alter anything. Moreover, we do not believe in collective salvation.

The father and mother, holding the little boy between them, decide on a leap that is met by volleys of gunfire.

We move away from the Unborn Girl and stand, silent, in a circle round her. There is no hope for her any longer and she knows it. We would weep if we could. Finally, we part from the one who will never be born to soften her fall into oblivion. I now leave Kempf and his patrol to look over this ghetto *en miniature* in which there is now nothing but rats. I promise them an interesting time.

place where the ghetto had been up until two months before, "but now," said Pan Stanisław, not without pride, "our town is *judenfrei*!", and he himself had liberated the Zimmerman tavern of Jews, only he didn't dare change the name of the business as it was so well established. In fact, could the German gentlemen suggest a name? What would be a good name for a bar in a small Polish town that had been "cleansed of Jews"?

There was something nauseating in the way Pan Stanisław bowed, and Sturmmann Kempf kept his hands buried deep in the pockets of his uniform, not so much because of the cold, but out of fear that Pan Stanisław would grab one of them and start slobbering over it. For the same reason, Kempf resolved in advance not to offer him his hand on parting, as the Pole could have twisted it off his shoulder out of servility.

Mlle Katarzyna evidently also intended to join the patrol, while the maestro Liszt scampered everywhere after her like a little dog. It turned out that they were an "artistic couple" who would perform for a small fee in bars like this in "the interior"; but, gentlemen, also in Warsaw, of course . . . that is everywhere and always when the circumstances of war permitted. All according to law and order, the "artistic couple" had a permit from the occupying authorities in the royal palace in Wawel. Drinking vodka out of Mlle Katarzyna's shoe was one of their turns, and the fortunate man who had to kneel beside the table of "the goddess Katarzyna" was drawn from a kind of tombola in which, for a pittance, all present participated.

It was noticeably colder, the south wind had died down and the breeze now blowing came from the north. It would be wise to return to the school as quickly as possible, collect the guards and get back to camp to sleep.

But they all wanted to see that wretched ghetto.

The patrol set off through the town, led by Pan Stanisław. In fact, he and the maestro "Liszt" took it in turns to lead, with the latter constantly making strange movements, as though he was still beating the keyboard. Panna Katarzyna made a half-whispered arrangement with one of Kempf's soldiers "for later". The Pole who had drunk vodka from her shoe was still hanging around her, wanting to stay in the game. But, objectively, his chances were quite slim. Might is right!

I'd be interested to know how it all turns out, thought Kempf. If someone could see us now. A ship of fools, that's us! Even that pale old man who rides on the clouds above us must be smiling. He must have sleepless eyes tonight.

Where on earth was that ghetto, and what was there to see in an abandoned ghetto? Garbage tip, death site, carcass dump, wasteland, nothing . . . Why had they let themselves be persuaded by the Polish gentlemen, particularly Pan Stanisław?

But the ghetto wasn't far. In fact the shtetl, a little settlement of Ashkenazis like the hundreds there had been throughout the Dual Monarchy, was a suburb of the small Polish town, and had there been no war it would have been difficult to say where the Jewish part began and the Polish part ended. But the German authorities in Kraków had ordered that the ghetto had to be separated off and now they were standing in front of a red brick wall, which reminded one of the patrol of the walls of churches in his homeland, in the north of Germany. The Ukrainians had seen something similar many times.

The wall was the best-preserved aspect of the whole ghetto; in fact it was all that had been preserved. The gate had been destroyed as it was unnecessary. The two lookout towers, concrete bunkers, were now home to bats, hanging in bunches, asleep. War veterans, they must have seen a lot, even though they were blind.

There was only one street in the ghetto. Kempf began reading the inscriptions on the shops, but soon tired of it.

"There!" exclaimed Pan Stanisław, spreading his arms. "This is where animals were slaughtered and salted according to the regulations. Until the war. Here things were bought and sold, day and night. Behind that window the learned Jews bowed over the Torah, also day and night."

The signboards were on the whole intact, but often barely attached to the buildings, which looked like rotten molars: teeth that had long since lost their enamel, of course, as well as their gold fillings. In fact, there wasn't a single intact house here. Kempf's practised eye calculated: that one had been torched. The house opposite had been destroyed by a hand grenade. That one – another fire. Further on, a heavy-calibre gun, right on target. A tank had passed through that one, the building had fallen onto the cupola, the tank had dragged it along.

"Nothing that happened here was against law and order," continued Pan Stanisław. "It was at Yom Kippur, when Jews pay off their debts to one another and contemplate their sins, that our police came with the S.S. They had, in black and white, the name of every Jewish man, woman and child. Germans don't make mistakes. When it's a matter of keeping records, the Germans excel."

"You worked on that list, of course, Pan Stanisław."

"Heaven forbid, Sir Storm Trooper. I could never have done so."

"Why not?"

"I knew only our Jews. But there were more than two thousand crowded into this ghetto."

"More than two thousand people lived in the space of three or four football fields?"

"Jews are capable of anything. But to say that they lived here would not be correct. They survived here."

"Of course, you couldn't have known those crammed in here."

"Why, they didn't even know each other, how could they, they had fled here from all over the place. But Jews always stick together I respect the Storm Trooper's intelligence, but I want to emphasise the fact that nothing happened here that was outside the law of the people in Kraków. Our town lived its life, they lived theirs."

Kempf noticed a commotion in a building with no roof or windows: as though they had been summoned to the *Appelplatz*, and in other ruins as well there was activity among the rat population. At the same time, Kempf detected a terrible stench, as though the rats had disturbed something that now smelled. A corpse, for sure, he thought. The Poles here are crazy. All the dead should have been buried, if not out of piety, then because of potential infection. He would give the necessary order to the locals in charge. The dead must be buried, however many there were. The town must be sanitised.

Kempf was relieved to discover that the terrible smell was not of a human corpse, but of a dozen dead rats, scattered around an entrance with no door (of course, thought Kempf, after the "evacuation" of the ghetto, the townspeople had wrenched off all the doors and windows). Those rats must have been killed by cats, or possibly dogs. Which was more likely as the rats were the size of an average Polish cat. Or perhaps the rats carried out "cleansings" among themselves? That had been known. The black ones were chased by the brown ones and the other way round, to a "final solution". Rats were genocidal. Was that the secret of survival?

"This is where the yeshiva was," said Pan Stanisław. "The school, that is. Before the wall was built round the ghetto, I used to come here occasionally, and I remember seeing young Jews standing by lecterns, even at night, studying the Torah. They spoke Yiddish among themselves, but otherwise Polish. Some never learned Polish, despite being born here."

The Pole continued to swagger with the gestures of a garrulous guide anticipating a handsome tip. Things may have been going better for him than for his patrons, but he still knew how to maintain the distance between servant and master.

"This is the mikvah, their ritual bathing place. There's water in it still. It comes from a stream behind the building."

Kempf noticed the remains of a wall lined with yellow tiles; with a ceramic facing on the top edge, at the height of a man, there were Hebrew letters and some decorative designs that conveyed something, but only to the initiated. There were no initiated people here now, so the signs appeared merely ornamental.

But Pan Stanisław did know a bit: "This is where their women and girls bathed when they were unclean, once a month."

Panna Katarzyna burst out laughing. "Why did that bother them?"

Maestro "Liszt" slid, like a lizard, off the remains of the wall from which he had been observing the mikvah. Kempf had noticed earlier that his movements were too abrupt, as though he was constantly playing the piano with special aplomb; but they were all fundamentally fawning. Just as the obsequious movements of Pan Stanisław always contained something deferential, oriental, Asiatic – a recoiling from a scourge combined with the wiliness of an artist of survival. For Pan Stanisław had risen, out of the class of the ordinary poor, out of the pack of people who had once served under one or other filthy Jew, into the class of the propertied.

"The Jews were taken, in a column, to the railway station. There freight trucks, a lot of freight trucks, awaited them. And that was the last check, in keeping with the regulations. Everything had to be proper, to be in keeping with the written orders. The train set off at exactly the appointed time. Generally, great store is now set by exactness in all things. This entire 'action'."

Here Kempf shuddered. He knew well what the word "action" meant in the slang of his unit: it was code for a round-up and "special procedure".

"It lasted less than an hour."

They paused in front of the burnt remains of the synagogue.

Part of the entrance, with the star of Solomon, and some side walls still stood; the roof had burned, the synagogue was covered by a sky over which clouds chased one another. But before those clouds covered the paths of the moon's meanderings, the entire ruin was bathed in liquid silver. Even the gushing Pan Stanisław fell silent, perhaps yielding to that unexpected onrush of beauty.

"What then?"

"About fifty of them refused to be taken to the wagons. They were locked in the synagogue with their rabbi, a renowned cantor. They sang the Kaddish for themselves. They offered themselves as burnt sacrifice, and so, according to their profane faith, such as they were, in one piece, as it were, they rose to the skies. They took their children with them. They gave a live and then dead performance of their new Masada, gentlemen!" Pan Stanisław spread out his arms in order, like a good guide, to explain to the ignorant chance travellers the significance of the place where they now stood. "Masada, the fortress in which Jews set fire to themselves in order not to fall into the hands of the Romans."

Kempf removed his cap. The other soldiers pretended not to notice and went on hopping about in their black helmets. It was getting increasingly cold, if this diversion didn't end soon, the men would start to freeze.

Pan Stanisław's mouth fell open for a moment. He was astonished. But then he too removed his hat. Even Panna Katarzyna, who had otherwise chattered incessantly, fell silent. Maestro "Liszt" slid off the ruins, like a lizard: then he too took his hat off his tangle of curly grey hair.

No-one could say how long the silence filled with liquid silver lasted. Even the rats were stilled, as though their army too had caught the sound of something.

Kempf ordered a quick march back to the school. As they

parted, he asked Pan Stanisław whether the school, where they now intended to spend the night, had once been attended also by Jewish children. "Yes," he replied, "when I was still in short trousers, I used to sit in the same class with some of them in the old school. The children of doctors and lawyers didn't attend yeshiva, because their parents didn't think they could learn anything useful there. It was the poorer Jews who lived in the ghetto, where there wasn't yet a wall. Those who were doing better bought apartments among us in the town, some even had whole houses, or inns like Mr Zimmerman. He didn't go to the synagogue or speak Yiddish. I swear he ate pork and especially loved pig fat. There was an inn in the ghetto that served only kosher food, but Mr Zimmerman's clientele weren't choosy. You saw for yourself, his inn was in a good place."

"Did you work for him?"

"Did I work for him? He didn't want to take me on. A long time ago," Pan Stanisław whispered into Kempf's ear, "I was a real orthodox Jew. Not by faith, but by choice. Zimmerman thought that was an affectation, he didn't believe me. But I admired the Jews and wanted to be like them. How indescribably stupid of me! Had the Jews had a shred of the secret power I ascribed to them, they would never have met the fate they did. The power of the Jews is a lie."

"So why does everyone persecute them?"

"I think, dear sir, they are persecuted because wherever they went, they always wanted to be and remain different. And that upsets people, it wasn't acceptable."

"Did you denounce them?"

"Heaven forbid. We're Poles, and decent people here. We believe in law and order. The trains here run on time."

"So there weren't any *szmalcowniks** here?"

"Two. But they're gone."

"How do you mean?"

Pan Stanisław ran his hand across his throat.

"Liquidated? By whom?"

Pan Stanisław shrugged. "Does it matter? What matters is that all of us here stick together and think the same way: our hands are locked together."

The parting was brief. Panna Katarzyna, who had carried her high-heeled shoes in a lacquered bag, had decided in favour of one of Kempf's soldiers, but Kempf refused him permission to leave. And so it ended with a noisy kiss witnessed by the rejected Pole with the sorrowful expression of a bedraggled dog; but now he had another chance.

The patrol set off towards the school through the sleeping town; in the occasional window there was a light or paraffin lamp. Wet snow stuck to their boots. Kempf ordered the men to turn their coats to the white side. Unlike in the winter of 1941, after suffering blow after blow, the Germans had learned to make themselves invisible in a landscape such as a Polish or Russian winter.

Like a group of white monks, thought Kempf. The Lord's dogs, *canes Domini* . . .

Here his film broke off, he hardly remembered how they reached the school and set up guards on each of the four corners of the building, scattered through the spaces that were once classrooms. He then gave himself up to the womb-like tranquillity of his sleeping bag, utterly exhausted.

---

* An expression denoting Poles who denounced Jews for money. [Author's note] rats rats rats

They come out of every hole in groups, evidently their kin. When the synagogue with the burnt roof filled with rats ranged behind one another, their
born leader and Messiah climbed onto a stone post. The speed with which
he did this was astonishing. Thousands of tails jerked upright, greeting him
enthusiastically and loyally.

"Until now," squeaked the supreme rat, "our nation has been trampled by
foreign, Norwegian rats," the troops at the foot of the column responded
with a shriek of contempt, "but that is now at an end and the providence of
our rattus God will from now on determine the direction of history: we were
crushed, we were shamed, we were poisoned, burned, plundered, we were
driven out of our native canals and holes, they stole from us everything that
could be stolen, our nation was on the verge of extinction . . . From all around
legions of Norwegian rats, in collusion with our eternal enemies, attacked us
and our age-old habitats . . .

"We endured it all because we are a nation that knows how to endure.
We endured loathsome accusations that we spread the black death among
Humans, while Humans are for us entirely irrelevant creatures as they belong
to the race of losers . . .

"Brother rats, let us be as one, let us no longer allow ourselves to be
crushed by inferior beings that would give anything to be like us. Let us gather in
ranks, form cohorts, let us go to a holy war for our threatened difference . . ."

Thousands of tails thumped the floor of the synagogue, stone-tiled, slippery
from the feet of thousands of Jews who had only yesterday prayed, sung and
traded here.

"Here, in this place, I declare TOTAL WAR against all sub-rats on planet
Earth."

The tails stretched into the air, as one, and thwacked the floor of the
synagogue, and that movement, accompanied by a swelling din, was repeated
without interruption. Like millions of wet shirts being beaten on a washboard.

In a victorious rhythm; a rhythm glorifying the Holy Word of the super-rat cavorting on top of the column, also thumping his tail.

Too many of the rats, with their long, flickering tails, began to entwine into a knot.

The super-rats thumped their tails, but the ball was becoming ever larger, the mass of tails could no longer be separated, it was too late for such a thing. The knot went on seething with hatred towards the enemy who was now said to be gathering on the borders of the grey super-rats' state; the knot grew, mesmerised by its own exuberance.

No-one dared cut off the tails. What would then be left of the rat nation? Could the tailless make history? What the losing races thought about that was unimportant.

This knot would not be able to survive even the first pangs of hunger.

Kempf woke from this strenuous dream drenched in sweat. He had become entangled in his sleeping bag, and now he needed to pee. The bag had almost suffocated him.

Sremska Kamenica, that I can understand, I often dream about it. But why not about my Hungarian?

Sremska Kamenica referred to an event from Kempf's student life. He easily found a connection with the previous night's dream: the tangled tails. That terrible event kept coming back to him precisely because he wanted to forget it. Every student knew that much "Freud".

Perhaps the day will come when we will be able to request our own dreams.

The night was too calm. The snow ennobled the ruins. As he urinated against the wall, he was aware that someone was watching him.

When he turned round, he saw before him, a metre away, a large rat: it had climbed onto the remains of the wall and now its muzzle was on a level with his face. It watched him attentively, calmly, without a trace of fear, perhaps slightly mocking. It seemed to Kempf that the rat was trying to catch his eye. The day before it was "Liszt" who had clambered onto that wall.

"Sturmmann Kempf, we expect a little more zeal from you!"

The rat's German was good. After this warning, it slipped off the wall and disappeared into a hole. It took a little longer to pull in its whole tail.

Interesting dream, for sure. A super-rat standing on a column . . . Could you, father, have eaten something at Zimmerman's that disagreed with you?

Like that Simon Stylites, the saint, who spent thirty-seven years on top of a post in the fifth century, with a multitude huddled day and night at its foot. A Rattus saint. He wanted to be closer to God, at least by the height of his column. But in fact God had absolutely no need of him.

I understand that Kempf, my father-to-be, is horrified by such visions. But that is mostly because, at the moment, he is living through them, he belongs to them.

Father Kempf, do you think you'll easily be able to preserve your tail? How do you think you'll escape without getting entangled with the rest of them? You've been told: "A bit more zeal, Sturmmann!" Don't jeopardise my chances and don't act out the despair of the righteous.

Operation Weiss

Who is Karlheinz Meier?

For some time now Kempf had been looking for an opportunity to talk to him alone. But for the last few days there had been constant alarms, the battalion had been on the move, it had been a long time since they spent the night in the same place to be woken by the unwelcome summons of the trumpet. He used to coincide with Karlheinz Meier when their bowls were being filled, but they had been eating on their feet, virtually with an eye on the target. There simply hadn't been an opportunity, the situation was serious, you could see it in the officers and radiotelegraphers' faces, in their constant haste, in that general tension on the verge of panic which must be regularly suppressed and was a greater enemy than the Soviets, although they were its cause.

Why did Kempf have such a lively interest in a soldier who had joined them on the eastern battlefield, where the statistical prospects of survival in that winter of 1943, especially in the units of the Waffen-S.S., were never more than 50 per cent, and who had been sent here as a punishment? The new arrival in the division was a veteran; in the autumn of 1939 he had participated in the German penetration to the East; he had, in so far as it was possible for an individual, contributed to the collapse of the Polish army. What is more, Karlheinz Meier also knew something about those first massacres of the Jewish vermin, who were in those days mainly killed by machine guns or crushed under tanks. But they had gone too far, foolishly. The winter forced them to dig in outside Moscow, which was an indication of their ultimate defeat. All the German soldiers who found themselves in that area, on that "magnificent advance", learned the Russian word *rasputitsa* – quagmire. The roads simply disappeared in liquid mud, which at a certain moment could not be passed by any vehicles with wheels or treads. You had simply to stop and wait for late spring. How could Hitler not have known? Hadn't he read Tolstoy? Had the terrible fate of Napoleon, whom they otherwise admired, not been able to give them some hints?

Karlheinz Meier had learned the butcher's trade from a friend of his father's and gone back to the family farm, but then, without himself knowing why, he was drawn to the big city. So he moved to Munich where he listened to a certain Adolf Hitler, who gave rousing speeches in a beer house. The butcher's apprentice belonged to the "first generation" of Nazis. His war journey up till now had been a real epic. His posting before Poland was called "the Balkans". The German soldiers, in discussions among themselves, called that area simply *Verdamtes Land Balkan*: "the cursed Balkan land".

Karlheinz Meier went to the Balkans as a soldier of the 7th S.S. division, which included tanks in its composition; it was on one of these that the S.S. volunteer Meier from Bavaria served.

So, he was a much-decorated veteran when, again who knows how or why, he arrived in the S.S. Galicia division.

After the constant changes of position, digging into the earth, moving their bivouacs, eating on the hoof, etc., it finally emerged that the Soviet formation had withdrawn deep into its territory; this was perhaps in part due to the arrival of the S.S. armoured division that had dug itself in behind the German

lines as soon as the decision had been made to defend those lines
at all costs. Had there been a battle, it would have been a real
mess, as Kempf's unit found itself between two artilleries. The
officers wrangled bitterly, someone had made a huge mistake,
but the scouts finally reported that the Russians were retreating
all along the front.

Things became livelier in the camp, post arrived (nothing for
Kempf again, the Balkans were far away), there was a prospect of
hot meals, and that inner war of all armies in the world began:
the war against lice.

Kempf sat down beside the butcher, trying to find a way to
initiate a conversation. "It's bad down there, isn't it, Karlheinz?"

"Hellish."

Kempf avoided asking why Karlheinz had been punished and
transferred to them. "It's not much better here."

"This is a walk in the park," Karlheinz said.

It quickly emerged that Karlheinz knew where Kempf came
from. Someone must have told him. Perhaps he too had been
waiting for a chance to talk with him alone? Perhaps he wasn't
as taciturn as it had seemed to Kempf.

"You should have seen what Operation Weiss was like, my
friend!"

Kempf had already caught wind of something about Operation
Weiss, as his fellow fighters would come running up to him as
soon as they heard anything connected with the Balkans. In
the case of Operation Weiss, the Supreme Command of the
Wehrmacht had informed everyone of the enormous successes
of the German and Axis unit against the Partisans; according to
that version Operation Weiss had ended with the complete defeat
of Tito's bandits; the Balkan battlefield was in practice cleansed
and pacified, which is what Hitler had always wanted.

The operation with the code name Weiss took place in the winter and continued until the spring of '43; somewhere round the time when Kempf had taken down his trousers in front of the S.S. medical officer at the recruitment centre, complaining of shooting pains in his knee.

"You should have seen those women," the German went on.

Kempf was all ears, even if he was expecting to hear Meier say something conventional about women, something about Balkan sluts.

"Those women gave us a real headache, they were a serious menace and temptation," he said.

Aha, thought Kempf, so that's it: temptation. The Siren call of sex!

"Those bitches of Tito's were a constant riddle to us. Not even our officers could understand their fanaticism!"

Fanaticism? Kempf winced. He hated that word, it belonged to Nazi slang. While Hitler's voice could still be heard on radio-receivers, he had thundered on about the "fanatical resistance"; "the fanatical persistence and courage of the German soldier secured a brilliant victory . . ." and so on. It was well known that in principle the S.S. units fought "*fanatically*".

"Operation Weiss really was to a large extent successful; that's not propaganda . . . The Partisans, the men, knew when to withdraw, but they would usually return at a quite unexpected location . . . in a way that was not anticipated in books about armies and warfare, they would appear behind us, but we usually dispersed them again. We had tanks, my friend, tanks will decide this war. But in the ravines of that benighted country tanks are sometimes powerless. And then it was a matter of man against man. Or rather man against woman.

"Do you think that was easy? On the contrary, my friend.

Those bitches protected their wounded until their sad end – and their own. They *never* withdrew and we never saw *a single one* run away. The men ran away, and we sometimes ran away . . ."

"You weren't always in the majority," Kempf wanted to interject, but thought better of it.

"I'll tell you," Meier said, as though reading his thoughts, "despite the fanaticism of the S.S., we sometimes fled, although less than the Wehrmacht. Quite simply, when something's not working, it's not working."

Is an observation like this the reason for Karlheinz's transfer, wondered Kempf, but he said nothing.

"So, those bitches fired with whatever they had, down to the last bullet. They never killed their wounded, even though they couldn't save them, or themselves. We could perhaps have spared them, we too desperately needed medical staff . . . Why, look who works in the medical corps these days, butchers, so I could join them," he said with a grin. "But we couldn't see them as soldiers, as fighters, you understand, that was something incomprehensible to a German. German women have different purposes, they live differently, they're quite different, except for down below . . . In their heads they are quite different beings . . . Those vipers of Tito's caused us considerable losses."

"And how could it have ended?"

"Above all, man, we were taking on the whole country. The country. On the territory they captured, those bandits established a real Soviet republic. They had schools, an economy, actors, they held, imagine this, doctors' congresses . . . They had underground hospitals on several floors. Operation Weiss was supposed to be the final blow to all those ideas in their hot heads. We fought for days, we mostly advanced, they fled, then re-emerged, behind us, as though out of the ground.

"But we're eliminating them, there aren't that many of them. Our scouts tell us that only the wounded are in front of us. And the women with them. The main force has probably been destroyed. We go forward, not understanding anything, somehow we're disarmed seeing those women of theirs, enraged vipers, and we keep falling, on all sides. Those women fire at us! And hit their mark. Then our commander sends a radio request for an armoured vehicle. That provoked a smirk in other units: all we had in front of us were their wounded on stretchers, a few donkeys and old nags, astonishingly resilient, admittedly, and those women who had a few rifles and hand grenades ... A tank would have trouble making it over the almost impenetrable karst, but then it did get through so that the whole group was within our reach."

"Then what happened?"

"Well, mate, you've seen what a barrel can do if the tank has someone on it who aims well."

Kempf had.

"We pulverised them."

They finished their cigarettes in silence and parted.

In his tent, after an evening that promised a calm night, Kempf tossed and turned in his bed. What he had just heard was the first authentic news from the Balkans. Up to now it had only been propaganda, which meant poorly disguised insults and curses: bandits, brigands, barefoots,* Bolsheviks ... rarely Partisans. Where he was now he had heard something about Polish and

---

* The original expression is something like "sock-wearers", used of the Partisans by the Ustashas in their propaganda: an insulting expression for a bunch of people in rags without boots who scampered about the forests in their socks. Thanks to the Germans, the Ustashas were always shod. They did have boots, but on the whole they ran away from the sock-wearers. [Author's note]

Russian partisans, after all that was who they were fighting. But here the word "bandit" was obligatory.

And now he kept thinking: women, girls . . . bitches . . . nurses . . . From Lika, Bosnia, Dalmatia, an insoluble riddle for the officers and soldiers even of the armoured S.S. divisions . . . fighting even after their last bullet . . . never surrendering.

Here a different figure came to Kempf's mind: Sofija.

He couldn't have known that she had long since completed her lengthy journey down the Sava to Kalemegdan in Belgrade, then down the Danube to the Black Sea, and then, instead of floating towards Trebizond, mysterious name full of promise, she had gone further south, into the Aegean Sea, to be caught up in the net of a Greek fisherman, fascinating the English officers, who examined the catch from all sides, smoking their pipes in a jeep parked on the quay, muttering: "Oh my God, oh my God."

For Kempf Sofija had passed away from pneumonia.

There was a great difference between dying and being killed. Kempf knew that very well, but what should he believe if not his mother's letter?

As well as letters, Christmas gifts were distributed: woollen socks, gloves, hats that could be worn under one's helmet, chocolate, alcohol . . .

There were also presents from German children with messages on little pieces of paper. Many of the packets were sent by soldiers' widows. On the whole they were gifts for "a German soldier on the battlefront".

As such, Kempf received a pair of socks and a drawing on which a child had written: "May the angels protect you, German soldier!"

The soldiers cut down a fir tree and decorated it as best they could, mainly with the cases of spent cartridges.

Idyllic, thought Kempf. My first year in the Waffen-S.S. is drawing to an end.

In the Field Hospital

When he was about eight years old, the boy Kempf pushed through the bushes along the Bosut river, fell and got up, carrying a branch in his hand, pronged, where the chub were caught, their gills penetrated so they could no longer slip off . . . here and there it was dark, with sudden bursts of sun as it descended for the day . . . here and there the boy moved branches apart and was showered with golden pollen from elderflowers.

Fearful of the dark, Kempf ran, with grass snakes rustling around him, and possibly an occasional viper. Kempf ran, beginning to feel he didn't know how to find the path he used every day.

The boy would have stayed a bit longer by the Bosut had someone not knocked against his camp bed, unintentionally, but provoking an intense pain in his shoulder.

The tent filled with people. They had brought someone in. Kempf saw that they were raising the man's left arm, looking for the Waffen-S.S. insignia, his blood group. They were evidently intending to give him blood.

Gradually and not of his own volition, the most recent events returned to Kempf like a nightmare.

They had run into an ambush. Why hadn't the company commander sent a scout? How come they had felt so confident? It was true that they hadn't seen a single Red Army soldier, at least not alive, for more than a month since the massacre at Kursk.

Kempf suspected that Kursk represented a new defeat since the initial influx of optimism had been followed by total silence. That is how it had been after Stalingrad as well. The same reasoning suggested to him that the front was being "stabilised", whatever that meant, but that the German penetration had not gone according to plan.

The Red Army was involved further east, both sides were consolidating . . . How come the Russians had so many tanks? Kempf sensed the constant surprise of his fellow fighters, particularly the officers. Sub-humans designed and made quite a good tank. The crews of those tanks were well trained. The Soviet infantry had learned to accompany and defend their tanks. Now the Russians were absolutely in a position to coordinate the movements of huge numbers of people and materiel. In addition, the forests were swarming with bandits.

How did these bandits breathe, politically? Whose bullet was it that had hit Kempf and which he now had to carry in his shoulder, because removing a stupid bullet had been delayed for more urgent cases? Had he been hit by a Ukrainian partisan? Belorussian? Perhaps a fighter from the group composed of young Jewish refugee men defined by their officers as born Bolsheviks? Or was it a fighter from the underground state? A woman? Or, Kempf continued the catalogue of potential enemies, could it have been a Soviet commando who had fallen from the sky by parachute? An angel with a star! "German soldier, may the angels protect you!"

Once the wretched bullet was extracted from him, it should be clear who had shot him. Probably. But rifles here go from hand to hand, rifles are prostitutes. We too use some tools we've captured from the Reds. They aren't as bad as people in Berlin might wish.

It was a stroke of bad luck, thought Kempf, his wound gave him ferocious pain with every movement, but it wasn't lethal. Touch wood. The bullet had entered just a few centimetres above the tattoo on the inside of his upper arm, above the bluish letter A which denoted his blood group. As a doctor-manqué, he was interested in why the Supreme Command of the Waffen-S.S. had chosen precisely that place to engrave their signature on the bodies of their soldiers the way livestock was marked for slaughter. He asked the medical technician from their field hospital. That hospital, like most of the German war hospitals, always followed a step behind the units in action. The German high commands, both of them, the Wehrmacht's and Himmler's, considered that the proximity of doctors was good for the fighters' morale. The explanation: the blood group was tattooed on the inside of the upper arm because it had been statistically established that in World War I wounds to the upper arm were rare.

It had become crowded in the tent, so it happened that a nurse had knocked into Kempf's bed and woken him. They had brought in someone Kempf immediately concluded must be a big shot. There was a commotion around the stretcher. The surgeon came in with his assistants, a butcher, therefore, thought Kempf spitefully. What had driven him, a surgeon, into this war, and to the East to boot? Undoubtedly this old codger had also volunteered. He was unlikely to be a "forceteer". He had abandoned his emeritus chair in Frankfurt and a hospital in which conditions were flawless . . . absolutely sterile . . . he had left his grandchildren, who had had to take shelter in the country, because of the Allied bombings . . . And now that professor was watching a male nurse stepping in his boots on a heap of bloody bandages, overflowing from the overfull bin . . . and, as he watched, wounds were being dressed with paper instead of sterile cotton bandages. And after they made their rounds, the old doctor stood to one side, because his rank was low.

How good it was, thought Kempf, that he had not opted for the medical corps. Not because he had fainted at their first dissection (a drowned body) in Belgrade . . . he would have got used to it, people get used to anything. The professor had got used to a lot that he would have considered scandalous in his own hospital. But there were things a person should not get used to. This was certainly a descent into barbarity. In field hospitals like this, on the eve of the decimation at Stalingrad, conditions had been like those of the Thirty Years' War. Sometimes, the only "narcotic" even for the worst amputations was a swig of brandy. Such "narcotics" were used also by the surgeons themselves because they needed them too.

Already then, in Belgrade, Kempf had been troubled by the fixed idea that the drowned man could come to life, sit up on the table lined with white ceramic tiles, and, holding onto his liver or lung with his hands, ask the students: "What on earth are you thinking of, gentlemen?"

Hostages lined up against a wall in front of a firing squad: "Gentlemen, what are you thinking of? You can't deprive us of life just like that!"

Jews in front of the gas chambers: "Gentlemen, what sort of idea is this? There are little children here!"

And so on. Those are questions that should be posed by – Europe. Disbelief like that should be expressed by – Humanity! Like a flabbergasted child in the face of all that "adults" dream up.

Field guns flared. The partisans don't have big guns, thought Kempf. Are the Soviets coming to thrash us?

Will someone from the unit finally come and tell him who it was they had run into?

Kempf didn't know anyone here in the tent.

It was as though they had all forgotten him, Sturmmann Kempf, particularly his own people. For the surgeon, the old professor, his wound was of no interest. In the end, the wound was hurting him, not the doctor. How many things in medicine would be simpler if a doctor could, at least for a moment, experience the pain of the person he was treating. But that was impossible, just as it was impossible for someone else to wash for you. Although one could die for someone else.

A face now leaned over his: he didn't dare move his neck because that would have hurt. So he had to endure the lengthy, questioning gaze of a woman: two blue eyes. Kempf had never come across such a clear blue in Slavonian girls' eyes.

"Are you in pain?"

The question was in German. But at the same moment Kempf realised that the woman was Polish. She spoke in that softened German, as though lined with velvet, that Poles spoke.

Two more days passed in the field hospital, filled with bustling, groaning and the death of the seriously injured, in the stench of carbolic, with the rumbling of the generator that gave a flickering light for operations, before Kempf managed to get the woman to acknowledge that her name was Ania and that she had studied medicine in Kraków for a year before "this shit" began. So, she too had enjoyed a brief flirtation with medicine that had been interrupted by the war, and now she was here and knew all there was to know about medicine.

After she said *diese Scheisse*, "this shit", she fell silent, watching him carefully . . . as though expecting some comment, or simply negation.

Ania Sadowska wore a white coat, and, like everything else here, it was dirty. All manner of bodily fluids had left their trace on the once white material. It was hard here to come by enough water . . . only the most essential things were washed. The frequent evacuation of the field hospital as it followed the battalion tended to exacerbate the water shortage . . . in this part of the world it was hard to find a well that had not been polluted, while down the rivers and streams floated the dead, horses, men, dogs.

"All the perfumes of Arabia will not sweeten this little hand!" Kempf recalled Lady Macbeth before Ania Sadowska's syringe sent him once more towards the Bosut, to meet the chub stuck on the forked branch, and the old oak, which he considered his friend. Ania Sadowska, student of medicine and his colleague, dissolved.

"Where the hell is that rucksack?" Kempf heard his voice and felt that he was sinking into a bluish mist, the pain in his shoulder had vanished, he was suddenly walking, light, as if emptied, he was walking the way shadows move . . .

In the corner of the kitchen sat his mother, the rucksack in her lap, sighing softly from time to time. Half-full or half-empty, that rucksack on her lap appeared like a grandchild. But instead it was their cat which was able to look at one like a person who understood (but was not interested).

"Where's the old man?" asked Đuka.

Knowing that Old Kempf was playing cards at his usual spot at the inn which had been Jewish until only yesterday, and was then sold for one kuna, his son was asking for form's sake, not expecting an answer. If form was no longer respected, if the only son's departure "to Stalingrad", or somewhere similar, was not reason enough for gathering round the family table . . .

Old Kempf was playing cards and sipping brandy at the inn,

which could have become his. He had not, however, been interested in its purchase, that is in its Aryanisation, for the simple reason that if he had become its owner, he would be playing cards in his own home, meaning that he would never go out "for company". And that would be death for him.

He'll moan about the soup being cold again, thought Kempf. The old grouch!

But late that night, both Old Kempf and his wife stood on the platform at Vinkovci railway station, like the parents of the other soldiers, waving. That was how Franja's mother, a widow, had also waved farewell to her son nearly a year ago now, and Đuka, who was with her on the platform, had consoled her.

"Don't do anything there that would prevent you from returning to the home of your birth!" his old man said, grasping his neck, as if intending to draw his son to him and give him a loud kiss.

"It's not true, it's not true . . ." mumbled Kempf, half-asleep. His old man was so drunk he could hardly stand upright, he didn't know where he was, and if his old lady had not held him under his arm, he would have collapsed onto the platform.

I must ask headquarters about Franja, was his first thought as he surfaced from the bluish mist of half-sleep. Let his division commanders ask Berlin where the Volksdeutscher Lauber was and whether he was alive. A man is not a needle to get lost in a haystack. Even if the hay now belonged to the empire, there must be some trace of him somewhere. Germans liked to record everything.

If Franja could only see this Polish girl. His mouth would be watering. Franja and women!

In his early twenties, he had already worn a tonsure on his head. In truth he had begun to lose his hair early. He maintained that it suggested priapism. At that time Kempf had the luxuriant hair of a young genius. Despite the fact that Franja proclaimed his priapism, young Kempf fared better with the ladies.

Franja, where are you now? Where have you got lost, my friend? It's not right that I should always fare better.

Ania Sadowska

Kempf suddenly had a lot of time to gather his thoughts. He didn't know whether that was getting him anywhere. Perhaps it was better to charge frantically through the woods, shooting at invisible targets. He tossed and turned on his camp bed, it hurt less if he lay on his right side. But inside his head was fairly chaotic.

It was calmer in the field hospital now. Here and there an occasional German word was heard, escaping from someone's dream; mostly a woman's name that scuttled away to a dark corner like a mouse. The Waffen-S.S. was a formation ashamed of emotion. During the day, the soldiers' lips were pressed

My prospective father Kempf is making his way through life. This Ania Sadowska is one of his passing – I hope – loves. She is an intelligent, mature person. When Kempf warned her of the risks, she told him that any child of hers would be conceived when she wished.

Sadowska was registered with the Underground. Her life constantly hung by a thread. She too wanted to change the world. Like Vera, her choices were dictated by her own will. The Home Army was not a good choice for Kempf, but he didn't know that. Kempf had acquired most of his information about Poland from leafing through his Baedeker. He knew that there was a good hotel in Auschwitz. He was capable of calculating that the value of the złotys with which they were paid in the General Government was weaker than together. The women came at night, obediently, as soon as their names were spoken. The Ukrainians invoked quite different names.

Kempf knew that most of the people lying here had more serious wounds than his.

The year '43 was draining away, and with it much of what was supposed to have been completed. But they were still giving out medicines to alleviate pain that would otherwise have been intolerable. After Stalingrad, and despite the "victory" at Kursk, limbs were again being amputated under anaesthetic. In the hospital there were still doctors who were partially trained and the amputations they did here were not their first. The experienced surgeon was still in the hospital, admittedly staying to one side like a scalded dog, and always following the others at the end of the morning rounds,

when he had arrived in Poland. He had seen the two Poles his unit had killed and those five liquidated hostages ... That was all for now, apart from the bullet he had acquired in his shoulder.

The people who signed up for the Armia Krajowa were on the whole decent and courageous people. These days, unfortunately, that was no guarantee that they held strong cards. On the contrary, their ultimate prospects were poor.

In a world in which politics and sheer power are the determining forces, we unborn have also to think politically. Poets are politicians, and they are proud of the fact.

From a political viewpoint, my prospective father was a dolt, an oaf, a blockhead. Ania Sadowska could ruin him.

I have to go on trembling with anxiety. For how long?

On the other hand, maybe it was better for her to hide him in the forest. Both sides were piling up previously unseen quantities of tanks, field guns, planes; the final reckoning was hanging in the air. Heaven help anyone caught up in that hell.

And if he happened to be between two firing lines?

Have you ever seen wild

but he was always asked for advice when something went wrong. The supply lines were not yet completely cut and the main body of the Red Army was only just grouping in the East. The German military machine, which seemed to have been dealt a fatal blow, came back together as soon as the storm of molten iron had passed. Admittedly, the losses of the German army, and par-

animals trying to escape from a forest where huge fires are raging? Often the animals make the wrong decisions and burn pitifully.

This could now easily happen to Kempf. Was it better for him to stay in his division or to join the underground army, politically correct but militarily weak?

That woman, that Sadowska, evidently had some hold over him.

ticularly the Waffen-S.S., were enormous. But the military glory of the latter had been consolidated: the Waffen-S.S. fought well. A German soldier could perish from a Russian bullet, but he would not retreat. There were huge difficulties in provisioning, but he did not go hungry. The Waffen-S.S. itself was in fact becoming a legend. The Wehrmacht generals pointed out in vain that their soldiers too were perishing in no smaller numbers. The two armies competed to see who would contribute the greater sacrifice to Hitler's cause.

After the first Russian winter that had so astounded the German High Command, the German soldiers were now better protected: even here Kempf was covered with an overcoat with two sides, one of which was white. The colours of his uniform, at different seasons of the year, tried to reflect the colours of Polish and Russian forests. The Waffen-S.S. had been the first to introduce camouflage uniforms; the Waffen-S.S. had been the first in this war to get new models of tanks. It seemed that in the notorious conflict with the Wehrmacht, Himmler was prevailing.

That was achieved by ideology: devotion to bronze idols. He himself was that idol in the absence of Hitler, who remained the supernatural deity, the German Caesar. That was just the way God-the-Father had instructed Moses to fashion a bronze serpent that would represent the absent God. Himmler's visions were more merciless, more consistent, because the bronze idol did not stop where ancient concepts of Prussian military honour nevertheless imposed certain limits. Before he was wounded, Kempf had seen it all with his own eyes, and what he had seen was the implementation of the "scorched earth" notion. The Waffen-S.S. fought with more fanaticism, hurtling into the fire beyond what was taught in military academies, sometimes successfully, sometimes not . . . That was all.

Kempf's wound was healing too quickly. The tendons were untouched; in normal times, that would be a cause for celebration.

It greatly concerned Ania Sadowska. It ought to have concerned Kempf himself more. He would soon be sent back to the front line. Every day, at Himmler's command, commissions would comb the field hospitals near the front, including the one that was now situated beside the main dressing station. The wounded were brought there day and night, some by aeroplane. Even the wounded who were still bleeding were inspected by Himmler's visiting commissions: armaments were arriving, but it was increasingly difficult to replace men. In the Waffen-S.S. racial criteria had long since been suspended. Dwarves were still not accepted into the Waffen-S.S., they were collected by Mengele for his experiments. But all other barriers had fallen. Beggars couldn't be choosers.

It took quite a while for the Polish woman and the Volksdeutscher to draw closer. Kempf had the impression that, like a bird, she was circling over his bed, endeavouring to gauge whether he would gladly be that prey: it was months since he had seen a woman other than as a corpse.

He inhaled the aroma of the woman who leaned over him, and the cross she wore would sometimes fall from her breasts onto his face: carbolic, some sweat and the scent of a woman which would open the nostrils of any male dog suffering from misery and deprivation. We're all dogs, thought Kempf, we'd all like to sniff.

Should he put his arms round her?

Who knows how she would have taken that. Perhaps she would have defended herself, perhaps not. In this large S.S. field hospital tent there was probably not a single male dog who would not have wanted to embrace her, even for a moment. Even if he was not fully conscious, maybe even if he was in a coma, like a vegetative being, like a plant twining its tendrils round a female body.

"Why did you refuse to shoot the Poles?"

Ania asked that question on the fifth or sixth day after Kempf was "delivered" to the field hospital. It echoed like a shot, so loudly that the patient on the next bed began to look round.

"Are you crazy, Ania!"

Kempf was now waiting for the Gestapo agent to appear in the tent. You couldn't say or think that the walls had ears here. There were no walls in a tent, just an ear.

"You didn't want to," said Ania, using the informal "you" and thereby erasing the distinction of the two forms between them forever.

Their drawing closer was dragged out over a few more days. And then, any time now, Kempf could be sent back to his unit. The day before he had been visited by lads with whom he had shared a whole bag of salt. They said it was calm in their sector now, but soon they could be sent off to where there was more action. In the end, that was the credo of the Waffen-S.S.: to go always where it was fiercest, where a gap in the German lines had to be plugged because the Wehrmacht types had screwed up again.

Like almost everyone in Poland, Ania was devout. The cross that fell coquettishly between her breasts, not large, but firm and nicely shaped, was no mere ornament, but a vow.

As soon as she heard him for the first time, Ania was delighted that Kempf, although a German, spoke a language she understood up to a point. And from then on she would lisp words in her Polish that sounded ceremonial to Kempf, like a Croatian dialect from a chivalric age of forgotten dragons and heroes.

The two of them understood each other . . . He used German only when something to do with the war had to be explained: officers' ranks, weapons, kinds of wounds, kinds of killing, *Totalkrieg, verbrantes Land . . . Konzlager, Juden, judenfrei, Endlösung, Aktion . . .* The language of Goethe and Schiller was now the language of war.

How could he explain to her the meaning of constructions such as *freiwillige Gezwungene* or "forced volunteer"? How to explain the difference between a "real German" and a "national German", a Volksdeutscher? Between a "German German" and a "Danubian German"? In this war language put up with it all, becoming one of its greatest martyrs.

Although she didn't think the Jews should be killed just because as a rule Poles and Jews didn't care for each other, Ania Sadowska herself couldn't bear them.

"Nonetheless, *we* are helping the Jews!" Sadowska admitted at one moment. "Well, you can't put all Jews in one basket."

"That's true. In a village near Kraków there was an innkeeper, a Jew, who wrote off all the widows' debts. People used to say: 'if you want to redeem yourself with the Jews, all you have to do is hang yourself."

There was no-one in the tent at the time, the medical round had moved away long before and all the nurses and technicians had been summoned urgently to the main dressing station because a plane had been heard arriving with new wounded soldiers. There were still patients in the tent, but in such a desperate state that they had to be given sleeping drugs. It was in that relative, perhaps deceptive, security, that Ania Sadowska uttered that *we* . . .

"We?" repeated Kempf, wanting to be certain of what he had just heard.

The torrent that poured out of Sadowska's mouth then revealed the following:

She was committed, in heart, soul and body if necessary, to the Polish underground state.

The Polish underground state included all Poles who thought in a nationalist, that is, Polish way.

The fundamental aim of the Polish Underground was a free, independent, democratic Poland, within its pre-war borders.

The enemies of an independent, democratic Poland, whose only legitimate government had fled to London, were of course the German criminals.

Her enemies were also all those who didn't want an independent and democratic Poland, as it was before substantial parts of the Polish land were amputated by the Soviets, without anaesthetic.

That amputated, crushed, dispersed and burnt Poland was screaming, but in the West no-one could hear. Poland was writhing in fantasy pain!

That was why the underground Polish state had a military wing, called the Armia Krajowa, that is the Home Army, Sadowska informed him solemnly. "It includes all patriots, all those who think and feel Polish, including foreigners" – here she looked seriously at Kempf – "if the ideas I've just expressed aren't alien to them."

"Does it include Jews?" Kempf said.

"It does. But they're fighting for themselves."

"Well, everyone in this war is fighting for themselves."

"We in Poland are fighting for a better world."

"And what are the Jews fighting for? World domination?"

Kempf had never heard that the Jews were fighting for anything. On the contrary, his S.S. comrades who participated in "actions" against the Jews always told him of the surprising fact that the Jews didn't resist either killings on the spot or deportations. It was known that sometimes they went into the gas chambers singing in praise of God. More often than not they entered them as though they were entirely absent, as though sleepwalking, as though they didn't understand what was happening to them, and started shouting only when the door was already closed . . . That's what people whispered in the army. A subspecies of S.S. soldier guarded the camps, the ones who served the Reich under the sign of a death's head. They were sometimes directed to units on the front for various reasons: often because they had plundered the state by stealing from the dead. Hence, everything was known about what went on in the camps. In this way Kempf heard things he shouldn't have heard. And he would have preferred to have heard them from that creep Schlauss junior, whose ugly mug he would then have punched again.

While he was still in Nuštar, in Slavonia, now in the Independent State of Croatia, Kempf had heard people saying something similar about the camp at Jasenovac: the only people who had resisted mass slaughter there on the Sava ferry were young Gypsies. Here in Poland he would often hear that this Pawelitsch* of his may have been a good lad, although he seemed to Berlin to exaggerate in some things. He had found his own Jews, otherwise called Serbs.

"In the forests, including here, around us, there are Jews who are organised militarily," Ania Sadowska affirmed categorically.

"Good, but what are they fighting for?"

"Don't you know that every Jew, every day, and especially when there are several of them together, must mutter: 'Till next year in Jerusalem!'?"

"Well, we too, especially when we find ourselves in churches, have to promise ourselves the Kingdom of God."

"That's not the same."

"The Jews are thinking of a heavenly Jerusalem."

"We don't know what they are dreaming of. The Poles have bitter experience with the Jews. They always stick together. The Jews are always dreaming of something. It would be best if they would move peacefully to Palestine."

"Arabs live in Palestine."

"Poles live in Poland."

As soon as Ania had gone to the dressing station where there was now an urgent need of every pair of hands experienced in washing and bandaging those covered in shit and piss, and the dead, it all sorted itself out in Kempf's head:

---

* Ante Pavelić founded and headed the ultranationalist organisation known as the Ustaše in 1929 and governed the Independent State of Croatia, a fascist puppet state built out of parts of occupied Yugoslavia by the authorities of Nazi Germany and fascist Italy, from 1941 to 1945. [Translator's note]

Underground Poland was proposing something to him. The Home Army was summoning him to its ranks. The Underground information service knew that he was a weak point, in terms of the fighting morale of his S.S. troop. Someone had passed on the information that he, the storm trooper, Sturmmann Georg Kempf, was a Volksdeutscher from Slavonia, who in Croatia, now Hitler's ally, had probably been recruited as a somewhat older novice-volunteer, who until 1943 had evidently not allowed himself to be volunteered for slaughter, and most importantly he had refused to participate in the execution of five Polish hostages, including two women . . .

Did this mean that now he, Georg Kempf, was being given a chance to really be a volunteer?

For the first time in his life to choose a side of his own volition? Or was it in fact Sadowska's decision?

When those who had been brought for washing and bandaging had been washed and bandaged, when the daily quota of legs and arms had been cut off in the operating tent, when those who could not be fixed in the S.S. field hospital, in reach of Stalin's "organ", had been flown to Germany, everything suddenly went quiet. Kempf heard someone groaning in his sleep, and once again the air of the tent filled with women's names . . . Those who were called to now were Ukrainian and just the occasional German woman.

How strange it is, thought Kempf . . . as early as the second generation of German colonists in Slavonia real German names like Hilde, Inge, Brigitte, Christine and Gudrun disappeared . . . The granddaughter of his great-great-great-grandmother, called Maria Theresia Kempf, of the house of Freundlich, named of course after her grandmother, had already been written: Marija Terezija Kempf. And the German-Slavonian girls were given names such as Tena, Zlatka, Zdenka, Jana ... Our national names, thought Kempf.

Then Ania returned, as soon as she was able to, and she seemed in a hurry; she combed her hair, bathed in a small bathtub, so small that in normal times she could barely wash stockings in it. But anyone who had seen her would have concluded that she was preparing for an assignation. She was tired, her shift (lasting a full twelve hours) had only just ended, but now, standing over Kempf, the fatigue dispersed; Kempf was pretending to screw up his eyes, but in fact his lips stretched into an inner smile, without stirring he was going to meet her full of expectation, without showing it on his face. Kempf was almost paralysed by the fear of spoiling something. First, she took off her apron, covered with stains of all sorts, including blood, then her white coat, and slipped, inaudibly, warm, coy and sweet, next to him on his camp bed, saying only: "Đuka!"

Kempf could just hear the soft hum of the generator emitting a flickering light sufficient only for basic orientation in the tent. And he heard his name, Đuka, for the first time after many months which seemed like years: and now he wished that this hour should last a "year", which was quite possible in the Polish language,* of course. And after that he heard in the half-dark: "Jurek! In our language Đuka is Jurek. That's what we'll call you."

Kempf understood that he had just been re-christened.

But perhaps very soon, in just a few Polish *godzina*, he could be sent back to the front line, into a trench where the earth was beginning to freeze; his attack rifle would be returned to him, and the insignia of his belonging to the military elite would again be

---

* The Polish word for "hour" is *godzina*, very like the Croatian for "year": *godina*. [Translator's note]

fixed on his collar and his wounded shoulder, which had healed treacherously fast.

Or, on the contrary, would he set off wherever he was guided by the invisible hand of the Polish underground state and the Home Army? Where was it that Ania Sadowska intended to send him, like a package with no sender's address, in the name of the Underground?

And in that case, would the only remaining sign of his belonging to the herd hurtling with braced horns into battle to the "final victory" be the mark of Cain, not on his brow but on the inner side of his upper arm? You can flee from a flag, you can move away from the group, from the "black hordes of Florian Geyer", celebrated by the cursed warriors on the basis of an inappropriate loan from history. The Waffen-S.S. had its deserters too. Captured deserters were summarily despatched. What you can't escape is your blood group. You can't that easily leave the community of blood, as the Nazis put it. But just because you can't run away from blood, it's wise to leave it out of any such decisions. Blood speaks only in ultimatums.

"Jurek Kempf," whispered Ania, passing him a little mirror.

A satyr, a wild man, thought Kempf, looking at the stranger in the mirror.

Ania was now sitting on him, clutching him firmly with her thighs, then expertly soaping and shaving him with a razor.

"As though you were shaving a corpse," Kempf said.

"They're cold, and you're hot."

He lay under Sadowska helplessly and that pleased him. We all ought to abandon ourselves to women, thought Kempf.

"Lift your chin!"

The moon now came into the limelight, in the glory of a full moon.

"Here's our Pan Twardovsky," Ania whispered. "A little longer and Pan Twardovsky will alight on the moon riding his red cockerel."

"?"

"Twardovsky is a wizard, he's our Faust, but not as serious. On nights like this he wants to escape to the moon on a red cockerel."

"And who's chasing him?"

"The devil and a woman."

"I'd put it the other way round: first the woman, then the devil."

"You're going to run away from me!"

After that they made love.

Ania asked him to stay inside her.

"You'll conceive."

"My baby will be born when I want it."

Ducats

The bad weather passed. Rain stopped drumming on the tent's canvas; what could now be heard were drops from branches tossed by the wind. It drove the clouds away, the dark rags in the sky joined into a single carpet: never so many stars. Pan Twardovsky was again sending greetings from the lunar disk where he had alighted the previous night.

The sky is the same as at home, thought Kempf. When Europe wants to sleep and draws the sky over itself, it's always the same blanket: Scorpio trying to grab Virgo with his pincers; while orange Antares squints furiously right behind him because, of course, for millions of years he's been trying to do the same thing, without success. Isn't that an image of failed desire? Even so it's true: anyone can read something of his own destiny in the sky, if Luna's glow allows him.

He had seen his Sofija for the first time when he came home from Belgrade for the vacation. Almost every Sunday, unless it was pouring, the Slavonian girls would dance their ring dances in the middle of the village. The village into which Kempf had come by chance (but is there such a thing as chance?) on that particular Sunday was near the small town of Nuštar, but was that the reason? There were many villages scattered around Nuštar, some just a stone's throw away.

He had in fact come to visit his friend. Franja was unwell, he had been ordered to rest. Franja was at home in bed, swallowing revolting medicines, vomiting from time to time and recovering from a problem with his digestion, but Kempf couldn't now remember exactly what.

Kempf had felt his pulse, peered into his throat, taken his temperature, self-importantly, and then thumped him on the shoulder. "Get out of bed, Franz, you don't have to perform for me, let's go look at girls."

And Franja had got up, in a mild trance, and his entire family, gathered in the doorway, crossed themselves. Not since Jesus roused Lazarus had there been a greater miracle.

He had barely left the veranda when they brought him a child with a fever. One man pulled his sleeve mumbling that his wife had taken to her bed, while another wanted to take him to a cow whose belly had swollen with clover.

Word soon spread round the village of the doctor who treated people virtually with a glance, but Kempf told them all that he wasn't going on any visits because he was on holiday. Then they started begging him and pulling him by the sleeve to grant them that glance of his, so they could take it, like a candle, to the sick. Aware that he would not be able to get off so lightly, he found prescription forms and wrote out, for one after another, in his doctor's execrable handwriting, the weather forecast for the day that he had found in the newspaper.

It was only then that the villagers let them go to the square where the girls were getting ready to dance.

Whoever has not seen such a *kolo*, or ring dance, hasn't seen anything.

When they finally reached the expanse of beaten-down earth that was considered a square in the middle of the village, the *kolo* was just getting underway.

In the centre the piper tapped his feet, and the young women each placed a hand on the next one's shoulder. Long plaits, some wound into buns, conveyed a message: these were the unmarried girls. It was exclusively a women's *kolo*. In their hair duck feathers competed with silk ribbons, their white blouses were luxuriously embroidered, their skirts pleated and stiffened with starch, their feet in leather peasant shoes, but some also danced self-confidently in little lacquered shoes, black or bright red . . . All the women were equal, but they were all different.

Whoever has not seen necklaces of gold ducats, who hasn't heard them clinking on the breasts of these women, has not seen anything.

And in that *kolo* was Sofka, Sofija.

Neither too tall, nor too short, but supple and charming.

Franja saw at once that his friend was losing himself and, as though he had already been captured by nymphs, couldn't take his eyes off those jiggling breasts and the gold ducats bouncing on them. He wanted to drag Đuka towards the cauldron where meat was crackling in hot fat, but he looked at him like a stranger, with two question marks in his eyes. Franja could see: the man was sleepwalking.

When the girls finally sat down on a large bench, Kempf somehow pushed his way through to her. He was flattered, almost overjoyed, when she greeted him as though she knew him.

And Sofija did know about him through her father, who traded with his father. Not often, now and again. Her father traded cloth, and in more recent times also vegetables. He had brought a few families from Bulgaria and settled them on his property. He planted those Bulgarians the way they sowed paprika. And then he traded paprika, the hottest kind.

Sofija was the richest marriageable girl in the village, but for Kempf it was more important that she was the most beautiful woman in this part of the world.

He tried to put his arm round her as they sat on the bench between two dances, but she removed his hand, saying: "Slow down, lad, take it easy!"

When the last *kolo* had been applauded, dancing in pairs began. Kempf stood up, bowed to Sofija and asked her for a dance, but she was, she said, very tired.

So it was with a "slow down" and a brush-off that their relationship began.

Kempf's wound no longer hurt. On his morning visit the surgeon told him he had been very lucky and showed him the little piece of lead they had taken out of him.

So he no longer felt pain in his shoulder, but something was ripping his breast apart.

Not only had he betrayed Sofija with a woman who had been a complete stranger to him until the previous day, but he had not thought about her for several days. What kind of man am I, thought Kempf. I have betrayed Sofija. I shall betray Sadowska as well. I am disloyal to women, I have incurred great debts with the devil and sooner or later he will coat me with the burning tar of hell.

Where was Sofija now? She believed in Heaven and Hell.

Incomprehensibly powerful forces prevented Scorpio from realising his intention of grabbing Virgo with his pincers. But in the sky there was far more morality than on Earth. It seemed that all morality had fled to the sky.

It was true that however far Scorpio moved to the west, endeavouring to approach Virgo, she would move away to exactly the same degree in the same direction. And Scorpio would never reach her.

Kempf recalled the black shadows that moved along the lanes towards the places of their secret meetings. He had a passing acquaintance with some of those who were conspiring. They talked, or rather whispered (just like prayers), about a new order. But a new order was also what Adolf Hitler was talking, or rather yelling, about.

The shadows of young people who were evidently prepared to sacrifice themselves for a better world and who were searching for their place in the world because they did not have one – and could not believe they would ever have one without a struggle – now filed past Kempf, as he lay on his camp bed, although he knew it was impossible.

But it may not be impossible, he went on thinking. There are visionary young people everywhere. In Poland too, for sure.

Should I have joined them, gone to their meetings, out there in the farmsteads on the other side of the Bosut?

Join which side?

Ania was a Polish nationalist.

Comparing these nationalists with the young communists wouldn't be right. The communists considered themselves inter-nationalist. In addition, old Kempf had always told him that in the damned Balkans, where everyone had it in for everyone else: "We Germans had to stick together. For the Bolsheviks who want communal women – O.K., why not, let the women decide – but they also want communal factories, and that's out of the question . . ."

His father's warnings were superfluous. He felt that the people who had sunk into the Underground in Vinkovci before the war were too rigid, too one-sided. As though they had already earned their memorial bronze. They wanted to persuade others, and if that didn't work, they would immediately flare up. To Kempf, that made them like priests. And he didn't like priests.

Nationalists were similarly inclined to flare up. Ania too became heated when she talked about Poland.

They all talked about freedom. The world was full of fiery people, the world was hot, and for all of them freedom was their first and last thought.

Yes, but the means by which that freedom was to be achieved were not the same.

There were moments when the choice of means was limited, an inner voice told him. Kempf was surprised, he felt occupied. As though someone else was living inside him, either as a calm co-tenant or as a devil's advocate.

Should he have gone with them? They used to wait outside factories for the workers and foist their flyers on them. The only workers Kempf saw were the tradesmen to whom his father used to give bread and the people he had worked with in the Jewish brickworks. They were so demoralised that they had no interest in any kind of flyer. The flyers talked of freedom, of a better life, while the workers wanted only to survive. And that was when Stalin got together with Hitler.

And what had Hitler and Stalin done with Poland? They had torn it apart with their claws, divided it. Raped and devoured Poland. They had spat out the few remnants now writhing beneath the Milky Way, neither alive nor dead. That was the way a young man whose legs had been cut off above the knee by a shell writhed, when he was trying to escape from a burning tank, leaning only on his hands. Half a man, trying to flee from a blaze. That was Poland today, a profoundly distressed space, raped by anyone it occurred to, and Ania assured him that it had always been that way, except between the two world wars.

Freedom is not gilded by every means. There are means that are simply not justified. Machiavelli asserts otherwise. But Machiavelli is not referring to freedom as an aim. Celestial mechanics prevent celestial rape; for the next several million years Scorpio will not be able to deflower Virgo. But there must also exist some moral mechanism that prevents ultimate savagery. That savagery cannot be crushed by the terror of a different savagery.

I didn't go with those shadows, I didn't let myself be drawn into their conspiracies. The extreme right disgusted me. My Germans also, although not all of them. What else could I have done?

Here he began to succumb to weariness.

Already half-asleep, he was visited once again by Sofija, dancing between two companions, her breasts swaying under the ducats. He had seen those breasts also without blouse or waistcoat . . . because Sofija had later withdrawn her "slow down", they had loved one another quickly, and as often as they were able to escape inquisitive glances. As though the two of them knew that it would not last.

Everyone knows everything but doesn't want to admit it.

Suddenly, still half-asleep, Kempf began to laugh, so loudly that he woke the wounded soldier in the bed beside him.

"*Was ist los?*"

Kempf remembered what his friend Franja had passed on to him: on Monday, the villagers for whom he had written pre-scriptions went off to the Vinkovci pharmacy and handed the pharmacist Kempf's prescriptions. The pharmacist put on his spectacles, shook his grey mane and started taking brightly coloured packets of pills off shelves and out of drawers. Finally, as a bonus, he added also plantain syrup.

He was old, he knew how to cope with doctors' scrawl.

And so, in Sofija's village treatment was handed out for the forecast of a dangerous deterioration in the weather, published in the newspapers.

Kempf laughed in his sleep, happy again after a pleasant lovers' tryst.

That Pan Twardovsky must have been a madman to run away from a woman. But nevertheless, if he was some kind of prophet, at least in his spare time, it wasn't surprising that he walked in his sleep.

As usual, particularly before he fell asleep, Kempf pondered and wandered a bit in his sleep.

Ania as a nationalist? What else could she be?

"There's more between her legs than between Heaven and Earth, my Horatio!" So thought Kempf.

And let come what may.

I am following this amorous adventure of Kempf's calmly. Ania cannot be my mother, not only because she is careful in bed, but because it is not written. And what is not written cannot be read as one's destiny.

White Ballet

There was sudden haste in everything: Vera barely managed to say goodbye to the women in the hut. Her patent leather shoes and her skirt were returned to her. Had she wished, she could have been a young lady again. Instead, she left them to one of the girls with whom she had grown close. They took away her "pyjamas", striped, blue and white, with her number. It would be drawn by another "lucky" one.

Five of them were crammed into a small truck, the gate opened and Old Gradiška was left behind them. Out of the corner of her eye she could still see the women going to the fields and, at the very end of that image, she saw the body of a man who had been hanged the night before: yet another failed attempt at escape. She had known him superficially: she had once smiled at him as they fetched water. He was the man who had told her about the field guns across the Sava.

The truck coughed, juddered . . . two or three times it stopped. The guards cursed. They would have preferred an old nag that they could at least have whipped, that would have had some sense and purpose.

At the end of the road there was a nag, harnessed. They were transferred to a cart and set off further along a washed-out forest track. Clearly the track was used for hauling tree trunks. The wheels kept getting stuck in the mud, they all got out and heaved with their shoulders . . .

Then the track became a little better, there were fewer puddles. The guards lit cigarettes.

"Why those sour expressions? You're going to your people."

The camp inmates were silent. Their faces tense, they were all looking straight ahead, into the forest. And they were afraid that they were hallucinating again, that at any moment the siren would wake them and drive them to the rallying point.

Then a statue of the Holy Trinity appeared, with a bunch of dried flowers. Then the carter halted the nag.

Then they all got out of the cart.

Then they were told to carry on into the forest along this same track. "God grant that we never see you again!" a guard spat.

That was what all five camp inmates were thinking as well.

Hesitant, they glanced at the gun barrels, which were, however, lowered, while some guards had their rifles on their shoulders.

They set off, not knowing where to.

They believed that they would now be liquidated by shots in their back, which would prove that they had been killed running away.

They looked around.

Then they caught sight of a figure walking towards them from the opposite direction, from the depths of the forest.

All was still unclear.

The figure was wearing a German uniform.

One of the inmates recognised his insignia: Oberst. Wehrmacht.

For a colonel in war his hair was too long. He pushed his plump belly before him as though on wheels. He seemed cheerful and, as he passed them, he waved. Casually, the way people on an outing wave from one boat to another.

They turned round, the camp guards were nowhere to be seen.

But they heard the carter rousing the horse. The tubby Oberst disappeared from view along with the cart.

Before them was a forest in which nothing stirred. But that calm was deceptive. Soon they were surrounded by armed people who began to touch them, kiss and hug them.

The exchange had succeeded. In this phase of the struggle exchanges were rare. Had not Goebbels in the Sports Palace in Berlin declared total war?

Vera was surprised by the size of the Partisans' camp. Wherever she looked, there were people or horses. She even noticed two small field guns. A few machine guns. Steaming cauldrons, a lot of washing hung on string stretched between branches. The clinking of tin dishes and cutlery, yes, even that. Under a tree, a few men were patiently waiting their turn to be shaved. Under another, a woman was breast-feeding a baby, another even smaller one was grumbling in its cot. Small children were learning the alphabet. A woman in uniform drew the letters on a blackboard set up in the middle of a clearing. Civilian life.

"Vera, daughter of Mijo?" asked the commissar, without lifting his eyes from the paper. When he did finally glance at her, he seemed surprised that she was so young. She was bronzed by the sun, thin, but she appeared robust and healthy.

"I've got two pieces of news for you, one good, one bad. Which do you want first?"

"The good news."

"You're free. You'll now have a chance to get your revenge on those brutes. But they've captured your brother. That's why they've given you in exchange. They don't need you as a hostage anymore."

"Where are they holding him?"

"Jasenovac. We're working on getting him to Mauthausen. He might survive there. The swine here will slaughter everyone before we kill them."

"So why haven't you done it already? Look how many of you there are. And there are all sorts of weapons here. You've even got field guns."

"We have, but we don't have shells. We've got five, only they are either too big or too small for our barrels."

"You've got horses. You've got machine guns."

"We have. But so have they. We have considered liberating the camps from a military standpoint. But the camps are on the plains. Then there's the Sava River. For the time being we can't liberate the camps, but tomorrow, who knows . . . ?"

"You've no idea of the suffering behind the barbed wire."

"We have. But there are more important war aims."

The commissar could not have known that he was echoing Winston Churchill, who had said the same about Auschwitz.

"What can you do?"

"Anything."

"Can you fire a rifle?"

Vera said nothing.

"Do you want to join the medical corps?"

"No."

"I understand. All those we have so far exchanged, or who've managed to escape, they all want guns. You look agile and alert to me. How are you on orientation? For instance, do you know which side of a tree moss grows on?"

"The north."

"Did you grow up in a village?"

"No."

"Did you go to school?"

"Two years of grammar school."

"So you can read and write?"

"Two years of grammar school."

"That's not what I'm asking. Are you literate?"

"For a year I've never been without a book in my hands."

"There's no library in the camp."

The commissar realised he had gone too far.

"Listen, girl, joking apart, we don't have many here with two years of grammar school. Me for instance, I only have two myself. We're roughly the same generation. But we have older people here too. We have teachers, doctors, we've even got a priest. There are all sorts among the people. The people are like a chest full of hidden treasure.

"Here's a Frommer 7.65. We call this pistol the 'Hungarian' because it was cobbled together by Hungarians. It's a good pistol. And here's a box of bullets."

Vera opened the box.

"Come on, kid, they're not toffees."

But the yellow brass shell cases really did look like sweets. "If you ever run into an S.S. soldier aim straight for his heart!" Vera put on the belt with the holster.

"You'll be on courier duty, that's like being a postwoman, only more dangerous. On the way you'll look around you and keep us informed; that's security work."

"Something like the police?"

"Reaction never sleeps. You'll go through liberated territory, but also where everything is still under their control. Well, good luck, and welcome!"

The commissar shook her hand.

"We've got an entertainment tonight. Have a wash, tidy yourself up, and come to the show. It'll be fun!"

He took her to a barrel of warm water, women screened her with sheets. For a moment the water paralysed her, she felt like falling asleep; a terrible fatigue spread through all her limbs. So, her brother had been caught, arrested, thought Vera. Their mother would surely know that by now.

She gave a start when she heard a violin wail. She dressed and set off to the show with the women who had helped her.

In a clearing in the middle of the forest, a stage made of rough logs had been set up and everyone was standing around it, apart from those who were keeping watch.

Vera was tired, but the fact that she was suddenly bathed and clean drove her to hope for ever newer miracles. She understood that something exceptional was beginning for her – admittedly at an enormous price that she would never have agreed to pay had she been asked: she had been exchanged because they had captured her brother.

On the stage stood a being in white, a perfect vision. It seemed to Vera to be made of white china and that it could shatter at any moment. But those fragile limbs were held together by the fact that they were being watched, absorbed by hundreds of pairs of eyes following the ballerina's movements with devout wonder. If anything, it was a collective hallucination.

Below the stage stood a tall, lean violinist, who had pulled a black tailcoat on over his uniform. From the instrument pressed under his chin he drew amazing sounds reminiscent of real human sobs; then the sounds calmed, to be followed by *staccato* – it was impossible to tell whether those sounds were setting the dancer in motion or, in some magical way, she was moving the musician . . .

Vera had lived in a provincial town in Eastern Slavonia in which there was not much music: generally speaking the muses barely associate with the poor. At that moment, she could not remember that she had ever in her life heard anything as beautiful . . . The Gypsies played the *gusle** and of course the accordion, which was drawn out and squeezed in every local lane, not to mention the *tamburica*,† but this . . .

And so, Vera didn't know, nor could she have known, that she was watching and hearing Chopin's "Les Sylphides", admittedly only in the singular, that this was classical *ballet blanc.*

Few of those present could have known that.

The women especially looked on with wide-open eyes and mouths.

Perhaps the loveliest moment belonged to the complete silence when the violinist stopped jerking his body, but the china Sylphide continued to dance, as though listening to some inner music.

A sylphide or sylph is a nymph, eternally young, living in the air and from the air. And it seemed that she wanted to prolong that special moment of completely entranced silence into eternity.

That's what revolution wanted as well, but it was the realm of human beings who age, and it ages with them. For now the revolution was still young. And indeed, all around her in the forest Vera saw young men and women who were probably her contemporaries.

There were some younger ones too, even children, with some of the boys carrying weapons.

When the initial enchantment had passed, a clamour was heard and some country people came dangerously close to the invisible ramp in the hope of touching the sylph. The people were

---

* A single-stringed instrument, usually accompanying the chanting of epic songs.

† A long-necked lute. [Translator's note]

hungry for everything and they all hoped that the revolution would answer their needs. People cannot live in the air or from the air. They had been promised a lot. And in this world what's more. The more thoughtful among them in the forest still wanted the other world to be left to the priests because there had to be something like that. The other world was the priests' world, the Partisan movement had nothing to gain or lose from it. Let's get this one sorted first! Let's not quarrel with God or the clergy, especially not the lower clergy. That was why some of the priesthood, those who had joined the Movement, were nurtured and cosseted. In the forest people were buried according to Christian rites, or some version of them. Only the communists, and there weren't many of them, were wrapped in blankets and lowered into the earth, accompanied by shots into the air, without being delivered to any god.

The enchantment had almost entirely dispersed just as the moon disappeared behind a cloud. But for a moment many eyes had still seen in the sky wispy winged beings, white sylphs, sitting on each of the downy clouds, now suffused with the pale pink glow of the setting sun: the whole sky was a white ballet.

The people began to disperse. A bugle sounded the last post.

Vera noticed that the sylph lived in her own tent and the musician in his. When he removed his tailcoat, she saw that he had the emblems of a captain's rank. The two of them were given dishes of stew and all the magic vanished as the sylph plunged her spoon into the steaming stew.

For a while Vera sat leaning against a tree trunk in which she could still feel the sun's warmth. Although she was dead tired, sleep did not come to her eyes.

She noticed the shadows of highlanders disappearing deeper into the forest.

Had there not been the noise of a military camp, the clanking of dishes, the barking of dogs and whinnying of horses, Vera would have heard men trying to fertilise the dry leaves.

War is a time of many deprivations.

All is well. They'll get over the deprivations. Vera is with her own people. My chances are growing.

I've nothing more to say. I'm quite exhausted by so much excitement.

Knot on the Anus of the World

Ania brought him news from the medical appraisal: his tendon was definitely alright, Kempf would be returned to his unit the following day. His company commander had even called to see whether he could count on "his lad", in the reasonably short term. He had been glad when he heard that it would be the next day.

The Rottenführer tapped him gently on the chest, as though inspecting its firmness, and said: "Your guys are having it tough again down there."

Down there? His guys? If he was now "up here", he ought to be able simply to abandon himself to the law of free fall, and after a while find "his guys down there" in the anus of the world. Because there was no doubt that the Rottenführer considered it the anus of the world, judging by the contemptuous contortion of his face. If "we" were not "down there", striving to maintain some kind of order, your guys would slaughter each other to the last man.

We here, thought Kempf, slaughter to the last Jew, and if we weren't here, the Poles would live in peace.

His commander seemed to read his mind.

"You're lucky that we're still keeping the Russians well away from your borders. And Soviet divisions, along with Tito's soldiers, are on the verge of liberating Belgrade."

When he was left alone on his bed, in a corner of the S.S. field hospital tent, Kempf endeavoured to put in order all he had heard that day about himself and the anus "down there".

Without doubt "down there" was a general slaughterhouse. How much could the officer have known? It wasn't likely that a junior S.S. officer received daily bulletins from Supreme Command about the Balkans.

He was merely allowing himself to have a "general impression". At that time the Germans and their allies were preparing larger-scale operations that were meant finally and forever to pacify "those damned Balkans". But the Waffen-S.S. had more urgent business here in Poland and it was improbable that its officers would be concerned also with the bloody tribes "down there".

And so Kempf, closing his eyes, wandered in his thoughts through the previous night, here, in this bed, where Ania had so surprised him with her initiative, and then complete abandon, in the game of love, until she became a thing under his hands. He, who had some experience of women, could not gauge how, or how prolific, her experiences with men had been. But that there was no calculation in her playful ways was absolutely clear.

Unlike the very experienced Ilonka, a Hungarian from Novi Sad, who, before Kempf had happened upon her, had accumulated, like an ace pilot counting numbers of downed enemy aircraft, dozens if not hundreds of "victories" over the middle-class sons who had paid for lessons in the subject of *ars armatoria*. Ilonka had done for Kempf everything the townsfolk dreamed of in the antechamber of their marriage beds. In that case, everything was calculated and paid for, but Ilonka had liked Kempf and, after her climax, she had whispered in his ear that, if he wished, she was ready to marry him. Kempf had burst out laughing, which echoed oddly in the deathly silence of the small sleeping Slavonian town, and she had slapped him soundly.

Just then, from the street outside, came the sound of many running feet, a police whistle, the neighing of horses, and Kempf's nostrils registered that something was probably burning.

We should now wind that film back. That day, in the morning, the city of Novi Sad had witnessed this scene: a group of young men had rented a carriage and, already fairly well-oiled, set off somewhere.

That "somewhere" was Sremska Kamenica. The young men were Kempf's colleagues, medical students. They had decided to celebrate their excursion to the "Serbian Athens" with a booze-up in Sremska Kamenica, where they had hired a back room in a tavern.

That was a time when in similar back rooms almost everywhere in the old Europe, fiery speeches were delivered, and Hitler had already long since accentuated the speeches with a bid for power. The innkeeper in Sremska Kamenica asked a bit sourly whether their gathering was political as then it had to be registered in the kingdom, but the lads had dismissed such a thought. However, seeing them tanked-up around noon, he had required them to pay a deposit against damage.

There was music and singing in the carriage. The names of these merry travellers to Sremska Kamenica – it was 1939, towards winter, Poland had once again, for the nth time, been dismembered like a slaughtered corpse – were a pretty accurate reflection of the numerical and "tribal" components of the Kingdom of Serbs, Croats and Slovenes, which by then had been called Yugoslavia for a long time. The German Kempf belonged to a "minority", but Radoje believed that "if things ever got bad", he would side with Josip from Osijek, while Marin was an ardent member of the Yugoslav Nationalist Organisation.

For years Kempf had been aware that innocent boyish scraps

at village fairs were an indication of a greater evil. A good village fair had to end with a few bloody noses, that was a matter of honour. But in the late 1930s, lads were not fighting over a pretty girl, or even for no reason: they were clobbering each other for "principles". These wars of principles carried on without end into our own times: Croatian far-right supporters of Josip Frank would wait in the dark for a Sokol* member and beat the hell out of him, then the nationalists would knock a Frank supporter into the dust, then the Frank supporters would grab a supporter of Maček's Peasant Party, or, even more readily, a communist, and so on in a circle; then the son of a Jew, shamefully rich of course, would be beaten senseless, which would be considered an accomplishment, and in that all, apart from the communists, were more or less united.

To come home with a bloody nose, bruised, because of a pretty Tena, was once a normal thing and part of male growing-up; but to be beaten up, or to beat someone up "on principle" made no sense to Kempf. For him, politics was something objectionable. At that time he devoured books, but no writers of the left were included in his selection. He read poetry, he wanted to create poetry. He thought that he understood Baudelaire up to a point; he made no effort with Marx.

And now, in the carriage, they wooed him as representing a "minority" to arbitrate in the matter of Croatian thousand-year culture and Serbian heroism. But he was already thinking of Ilonka, whom he had booked for that night and who would be

---

* The Yugoslav Sokol movement was one of the most influential non-governmental organisations in the interwar Yugoslav Kingdom. In the course of the 1920s, it shifted from an independent, idealistic organisation celebrating brotherhood between the South Slavs to being a still independent but Serb-centred organisation. [Translator's note]

waiting for him in a little room a few houses away from the inn. At a safe distance from this drunken group.

Sremska Kamenica reminded him of Nuštar: the houses were arranged at right angles, with their narrow ends to the streets, like a kind of exclamation mark, their gables often made of wooden beams painted red. They were set apart at a regulation distance because of the danger of fire. It was Sunday, the little town that was in fact part of Novi Sad appeared to be asleep, nothing moved. The arrival of their carriage, accompanied by loud laughter, provoked a small disturbance. The innkeeper was standing outside his tavern, waiting, bowing to the ground. Beside him was his wife, the cook, a being who exceeded the normally accepted dimensions of the human race. That certainly boded well, for if she liked to eat, she would also know how to cook.

The lads went into the back room which they had hired for their "celebration" (they had invented someone's nameday for that purpose). As it was a cold day, the innkeeper offered to light the stove. The flame in the cast-iron stove started to flicker cheerfully. Rounds of drinks began, and the agreement was that everyone should drink as much as he could; it had all been calculated. Plates of meat appeared, it was increasingly warm in the room, in reality and symbolically, as the debate begun in the carriage as they left Novi Sad continued without interruption; in fact, that debate had been going on forever, and now there was reason to fear it would never stop. They were the only people at the inn; on Sundays the locals ate in their own homes.

The innkeeper frowned because what could be heard through the walls and trickling out into the street contradicted the assertion that the celebration would not be anything like a political gathering. But then he sighed and persuaded himself that he was an innkeeper, not a spy. If one of these boys threatened law and order or even the king, let the appropriate authorities worry about it. As far as he could make out, communists weren't represented in this little group, and they were the ones most pursued; so it was probably alright.

In truth, in the fairs and fist fights Kempf was recalling on this night as he lay in the field hospital, there were hardly any young people who could be suspected of being registered communists. They had always behaved in a conspiratorial way. Or rather they were absent from the present as their eyes were fixed on the future. They put Kempf off with their sectarianism, but they really were persecuted. All the others could count on the support of "wider political forces" in the kingdom, and, as always, on the support of their own "tribes", as they were good "nationalists".

By the early afternoon virtually all the ammunition of the political wars in the Balkans had been used up; historical victories that were in reality heavy defeats had been evoked.

Tangled theological questions that tormented the followers of opposing sects had been produced, like rabbits from hats: about the holy trinity, about whether the Virgin Mary could really have given birth without being deflowered; about the human or divine nature of God the Son – these were all debated around a table at the tavern, in the middle of Sremska Kamenica, with the virulence of the church fathers at ancient councils. And those fathers could be so ferocious that the more moderate would separate them with wooden barricades.

At dusk on that winter day Ilonka appeared at the tavern like the proclamation of the Eternal Female. Đuka Kempf had foreseen this impact and looked forward to it. Of course, he did not tell anyone that the love that would follow had been paid for; on the contrary, he had said that a lover was coming for him that evening from Novi Sad.

The tipsy young men halted their "war of ideas" for a moment and all of them stared at the supernatural phenomenon. It even seemed that the Eternal Female would be victorious, and that it would occur to at least a few of them that there were in the world more important things than fallen kingdoms and glorious defeats.

"Congratulations on your woman," said one of his colleagues. "Hungarians are hottest."

"May her haunches set you ablaze!" shouted a Slovene, who also scribbled verse.

"May her hot paprika set you on fire!" mocked another, raising a glass in honour of "the 'young lady', a Hungarian, a girl from Magyar land, and we know how the famous King Tomislav sent the Magyars packing across the Danube . . ." He raised his glass in honour of the national Croatian dynasty and at that moment Ilonka, who had observed all this with impatient indifference tinged with contempt, seemed to disappear in the thick exhalations of the sweating males, who were then only interested in throttling one another.

Kempf said goodbye to the innkeeper because he could see that Ilonka had had more than enough. The innkeeper's wife took the opportunity to come out too and she shook his hand firmly; she had concluded that this "Swabian" was the only decent one among this student rabble. The innkeeper was already fearful that he would never get his damages paid. His intuition turned out to be correct.

What happened afterwards, Kempf could not, in the nature of things, have known exactly, but he could imagine. While the tragedy was unfolding, Ilonka, combining hot paprika and her

Hungarian heritage, did things with him that went far beyond the routine of paid love.

But he could nevertheless reconstruct what had happened and dictate to the policeman's pen; there was no better witness than him, although he had not been present. For the others had gone up in smoke, that is, they had burned.

Around midnight, the war of ideas had developed into a real boxing match when no-one could any longer make out who was hitting whom, followed by wrestling on the floor, freestyle. In the turmoil someone had kicked the cast-iron stove, the door fell open, the flames flared and immediately took hold of the woodwork. It wasn't possible to get out, because the stove had fallen across the threshold. The room immediately filled with smoke, and at that moment they could have escaped through the window, but individual escape was not on anyone's mind: the nation's salvation had absolute priority. The young men went on fighting, writhing on the floor which was now burning. Had anyone been able to see in from outside, they could have thought that it was a matter of particularly ardent embraces.

When hoses, brought on a horse-drawn cart, finally began to pour water into the room through the windows the firefighters broke with hammers, it was already far too late.

They found them, more coal than flesh, entwined on the tavern floor.

Like rats, whose tails become entangled in an inextricable knot, they hadn't had a chance. That's how "down there" arguments about "us" and "them" end. They are waged, and in them people reduced to ashes, in the anus of the world. That is our inextricable knot, and woe betide anyone who touches it. He will be damned for all eternity, amen. He will forever be an outsider.

In the notes there was nothing about the national destiny, the

Virgin Mary, or the fact that virgins don't give birth, nor was there anything about heroism or a thousand years of culture. To the sergeant's question as to what they had been quarrelling about in that room, Kempf replied: "About everything and nothing." The sergeant added in his notebook: "They were evidently dead drunk."

And now, thought Kempf, we Germans have gone to maintain law and order "down there". What the Poles of the Underground Army who had shot him in the shoulder thought of that law and order "up here", S.S. Storm Trooper Kempf had a pretty clear idea.

That Red Army soldier and that German in an embrace – they froze to death, while those guys of mine were incinerated. The former could not be separated, not even with a saw. People had tried to separate the ones in Sremska Kamenica, at first it had seemed it would be an easy task, but then they realised that the bodies would crumble into ash. The remaining heaps of coal were collected in one single coffin. Then there was the question of the appropriate native soil for each of them individually, the dilemma of the so-called native sod ... The question was insoluble, and a compromise was arrived at: they would all remain in the local cemetery, in Kamenica, where of course not one of them was born. Kempf had not dared attend the burial for fear of being asked questions he would have to answer.

And even today he had no answers to those questions. All in all, it was terrible and stupid. And you couldn't say that to the dead.

Immediately after the funeral, the Hungarian girl sent him a postcard: *Dear sir, someone from Kamenica is thinking of you. Ilonka.*

Ilonka saved me, in Kamenica, he reflected. Just as Ania was going to save me now. Let us leave the world to women, that's the best thing we can do. It would be good for both us and the world.

Across the River, and into the Forest

It was now as quiet as the grave in the tent. Kempf, dressed, with his boots on, was lying on his camp bed. Under his pillow was a loaf of bread and a piece of sausage, under his bed a rifle. The hours dragged on, he was no longer surprised that the word for "hour" in Polish was the same as "year" in Croatian.

How had he succeeded in gaining so much trust from his Polish friend? How was it that the invisible finger of the Home Army was pointing at him? Who was it, in the Underground, who had concluded that he, a Slavonian Volksdeutscher, who had for a year now worn the S.S. insignia on his collar, could be "one of them"? Just because he understood some Polish? Ania Sadowska knew very well what the Gestapo were and where they could be found. But how could she have known that S.S. Sturmmann Kempf would agree after he had asked the Underground to allow him just two hours of his remaining life to spend on considering his future involvement in the war, as he had put it.

Who was this Ania Sadowska? Kempf knew little about her. That is, he knew only what she had told him. In war tedious formalities are skipped. Was she a loose woman? One of those marauders who always circle round soldiers, in every war? Definitely not. Women are good at acting in bed, but not Ania Sadowska. But if this was something like love, why was she now sending him as far as possible away from this field hospital, and therefore from herself? In the Kraków castle on Wawel hill Herr Frank still held sway, master of life and death in the occupied part of Poland. This was now that moment in the war when, after the intense conflict at Kursk, everything had gone quiet, it was the calm eye of the storm that would soon break with all its force over everything that was still moving.

Where in fact was the Home Army? On Polish ground? Or rather underground. Barely armed, it was preparing for the new storm, intimated on the horizon anywhere you looked. The Soviets were again piling up war stocks in quantities the world had never seen. Let us imagine for a moment that in the campaign against Rome several hundred thousand of Hannibal's elephants were descending from the Alps!

Ania was a Polish patriot. She spoke with the greatest contempt about political parties, about political folklore, about the right and the left in pre-war Poland. Now and again she would remind Kempf that the Polish Catholic church did not collaborate with the Germans in any way. She did not know of a single case when a priest had betrayed his country to the Germans. On the contrary, Poland itself was a Christ among the nations, sobbing, crucified between East and West . . . The Soviets, it seemed, were winning. And they would prevail when it suited them, not before. In other words, not when it was essential for the Poles.

This woman had foreseen lucidly what would happen with the Warsaw uprising. She was lucid, although she thought in an exclusively linear way, in an exclusively Polish way.

Kempf thought that he could come to love Poland.

"We will prevail with the force of our ideas," Ania maintained. "Not with tanks."

"Thoughts that come on dove's feet guide the world!" Kempf recalled Nietzsche.

But communism was advancing with tanks, indicating a new iron age and the triumphs of a drawn-out "empire of necessity". What would have happened had those tanks not existed?

Georg Kempf had often wondered: what would have happened if the Master Race had succeeded in enslaving the inferior races?

What would have become of him, a Volksdeutscher from Eastern Slavonia, whom the Germans had recruited, as a "forced volunteer", into their army, dragging him into their plans to establish world domination, had "his people" not been stopped outside Moscow in 1941? If, at the beginning of 1943, they had broken through the ring where they found themselves at Stalingrad? If they had overcome the material superiority of the Soviets in the summer of 1943 at Kursk? If things had gone better for them in Africa? If they had bribed the U.S.A. and left them in their blessed isolationism? Or even, back in 1939, had they succeeded in their invasion of Britain? If they had been at least a little more lenient towards the Jews, who – as Ania Sadowska, otherwise infected with a germ of populist antisemitism, herself admitted – had not on the whole been communists? Or towards the Poles, as they would soon be advised by the governor of Poland, Hans Frank, himself?

So, how would Georg Kempf have behaved as a German and Superman? How would he have taken "our" German victory? How would he have conducted himself as a member of the Master Race?

That night a simple thought was conceived in Kempf, and it seemed to him to have spread right through him, enlightening him: he would be a civilian to the end of the war and see what happened. He would run away unarmed. Along with his S.S. insignia he would leave his attack rifle, here, under the bed. He would run away with a loaf of bread and half a sausage. With a piece of bread in his soldier's rucksack, that way his idea was all of a piece – the idea of a poor civilian who did not intend to distinguish himself by particular courage, did not intend to fight, but simply proposed to withdraw through the opposing sides, southwards to his real homeland. He wouldn't even have a compass, but as a Slavonian who had spent a lot of time roaming through forests, he knew that moss grew on the north side of trees. He looked forward to meeting fawns and feared meeting wild boar, hoping they would not grunt in the language of Goethe and Schiller.

Unarmed, he would be the person who did not wish to wrong anyone. He wanted to be as innocent as existence itself. Was that possible? Was it not necessary to accept some responsibilities?

Existence itself was not innocent, nature was cruel. So, which responsibilities?

Kempf stuck to his decision that he considered enlightening. But he had to admit that he had no answer to that question.

As with all such plans, so the soldier Kempf's plan of escape required a degree of luck. Ania knew that the unit of the Home Army was going to attack the German position from which the field hospital was defended. She couldn't yet say when. "When the snows melt," she had laughed. "Until then you are only mine!"

The unit had no heavy weapons, mostly revolvers and rifles; they had a few hand grenades. That had horrified Kempf as he well knew the elevation his squadron was defending and he knew how many heavy guns were buried there. It seemed fairly crazy to rush out of the forest and fire pistols at buried guns that could pulverise them in an instant.

But that plan was in keeping with the methods of partisan warfare: burn and run! The underground army was far from being able to hold a front line of any kind or let itself get into an open engagement with Germans with greater scope and style. An attack would serve solely to make the enemy insecure; would do little more than disturb their night's peace. So that Pan Twardovsky, riding his red cockerel, could see what was going on down here, in Poland, and that Poland was fighting. Casualties were taken into account. Poland too needed heroes.

Those who fell were supposed to gladden the prophet on the red cockerel, but also to show the world that Poland could liberate itself by itself and that in the holy matter of its liberation it did not need either Russian fur hats or Soviet tanks.

At that moment, when the unit attacked, the whole army would rush to help the position under attack and Kempf would simply walk out of the tent unnoticed. In the morning the commanders would assume that he had in all probability joined in the battle and disappeared in it. Nothing, that is, suggested that he of all people would have run away from the flag. After all, of many Volksdeutsche, he was one of the few who really understood German. Sturmmann Kempf had been wounded in battle, and those who had injured and almost killed him were Poles. He had not wanted to fire at Poles. Fair enough, but he was not so stupid as to run away and risk his life. Real challenges still awaited him, he was a *soldier.*

Kempf now intended to walk away into the forest, but as a civilian.

And when they found that he had left his rifle under his bed, they would think that he had sleepwalked off into the forest. A soldier who in the midst of war wants to be a civilian was a textbook example of somnambulist disorder.

The snows had not yet thawed when Sadowska, sad and joyful at the same time, came into his tent. Her instructions were simple: "Straight to the river, going west. It's shallow there, you'll cross easily. Hide in the bushes on the other side, you'll spend the rest of the night there. At dawn set off towards the sun, further into the forest. There you'll find a tank that looks whole, but is forever *kaput*."

Kempf did not reveal that he knew the appointed place. He knew for instance about those five black helmets of S.S. design that indicated the five graves beside the tank: it was like a crushed hen around which her trampled chicks had gathered. A hen, not a Tiger, as the tank was called whose official mark was Pz.Kpfw.VI.*

"Go west for roughly seven kilometres. You'll come to a village with just a few houses. Not many of them are occupied. Go into the largest of them, painted white, and ask for milk; say that you will pay in złotys. From that moment you will be a soldier of the Home Army."

"I want to be a civilian!" muttered Kempf.

"You'll be a soldier!"

Kempf felt that the woman had tapped his shoulder that no longer hurt with an invisible sword. She has just ennobled me, he thought.

---

* Panzer Kampfwagen VI.

Ant Nation

The shots had either died down or Kempf had moved too far away to hear them. Now he heard only his footsteps on dry leaves. The pole star led him, almost by the hand: it was easy for him to work out where west was. In the southern sky Scorpio was waving his pincers, and at his nape, as from the cupola of a tank, he was watched by Antares with his reddish eye, as though suffused with blood. The sky could be as clear as this in Slavonia, but only in winter, on cold, cloudless nights.

Kempf paused from time to time, stepping off the path to hear whether he was being followed: he had seen in some film or other that it was good to kneel and put one's ear to the ground. He would certainly have heard tanks. At one such moment in a shaft of moonlight he caught sight of a procession of red ants, bigger than he had ever seen. He had thought that ants slept at night, like people. Evidently not. The night hunt was happening all around him.

Now and again he clearly heard the grinding of teeth, the squeal of a victim, signals from those hunting and the warnings of the pursued ... The ant formation was advancing without a sound audible to the human ear. Not knowing why, Kempf thought they too were probably at war, because it was only in war that such formations moved at night. Was their undertaking defensive or offensive? Were they defending their own anthill, or

attacking another? A just or unjust war? And of course, it was
only in war that a deserter like himself, now a civilian, would be
moving through a forest, orienting himself by the stars. He came
across the destroyed German panzer immediately; now he knew
that killing machine far better than when he had first seen it. In
this same place, where its advance had been halted by a shower of
small-calibre shells straight from the sky, it too looked black, like
the five S.S. helmets. Should he mention that Ania Sadowska was
convinced the tank had been destroyed by a Polish soldier? She
had mentioned a grenade. Women know nothing about weapons
so they make up their own truth. The truth was that the tank
had been destroyed not by a fighter of the Polish Underground
but by a Soviet aeroplane.

Kempf knew that the wreck of the Soviet plane was somewhere
nearby. It was on his way. The star was still shining on its carcass, but where could it have gone? Not, presumably, to the sky.
Here beside the plane the pilot and machine-gunner from the
back hatch were still lying. Where could they have gone? To the
sky? Why, they had fallen from the sky. There was no marker on
the mound, then, when Kempf first came across them, and none
now, either. But where the head was probably resting lay a bunch
of wildflowers. That sign of respect in this black forest, which
seemed like the end of the world, astonished him. He understood
that the little graveyard of the fallen S.S. soldiers was tidy; that
the graves were bordered with white stones marking them clearly
in the moonlight. He understood that their helmets were arranged
with the strict regularity of Prussian pedantry. He read the names
of the fallen Tiger crew and the date of their demise, the same
for all of them. He also knew that in the German army, in both
armies of course, the Waffen-S.S. and the Wehrmacht, there was
an office in charge of war graves.

But who had decorated the nameless Soviet grave?

What had happened here was this: the Tiger tank had mistakenly separated from the formation, it had got stuck in the forest, despite radio contact. But the crew did not panic because the Red Army was a long way off. The clash on the ground was still being planned.

But in the sky, a battle was already going on between the Luftwaffe and Soviet squadrons. There were more of the latter, just as there were increasing numbers of tanks; and their crews were better prepared. The lesser race was learning in double-quick time.

So it happened that the pilot of the Ilyushin had spotted a tank, which seemed to him like an enormous wild boar in too narrow a pigsty. And it swooped down, just as a hawk swoops on its prey in a thicket. But the prey was able to defend itself and the gunner aimed his heavy machine gun, 12.7 mm, at the swooping plane and hit it. The pilot demolished the tank with a practised move: he released a rain of small-calibre shells from a height of some one hundred metres; some of them destroyed the tank and killed the crew, falling through its openings. It sounded like a child's game in which peas are shot at lead soldiers. But as it flew over, the plane was riddled with bullets from the tank's cupola. The Ilyushin, *shturmovik*, as the Russians called it, ended its war journey here.

Ania had told him that, as soon as he had gone far enough away, he should sleep the rest of the night in the forest so that with the dawn the sun would give him a clear indication of where to go. The night was cold because the sky was clear, but, given that summer was on its way, he would not freeze.

How had "his" men fared in that attack? Superior in every sense, they would definitely have fended it off and gone in pursuit.

Was there work for the dressing stations? Was there work for the chaplains and priests? How did the Poles fare in this whole undertaking?

Were the reflections on the horizon an indication of a coming storm? For the time being there was no thunder. If that was the Russians, they would have made themselves heard.

That damned T-34! How often had the men in his unit talked about Stalin's tank. The soldiers who had served for a long time in Poland and Russia had said how stunned they had been when they first saw it.

Kempf felt a profound weariness that weighed on all his limbs. He stepped away from the path and leaned against a tree. The Milky Way moving its opulence to the west produced no sound. The music of the spheres was a lie.

Now he had to sleep. He slid down the tree trunk onto its roots. He felt that he was being besieged by columns of red ants. Without a doubt, this was a military operation on a grand scale, and he was in the eye of the storm, surrounded. He must explain to these ants that he was not their enemy. He was a civilian who gave himself the privilege of understanding nothing.

Stalin would explain to him how mistaken that was. Josif Visarionovich was summoning him with his forefinger. Kempf climbed the steps to the top of the rostrum while millions of Red Army soldiers shouted as one: "Hurrah! Kempf! Hurrah!"

A military parade was underway. On top of the rostrum, which millions of sexless proletarian ants had created by sticking leaves together with their saliva, stood the Generalissimus of the ant state and the supreme commander of all branches of its armed forces; this was also the supreme headquarters and the seat of the enlightened drones with whom the Generalissimus occasionally consulted; from time to time he would exterminate them and then at similar festivities such as this millions of fervent proletarians would tear them to pieces with their jaws.

But the elite of the ant army consists of a different sub-species of ant: the soldiers are far larger than the female workers, who, without the slightest objection, carry out tasks such as building anthills, defence ramparts, chambers for storing food, nurseries where the pupae are placed and quarters for captive ant queens that produce, as required according to a special plan of the enlightened wise ants, workers, fighters and even artist ants . . .

Which now, drumming with their hind feet against their napes, produce a solemn rhythm which determines the progress of the army in front of the rostrum.

The Generalissimus drone greets the procession with its upper extremities and they respond with joyful cheers produced by moving their huge jaws, that sounds like human grinding of teeth.

The Generalissimus-ant raises both its front extremities into the air and everyone down below, millions united as one single organism, know that this means war; and that was to be expected. That age-old enemy of everything antlike, the black super-ant, had only the day before (an ant's day is somewhat shorter than ours) declared war on the red ants, and particularly, by special envoy, on the Red Generalissimus . . .

That is why since yesterday military production has taken priority in the anthill and now millions of female workers, whose vaginas have been blocked for the good of the state, produce only for the war: ammunition in the form of poison . . . And since yesterday (ants live rapidly) the queen ants spit out, along with their saliva, only warrior-attackers, capable of crushing with their jaws all the armour of the black ant, halting their advance and deciding this unjust, imposed war in favour of the red ants' anthill. The vaginas of these female workers, these queens long since removed from their thrones and imprisoned by the customs of state command, glow with a red shine, looking for all the world like Siemens-Martin furnaces in which white iron is smelted to produce steel. As the anthill has been on a war footing for some time already (time passes vertiginously fast for an ant), special measures are in place requiring special attention to everything and everyone that perhaps from the outside resembles an ant of the same colour, but is in essence a quite different creature, only that is not obvious to the casual eye.

So, just a few seconds earlier a red ant, in all its external appearance one of their kind, genus, even, had had the misfortune to enter their anthill, and attempted to conceal the fact that, although of identical appearance, it had hatched in a different anthill ... We repeat, that ant was not black but red, like the rest of us.

The appropriate services had immediately cut that unfortunate creature to pieces and tossed them out of the anthill because among several million identical red ants, although identical in everything apart from its origin (and that was no innocent matter), it had been immediately denounced as different, in other words necessarily aggressively inclined towards a community that was preparing for a battle for survival. It was a question of smell, and a difference in smell will be instantly and infallibly detected by every ant that the anthill had charged with differentiating aromas.

It was customary for the Generalissimus not to play a

prominent part in the anthill. He was still just standing, his jaws a little open, from time to time raising his front right extremity as a sign of final greeting to the formations going straight from the parade to the front, among the fanatical cries of millions of sexless females of the united ant proletariat.

A ray of sun found Kempf's face and only then was he aware that he had lain down on the roots of an oak tree, his back against its trunk. He leaped up in horror because he was covered in ants. He must take off everything he was wearing and shake every piece of clothing thoroughly, as he had been occupied by ants. Beneath him, in the anthill, panic had broken out. It had simply undertaken measures of self-defence.

For some reason he did not want to tread on the ants, just shake them off.

The man had spent the night on an anthill and discovered totalitarianism. Soon he would not dare fall asleep so as not to dream. Father Kempf, leave political analyses, there will be time for that. Look in front of you, behind you, listen to the voices of the wild and, particularly, of people. Here everyone has gone mad. I have a greater interest in the matter of your safety than even you yourself, because I have not lived and you have already lived part of your life. You know what you could lose, I don't know what I might gain.

Kempf had quit the Reich. He had served it for a year. Enough.

Judging by the sun, it must already have been eight o'clock. It was good that for us humans time passed a little more slowly, thought Kempf, who knows what year of the war it was, down there. Stepping out of their circle, he turned his back to the ants' front line. Now to follow the sun!

Godfatherhood

I shouldn't hang around, thought Kempf. The fighting round the
field hospital would surely have died down long ago and now
they all knew that he had disappeared. It would not occur to
many that he could have gone voluntarily: up to now he had done
nothing voluntarily. Ever since the day he was told that he would
have to go to Stockerau for training, he had done nothing of his
own free will; except once, when he had stuffed his mouth with
raw potato so as not to have to shoot the prisoners.

I shouldn't hang around. His men will go and look for him to
save him, or to bury him. The fatherly concern of the Scharführer
required that his story be told to its ending, to the corpse. He would
send a letter to his father and mother in the small town of Nuštar:
"Your son, S.S. Sturmmann Georg Kempf, was found in the form
of a corpse on the field of glory, and, in the name of Reichsführer
Himmler, I send heartiest congratulations!" Or "Most respected
Mr Kempf, in response to your enquiry as to why your son did
not come home from school yesterday, we can say that he was
last seen in the school playground, and that afterwards he walked
away into the forest. We regret that we have not so far been able
to find your only son and suggest that you approach the German
Red Cross, which concerns itself with runaway pupils . . ." Kempf
makes a wry face. No-one in the unit would think that he had
run away from the flag. Apart perhaps from that old Prussian who

dragged himself around like a scalded dog in the wake of ward rounds because his military status was low, but he was still needed. A gesture of his hand could mean farewell to a leg or an arm, for instance. In some cases, he seemed to make the sign of a cross in the air . . . He was known as Dr Death.

On one occasion, out of the blue, that old man told him that in 1939, as he worked in a dressing station near the front, he had witnessed, from close to, a Polish cavalry attack on an armoured division of the Waffen-S.S.; it was slaughter such as he had not seen even in the Great War in 1915, when he had served as a young medical intern. As a medical student, mobilised into the medical corps, in the war that was not yet counted as the first as it was meant to be the last, he had seen from close quarters the consequences of the first mass use of mustard gas. On that occasion he had been standing beside a tall Prussian officer watching through a telescope as hundreds of British soldiers crawled in all directions, suddenly shrouded in darkness, then most of them fell onto their backs and stopped moving . . . like squashed insects.

"That's not warfare," the Prussian had said then. "That should not be done. There are things, even in war, that should not be done. We should not have done that to them."

They continued to do it, they were doing it still; Dr Death did not say what had happened to the Prussian officer.

At that moment Kempf was not particularly disturbed. He felt that he had made the right decision. In fact, warmed by the sun that was shining increasingly strongly, he was congratulating himself.

For the time being, the plan was "holding", nothing had yet started to go wrong. The Underground was watching over him, Ania Sadowska was following him. "German soldier, may the heavenly angels protect you!"

A white, freshly painted house.

The hamlet was virtually deserted. But the orchards round about had been whitewashed against an influx of ants, evidently not long ago. Kempf heard barking, and where there were dogs there were people. A cow lowed: Want some milk, passer-by? And there was smoke rising, admittedly only from two chimneys. People were living here and it would be possible to come by a cup of warm milk. For złotys.

The peasant invited him into the house. Nothing in that house could surprise Kempf; particularly not the poverty of the peasant's surroundings that nevertheless suggested life here was being carried on and borne in a kind of seclusion, that in the end people were giving birth, living and dying under a roof, and that at a given moment a passer-by could be offered a cup of milk.

The peasant, as thin as if all the flesh had fallen from him, with a pale complexion, his face covered with freckles (strange that a country man should look like this), disappeared. He must have gone for the milk, thought Kempf.

But that threat did not materialise. The peasant brought two glasses and a bottle of vodka. His name was Jerzy, and Kempf, who liked a drink, also liked to know who he was drinking with. So, he was drinking with a namesake. It wasn't good to drink with strangers. Even so the conversation just could not get going.

To start with the peasant had never yet heard such a version of "Polish". If he had met a German before now, that person would not of course have tried to speak "Polish". But this stranger was trying, which the farmer found above all amusing, but it wouldn't have been nice to show a visitor from far away how comical it was. He could not fathom that a grown man didn't know how to speak, like a child who was just learning to talk. It was incomprehensible that this stranger said he was a German, but then that he wasn't really German. But the peasant believed that the Underground always knew what it was doing. It wasn't his job to assess the stranger. His job was to hand him over to a courier of the Home Army. He was meant to come today, before sunset. So everything had to happen between dawn and dusk, in the course of a day.

Like a Greek tragedy.

The foreigner, who nevertheless confessed that he was German up to a point, enjoyed the trust of the Underground and intended to join the Home Army, probably its medical corps. He evidently liked Poland and wanted to tend its wounds; he saw Mrs Sadowska (the peasant knew who she was) as a Maid of Orleans, but in Poland one had also to mention Our Lady of Częstochowa; the stranger was careless because he mentioned the name of a woman who was an officer of the Underground.

After the third glass Kempf wanted to know something about the Jews, were there any here, what had become of them and what did he, a Polish farmer, deeply rooted in his property, bordered by white-painted fruit trees, who milked his own cow and ploughed his own fields, think about the people who followed Moses . . .

The farmer spat and crossed himself as though wanting to drive a jinx away. Kempf didn't ask about the people who followed Moses again.

This conversation, in fact more of a pantomime, ended in silence. The vodka kept flowing as the shadows of the trees lengthened, looking as though they wanted to tear themselves away and live independently; as though the shadows wanted to desert their posts.

The peasant was now more agitated than before. There was no sign of the courier. It was dusk before a breathless young man burst in with news that was not good.

The local detachment of the underground army had been completely demolished in the previous night's attack on the S.S. field hospital. It was not known if anyone had survived. The Germans had two dead and a few injured. They were now undertaking revenge action by cleansing the whole area.

The peasant frowned. All at once he realised that he had no-one to whom he could pass on the stranger who tried to speak Polish in such an entertaining way. And what's more, he evidently liked Jews, since he was asking about them. Maybe he was a Jew himself?

The stranger grasped that this was the end of his hospitality. The Germans were scouring the terrain. Kempf knew very well what that meant. He also knew what the Waffen-S.S. always did in such circumstances and how they exacted revenge for their dead.

A child's crying was heard from the only other inhabited house.

The peasant leaped up from his chair.

The stranger understood that someone had just been born over there.

That was soon confirmed.

The peasant brought out a new bottle of vodka and said that, if he wanted, he could spend the night in the pigsty. It was virtually leaning against the forest, so if anything happened the stranger would be able to jump the fence and disappear into the forest.

The stranger took out a large złoty note, saying that he would gladly be godfather to the child.

The peasant brushed the money aside, saying: "Passwords serve to tell you who another person is. Godfatherhood can't be bought here like a cup of milk."

Kempf stood up and set off towards the forest.

The peasant didn't try to stop him. Kempf didn't look round, but he knew that the inhabitants of both houses had sighed with relief.

It was only after a couple of hundred metres, when the darkness around him began to thicken, that Kempf realised what had happened.

The plan had collapsed. The underground army was no longer following his movements. Ania Sadowska knew that the contact had not arrived and that he, Kempf, was now left to his own devices.

To be left on one's own in such a situation was not a promise of good fortune.

Whoever did not succeed in fitting into some larger whole or other, into a turbulent anthill, was lost. Kempf came out into a clearing just as the hitherto pale moon began to change into its golden gown: before him was a mountain. He didn't know its name.

Its name was Babja Gora. He would learn it, as he would many things. Kempf was in southern Poland, in the Polish Beskids. Further to the south was Slovakia. Somewhere even further away was the Pannonian sea on the bottom of which was the small town of Nuštar, a tiny pebble on top of layers of ancient shells and the skeletons of monsters from before the Flood. There were also the wrecks of tanks and downed aircraft; and a lot of graves and graveyards.

Kempf got his bearings. He easily found the North Star at the end of Ursa Minor's shaft. Ursa Minor winked cheerfully at him, as though someone had tightened the reins of a showy carriage. Behind him, to the east, the Russian ants were piling up their monsters. The Generalissimus was training more and more new crews for the T-34, dragging "organs", multiple rocket launchers, to the current front line . . . Soon he would again shower, burn, pulverise the Germans with enormous quantities of smelted iron. The Germans were consolidating their position in the west ... digging in and waiting for the final blow from the direction of the superior anthill. The front was increasingly close to the eastern frontiers of the Reich.

Kempf knew roughly where he was. But that was no use to him. Behind him was the huge expanse of Galicia, and then the steppes. In front of him was Babja Gora, 1,700 metres.

"Open up, mountain! Take me into you!"

Because, he thought, presumably Transylvania lay behind that mountain. The land on the other side of the forest. The land of Dracula and the seven German towns, Siebenburg, the land his ancestor Kempf had sought as his Canaan. The epic called "Volksdeutscher Kempf" had reached a critical point. Now things would go one way or another, but it would be hard for them to turn out well. Epic fortune does not exist.

"Take me, mountain, hide me!"

While he was still in the field hospital, he had heard from an officer what was known up to then of Franja's fate.

Virtually nothing. For the Waffen-S.S. Franz Lauber was missing. In fact, a whole formation had vanished, nearly a thousand soldiers. As though a mountain had swallowed them.

"Was that in Transylvania?" Kempf had asked.

"The Urals," the officer replied and could not say anything more.

Cats

As a child, Kempf was of the firm opinion that his senses were exceptionally developed, that is that he could see better in the dark and hear better than the other boys, to say nothing of his sense of smell which was said to be as sharp as a dog's. He boasted that he could recognise the call of a dozen birds in his homeland and even guess their state of mind: were they in love or just angry? The latter was more common: chirruping to turn away usurpers. In brief, he considered himself closer to nature than other people were. That was his personal myth.

But now all his senses had indeed sharpened. He was not interested in birdsong in the trees where, for fear of wolves and wild boar, he strapped himself with his belt to a branch. In fact, although his day dragged on like a hungry year, Kempf had no time for nature. All possible sounds produced by humans, not the forest, were the danger signals that drove him to heighten all his senses.

So now a barking dog warned him that he was near a settlement. He could smell smoke on the light breeze and decided his direction accordingly: let come what may!

Just a *chutor** for now, the village was probably on the other side of the wood surrounding it.

---

* A single farmstead. [Author's note]

He looked at the yard through the branches. There was life here. A child was floating a little paper boat in a puddle, another was driving a small tortoise with a stick. A cat was stretching on the threshold. What an idyll, the other side of time.

As the Jews would say: the Messiah, the Saviour, chose to make himself known to the people: "Come to me, little ones!"

The children looked at him astounded, even the tortoise stretched its head out of its shell. A dog came up and sniffed him. Kempf had always got on better with dogs than with their owners.

Was this a little land of children? Had these children been lured away by the pied piper of Hamelin? Were we in Transylvania?

If only he had a small piece of chocolate.

All he managed to ferret out of his pockets was a brass cartridge case.

Kempf knew how to whistle on it, he could even entice something like a tune from it.

Then a plump woman appeared in the doorway of the house and called the children in. The stranger said that he was hungry and could pay.

The woman disappeared into the house with the children. Only the dog was left in the yard. In the house, they were evidently consulting.

A barn, pigsties, stable . . . This was how it had always been, Kempf thought: the early Stone Age. This farmstead would have looked the same anywhere in Slavonia. Meadows, some scythed and some still waiting. Fields ploughed and fields lying fallow. Potato patches and compost heaps, everywhere piles of dung. A lot of chickens. A garden with huge tomatoes, bursting with ripeness. Above the entrance deer antlers showing that the peasant was also a hunter.

The stranger repeated his story to the man who appeared in the doorway, emphasising again that he had money. The property was in good order, as though a lot of hands worked here. This could not be done by children or an adult couple no longer in their prime.

So, there they were, sitting under the eaves, drinking vodka; from inside came the aroma of sizzling pig fat and the stranger was soon served fried eggs. More than the vodka, that aroma made his head spin. But I mustn't be a sentimental cow, thought Kempf, it'll cost me my head.

It was hard for the stranger to explain who he was and where he had appeared from. He said that he would be grateful for a wash. They brought out a tub that the peasant filled with water from the well. They didn't have the good old draw-well of the Slavonian plains, although they could be found in these parts. The stranger stripped to the waist, rubbed himself and washed; he seemed joyful. An avenue of children lined up around the tub, watching each of his movements. Ever since he had given them the brass cartridge case, he was *their* stranger.

"You can stay," the peasant said, and his wife nodded in agreement. "But it would be better for you to go."

"I'm going on," Kempf said and they were evidently relieved.

"Where to?"

"Is there anyone who could take me over to the other side?" He pointed south. "I can pay."

"You don't know what that mountain's like."

In the ensuing conversation, Kempf was informed that this village was constantly combed by the blue police and that the S.S. were also known to turn up. Everyone here was hunting Jews. But there weren't any Jews here. How can we assure them that there aren't any Jews here? They'll burn everything and kill us all before we convince them that we are – *Judenfrei*!

A young man burst into the yard, panic-stricken: "They're here, they're coming!"

"Hide in the forest, man!"

Kempf withdrew some fifty metres into the forest and climbed a tree from which he would have a good view.

The farmer's wife, he could clearly see, poured a can of petrol out in front of the house. Was she mad? Were they intending to set fire to their own property? Kempf saw the children peering out from the attic. If this all went up in flames, who would get them out? Double madness! You could only get petrol here on the black market and it cost a fortune.

The property was surrounded by a dozen blue policemen and three S.S. soldiers. They also had a pack of dogs trained to hunt Jews. The farm dog retreated in the face of such superior opponents. He was merely an ordinary Polish mutt, a freckled mongrel, which had no chance in a skirmish with the super-dogs with flashing teeth.

The blue police and German soldiers told the householders to hand over "their Jews". It turned out they had come on a tip-off from a neighbour. It all stinks of Jews here, they yelled.

"Where are the Jews, where are *diese stinkende Juden* . . . ?"

The officer gave the order to release the dogs. The farmer and his wife stood at the door of their house. Now the dogs will charge through the property, thought Kempf. If there is one single handkerchief left by a Jew, they will bring it.

But the dogs didn't cross the imaginary line along which the farmer's wife had poured petrol.

A Polish policeman came back from the barn with the news that there was a lot of trampled hay.

"Someone's definitely sleeping there."

They all went to look. The barn was big, there were three cows in it, and in the depths a lot more hay.

When they had all emerged into the light of day, the commander ordered that petrol be brought and everything burned. "Then the rats will come out!"

The woman fell onto her knees, wailing and praying. Her prayers were directed mainly to Our Lady of Częstochowa and to God the Father in Heaven, and finally to the gentleman commander.

"If you set fire to the hay, everything will burn. What will we live off? Who'll feed these children?"

He decided against the fire.

After all, the dogs would have picked up that special Jewish smell. It's hard to trick a German S.S. Alsatian. Wherever there are Jews, there is their stench. There was no stench if they aren't there, end of story.

"What did we tell you?" the householders said, as though apologising. They brought out vodka, the blue police and soldiers left. All according to the law, they don't like to pester peaceful, hardworking people, they don't interfere with loyal Poland.

It was not until it was properly dark and Kempf finally went back into the house that he understood what had happened here.

The farmer invited him to spend the night in the house because there would be no more raids for a while.

Then Kempf saw an incredible sight: the pigsty and barn suddenly seemed to swarm with people.

Some figures – men, women, two or three children – emerged from the buildings and stretched in the moonlight which now bathed them in silver.

"Petrol. Do you understand, Jurek?"

Kempf had been rechristened at the farm and immediately

diminished, according to the Polish custom: Georg = Jerzy = Jurek. They couldn't know that Ania Sadowska had already rechristened him.

It dawned on Jurek: the petrol had dulled the German Shepherds' sense of smell.

They had been trained, among thousands of smells, gifted by nature, to differentiate infallibly the smell of Jews from every other smell, and especially from the smell of Germans or Poles, even though the latter were a lesser race. Of course, the dogs weren't racist, they simply picked up the smell of a person, but their trainers had different ideas. That training wasn't worth a piddling fig if the searchers' nostrils were filled with the stench of petrol.

"There, you see how good it is, although dangerous, to have a clever wife!" the farmer said, scratching his ear.

On the one hand, a Pole who informs, perhaps for money. On the other, a Pole who gives shelter to Jews.

Moonlight everywhere, in the smallest corner, everything was bathed in silver.

In the middle of the meadow beside the house, men with tangled beards, in kaftans down to the ground, swung their thin plaits, while the women gathered sheaves of leftover hay.

The farmer invited him into the house. He took an oil-lamp and led him to a small door hidden by a heap of hay.

On the hay, in a tiny space, lay a man of indeterminate age: a sack of bones. Sunken eyes that rarely squinted towards the light. Grey complexion, scattered with scabs. But the eyes were large, as though gathering into themselves all the leftover light of the world over which darkness was falling. The eyes of a half-alive, crushed cat.

"Treblinka!" the farmer said. "He escaped. Like you, only you,

Jurek, are alive and in good health. You probably put on weight, the S.S. fed you well, and would have overfed you."

The peasant laughed. When Kempf had first seen him, a matter of hours ago, the last characteristic he would have attributed to him was a sense of humour.

It was in that farmhouse that Kempf understood for the first time what a concentration camp was. He had not participated in the extermination of Jews, but that was only because there were no longer any in his unit's operational territory.

In the morning, after an unsettled night in the barn (but at least he hadn't had to tie himself to a branch with his belt), Kempf was sipping coffee, or something similar, at a barely hewn table.

"How many have you got?" Kempf asked.

"I've got nine *Katzen*!" replied the farmer gruffly. Kempf understood that in war slang hidden Jews were called cats. Cats are nocturnal animals.

"More exactly, now there are eight of them."

They took spades and after they had placed the body, light as that of a child, on a cart, they went into the forest, to a place that they had decided would be the final resting place of one of the farmer's nine cats.

The ground was still frozen, it was hard to dig the grave. In the end, Kempf placed a little stone on the mound, the way Jews do.

As they parted, the farmer's wife gave Kempf a loaf of bread and a whole salami, while the farmer said: "Hide that mark under your arm. You never know who you might run into. Maybe your own people? Use your head, Jurek. And find yourself a clever wife. Good luck!"

I washed in the open air, thought Kempf, calmly, and the farmer had seen. I must be more careful.

The Brass Age

The shadows were lengthening, the sun had almost set. Like a wild animal, Kempf crept towards the voices carried towards him on the wind. Although he was not a real hunter, he had gathered some experience by accompanying those who hunted in the Slavonian forests. He knew that wind could ruin any hunt. He knew, on the other hand, that wind blowing towards a hide-out could be fatal for the prey. This one was blowing out of the depths of the forest towards its lighter areas, where there were birches, slender and still young, now tinged with the first hints of autumn.

Kempf longed for the warmth of any kind of

While Kempf wanders through the forest, I am reading mankind's holy texts. Fortunately the contact that Sadowska had set up did not work out. Up to now Kempf has done well. He works like a Trojan for farmers, some are agreeable, others treat him like a slave, and sell him on. But no-one has yet betrayed him. All that mattered to them was that he was not a "cat", that is, a Jew. If his people are looking for him, and that is certain, let them find him. The farmers do not fear sanctions for having a German deserter digging their fields. Besides, he's strongly built, he does what he's asked. Now they have to hide their crops, all armies are always hungry, they reap, but do not sow.

I do not have much time, but at present my constant watching does not bring me any particular negative concerns.

shelter. The nights were already freezing. He remembered how, in his army tent, he had shared the warmth of his body with the other lads in uniform. For two days now he had seen nothing alive, apart from a wild boar that had stood in his path, watching him with the greatest dismay, then the aggressor had after all abandoned its attack and disappeared into the forest. The rat that had fixed its eyes on him in that visit to the ghetto had seemed to him far more malevolent.

It looked as though no human foot had trodden here for a long time. Kempf didn't know whether this should be a cause for celebration or despair. If it had fallen to him to be the last Adam, then it was very bad, as he bore the mark of Cain. With him mankind would have ceased to be, without redemption. That was how it all appeared: either all people had died out, or there were not yet any people on

I advise all those who keep watch in vain to find the fourth book of Moses, verse 21.

It was this place, found by chance, that helped me to contend with the worst experience towards which my prospective father Kempf was hastening at precisely this moment.

In brief, in that spot in the holy book, there is this instruction:

When the people became capricious because things had not gone as had been promised from above – and what is more the people had been attacked by fiery snakes – the Bible gladly uses images, and I have the right to think that these fiery snakes stand for doubt in God's works: God orders Moses to make a serpent of fire and brass. Then, "Let as many as are bitten look upon it and they shall live." The fiery snakes will no longer pose any danger.

Later, in Matthew, Jesus Christ takes the place of that serpent.

Later still, up to the present day, many people with various names and with various ideas in their heads have been climbing onto pedestals where there was once a staff with a brass serpent wound round it. They all believe that they

Earth: the time before and after our ancestor Adam. That Russian plane and the German tank into the cupola of which the metal bird had cast its eggs were perhaps two prehistoric tyrannosauri? Maybe mammoths?

Kempf was careless: he hurried through the branches and scrub towards the voices carried on the wind. Now he was close enough to distinguish words from exclamations and laughter. Yes, someone in this forest was laughing, Kempf could clearly make that out. They had to be people. Animals do not laugh. Only hyenas are thought to laugh. Just as it is quite mistakenly thought that birds twitter love sonnets, when in reality they only want to mark their territory and warn potential usurpers.

are men of vision and they all demand, under threat of terrible punishment, that others should look only to them.

In essence, there is just one idea, and it is constantly stolen from the One God: YOU MUST OBEY THE IDEA! ESPECIALLY WHEN IT ACQUIRES A BODILY FORM!

It is curious, nevertheless, that the leaders of humankind do not seek to be Apollos, but rather to reveal themselves to the people as brazen serpents.

As a rule, a snake provokes unease. That seems to have been taken into account.

In the Brass Age, in the name of the Idea, unimaginable horrors are committed. Worse still are those horrors that the victims themselves are forced to commit. And the worst of all are those that the victims perform by their own choice and will. That is coming now.

Warning! Disturbing content!

Kempf was now certain that in the murmuring of many voices he could make out also the laughter of women. He moved a couple of steps closer and now realised that it was Yiddish. They could not, therefore, possibly be hunters. They could only be prey.

Kempf didn't understand Yiddish, he just recognised it. "*Bist a Yid?"* he recalled the way Pan Stanisław, who had acquired the Zimmerman tavern, had characterised the Yiddish of Polish Jews. "Are you a Jew?" There, he'd understand that when he was asked by these people who were strolling in the clearing as though on an excursion. *"Nein, ne, nyet!"* Kempf would say. And he'd find himself again in that uncomfortable situation of having to explain who he was exactly, when he didn't himself rightly know.

Unnoticed, for the north wind was obliging, he watched from the scrub a group of people wrapped in rags of unimaginably varied colours, as though they had passed through some kind of machine that had ground them up, then by some miracle put them back together as human beings, clean and crumpled. Admittedly three of the men were dressed in kaftans that were more or less whole. The women were like Russian dolls, you could imagine that each one was composed of several women, the smallest of which was presumably a child.

Amazingly the sun came out and a ray benevolently, gently, sought out the people who were moving over the carpet of recently fallen leaves, stretching their limbs with obvious satisfaction. A pastoral idyll of poverty.

If they had not been so ragged, it would have been a charming sight, framed in branches dappled with the whole spectrum of colours of early autumn. How dull green is, thought Kempf. How festive is autumn!

The Jews began to dance. The oldest, in a kaftan, would take a couple of steps then raise both arms into the air, the others followed him and the procession then moved in a circle. Knocking one stone against another a woman, wrapped in a blanket that could once have been red, gave the dance a rhythm, slow and solemn. The people danced unnaturally slowly, as in a slow-motion film.

Kempf had time to count twelve adults and five children. These were undoubtedly Jews who had fled from a ghetto that was about to be liquidated. The children carried unlit white candles. The kind Kempf had seen burning in the Osijek synagogue.

Kempf weighed up what he should do. He would have liked to greet them without frightening them. He would like to reveal himself to them, as the Jews put it, thinking of the Messiah, but making it immediately clear that he, Kempf, was not the Messiah, nor did he wish to be, so he was not that longed-for saviour sent by an angry God, whose anger had just passed; at the same time, he, Kempf, was no threat to them and he was himself being pursued. That he, a civilian as he wished to be, and not a soldier, was being led by just one idea: could this chaos lead to a world in which no-one would need to be saved?

He imagined that they would be fearful, that they would scatter at the very thought that someone hidden behind the trees could be observing them; that a stranger was watching them, one who didn't understand their language but knew it was Yiddish. If it was just that he didn't understand it wouldn't be so dangerous.

Undecided, Kempf stood behind the tree. He even considered turning away and disappearing into the forest. But on the other hand, he craved human contact. He was already half-crazed with solitude. He had grown into a solitude that was longer and more onerous than his dishevelled beard full of thorns and berries.

The same wind that had offered him the pleasure of undisturbed observation prevented him from hearing two men creep up behind him: he didn't even see them when a knife flashed under his chin. How could he have imagined that the Jews would emerge from their holes in this forest without posting guards? Judging by the tatters of everything they were hauling round on their bodies they must have been here for months; maybe even a whole year. Ever since the Germans, with the help of the blue police, had begun to empty the ghettos in the General Government systematically, a small number of Jews had fled to the forests, so escaping the gas at least for a while.

Kempf didn't resist. If they slit his throat now, alright, if they didn't that was alright too. He felt no fear. But still, he muttered something like "*Nyet, ne, nein.*" The tight hold on his neck relaxed.

The Jews stopped dancing and surrounded him, one of the two who had approached him from behind still held him by the neck, the other by the arms. And those hands of his were empty, he was a civilian like them, he did have a knife in his jacket pocket and that was his only weapon for defending himself from wolves and wild boar. His jacket was German, but that didn't mean anything. Many people wore those jackets, including those who were fighting them.

Then, visibly panic-stricken, guards rushed in from the opposite direction: "Patrol!"

But experience told Kempf that this was not a patrol. Something, someone was breaking branches in front of them, unconcerned whether or not his progress through the forest was heard or not. Soldiers never move like that. It could be a tank, but what would a tank be doing in the forest? Almost certainly, it was a herd of wild pigs led by a furious boar, their Messiah, and that herd wasn't afraid of anyone.

All the Jews disappeared from the clearing. As though it was a performance by a circus magician, as at a hand clap, they simply vanished. Including the two who had surprised him from behind.

Kempf thought that he had simply dreamed those dancing Jews, their kaftans and their children with the candles. The shadows were long, everything was dreamlike, he was tired and sleepy.

Out of an opening well-hidden with branches, a hand appeared. That hand appeared, quite ghostly, from nowhere, out of the darkness of that opening, a woman's hand probably, in a white lace glove, and invited him in.

Doner-veter-parapli, thought Kempf, suddenly remembering his uncle Johann's three-part curse. No-one had looked at my trousers. No-one had asked whether I was circumcised. They hadn't even asked: "*Bist a Yid*?" And now they were offering him shelter, believing that they were being sought by an S.S. patrol. And not a herd of wild pigs that were not looking for them but for oak trees and acorns.

Kempf slid into the hole. It took his eyes a while to adjust to the darkness. However, he knew where he was from the first moment. It was a long tunnel-like hole, dug in these woods long ago, in 1941, by Red Army soldiers who had managed to escape from German camps. On his wanderings, Kempf had made use of such dugouts. The Poles called them *ziemlanke*. Polish Jews as they fled had dug similar hideouts.

On the other side, there was a hole for ventilation, also well hidden with branches. Why, I was standing virtually on top of it without noticing a thing, Kempf thought. May God on high, whoever's You are, whoever believes in You or has given You up, ensure that the Germans never find this hole!

Here I am again in a burrow, thought Kempf, as though I was a vole. I'm smaller than a mouse, I am mortally afraid of those whose language I speak and understand, but I am being warmed, saved, by those whom I can't understand. Nor they me. They grabbed me then let me go, without asking me a single question.

To be honest, for a long time I haven't looked like a German soldier. I've grown a beard like the ones these people have, my uniform is in tatters like the ones they cover themselves with.

My eyes are sunken, my ribs stick out, my stomach has shrunk, I'm the image of hunger, if anyone needs such an image. I'm far more like an ageing satyr, a forest creature that lives off berries, and starves in the winter, because he doesn't know how to find a lair, like a bear, nor does he know how to collect supplies for the winter, like a squirrel. I'm a satyr, a wild man. Even worse, I'm a man grown wild. And this group here is just like people from the Stone Age, trembling with fear of attack by a maddened mammoth, whose weight alone could crush all these ancient people concealed here. And this heap of objects dragged here, hand tools to solve this or that problem, everything is simple, improvised, that heap of dishes, cutlery, everything that prehistoric cave people could have had, albeit made of stone.

If I'm caught with them, my life will end here, as will theirs. But that's still better than freezing stupidly and forever.

The herd of pigs had thudded over the hideout, nothing was heard from outside anymore, apart from owls announcing that their nocturnal hunt was beginning.

But caution had taught these people that every event must be separated from every other by lengthy intervals. Kempf squatted in the corner he had been directed to by its other inhabitants.

Then the white candles the children were holding were lit, all at once. There was a solemn silence in the hole.

The oldest of the women in the group took one of the candles to illuminate her face as she began to speak softly, almost in a whisper, but Kempf could hear every word clearly, which didn't help him understand her: "*Baruch ata adonai eloheinu melech ha'olam asher kidshanu . . .*"*

---

* Blessed art Thou, our Eternal God, King of the world, who has sanctified us with your commandments . . . [Author's note]

Kempf gave himself up entirely to the magic of the unknown words spoken by our foremother Eve or Sarah or Rachel . . . He thinks he must have happened upon the *shabbat*, the Sabbath.

He did remember, from his childhood, the flickering of white candles that he had seen in the Osijek synagogue, he knew that the Jews celebrated their holy days, that they are not concerned with the birth of the Young King, that for them the Blessed Virgin Mary is Miriam, that, like Orthodox Christians, they do not believe that a woman can conceive without semen, that they do not know about Saint Sylvester, and that they had waited for the baby Jesus, born in their midst, to grow up so that they could crucify him on a cross, according to the Roman custom.

When the foremother's blessing ceased and all abandoned themselves to their own thoughts, a few German words, as though they were spoken in the shelter itself, rent the silence of the dugout.

A tiny bundle, to which no-one had paid any attention until then, began to whimper. Kempf understood that now things had become really dangerous. Overhead a herd far more threatening than wild pigs was strolling, digging and sniffing.

The young mother, almost a child, endeavoured to calm the baby. She had no milk, they had been suffering black hunger for months already. The child wouldn't be soothed. The mother pressed it to her breast, in vain. Not only would it not calm down, but it began to cry increasingly loudly. And no-one and nothing could soothe it. They all looked at the girl as though she was to blame.

Two older women, two foremothers, Sarah, Rachel, took the bundle from its mother, the girl was led away into a corner of the hideout. A man in a kaftan pressed a pillow with feathers leaking from it over the bundle . . .

The young mother was held tightly by the arms in the depths of the shelter.

The candles had been extinguished at the first German word from outside. One single short candle still smouldered, like a small wax finger.

The child jerked its little feet frantically. Not in all directions, as those who have not yet learned to walk, but as if running, like a young dog dreaming it was charging over an endless meadow.

Then it stopped.

The mother! Rachel, Sarah, Eve: indescribably huge eyes, dark hair, light complexion: just like the perception common in the West of *la belle Juive* . . .

Kempf could still clearly see her face before that last finger of wax went out.

During the night, Kempf thought the following: Holy God, what have I just witnessed?

It was only now he noticed that once all the others had fallen asleep, an elderly man was watching him from a corner of the dugout. They were the only two people awake.

Perhaps my idea of slipping through the war as a civilian is mistaken, thought Kempf to dispel the unease caused by the old man's gaze under his hat.

Before he drifted off to sleep, he longed for his attack rifle, which he had fired so often at animate and inanimate objects, which he had so pampered, rubbing it with machine oil, the rifle he had left under his bed in the field hospital. When that was discovered, Ania Sadowska would certainly not have understood. He almost prayed to that rifle of his, invoking it. It seemed that his desire for absolute civilian status had lasted just a few weeks.

In the morning, as he was washing, the shadow of a long-legged man fell over him.

He had of course seen him in the hole under the earth, he was the man who had been dozing in his corner, he was evidently much older than most here and had hardly covered his nakedness with an assortment of rags. They could have been the remains of a kaftan, though threadbare. He wore a hat with an unusually wide brim. As long as he had been lying, curled up, it was impossible to judge how tall he was.

"You're coming with me."

This was spoken in such a commanding tone that Kempf was surprised. The whole night the man had looked absent, as though he had been sleeping for several thousand years, the kind of half-sleep that was his enduring state of consciousness.

Treblinka

"How much further?" asked Kempf.

He was finding it hard to keep up with the Jew. Leon Mordechai seemed like a bird trying in vain to take off, but each time he jumped ahead just a few paces. As though he was in a terrible hurry. Or as though someone (something?) was chasing him.

Kempf asked where the railway track they were following led. Mordechai stopped, in half-flight, and solemnly disclosed, as though it was an epiphany to be greeted with applause: to the west, Warsaw. To the east, Białystok. On the right, soon, ladies and gentlemen ... TREBLINKA! (Kempf was the sole audience.) By the bunker.

What now follows fills me with ever greater dread, but dread is the enduring condition of the unborn. My future father Kempf is risking a lot in now deciding to follow a Jewish man, not knowing where to or who he actually is. That man, who declared himself to Kempf as Leon Mordechai, had been watching him for a while. He had seen Kempf truly appalled by the suffocation of the child in the dugout, and he now thought that horror a recommendation for further instruction. Mordechai was the man who had huddled in his corner, pretending to sleep, or else doze. He had not taken part in the rituals, he had not sung.

Leon Mordechai was an apocryphal name. Because the current age ridiculed myths, the Stranger had adopted a different name. Admittedly, in

Kempf knew, he had agreed to it, that this man was leading him to Treblinka, from which, only a year ago, Mordechai had miraculously escaped. He knew that the Soviets were there now, he knew that, immediately after a failed uprising of the inmates, the creators of the camp, afraid of the red tide, had liquidated it, destroying virtually every trace. Kempf had not yet met the Soviets, but he had heard them. The language of their heavy guns was more convincing by the day. But the situation on the ground, including that over which he and Mordechai were cautiously moving, was still "raw". They were keeping to the railway track; it was debatable just how sensible that was.

A train was coming, they heard it by laying their ears on the track. They sped across the open ground trying to reach the forest as fast as possible. The Germans had cut down

neither his appearance nor what he was wearing did this man correspond to any given preconception of the Eternal Jew. For instance, he did not have a violet-coloured coat buttoned up to his throat, nor trousers of the same colour, he did not have white socks ... Instead he wore rags that were the tattered remains of clothes worn by peasants in the Polish backwoods. Only his wide-brimmed hat was vaguely reminiscent of the famous series of engravings of Ahasver by Gustave Doré. He was the Jew, a cobbler by trade, who did not recognise the Saviour, weighed down by his cross on the road to Golgotha. Such a thing – not recognising the scriptural Saviour – was a great sin among Jews, not to mention Christians. Along with the towns where the unhappy shoemaker, whose punishment was eternal life, was seen in the past – Hamburg, Lübeck, Paris, Munich – is also Polish Gdansk, while it was still German Danzig, and Kraków, where Hans Frank, the all-powerful master of the General Government, now held sway. That this really was Ahasver was supported by the fact that Leon Mordechai spoke a lot of languages. With the bushes along the trainline to pre-empt sabotage.

The composition seemed endless. Then came open freight wagons, on each of them was a T-34 that would be the real victor of the war in the East. New, in mint condition. And war had been waged on this territory for five years. In his aimless wandering, Kempf had seen hundreds of destroyed tanks, armoured cars, howitzers, heavy guns . . . perhaps ten times more Soviet ones than German. And now, brand-new tanks with red pentograms, their paint not yet properly dry. Stalin had evidently won the materiel war against Hitler.

Kempf conversation would be in German because that was the language of philosophy and its breakaway sister theology. Be that as it may, there was no chance that this would end well. The name Leon is found among the Ashkenazi, while the surname Mordechai suggests the Sephardi, so in a way Leon Mordechai represented both.

Treblinka no longer exists, it is now a field sown with broad beans.

What is my father doing in a field full of broad beans?

But I can't change anything here. Kempf's natural curiosity was stronger than anything. The matter of my birth can again easily be gambled away. I was allocated that man as my father also in a game of chance. I am not to blame, but I must continue to be apprehensive.

These monsters were undoubtedly headed for Berlin.

Mordechai and Kempf tried to withdraw in the opposite direction in the hope that the Red Army was already far behind them, hurrying to Berlin.

At last they came to points where the trainline turned to the right. The other branch was evidently long out of use. As though nature wanted to swallow it up, it was overgrown with weeds and scrub.

"A little further!" Mordechai said, but it seemed to Kempf that he had bent his head as though expecting a blow.

They passed a bunker, but it was just a rotten tooth: clearly a multitude of direct hits from close range. The Germans had ordered the Ukrainian guards to destroy any trace of what had happened there. Then they disappeared. In the end the place where many Jews had been murdered (how many, even Mordechai could not say, he expressed himself vaguely, taking hold of his throat as though suffocating, gesticulated, groaned: "In Treblinka many were killed!") had been guarded by only two Ukrainians. The Treblinka concentration camp had been transformed into a little country farmstead, standing in the middle of fields sown with broad beans. It was unclear what the Germans had wanted to achieve. When the Red Army began to advance, the Ukrainian guards too disappeared.

Mordechai hastened his step. Now he was again scampering through the undergrowth like a bird trying to fly. In the scrub his hat kept catching on branches but he wouldn't take it off. It seemed to Kempf that this tall man had no weight, his bones were bird-like, delicate. If he really was a prophet, then it was clear that other laws applied to him. All prophets were to an extent sleepwalkers. That was why in their presence everyone had to speak softly, not to wake them. Indeed, Mordechai kept admonishing Kempf that he was speaking too loudly, while he himself, whenever he felt it appropriate, almost shouted. That too was a characteristic of prophets.

As the wind under the sun was blowing from the direction of where Treblinka had to be, it brought them human voices.

"Ukrainian?" asked Kempf. "Or Russian?"

Mordechai turned round. Neither Ukrainian nor Russian. "And definitely not German."

"It's Polish."

Fine, thought Kempf. We were in Poland. Admittedly, the Russians would not acknowledge it.

But from the Poles he had met, in various uniforms, he knew that they would never renounce their country the way it had been before the various partitions; and it had been largest and most powerful when it entered an alliance with Lithuania. So, we were in Poland, and here people spoke Polish: a Polish Commonwealth. Ania had talked of this in ornate language. That was the "official dream" of Polish patriotism in this more enlightened version, without chauvinism: a Poland around which Central Europe gathered.

Mordechai put his finger to his lips, they both crouched down and crawled in the direction of the voices.

"Treblinka Number II," he said, parting the branches solemnly. "That is, this is where it was."

Now it was an expansive meadow, on which fires glowed, scattered, spread out. Round the fires sat men and women, even children. They were dressed like peasants in this part of Poland, the women in long skirts, the children no matter how.

In Kempf's eyes Mordechai saw a question mark.

Kempf suddenly remembered a distant excursion to the Kvarner region of Croatia.

And he recalled the lights strewn over the sea: the Kvarner fishermen fishing by candlelight. That's what the meadow looked like.

Astonished, he observed that Leon Mordechai's eyes were wide open like a cat's and in them was gathered all the light from that open space, all the stars above, all light ... all those sparks the invisible Creator had divided among the people as the Jewish Kabbalah maintained. Something was happening to Leon

Mordechai in which Kempf could no longer participate. His own eyes still registered the banal question marks: what were these farmers doing, what were their wives doing here, why were their small children not asleep, on that meadow where Treblinka clearly was no more? Why had the two of them come such a long way?

"Wait for it to get light," Mordechai said.

The two of them leaned against a tree. They had just one heavy coat between them and tried to cover themselves with it. The night was clear, it would be cold. They shared a piece of cheese and bread, green with mould in places.

Utterly exhausted, before he dozed off, Georg Kempf thought: How strange the name Leon Mordechai is. As if he wanted to include all Jews in his very name, as though he wanted to be both Ashkenazi and Sephardic.

Then he remembered that a Jewish man in Nuštar was called Klaić. They were everywhere, the Jews, he thought. And you could tell only some by their names. Why even his ancestor Kempf, who knows, could have had some Jewish blood. Our forefather Abraham certainly. Jesus Christ, of course, what else could a poor Palestinian peasant be? The fact that his Father gave him to a carpenter to adopt and feed was because he wanted to advance his class status. That's what the Bolsheviks wanted as well. Their first leaders were all Jews ... The Poles rejected Bolshevism because they feared the Russians who had appropriated it as their thing, once it was palmed off on them by Jews. How complicated it all was!

And now, here were the two of them, two human bodies lending each other life-saving warmth. The Jew was warming the Volksdeutscher, and he the Jew. Before them, on the open ground, was a curious gathering of Poles who were not sleeping. The wind wafted their voices, and occasional women's laughter.

A terrible explosion hurled Kempf, like a bullet blasted from a hot barrel, out of the world of his dream, which had just become pleasant, even exciting . . . recently Sofija had begun more often to visit his sleep . . . Kempf leaped to his feet, Mordechai had already crept nearer to the meadow.

The explosion reminded Kempf of the blow of a howitzer large-calibre shell that could bring much misery without anyone knowing rightly where it had come from.

Mordechai calmed him with a gesture of his hand and invited him to a place, on a slight rise, from where almost the entire open space could be seen at a glance.

The explosion had opened a hole in the earth that could have been made by a 105 mm howitzer shell, but in fact it was dynamite.

The Poles rushed to the hole with picks, their wives with spades. Around the hole were now scattered bones and other body parts which had not yet completely disintegrated. There were scraps of clothing, toys, wigs.

Mordechai began his explanation with the following litany:

"This is where almost all the Warsaw Jews were murdered. Many Jews lived in Warsaw. Warsaw was the starting point on the railway line that ends in Białystok. It isn't a long journey. Not remotely as far as from Thessaloniki to Auschwitz, or from Zagreb to Auschwitz . . ."

"Why Zagreb?" asked Kempf, but Mordechai went on, and Kempf realised that he was talking to himself. As the only person "in the audience", he had finally crossed him, Kempf, out.

"The trains were full of Warsaw Jews who could have read on placards: 'Take money and valuables with you!' The wealthy Jews took with them whatever they could carry and what they believed could save their lives. Here, at the end of that branch line, the men emerged in their best clothes, the women with new hairstyles, the children in sailor-suits . . .

"In less than an hour, it was all over, a new contingent was expected. They were put to death with the gas from diesel motors spread through 'showers'.

"The Jews handed over almost everything they had brought with them, but not all could be thoroughly searched so some were tossed into pits along with the remains of their hidden money or jewels.

"That treasure was used to trade; the Ukrainian guards bought women and vodka with diamonds.

"The guards vanished, as if swallowed up by the earth.

"Since then Poles have been digging up what the earth had previously swallowed.

"Many have learned what an emerald is, or a sapphire, and what a napoleon or a gold dollar looks like.

"It's hard to dig up the deeper layers by hand. Hence the dynamite, grenades; when tanks are once again transformed into tractors and power shovels, they will come too. Progress in everything, technology for the people!"

Horrified, Kempf watched a man trying to saw off an arm with a bracelet that would not come off. Then it was the turn of the finger of a girl who would not part with her ring, a pledge of faith to someone lying somewhere around here, in one of the layers recently doused in lime.

They kept chasing dogs away from the hole opened by the dynamite; a flock of crows as big as a plundering army occupied every branch of the surrounding trees.

The dogs and the crows were waiting for the people, having satisfied their greed, to leave, but that would not happen. There are hungers that cannot be assuaged.

It was now broad daylight.

All those who had sat by the fires the night before were now digging with tremendous zeal, the kind celebrated in the U.S.S.R. as "Stakhanovite". One peasant used his pick to drive the others away from "his" hole. Earthy Polish curses flew around, along with the bones thrown up by dynamite stolen from the Germans.

A group of peasants was heaving bones, the remains of flesh still on them, with spades into a threshing machine. By another hole people were sifting earth, while their offspring played with the toys of departed children.

This was called the Treblinka gold rush.

The open space was rutted, many holes had been opened up, the landscape resembled the moon.

The merry Pan Twardovsky on his red cockerel, alighting on the moon, was nowhere to be seen.

He also observed that the land under their feet was raised; both were standing on the corpses of Warsaw Jews.

Healing the World

For days Mordechai and Kempf tramped through the forest, listening to every sound. They were looking for a roof over their heads as the nights were cold. Snow had not yet begun to fall, but the rain was worse. The tree canopies, now bare of leaves, no longer protected them. During the day, there was still some sun and the two of them, when they were not walking, sat beside a hollow, a ruin, a burnt church or destroyed bunker to warm themselves on the sun's rays. Like forest mice, they would scuttle into a hole at the first opportunity.

Mordechai and Kempf argued about God. Anyone would have thought that their primary concern would be finding a roof over their heads and anything at all to eat, even tree bark, berries such as abound in the Polish forests in late autumn. But they argued about whether there was a living God or whether He was just a phantom of the dead for the dead. Two dead men quarrelling about a living God. They began to address one another as "colleague", for their dispute was becoming learned, scholarly.

Leon Mordechai instructed Kempf about the Jewish Kabbalah. That word meant simply tradition. If God were to hear them, thought Kempf, he would have concluded, well, here are two pathetic creatures, one of whom thinks he knows something.

God is unknowable, as his colleague Leon Mordechai readily

admits. There is no point in proving the existence of God. That is the great truth that does not require proof.

For Kempf that is not enough. Compassionate consideration prevents him from informing Mordechai that God is dead.

"The question of all questions," says Kempf at length, "is if your God is so powerful, why did he allow Treblinka to happen? If God made everything out of nothing, could he not have left Treblinka out? Would that have meant that everything was less complete?"

"That's the question people with no talent for religion always ask."

"What is a talent for religion?" asked Kempf, forcing himself to swallow a piece of sweetish rind.

"Not everyone is born a theologian."

"Fortunately," Kempf said. "Some are born free."

"You don't understand anything. God implanted in human beings freedom of choice."

"Including the freedom to choose to burn each other?"

"Yes, that too. For if man was not free, he could not be accountable before God."

"Do you, Mordechai, claim that Heinrich Himmler will be accountable before God?"

"Of course. What is currently happening in the world only serves salvation."

"Jews will therefore be saved by being burned alive?"

"The world is an arena of salvation."

"That's presumably what the first Christians thought, whose limbs were torn off by lions. Incidentally, will Himmler be saved as well? Someone should pass that good news on to him. The Allies assert that all Nazis who committed crimes will be brought to justice."

"We are speaking of divine, not earthly, justice."

"It seems to me that many could scrape through. Goebbels for one. He could compete for the position of devil's shyster."

"Let him try."

Through the shrubs, they spotted a village, seemingly deserted. Every other house was reduced to ashes. There were no cows lowing, now and again a dog barked, perhaps rabid. The peasants had taken their livestock, or it had been seized by the Waffen-S.S., because the supply lines, seriously disrupted by the Underground and Home armies, could not function as before. There was a shortage of meat.

Kempf and Mordechai decided to spend the night in that village. They felt confident, but you never know. The silence was absolute, the dog was not rabid, it rubbed itself against their legs; it was simply lonely. In the discussion about God it could be the decisive voice.

The two of them sat down in front of a house in which everything had been turned upside down; they didn't find anything edible. To the left was a large hole full of stable manure that was still warm and steaming, like smoke from embers. Whatever had happened here, it was not that long ago.

Mordechai did manage to find a few tea leaves in a tin. They were afraid of lighting a fire in the stove as the smoke would have been seen a long way off. They drank cold tea, hoping the water in the well had not been poisoned. They had long ago exchanged addresses in case anything happened to one of them and the other survived. Mordechai had given the name of a village on the Ukrainian–Polish border, Kempf the little town of Nuštar. Mordechai showed him the number tattooed on the outside of his left forearm; it was his personal identity card. Kempf didn't show Mordechai his sign of Cain. It seemed too complicated to explain how it came about that he was marked. He hadn't told the Jew anything about his own war journey. Mordechai could legitimately have thought that this eccentric man had appeared here like the prophet Mohammed, travelling through the night sky, which was the only true miracle Islam acknowledged.

Unlike Islam, their faiths, Kempf's nominal, Mordechai's real, recognised many miracles. That they were both alive they had the right to consider a miracle of miracles.

"We live in the worst of worlds, some mystics have asserted. But in it hope also lives."

"Explain, colleague Mordechai."

From the forest they heard footsteps on dry leaves. It must have been humans because animals are far more cautious in their movements. If they were humans, there must have been quite a few of them. They evidently had no reason to hide.

Kempf retreated into the house. Mordechai, in deadly fear, jumped into the manure pit: it was so deep that only his head could be seen above the surface and, when he sank in deeper, only his hat. One might have thought the hat had been brought by the wind, but never that there could be a man under it.

"Hope is the remains of light. In the cosmic catastrophe the vessel of light shattered, we call that *shevirat*, billions and billions of sparks . . ."

Mordechai plunged into the manure, holding his breath for as long as he could. Only the top of his hat shifted a little.

Through a window long since without glass, Kempf observed the edge of the forest. Perhaps an animal after all?

"Those sparks are retained in some human beings," his colleague Mordechai continued, "when the aeons pass, and when all the eternal light is again gathered into One, the world will be saved. That's what we call *tikkun olam*, the repair of the world."

So the world will be saved by the one who jumps in time into a slurry of cow droppings, thought Kempf.

"When that will be, no-one knows. Only Moses on Sinai received the prophecies directly from Jehovah. Everything else we know only at second hand. Even the Saviour, who is perhaps already among us, does not yet know he is the Saviour."

"If I understand correctly," whispered Kempf, "for the Jews war serves to save them, and not, as Hitler says mistakenly, for them to be destroyed."

"I'm talking about all people."

"Including Hitler?"

"Including Hitler."

"Well, if Hitler is in fact helping the Jews to save themselves, why don't they just burn themselves? Why put Hitler to that trouble?"

"They did that. The Maccabees chose to burn themselves alive rather than fall into the hands of the Romans. And many Jewish sages have preferred to be burned at the stake rather than deny their insights."

"Insights?"

"Their faith. But it is achieved by asking questions."

"I would have thought that asking questions would take one away from faith. You know what, colleague Mordechai: the world is crap. I think God simply messed up with this creation of the world. He was too hasty. What could one decently do in six days?"

"God has nothing to do with this 'creation' or 'this world'."

"How come?"

"One of the greatest secrets of the secret knowledge passed on to the Jews holds that the world was not created by God, because creation would have been beneath the demands of the purity of his being."

"I understand that. There are always splinters when something is being created, 'between piss and shit, we are born . . .'"

"The true and only God is not God the Creator. Whoever does not understand that, whoever thinks that God is the creator of the world, thinks of God as a kind of carpenter, a craftsman. There are mystics who have forever relieved God of concern with the creation of the world and its imperfection."

"That, colleague Mordechai, is brilliant."

"But we Jews still ask questions. We look for proof. That's why we are so successful in scholarship. However, colleague Kempf, the greatest truth cannot be proved and is therefore above proof."

"So why do you ask questions?"

"In order to penetrate to the level where questions are no longer possible. But that is very high, those are spheres far above our heads and our powers. In the Belzec extermination camp a little boy of perhaps four, outside the gas chamber, asked his mother: 'I've been good, so why have they turned out the lights?' That's a Jew asking questions."

"All I see there is a terrified child."

"I see a small Jew who doubts. From that doubt evolves the need to liberate God of responsibility for the state of the world. In the Old Testament, there is an interesting passage that points to that need and offers a solution. The Bible likes images: in this passage, doubt takes the form of the bite of a poisonous snake. God instructs Moses to fashion a serpent of brass and place it high up where everyone can see it. That is how they are relieved of the poison of doubt. And God is absent, occupied with more important matters. Or in fact with nothing, as befits Him. That is not far from the idea in Jewish mysticism of the Demiurge who is in fact a god of lesser rank. Are you familiar with that place in the Bible, respected colleague? They were inspired, but also literate, and came to the problem of the imperfect world, but they only half solved it."

"I only ever underlined the Book of Books. Sulamith was always closer to me than Jehovah."

"You're a cynic."

"Someone has to be. What I see is that God wanted to impose an idol on people."

"Yes. The idol wraps itself round its column, high above the crowd of skulls, showing the way with its tail. Doubt is removed from those skulls, they will follow the Leader's tail. That's the meaning of the brass serpent."

In the forest by the village, something was constantly moving; in all probability pigs on the loose, but in these parts there were a lot of gangs. Had those been pigs a little while ago? It hadn't sounded like them.

Mordechai dried his clothes in the sun and they now really stank. Kempf wasn't fragrant either, he hadn't washed for days. They didn't dare draw water from the well. The well was a little way from the house, in a clearing and clearly visible from the forest. So there was no prospect of washing.

Those sounds had deceived them. Nothing had happened. Other than that now Mordechai smelled worse. That was no doubt entirely at odds with the purity of his prophetic being.

The night found them in the small Polish town that Kempf knew slightly: this was where he had brought the S.S. patrol, here the sign *Zimmerman's Tavern – traditional Polish cuisine for gentlefolk* still flapped in the wind. But the little town had evidently been completely evacuated and not a single building was left whole. Kempf's experienced eye immediately judged that things had been bad, that howitzers of at least 105 mm had been at work, and probably tanks as well. He recalled that during that patrol a candle or oil-lamp had flickered in the occasional ruin. Now the town was shrouded in complete darkness, waiting for the celestial light to be lit. There was no-one here anymore, the town had been emptied.

The two shadows traipsed along the main road which Kempf remembered at the end turned right and led into the ghetto. If the town was ghostly empty, it was less likely there was anyone other than rats in the ghetto. That judgment turned out to be accurate.

Of course Mordechai proved himself an infallible guide in the shtetl which had been transformed into a ghetto as early as 1939 by being enclosed in barbed wire and a brick wall. "That's where the school was." He pointed. "Here's the synagogue . . ."

"And this must be the mikvah, our holy bathing place, my ignorant friend . . ." he exclaimed joyfully.

Kempf wanted to say that he knew what a mikvah was, but Mordechai had already begun to strip to his bare skin, tossing his stinking rags in all directions, and he hung his broad-brimmed hat on the branch of an apple tree, like a child intending to dive into water.

Without much thought, Kempf did the same and before long the two were in the little pool full of rainwater that was surprisingly clean. Another miracle: the autumn night was as warm as summer. Wonders upon wonders here, thought Kempf. What was left to Jewish mystics than to believe in miracles?

The full moon too was amazed by this miracle. Two naked bodies washed in silver that ennobled everything. Kempf now saw how much Mordechai had declined physically, how pitiful and thin: a sack of bones. But with pleasure, almost greed, Mordechai abandoned himself to the rainwater in the mikvah, endeavouring to catch fragments of light in his palms. *Tikkun olam!*

So the two of them spent some time splashing about, spraying each other.

"This was where unmarried Jewish girls came. They were usually afraid. They had to dunk themselves in the water, over their heads, three times. Men were excluded. Their mothers and the older women encouraged them in their bathing. Women who were not Jewish were also excluded."

The worst imaginable moment was when they both had to pull their stinking rags back over them. That was their reality.

At dawn the sun found them on a bench beside the mikvah. They were sleeping soundly. Dreams do not carry over either scents or stench.

"This is also where our women and girls bathe when they wash themselves of their monthly blood. I've told you that already. But you don't know that this is where Jewish men also bathe, with the aim of symbolic cleansing. Such bathing is compulsory for anyone who wishes to convert to Judaism. It's like your baptism. Only, you baptise tiny children who aren't in a position to make decisions. We do it differently. If you are not born to a Jewish mother, you can become a Jew, but only of your own free will. Do you want to be a Jew?"

"No," Kempf immediately burst out. "I want to be nothing."

"Well, that's the same these days."

"But you want to save the world."

"Kempf, you don't understand a thing."

"I would like a world that would not in the end need saving."

"You haven't passed the test, you can't be a Jew. You don't understand that the Unattainable, Silent, Distant God has set man a challenge and overcoming that challenge is the greatest freedom and joy."

To himself, Kempf thought he had answered well. Ever since he had lain on his bed in the S.S. field hospital musing about his chances, he had resolved to pass through the frenzy of war as a civilian, he had in fact wanted to be nothing. He would most have liked to be invisible.

In the heat of their debate, neither of them, not the theologian nor the agnostic, had noticed that they were surrounded.

Five men, with a mixture of fury and revulsion on their faces, had formed a circle round them. Kempf immediately concluded that they were some kind of gang, as they were so haphazardly dressed that it would have been too much even for the Underground army. They were wearing bits of uniforms from all sides in the conflict, for the most part in shreds. Only a large man who was evidently the boss was wearing a preserved uniform of a tank corpsman from one of the surrounded S.S. divisions. That uniform was completely black, tight, so that it appeared to be his skin. All five of them were playing with iron rods.

"Pants down!" the gorilla commanded, and Kempf judged from his accent that he was Ukrainian.

"Damned stinking Yid," said another lifting Mordechai's circumcised member with the tip of his rod.

Kempf felt the painful blow of someone's boot on his backside and pitched forward. "Get lost, stench!" the leader ordered. That was unjust. They looked pathetic, but after their ritual cleansing they didn't reek any more than the gang did.

The leader whacked Mordechai across his forehead so that blood immediately gushed from it.

"What're you waiting for?" asked another of the gang, evidently a Pole. Kempf crawled away into a bush, holding up his trousers.

The five of them threw themselves on Mordechai. They didn't mention the abduction of a Christian child with the aim of preparing the ritual bread. Nothing about the world conspiracy of Jews, not a word about the Sages of Zion. Nothing about the greedy Jews who plunder the Polish poor. Because this was all too well known to every Pole.

Mordechai's skull fractured at the first blow and Kempf hoped that his merciful God would have immediately taken his consciousness.

Mordechai fell into the stream that flowed past the mikvah. The water washed away clumps of blood and the greyish-pinkish matter of his brain scattered over the pebbles. A ray of sun played with the flowing water and those remnants of the skull of Leon Mordechai, his colleague. He had been right. The vessel of light had shattered into pieces, sparks; scattered out of the vessel were now little stars on the pebbles waiting for someone (and not no-one) to gather them once again into One, Only and Eternal Light.

Pants Down!

Just as he was afraid of rabid dogs, Kempf avoided villages with abandoned cows lowing in the barns. For a massacre had either happened there or was about to.

A farmer would leave his property only when faced with a deadly threat. The mourning of a cow over her overfull and painful udder was among the saddest things Kempf remembered from his "little Polish war".

The village behind the thicket appeared to be inhabited. At this time of day the livestock was in the barns, lowing could be heard, but Kempf knew how to distinguish the messages. These cows were fed, safe, they would be milked. Farmers could be heard calling. They were loud, they too, like their animals, felt reasonably safe.

While he was "observing" the village, and as his decision was forming, someone came up behind him and pressed a barrel into his back. Kempf recognised it as a hunting rifle. It was his future employer returning from the forest where he had hidden part of his summer crops.

"Pants down!" the farmer said calmly, knowing that he had the upper hand. Kempf removed his trousers. The result of the inspection, he suspected, was a disappointment to the man as it deprived him of a reward for handing over a Jew.

The farmer's reflection – what to do with the stranger he had so cunningly captured – was interrupted by cries from the direction of a fishpond. On its bank peasants were standing round a child lying on a heap of leaves, not moving. Kempf concluded that they had just pulled him out of the pond. He hurried to the scene, followed by the farmer pushing his rifle into his back, and told them he was a doctor.

"Step back, give the child air."

Full of respect, the peasants moved away.

Kempf knelt beside the child, felt his pulse and began gently pressing his rib cage. He turned him onto his stomach, the little boy spewed up water and, to the astonishment of the villagers, came to life.

The doctor asked whether he could stay in the village.

The more prominent villagers consulted. They pointed out to the child's father that all doctors were Jews.

"He's not a Jew," said his employer.

The farm where his new employer took him on as a servant was in an area under the protection of a Cossack and his gang. That band didn't flinch from anything, they weren't interested in politics, only plunder. For them the war was good, but the more thoughtful among them knew that the downside of wars was that sooner or later they were over. And then fools were made to pay what they owed. Kempf could not have known whether he had already met them: whether they were the ones who had slaughtered Mordechai. Winter was on its way. Kempf knew that he had to look for shelter and that he could not be choosy. Moreover, the heavy guns that could now be heard almost every day announced that the front was getting closer.

The Cossack and his gang too would have to look for a hole to hide in and wait for the storm to pass, and afterwards who knew what might happen? It was always possible to grab a Jew who had escaped from a ghetto or camp and get a reward. But they had to fear that higher powers would impose their own monopoly. For honest people and true Poles there would soon be no business here. The question was whether they dared continue to plunder the peasants. The Soviets could impose a monopoly here too.

For the captive and servant Georg Kempf, the fugitive low-ranking S.S. officer, born in a strange land in the back of beyond, who spoke the oddest Polish anyone had ever heard, the chances were slim. But he was not a Jew, he could have sworn that on his life to the Cossack and his gang. His landlord would not have dared conceal a Jew. There were Poles brave enough for such madness. This farmer was too clever to have kept and fed a litter of "cats".

As the farmer's inspection had turned out favourably for Kempf, and on top of that he had declared himself a doctor, the fugitive was permitted to stay under his roof. On condition that he did not touch his wife, because if he did the farmer would immediately blow his brains out with his rifle for hunting deer.

It was not hard for Kempf to agree to this condition. The wife was plump and dirty, and well advanced in years. But different criteria apply in wartime and the farmer had learned this, paying the Cossack and his gang not to pinch his wife's behind, at least not in his presence (the tariff for them not pinching her at all was too high for him).

Kempf had slightly misjudged the farmer's wife. Admittedly, she didn't appeal to him as a woman, but she was a good soul who took care of him in every way. His external appearance began to show a woman's touch. His clothes no longer fell off him, she drove him to shave from time to time, she washed the underwear she gave him. Kempf now thought of her with gratitude.

This farmer's wife instructed him in "the brief essentials of Polish antisemitism", as Kempf privately called her expositions on the Jews from the neighbouring town, who had now all vanished.

She asserted that she had heard with her own ears Jews talking of having to snatch a Christian child . . . then they would spin it alive in a barrel with nails sticking out on the inside . . . When it was completely mangled, they would use it to make their *matzos*, by baking flatbreads with little holes in them . . . and the long noodles that hung in their houses . . . Jews drank raspberry syrup, alright, that was acceptable, but to snatch children, like Gypsies, that couldn't be tolerated. Most of them had never learned Polish. They could hardly wait for the Germans to come to Poland because they understood them better. The red onion fried in duck fat would have made his mouth water too.

Kempf said nothing to all of this. The woman, of otherwise such a gentle nature, was quite convinced that she was simply passing on what she had seen with her own eyes and heard with her own ears, and that from Jews themselves.

"Jewish women have their own bathing pool that they call a mikvah. That's where young women wash off blood, older ones as well, as long as they still need to. I'm sorry that these baths are inside, so I've never seen them. Because they do everything in secret, and they bathe in secret.

"And how crudely they yelled from their market stalls!" the woman went on. "When Poles are selling something, you can hardly hear them."

There was no doubt, this simple-hearted Polish peasant woman hated Jews with all her being and thought she knew why.

The woman used to put the remains of the evening meal every day onto the windowsill, inviting Christian souls who had not yet found their way to Paradise to help themselves.

In other words, she had a kind heart.

Kempf had come across this "popular antisemitism" before. It grew in Slavonia as well, like vegetables, in every kitchen garden. What is more the church press thundered against the Jews who wanted to take over the world. But the Church had rejected racism, so it didn't condemn all Jews, only those who had "abandoned their faith" and subscribed to godless Bolshevism. None of that would have led to a major pogrom, nor, without the Nazis would "our" Jews have been annihilated. Kempf mocked both populist and church antisemitism. At the table in his family home, no-one spoke badly of the Jews. His father had done business with many of them, albeit not involving pig fat. When the persecution of the Jews began, his father said it was an outrage, but his resistance went no further than that.

So, the Polish peasant woman's views of Jews did not surprise Kempf. He just couldn't understand the connection between these views and Treblinka, and particularly everything that he had been shown there by the self-identified prophet with the smashed brain, his colleague Leon Mordechai. In his "little Polish war", Kempf had as yet to meet a Pole who could explain that to him. Not even one who would have tried. Ania Sadowska didn't of course believe in the myth that Jews steal Christian children to bake bread from their blood. But she had still maintained that the Jews were a Polish misfortune, immediately after the Germans and Russians in magnitude.

On one occasion, Jurek was invited to a celebration. There were more girls there than young men.

There were only older men left in the village. Kempf had of course noticed that the women took food to their men in the forest. But their men were not partisans. They were hiding because the Germans and blue police occasionally collected men and forced them to dig trenches. In addition, most of what the village produced was hidden in the forest. It had to be guarded. Every attempt Kempf made, in a roundabout way, to get a clearer idea of whose side the village was on was fruitless.

Now all these women. Red skirts and scarves, red stockings on chubby ankles. Green bodices, with gold thread – at home ducats would be quivering on their breasts ... Lads in white jackets. Everything was so similar, if not quite the same. In Nuštar the men would wear black waistcoats embroidered with yellow thread. But it was all the same world.

They were served borscht with potatoes. The village was not yet seriously hungry.

Small stringed instruments were played, Jurek now knew that they were called *złobtsoki*, someone played an accordion. These women drank quite a lot. People liked beer here, often hot. Their songs were sad, mostly about partings and unhappy lovers from past ages.

Would Kempf have been able to help himself to any of the femininity that filled this large room, in which, apart from a big table with chairs around it, there was virtually nothing else?

He would not have dared. He knew that the girls were not intended for him and that everyone would have known about it straight away. That was why he pretended not to notice a couple of pairs of women's eyes that were weighing him up.

As the gathering broke up, late that night, Kempf heard and remembered this exchange between two of the girls:

"How are your cats, Agnieszka?"

"Fine. Only they're not exactly catching mice."

Laughter, silvery, spilled over the field to Kempf's great delight.

Blessed Be the Fruit of Thy Loins . . .

The small town of K. was one of the larger towns in the Dukedom and had been quite prosperous before the war. Now it seemed neglected: just the occasional passer-by, a kid playing with a hoop, a shopkeeper standing outside his shop warming himself in the sun. The shop had no doubt previously been in the hands of a Jew, the signboard was strikingly new.

Kempf's present master stopped his horses in front of an inn. And opposite, set back from the road, was a small wooden church in front of which a few women were standing in a circle. It looked like a ring dance that had for some reason stopped, forming a still life.

"I'd like to see the church from closer to."

"This is the Church of the Assumption of the Blessed Virgin Mary. From the start of the war till now we have called it the women's church. Only women enter it. Until the war, as I said, it was called the Church of the Mother of God and, in addition, I remember well, if you please, the Church of the Holy Archangel Michael. The one who defeated Lucifer."

"So why is it not still called that?"

"Because Archangel Michael is the saint of soldiers and policemen. And soldiers and policemen are men. Now it's full of old women snivelling and wailing instead of cleaning their houses and taking care of the stock. You go and look at the church, I'm going to search for nails. I'll be back in half an hour."

Kempf jumped down from the cart and set off towards the church.

A church that had once been called after the Archangel Michael? Was he not the protector of the Jews? It was strange that he had been taken over by the Germans, for them to call a naive and kindly man from their own fold *der deutsche Michel*.

This little church was charming. Most unusual, because churches can be arrogant. Many Polish churches have strong bulwarks and look more like fortresses. But this little church was made of wood and as a fortification would not be able to protect anybody. There were a lot of them in Lower Poland, they were erected by the Polish aristocracy as their covenant. It was carved, like a toy bought for a child at a church fair. War Gothic, thought Kempf, late Middle Ages. There was still real piety then.

He himself was a fairly indifferent believer, mechanical, customary: baptised, confirmed, now and then confessed. He rarely attended Mass. His rebellion against his father coincided with his rebellion against God. But there was nothing excessive about it. He was not an atheist but admitted to being agnostic. A rationalist. That had so irritated poor Mordechai, who was a believer and didn't reproach God for anything. But that was possible only because his colleague Mordechai had introduced, between God and Creation, a lesser god, a craftsman, a worker, an engineer who had taken on himself the risk of failure. His colleague Mordechai had granted God something like universal indulgence.

The wooden chapel was full, Kempf could see this through the wide open door. There were only women in it. As there were no pews, they huddled together by the altar. A priest, of very fair complexion, young, pink-cheeked – an archangel could not have looked less warlike – a being therefore with no kind of military qualities or views, was singing the Mass. Well, tunefully.

The women responded with murmuring and soft singing. There were some older matrons, young women and some who were still little girls. There were women dressed in the traditional costume of this Dukedom of Lower Poland, but there were also townswomen.

Kempf abandoned himself completely to the sweet flowing of the Polish language. He couldn't follow the priest very well. Between him, standing to one side in a dark corner, and the priest, there were at least thirty women. They absorbed his voice and nothing could reach Kempf over their heads. In addition, it all blended with the aroma of incense.

Kempf tried to remember how the prayer to the Virgin Mary went in Croatian. How would it sound in German, in Luther's translation? Then he gave himself up to the Polish, which flowed for him in an incomprehensible way: like an ancient, forgotten language, spoken he believed by the Croatian nobles, the Zrinskis and Frankopans.

When the young priest had finished the Mass, he apologised that he would have to rush off to tend to a sick person and he took his leave of the women. Holding up the skirts of his cassock he set off towards the door and the lake of women parted to let him through, the way the sea parted to make way for Moses.

His bicycle was leaning against the church. Sensible, thought Kempf. These days a bicycle was the most reliable means of travel. It didn't depend on diesel from Romanian oilfields like tanks.

Kempf now thought that the women would disperse and go to their homes to cook the midday meal. But at that moment a figure dressed as though it had just emerged from a museum stepped

out in front of them: *Dark Lady*! And she, like the priest with
his cassock hoisted her skirt that otherwise reached almost to the
ground and then sat down at the organ. Kempf had never seen
such a tiny organ: hardly the size of two Pfaff sewing machines
such as the Kempfs had had in their house. Of course, like all
German women, in addition to housework, Kempf's mother knew
how to sew. Of course, she was literate, of course she had been
taught by nuns. And of course she read the Berlin magazines
about nature and fashion.

And of course she prayed to the Mother of God.

It seemed that the women had just been waiting for this. Kempf
noticed a small foot in a little black lacquered shoe pressing the
organ pedals. A melody emerged that Kempf had never heard,
more cheerful than devout. And now in the wooden chapel the
women started singing wholeheartedly, their voices, harmonious,
now rose towards the image of the Holy Virgin above the altar.
Perhaps real piety required misfortune. Perhaps to know both
one had to be in Poland.

The organist's alto voice was pleasant, confident, probably
trained. The peasant women and the townswomen sang about
everything to which they were enslaved. Full of anxiety about the
fruit of their wombs, which could hardly count on blessedness,
whether they were unborn, already born or already fallen.

Not one of them glanced towards the stranger. He didn't
bother them. He simply wasn't there.

Kempf stood for a while in the sun's rays, trying to get used
to the glare after the half-dark of the little church. He was near
the door, he had slipped out before the women began to emerge.

On his seat, his landlord was crossly banging his whip. "But
you said half an hour."

He took out his tin watch and shoved it in front of his servant's nose. "It's been a whole hour. What's so interesting in there? Old women wailing, so what."

It hadn't seemed to Kempf that so much time could have passed, but the clock had said so.

The Pole was perfectly right. Father Kempf, what has the wailing of women to do with you? Recently, I have suffered a great deal. I could hardly wait for the end of that picaresque journey of the two madmen who thought they were travelling through the sky and that they had placed themselves outside space and time, which together make history. One of them is no longer alive. Kempf is still alive, but it's debatable for how long. How irresponsible!

The news of the murder of Leon Mordechai would spread quickly. But that would not prevent his appearance in many towns. The Eternal Jew greatly annoyed Jesus Christ under his cross, and he would continue to wander until Judgment Day, as a reminder of the guilt of all Jews.

The same goes for our Lord: when the news of the death of God spread, that did not prevent Him from continuing to reveal himself to the visionaries.

Whither and Where To?

At dawn, a husband and wife came to ask for "Doctor" Kempf, after an evidently sleepless night: their little girl had a fever.

If I really were a doctor, thought Kempf, I would now be waving my doctor's bag, which in Vinkovci was indistinguishable from a postman's satchel . . . But here I have nothing. Every old woman knows more about medicine than I do.

Is that the teaching of Hippocrates? Make do and mend. That was why in the village there were more than the usual number of pale people whose blood the "Doctor" regularly let. At the very least, after leeches had sucked at them a bit, they didn't hit their wives so much. So, there was no harm done, thought Kempf, that's according to Hippocrates, at the very least: Doctor, do no harm.

The "Doctor" went into the house whose roof was so low that he had to bend down: the little patient was lying on a high bed, dressed in white, which immediately shook Kempf. In his homeland little bodies were buried in white clothes and a white coffin.

His intuition was confirmed, but he didn't say anything yet.

A temperature, evidently. He told the little girl to try to touch her chest with her head. She couldn't do so.

Kempf had been afraid of this. Even in the conditions of the best-ordered hospital like the one in Frankfurt managed by the aged Prussian from the S.S. field hospital, it would have been difficult to save this child. It was clearly a case of advanced meningitis.

"Take the child to town, to the doctors," Kempf said.

"We can't afford it. Why do we keep you and feed you?"

Kempf "prescribed" damp sheets in the hope that this would at least lower her temperature.

"It'll be alright," he said as he left and that news quickly spread through the village.

The news that the little girl had passed away that same night spread even more quickly.

That was the end of Kempf's renown. A doctor who saves once but not again – there was evidently some calculation. He wasn't a doctor, but a murderer. He killed a little girl with wet sheets.

Kempf did not have the heart to explain to them what meningitis was and how dangerous.

Soon after that event, his landlord informed Kempf that he had sold him to another master. He had a large farm, a lot of livestock, horses, cattle, and needed a lot of hands. They'd manage here without the "Doctor" because they knew how to catch leeches themselves, and they would make a point of avoiding wet sheets.

Whither and where to, thought Kempf, wielding a pitchfork, stacking the aftermath, the last scything of hay.

Who knew who this new master was, to whom he had just been sold? Everyone was a master over him, from the one on high of whose existence he was not convinced, but whom he sometimes feared, to the ones down here who kept shoving their existence into his face. The deity he feared Kempf called Bad Luck, and there was little point in praying to luck.

So, that was how serfs were sold on. Although generally with land. In truth, Kempf had already been labouring for months, from farm to farm. Although, in the course of this war, many women had taken over the work of men in industry, in the country there were jobs that had to be done by a male hand. But the men had either been taken away already, become outlaws, or were hiding in the forests near their homes. Kempf was young and strong, he could withstand the efforts that resulted from his situation and temporary "class position". The young bourgeois had become a servant and a serf.

Kempf understood that he had been sold, from hand to hand, like a slave. He could not be certain, but he presumed that the all-powerful Cossack had played his part in this trade.

That idea didn't appeal to Kempf at all. He had grown accustomed to his old master, he had even thought that he might be able to wait here till the end of the war, indicated by the almost continuous thunder of Russian tanks. Kempf had also grown used to the small services of a woman's hands, in the absence of which even the most inveterate fighters are at times helpless. That plump matron had turned a man who had grown wild with solitude, tramping through the forests, into an almost civilised being. He was a servant and a slave, but a civilian.

And now, once again, complete uncertainty.

More than the Russians, Germans, Ukrainian bandits and local Polish gangs, more than partisans of any flag, Kempf was afraid of that white one: not the flag of surrender, but of winter. Kempf would not be able to survive winter alone in the forest, and the autumn was already colouring the woods deeply.

He had tried in various ways to find a new contact in the underground army. Because who knew where Ania was now, did she even know who he was anymore, did she remember how good it had been in his camp bed in the field hospital? In all likelihood she had fallen into the hands of the Gestapo. If she was alive, she would be retreating with the field hospital towards Germany: at the moment all roads led to Berlin. Maybe she too had deserted? Unlikely, because as a mole in the middle of an S.S. formation she could be of far greater use to the Underground. Who knew how many like him she had despatched to the forest, probably with a better outcome.

Had he found a new contact, could he have passed new checks? A runaway S.S. soldier? How could he prove it? Of course, under his upper arm he bore the mark of Cain. It was easy to prove that he had belonged to the Waffen-S.S.

But how to prove that he had deserted? How to prove that he really had wanted to join the underground army? The only person who had known that for certain was his contact, the one organised by Ania Sadowska. The business of his transfer, his change of flag, had unfortunately not succeeded. And where was his weapon? The man had strolled off into the forest as though he was going to pick strawberries. A mushroom-picker. Had he collected birds' eggs to survive? How many such mushroom-pickers talk nonsense when a knife is held to their throats? How many are there who steal from birds? Could he be a Jew?

Pants down! He wasn't a Jew.

That was better than nothing, but not enough. Was he in favour of an independent, free and democratic Poland? Could he be, on the contrary, in favour of Poland as a Soviet republic? He was a Volksdeutscher, just like these Germans in Silesia who would soon be driven out with the same cruelty with which they persecuted the Jews. They would be subject to terrible revenge, not, of course, through love of the Jews – there was no-one to avenge them anymore – but for love of German properties, homes, mills, factories, land above all. Peasant hunger for land was insatiable.

What if this new master sold him again, this time to Germans?

They would instantly put him against the wall. Taking his trousers down wouldn't help at all. What if he was handed over to the Soviets? They would leave his trousers where they were, but would look for the mark of Cain under his left upper arm. What would Kempf have to say to a Soviet commissar? That he had run away from a unit that was defending an S.S. field hospital on the eve of Soviet victories at Kursk?

He could have said that, as an S.S. soldier, he had refused to shoot prisoners. The commissar would have found that highly suspicious. The Russians did not take prisoners. The fronts were moving too quickly, there was always too little food. He hadn't shot hostages? Nice. And had he been punished for that insubordination? If so, how? An officer's boot to his butt? Being wrapped in a woman's apron?

The following morning his master harnessed the horses. Kempf collected his bits and pieces, the master's wife concealed her tears. She had grown used to this mysterious stranger who never talked about himself but had golden hands. He hadn't touched her as a woman, which she regretted. He was somehow more refined than the others who had happened by the property, he had smelled better as soon as he had begun to wash more regularly. Yes, she had flared her nostrils in his direction like a doe when her time had come.

At a crossroads, his master said: "Listen, man, I did what I had to do to save my farm, my cow and my wife. The Russians will be here soon. They burn and raze, and they especially hate farmers who have more land than what is immediately around a house. They trample everything, they rape. They are worse than the Germans, they are worse than our brigands who at least understand Polish. The fool I have sold you to knows nothing about what's coming. He hasn't heard that there's such a thing as a radio. That peculiar box can tell you about the final victory of Hitler's men and then, if you just turn a small button, you will learn that the Russians are winning. With the difference that you see nothing of that ultimate victory of Hitler's, while you do indeed hear the Russians, there, they're greeting you in their own way."

It was true, they were thundering again, in their own way.

"For the Poles, none of this is good, there are too many victories here. And so, Jurek, think for yourself. My advice to you is to jump off this cart and vanish in the forest. You're a good man, you know life, you have a way with animals. Your would-be master will be sorry, but I will say that you ran away, ungrateful as you are by nature."

Kempf gaped. He had never heard a radio in his master's house. Who knew what secrets that property hid? There certainly weren't any "cats" there. Had there been, the Cossack could not have been cheated by petrol. He would have handed them over.

"Then you'll have to return the money you got for me to my new master."

"I haven't got anything for you yet. We trade by the word here. My loss in all of this is one pig."

"A pig?"

"Come on, that'll do, what are you waiting for, my friend? That's not such a small price these days. Now, goodbye, Jurek, and good luck. Watch out for the Russians, they're pissed off with the S.S."

Kempf stared into the dense forest for a while.

"Off you go, man," muttered Kempf. "Let's get that pig."

Swan Lake with Dog

Georg wanted to be alone for a while, he needed to get something straight in his head that very morning because he had dreamed terrible dreams, he had tossed and turned under his sheepskin coat, pursued, who knows by what ... The previous day news had reached the farm that in the nearby market town of K, the Waffen-S.S. had court-martialled and immediately set up a firing squad for two men who had deserted the flag. From judgment to execution had taken less than fifteen minutes. Young men, boys. Passing on the news, Bartek had said that the Waffen-S.S. was either increasingly young or increasingly old ... "The prime of life" was already rotting somewhere. German power now consisted of decaying crust and seed that would not have a chance to sprout.

Bartek was a young man with whom Kempf had made friends. They were the same age, they used to go together by boat to an island in the lake to fish. But now it was all frozen.

Kempf recalled that a few days before he had again come across several graves with black steel helmets on their crosses. There had evidently not been time to inscribe the names of the fallen. The Germans were retreating everywhere, increasingly rapidly. There was no panic yet, but nor was there time to inscribe names. Any of those graves could have been Franja's – but also his own.

Kempf often dreamed that he had been caught, questioned,

tortured. Even more than the Germans, the inhabitants of the Polish hinterland feared the Ukrainians: three letters – U.P.A.* – stood for unimaginable violence. However, those hordes controlled the Carpathians; here in the Beskids the Ukrainian nationalists had not succeeded in perpetrating so much evil. But still, after so many years, experience had taught the villagers that they should be afraid of anyone with a gun. And everyone had a gun.

There were supporters of the Home Army in the village. Georg had discovered this by chance from a girl who had confided in him that her young man had gone to the woods, to the Polish army. She would join the Ursulines if he didn't come back.

No-one here in the village would have called the national army the *Polish* army. And three months earlier, a unit of Polish partisans had driven off a formation of the Waffen-S.S. that had evidently lost its way and intended to set fire to the village out of pure fury.

That certainly improved the image of the Polish partisans of the Home Army, but, as far as Kempf was able to discover, none of the villagers old enough to hold a gun had joined it. Of course, after his initial hesitation, Kempf had confided in them: that is how they knew that his contact with a unit of the Home Army had failed, and the village elder had reassured him that everything could be put right, although for the time being in this part of the world the only real masters were the Soviet background troops. Naturally, the old man didn't reveal that he was himself a supporter of the Polish Underground, like Sadowska. Kempf had stopped hoping that Ania's plan in connection with him personally would be realised, he abandoned himself to events

---

* Ukraińska Powstańcza Armia, the Ukrainian Insurgent Army, fought against the Soviet Army up until 1949. [Author's note]

and to the fears he tried to keep at bay by imagining things. And for that, he needed to be alone, at least for a moment.

This morning the north wind was less biting, the weather calmer. Well wrapped in his fur coat, Kempf set off to the lake. It was frozen, but in some places the ice was evidently thin. It would have been risky to skate on it. He was surprised to see a pair of swans: do swans not fly south? The villagers had broken the ice in two or three places, evidently to help the birds. Did they eat them? In Slavonia no-one had eaten swans for hundreds of years. Why was he thinking about roast swan? The village, despite all possible requisitions, had not yet been driven to starvation . . . a life could still be bought with a squealing pig under the arm, or a sack of flour.

Just then, the sun rose above the dark edge of the tree canopies; what a dazzling moment. So much beauty serving no purpose. Everything material, fixed in its colour and dimensions, with firm outlines, now dispersed in a blend of blue and gold. Under the whiteness of frozen snow any rubbish heap would look lovely, thought Kempf. To give oneself up now to bad thoughts would itself be bad. All of this together, this whole spectacle, had no meaning and that was why it was beautiful.

Then a ray of sun found him, he had to close his eyes tightly. The sun was not yet warm, although it was high in the sky. Beauty should never have any purpose. That was the only way it was real.

At that moment, Kempf was an entranced person offering his programme on the altar of poetry. He found himself shivering for no reason; he wasn't cold, although everything was frozen. He wasn't hungry, although he hadn't eaten since he woke. He was breathing deeply, quietly. He wanted to participate in it all without participating.

Behind his closed eyelashes he had a vision of a flock of young women dressed in dazzlingly white feathers. He abandoned himself for a long time to these feathered women, never thinking how good it would be to get closer to that flock and so enter the fairy tale. To watch, to watch . . . just let the gaze slide over those white costumes . . . over those long white legs, opening the space between them, covered in white silk, to the gaze . . . What a triumph of voyeurism!

No, that too was something with a purpose! Let us accept beauty with no purpose.

When Georg finally opened his eyes, he was brought back to reality by wild ducks, colourful, but somehow too concrete, not at all elegant. The sight of the ducks skating over the frozen surface of the lake made him laugh. With each step one of their little webbed feet slid either left or right – as though trying to dance the Charleston. And now on the polished parquet of the frozen lake a whole procession of ducks were all dancing the Charleston, a social dance of pre-war capitalism. But this here was the Middle Ages.

Kempf began stamping his feet and drawing his coat closer to his body, which had begun to feel chilled: as soon as the sun hid behind the clouds, it was cold again. And the beauty had vanished, the world began to emerge in sharper outlines, as it is, in need of warmth and so much else, rather more hostile than benign, and already half-destroyed, desperate and wretched.

At that unpropitious moment a small dog scurried onto the frozen lake, driven by its insatiable need, for it was "hungry as a dog", it didn't know the steps required by the libretto or much care for Tchaikovsky's immortal kitsch or fairy tales in general. Nor was the ice-bound lake well disposed. And, right beside the little ducks, preoccupied with their dance, it cracked under the unfortunate dog some five or six metres from a willow on the shore.

What now?

The dog's hindquarters had partly slipped into the hole that had just opened up under it. For a while it waved its front paws, even pulled itself up a bit, but then its paws, without purchase, began to slip over the ice round the hole. Kempf called and encouraged it with all the names given to dogs in his part of the world; he threw it a little piece of bread he found in his pocket, jumped up and down and shouted, but the imprisoned dog was barely moving. It raised and lowered its paw, as though in greeting, and looked sorrowfully at the sublime beauty around it.

"Bartek, Miłosz ... Zofia ..." Georg shouted all the Polish names he could think of. He could only call a few people by their names, but now the dog's fate seemed so vital and he felt so sorry for it that he wanted to rouse a whole regiment, the whole village, all the villages around and all the Poles, and others, if they hadn't become completely callous, believing that a mere glance at the scene would elicit sympathy and set salvation in motion.

As the lake was not far from the farm, half a dozen villagers soon assembled, some had just risen from their beds, as there was no need to rise early in winter, if there was a woman in the house who would feed the animals. Their own dogs came as well, themselves uneasy, winding round the legs of their masters, inspecting the scene, panting and yelping.

The villagers observed for a long time. There was beauty in just observing. Some scratched their ears, all stamped their feet because it was still cold and the sun was still hidden. They muttered something among themselves that Kempf couldn't follow. Ever since chance had cast him among these Poles, he had had the sense that they spoke two languages: one among themselves, the other when they wanted him to understand them. As a Slav, as Jurek, and not Georg. Both languages had to be Polish. Jurek Kempf, the second part of this name was not far from the German word for battle, *Kampf*, but for a long time he had not been up for any kind of battle and these people knew that and valued it.

Jurek pointed to the sky, calling on God, in whom all believe, particularly in His goodness, because He is a loving God who loves all His creatures equally because He created them all, even the last little dog threatened by a terrible and unjust death from freezing, and, if not sooner, then as soon as the sun began to disappear over the horizon, by evening at the latest, and it would stay there frozen in the lake like all those far too numerous soldiers who had remained frozen on the battlefronts, not felled by bullets but scythed by a death they call white . . . so what if the dog had no soul, not an entire soul, that is, so what if it was not baptised, it must have something like a soul as it was suffering, souls generally exist because of suffering although they are immortal, so come on, let's save this dog with our combined efforts, you presumably know what to do in such a situation, surely you have yourselves more than once fallen into a frozen lake that can be deceptive for a human, let alone a little dog driven by its canine hunger and drawn by those alluring ducks which had of course flown away, they didn't give a damn about a dog that had in any case wanted to devour them, there was nothing beautiful here, there was only need, misery and distress, and death was unjust as it always is, even a dog's . . .

The Poles listened to this monologue of Jurek's, whom they had named Battle at this farm, and he wondered: Why aren't they stirring from the spot? Why are they standing like statues, as though frozen? Do they understand me? Why I am doing my best to help them.

And again Jurek raised his arms to the Creator, hoping that they feared the One on High more than the "Ukrainian Insurgent Army", more than the Germans, more even than the Russians. After all, it was all one world in which the One on High saw everything, meting out good and bad, and if it was bad, it was a punishment, and if it was good, it was a good harvest and a full pigsty . . . In essence the world was justly set up. The dog hadn't harmed anyone, not people, not God, not Poles, not Jews . . .

"It's one world!" yelled Jurek, as though the fate of the entire world depended on the fate of that small dog.

At that moment the wind changed direction, now blowing from the west. And the whole scene was imbued with a sweetish stench which in this part of the globe, in the Year of our Lord onethousandninehundredandfortyfour, was unmistakably distinguished as the smell of burnt corpses brought by the wind from a camp barely twenty-five kilometres away as the crow flies from this farm.

The villagers stopped stamping their feet. Jurek the Battle fell silent. Some of the Poles took off their fur hats. The women, as though it was some superstition, some terrible threat, ran back to the farm. The dog's story was over, thought Jurek, intuitively, not really knowing why.

But the men were still standing and looking, now at the dog, raising and lowering its paw, still saying farewell, now to Jurek Battle. It hadn't yet frozen, Jurek noticed out of the corner of his eye. This is how Battle interpreted those gestures – "Save me," the dog said, "only don't take any risks. Save me, but don't make the same mistake as me. Adieu, farewell!"

If such a rescue could have been possible, the world would be full of good people, Battle concluded.

Eventually, one of the villagers turned and hurried towards the farm, with the others following. Jurek fell onto his knees, sniffing the air, and, not knowing what to do, started throwing balls of snow after the departing group. He thought for a moment that he could try by himself to pull the dog out, but there were no branches nearby long enough, nor anything similar. It would be utterly pointless to try to get to it by walking over the thin ice, which by now could only be thinner than it had been that morning.

Why was all this so terrible and at the same time so ridiculous? At that very moment, there, beyond the fence, men, women, children, mostly Jews, were being burned, while here this little dog was expiring, and what was the connection and would the rescue of the dog help any human being in any way?

Jurek Battle relaxed a bit and sat down on a tree stump.

He was roused by the sound of breaking twigs. At first he thought that must be wolves coming to finish off the business, well, they wouldn't be able to, he wouldn't let them . . .

But it was the villagers, almost everyone who lived there. They were dragging after them a long ladder, which they laid down on the shore of the lake. They didn't so much as glance at Jurek. They were focused on doing something that was obviously not new to them: as though it was practised choreography. A display of exercises by a voluntary firefighting society.

They laid their ladder down on the frozen surface of the lake. Five of them, at least two of whom must have weighed a hundred kilos, stood on the end of the ladder on the shore. Bartek, inclined to joke, Bartek who knew about fish, but Jurek would never have taken him along into any fight, Bartek, skinny and too refined for the country, carefully stepped onto the rungs and set off towards the dog.

The dog abandoned itself so completely to him that Bartek, breathing heavily, groaning and cursing, was able to pull it out onto the ladder.

Throughout this whole event no-one, apart from Bartek cursing, said a word.

He took the dog, threw his coat over it, shoved a piece of bacon into its mouth, which it swallowed whole, and gave it a swig of vodka.

The sun illuminated the scene. It must have got warmer, or it just felt warmer. The stench from the west still pricked their nostrils.

As they were all working on the rescue, like a well-trained team, no-one there noticed that they were being observed.

In truth, three men were standing on a small pile of peat, among birch trees gleaming in their white apparel. Wrapped-up, the men probably appeared much heavier than they were. Under something that could have been white sheets, they wore the remnants of uniforms of many armies; of all the armies, it seemed to Georg, that had rumbled past here since the Thirty Years' War. Kempf noticed the jacket of a Waffen-S.S. armoured division tank crew. In terms of war fashion, those jackets were popular, not only because of their black colour but for their elegant cut.

But the basis of all these uniforms was that of the Red Army. And there could be no doubt about the three red stars that could be seen clearly, menacingly, despite the haphazard camouflage of something white.

It seemed the villagers were waiting to hear which language would be spoken first: Russian or Polish.

This time Russian won.

"Where's that German of yours?"

Kempf froze, but an absurd, albeit correct thought came to his aid: If they're Soviets, and if they shoot me, at least they won't order me to take my trousers down.

"S.S., damn his German mother!"

"We don't have any Germans here. We don't hide Germans. This is Jurek."

He, that Jurek of ours, that is Jerzy, as the Poles translate his name Georg, isn't German, he ran away from the Germans as any intelligent person would have done.

"Where is he?"

None of the Poles pointed out Jurek Battle.

And so Georg made himself known, since he had no choice, and it looked as though things could get tense.

"He's not German. He refused to shoot Poles," his Poles muttered.

As though the dog wanted to say something, in its own language, the third one being used here, in Jurek's support, it began to sniff around the boots of one of the patrol, whining and wagging its tail.

"So you rescued the dog?" the soldier said, scratching the dog under its muzzle. He knows about dogs, ran through Kempf's head. Maybe he's not a bad man.

That was Sergei, a Russian with whom later Kempf became friends. For life, one could say – had anyone known whether Sergei perished, and if so, where; in what ice, like a Siberian mammoth.

With the Bolsheviks

Kempf spent his first night with the Reds in a German bunker, on the concrete floor. The words *Gott mit uns* were engraved on the wall. Now, at the end of 1944, it appeared that the Lord, *Gott*, had abandoned the Germans. But that didn't mean that God had moved onto the Polish side. *Gott* was reluctant to change His position. He mostly dozed, unimpressed by being constantly disturbed by Polish prayers. In truth, many Poles, men and women, prayed fervently.

For months, since August 1944, Kempf had been hearing a whisper under the roofs of hamlets in the Polish hinterland: Stalin was in Prague, he had halted his divisions on the eastern bank of the Vistula, less than half a kilometre from the German lines. It did not suit his plans for the underground army to liberate Warsaw. Crucified Poland, the Christ among nations, was once again sacrificed. Warsaw was no more.

That was the loudest whisper Kempf had ever heard.

It was to be expected that the Polish-Soviet groups of partisans operating behind the German lines would hardly have been able to count on strong support from the Poles. One quite frequently heard that the Russians were worse than the Germans. The war in the background looked like a war against everyone. There were temporary alliances, but also many betrayals. To say that the situation was chaotic was putting it mildly. The only genuinely consistent group were the real bandits, who murdered and plundered for their own ends. The Soviets did not kill Jews. Hence young Jews, capable of resistance, sought contact with Soviet saboteurs. Although they were few, there were some Polish communists who were also in a sense "Jews" in that they were outsiders, not by birth but by political choice, although they were Poles. They too had no choice but to ally themselves with the Soviets. And so the surviving Jews and Polish communists almost found themselves on the side of the victors. Many Poles would never forgive them for that. The heroic defence of the Home Army at Warsaw, superhuman as well as fruitless, would become a myth. The Jewish Uprising in the Warsaw of a year earlier had sunk into oblivion.

Kempf had calculated that if he survived the war on the side of the underground army, his mark of Cain would be the deciding factor on his "war journey" that would plunge him into nothingness. Radio Moscow spoke increasingly frequently of the Home Army as Polish fascists.

Kempf had little choice. He was not the one making decisions. He was an object, a thing, and his status had not changed at all since he became a "forced volunteer" and was recruited into the Waffen-S.S. Then he became a village servant in Lower Poland, with barely the rights of a medieval serf. All told he was nothing but wild game, pursued by everyone.

Besides, it was only by chance that a bullet fired from the rifle of a fighter of the underground army had hit him in the shoulder and not in the head. Incidentally, he had noticed that the pains in his shoulder had recently ceased. In truth, pitiful as he was, he could still have seen himself as a child of fortune. Nonetheless, he would gladly have changed his skin, had that been possible. It was cheap.

In the Bolshevik headquarters, where his new "owners"

brought him, things were lively and Kempf was most struck by a cauldron from which rose the aroma of something edible, hot. Why, he had spent the whole morning saving the dog, he hadn't eaten anything since the previous day.

Under a tent flap attached to a hazel branch, some young women were dressing a wounded man who was moaning. Judging by the leather satchel and maps scattered over the table in front of the man to whom they brought him, Kempf gathered that he was the commissar or commander, if they were not one and the same person. He recalled Hitler's command about commissars, which was read out in S.S. divisions every day as a litany, and which all the soldiers had to remember well. According to that command, every captured Soviet commissar had immediately to be shot, with no formalities, no court, and particularly with no thumbing through the paragraphs of any war laws or conventions. This last was entirely outdated and had fallen out of use in the final war against Bolshevism and the inferior race.

But at this point in the war the commissar Sergey had no time for him. He had to study a special map. They took Kempf, somewhat disappointed, back to the bunker. Kempf presumed that was some kind of softening up. As though he was still capable of any kind of resistance, if only intellectual.

Kempf crouched like a dog in a corner of the bunker, endeavouring not to think about anything.

The longest nights are those when one doesn't think about anything.

In the morning, he was brought shaving gear, which astounded him. After he had shaved, they took him again to the commissar and one other officer, probably a commander. This was Alyosha, with whom he later became friends.

Kempf wisely decided to keep his German quiet. The

conversation took place in some old Slav language, from the time before Russian, Polish or Croatian emerged from it. Of course it included the language of gestures, older than words, they couldn't have done without that.

To begin with, the Bolsheviks thought that this confused man, born in Yugoslavia, had escaped from a German concentration camp. Kempf thought that was too big a lie. He then said that he had fled from a German hospital. Anything could be added to that; besides, it was true. The truth is always better even if the other side cannot fully understand it. He admitted at once that his name was Kempf, first name Đuro. "Would that be Yuri?" asked the commissar and the ice was broken. It's a great thing to have a name that functions in all languages.

"Are you a soldier?" the commander asked. "Do you know how to take cover, to shoot, to use grenades? Do you have any experience? What do you think about Tito?"

Kempf didn't think anything about Tito. What he had heard in Poland was meagre; Poland was preoccupied with itself and dressed its wounds fearful of the impending still greater catastrophe. Now and again it was possible to hear on the radio that the Balkan forests were swarming, but it was not clear who was with whom, who against whom. As in Poland, Kempf felt that down there everyone was fighting everyone else. The Yugoslav government in London seemed to him similar to the émigré Polish government that was trying unsuccessfully to govern Poland from that same London. However, what he knew for certain, from his own experience, suggested that the Home Army, that is, the army of that government, did not cooperate with supporters of Hitler. The Allied radio stations, after some initial uncertainty, could not say the same of the Serbian Chetniks, recognised by the Yugoslav king in London.

But Kempf had barely heard of Tito.

"Tito fights well," the commissar said. "We liberated Belgrade for him, and now he's sending us packing. But he's a good fighter, Tito – first class."

That was the first time Kempf had heard that the Soviets had participated in the liberation of Belgrade.

"Off you go now, wait on that bench," said Alyosha, ordering his men to give him something to eat.

It seemed to Kempf that the investigation took hours. What could they find out about him? Where was his S.S. division now? It was true that the Germans were retreating, but not as fast as could have been believed last autumn. Where was Panna Ania Sadowska? Could she have perished in Warsaw? Perhaps she had been seized by the Gestapo? Where were those who could have provided any kind of

I am speechless: Kempf with the Bolsheviks? The only good thing about them is that they are strong. The strong survive. So far my father has had good fortune. He's going to need more. If I am ever born, I shall be able to consider myself a child of fortune.

If at all, I will be born in Zagreb. Kempf has no premonitions about that. We are conceived without premonitions. Kempf's concepts of Zagreb are equally vague. He didn't know that on 22 December 1944, Zagreb had been under alert since 10.45 and that bombs fell on it. My prospective father had been in Zagreb twice: for three days on an excursion with his school and the second time when, on his way to Poland, he got off the train at the station to drink some water.

Today two shells fell on the Botanical Gardens. Kempf might have remembered it, because the excursion itinerary included introducing pupils to some rare plants. But about Krešimir Square, where shells had also spread devastation, Kempf knew nothing, nor that today in that town one egg cost 450 kuna, while a haircut was not less than 500.

information about Kempf's "war journey"?

In what Polish back-woods was "Liszt" tonight playing Chopin's mazurka or "Hungarian Rhapsody", somewhat wild; on what table was the better half of that artistic duo dancing? Where was his colleague Mordechai, had he been buried or had they left him to the wild pigs? Were those Jews who had to kill their child in fact still alive?

Fortunately, it was just as hard to find any of those who could have compromised him. While he washed, he took great care not to reveal his mark of Cain. That was routine now. And so the Reds never did discover what every villager for whom he had worked had noticed. Peasants have sharper eyes. Commissars take a broader view.

After several uncomfortable hours sitting on tenterhooks, he was taken back to Commissar Sergey and Commander Alyosha again.

Be that as it may, the very mention of Zagreb sends shivers down my spine, as that was to be my birthplace. Hence I loyally reject the comment on the price of a haircut as slander. And that name – Zagreb – first rang (as a sign of joy) when news came of the happy conception of one of us in that very city. But the other mention was not happy. It was recorded in May 1943, when the woman who was carrying her unborn child was shoved into a cattle truck, in the direction Zagreb-Auschwitz. A few days later he had just peered out between his mother's legs, it was dark, and his first breath was his last. To be precise, he came into the world in the gas chamber of Crematorium No. 2. They did not separate him from his mother on the way to the chamber because it was clear that the tightness of her birth canal was an insoluble problem. In addition, among the special unit that cleaned the gas chambers there was not a single midwife so that nothing suggested the possibility that fortune could have smiled on the child. We think he may have lived for perhaps one minute. They were found, the mother and the not fully

The commander took a rifle out from under the table. "Well, young man, tell us what this is."

"*Sturmgeweher vierundvierzig*," Kempf rattled off, then bit his tongue.

> emerged infant, on the side opposite the sealed door where the others all pressed, one over the other, the stronger over the weaker, in search of air.
>
> The woman had moved away to prevent him from being crushed.

"It is indeed a *sturmgeverka*, fuck it, the Germans make good guns," the commander said. "Hold it! Take a good look, have a sniff! You'll see two letters on the butt – S.S. Don't worry, the person who engraved S.S. on it isn't going to come and ask for his gun back. Let this gun now be your father and mother."

Kempf realised that this was something like an initiation. He was going to be rechristened and baptised. But they weren't asking him to take his trousers down. They were giving him back his rifle.

"Care for it like a woman, pamper it, grease it, and it will watch over you. Good luck, Comrade Yuri."

Well, so I'm a "comrade" now, thought Kempf.

From somewhere a fur coat and hat materialised. That same afternoon Yuri Đuka Kempfosky was marching with the Reds, chatting in a peculiar Slav language with Poles, Ukrainians, Jews and Soviets. The latter were not all Russians by nationality, as was indicated by their slanting eyes and sunken cheeks. Members of Caucasian tribes, like the Croats, fought on both sides.

That's presumably the Asia so feared by the Nazis, thought Kempf. The peoples of the steppe who will defeat the Aryans.

War and Peace

Kempf had first seen a five-pointed star on the destroyed *shturmovik*. And, in the distance, through a telescope, he had sometimes seen the star on a T-34 tank. That was long ago it seemed to him now, when his detachment had secured the supply lines of the S.S. divisions as they hurried towards Kursk. Seeing such a thing in the eyepiece had regularly been an alarm signal. Up to now, Sturmmann Kempf's war journey had been marked by skirmishes with Polish or Ukrainian bandits. The Polish Home Army had not been acknowledged by the Germans as a party in the conflict. They were, officially, all bandits. Kempf had never participated in large-scale combat and his escape from the field hospital had saved him from the disaster at Kursk, not to mention the massacre at Brody, where the S.S. Galicia division had suffered heavy losses. When he was panting through Poland under his black helmet, his unit had always been superior in both equipment and numbers, while military skill went without saying.

But those times had passed. The fortunes of war had completely turned in favour of the Reds. In the village where he had found shelter and spent the winter, everyone knew it. That village, like many others, supported the Home Army. But in this region, the superiority of the Soviets was such that all contacts with the Underground headquarters were broken off.

The villagers had tried to find a contact for "their German",

Jurek Battle, but without success. Kempf guessed they had tried, but no-one ever said so openly.

And so that period of Kempf's destiny was decided in the context of the "global situation" on the battlefields of Poland and Europe. In this, as in his recruitment to the Waffen-S.S., his will was not involved.

He had been accepted into a small, well-armed group led by Russian Army soldiers specially trained for sabotage. They attacked larger formations, striking and withdrawing; but more often they attacked objects: trainlines, military depots.

In its tactics, this Soviet-Polish company was similar to the partisan unit of the Home Army which had attacked the field hospital and had counted on him, Georg Kempf, to augment it, but had been shattered. This formation was more experienced and better equipped. It had left in its wake broken railway lines, demolished bridges, wrecked engines and whole trains. What is more, they fought well, coordinating with similar groups, following the tactics of the Headquarters of the Red Army, doing nothing of their own accord. In that sense, they were not a real guerrilla force, relying on their own judgment. The tactics were similar – wreck and run – but at times Kempf now felt part of more extensive events leading to the likely end of the war and victory.

There were several young Jewish men in the unit, who fought fanatically and often exposed themselves senselessly. They spoke disparagingly of the "darkness and backwardness" of the shtetl and mocked Hasidic mysticism. They were socialists, and the more educated of them, who had studied Marx in German, saw themselves as "doctrinaire", rational communists.

There were also Poles, who had been through all manner of things, and some younger communists, but they were all subdued once the news reached them that Stalin had halted his divisions on the bank of the Vistula, abandoning the Warsaw rebels to their fate. That was taboo; the Warsaw uprising was mentioned only in distant allusions. Commissar Sergey never mentioned it. Commander Alyosha, a young man who had evidently mastered the craft of war brilliantly and so was the authority on military matters, was also silent. He had been parachuted as early as 1942 behind the German lines and the unit he had formed after that was still holding now, inevitably with considerable losses. Only a few of those who had jumped with him were still alive. Alyosha never got involved in political discussions. He was interested in weapons, in the technical side of war, and if anyone had had the nerve to ask him, he would probably have admitted that the Waffen-S.S. fought well, even if their aims were criminal. All in all, he had a respect for the Germans, particularly in matters of technology. For instance, he was inclined to admit that the German Tiger tank was a technological wonder.

Commissar Sergey too was by nature taciturn. He never got involved in discussions either. Judging by the dark rings round his eyes, unusual in such a young man, he must have carried on such discussions with himself. His very appearance corresponded entirely to the Nazi preconception of Soviet commissars: he always wore a leather coat, he had a revolver at his side and he was never parted from his officer's satchel. But Kempf never saw Sergey using his gun to drive anyone to fight. Sergey liked dogs, it turned out that he had spent his childhood in a village near Moscow and that his father, who was a hunter, had a lot of dogs.

In truth, there was no need here to drive anyone to fight. On the contrary, the Jewish lads had sometimes to be reminded not to take needless risks. The Poles fought well, too. But in all military matters, Alyosha had the first and last word.

THE BRASS AGE

Kempf grew close to both Alyosha and Sergey. In Alyosha
Kempf saw a young man like himself, and like those lads who
had been recruited to the Waffen-S.S. as "forced volunteers". He
fought more like a sportsman. Sergey was of course "indoctrin-
ated", but not a bully. Dogs can smell a bad person. Sergey was
not that.

Just as Sergey fitted the Nazi image of a "commissar", he also
corresponded to Kempf's preconception of a communist.

That was vague though. What could he have known about
communists?

In Yugoslavia they were a persecuted sect that, Kempf learned
later, had prepared for the world war by stealing a couple of
field guns from the Royal Army. He had met young people with
leftist inclinations they didn't hide, until laws of the kingdom
proscribed them, forcing them underground, along with Croatian
nationalists for that matter. But it was strange that those young
men and women were either the victims of poverty or indulged
by wealthy families, as though communism attracted extremes.
Kempf could easily understand that the former should be drawn
to the left. He found it harder to grasp why sons and daughters,
brought up with every comfort, should sign up to communism.
As the son of a well-off German tradesman, Kempf had stayed
out of it.

That Kempf had not wanted to take sides politically was not
unwelcome to his father. However, when he noticed that his
son was not turning out to be a "good German", and when the
Kulturbund started bandying its slogans about, his father didn't
particularly encourage him to join it, but he did say: "You can
do nothing on your own!"

Kempf had fallen short in everything. According to the local
Volksdeutsche, he was a bad German; according to the Croats

allied to Frank, he was a bad Croat. According to the communists, he was nothing. The followers of Maček thought that this young man somehow belonged to them, but he had boycotted their approaches as well. In all of this, Kempf was far more interested in girls with whom he acquired his first experiences in the vineyards and farmsteads around Nuštar, the only really important experiences in life. And then the Waffen-S.S. had knocked on his door, having discovered that this young man in fact belonged to them. But he had wanted to remain no-one's.

In a word, Kempf thought about communists the way Hadrian had thought about Christians: that they were a persecuted and unimportant sect of fanatics from the East, of whom there were in Rome admittedly growing numbers, that women were particularly susceptible to them, but they had no chance of taking part in world history about which Rome alone decided.

However, standing beside the destroyed Ilyushin aircraft, where he had first encountered the red five-pointed star, Kempf had wondered whether that star would not in the end be victorious. That was between the collapse at Stalingrad and Hitler's new effort to take the "strategic initiative" once again in the clash of the two huge iron-clad armies at Kursk. But at the same time, the sight of the armoured divisions, in which the T-34 was king, making their inexorable advance after Hitler's "victory" at Kursk, had driven Kempf to wonder seriously who these communists were. From then on he associated communism with tanks. And their arguments were getting stronger by the day.

It sounds strange, but Alyosha too thought in a similar way about communism. It was not far from Lenin's old slogan: Soviets + electrification = socialism, after which, presumably, in the timetable of history, communism would soon follow. Although Alyosha's view of it was translated into the conditions of war. Communism was something that came with technology, with progress. It didn't occur to them that fascism too was a modernist movement based in large part on technical progress in two areas: fighting a war and propaganda. Both movements fought for the masses by similar means. A better life for the masses meant light bulbs in villages. And a tank with a red star that crushed fascists in grand style.

Alyosha did not wish to reply to the question of whether the Tiger tank was better than the T-34. He was objective.

Kursk had answered that question: the Soviets had deluged the Germans with enormous quantities of smelted iron and won the war of materiel. Quantity had definitely dictated the quality of the victory. But the Soviet losses were huge, acknowledged only many years after the war.

For Commissar Sergey, Stalingrad and Kursk were the ultimate proof that in history the law of the kingdom of necessity reigns. He would sometimes move away from the group, reading and reflecting; then Alyosha would say Sergey should be left alone: that he was working on theory.

He was an ideologue, an intellectual, but the mere presence of the commissar ensured that the unit would be equal to its tasks. In Western armies a similar role was played by military chaplains.

Their column was in constant movement, spending the nights where they could.

They were given shelter both gladly and reluctantly. Kempf could clearly see that some Poles were ill-disposed to his unit and that in many cases the door was opened in the dead of night only out of fear. Sometimes they had to take their food, at other times it was offered them, but outside the house. At times they all got drunk, but then again their lair would be wrapped in icy coldness. Their great fear was losing contact with the headquarters of the advancing Soviet formations. But that never happened.

The Polish communists were even more taciturn than the Soviet commissar. Kempf supposed that they were all well informed and that they too knew the law of iron necessity, which would prevail completely in Poland too. But that knowledge did not make them either calmer or happier. Many had passed through the school of the Comintern, which meant they had learned to suppress their doubts.

Some of them were more afraid of peace than war.

The situation on the front was clear: the Germans were withdrawing everywhere, admittedly in an orderly fashion. Both sides had long since scheduled their final encounter: Berlin.

But the *final, decisive battle* would be fought in Poland as a settling of accounts with the Home Army. The Internationale would be largely reinterpreted here.

But for now all roads, of both Germans and Reds, led to Berlin. At the same time as the advance, energetic means were also "putting the liberated hinterland in order", whatever that meant.

When they found themselves for a second time near Auschwitz, now liberated, it occurred to Kempf that they should look at the hotel he had read about in Baedeker in the train on his way to Poland, after leaving Stockerau. No-one in the unit understood what the poet meant. Nor could he himself recall its name. But maybe the Polish citizens of Auschwitz could give him directions?

Saboteurs

Kempf could no longer remember how he had come by the British jacket. It had the insignia of a British major sewn onto it. He thought it suited him.

They must have thrown it to him in one of the distributions of loot. The Germans had probably kept it as a trophy. In war a lot of objects travel around like that and their origin is unknown. And, like objects, people too move around. There were increasing numbers in the reception centres for displaced persons.

And so that jacket too had been displaced, found its way to the unit, and was allocated to Kempf.

Indeed, their company was dressed up in the remnants of uniforms of all the armies then thundering through Poland, fleeing or advancing. That ragbag was unimaginable and in winter made still odder by white sheets.

Today they were moving with the utmost caution, adding to their fantastic uniforms branches graced with fresh green: Birnam Wood, Macbeth's, the one heralding the end of the tyrant. They moved, but in complete silence, along the edge of a forest. In a clearing they flung themselves to the ground because they heard the hum of aircraft. Two Messerschmitt planes passed over their heads. They would come back. The forest was birch, giving little protection, but better than nothing.

However, for now the planes didn't return. It was a long time since they'd seen any here, such was the superiority of the Soviets over the Luftwaffe.

And now on the horizon, the German advance guard they had been expecting appeared. On the road stretching out white below the branches there was a commotion: sun was playing on the polished barrels of heavy guns. Sergey passed his telescope to Kempf without a word, but he clearly expected confirmation from one who would know best what it was: a Waffen-S.S. division.

The black helmets were marching in perfect order. Foolishly exposed to attack from the air – two Messerschmitts would not have been able to defend it – the Waffen-S.S. division was moving west. For months now, towards the German borders. They could still launch attacks, Soviet soldiers were still perishing in large numbers. In Poland there were a few towns left that the Wehrmacht and the Waffen-S.S. were still irrationally defending, regardless of losses. They rarely surrendered then, often fighting to the last man.

It was as if the men around him, as they observed the procession from their hiding place, were expecting him to recognise his own people. Even by name. They didn't say so, it was just Kempf's paranoia. It was clear to everyone that here before them was a Waffen-S.S. division, not admittedly called Galicia, like Kempf's. No matter, he was the only S.S. soldier, albeit penitent, among them. The formation would soon turn right, towards its objective. The Germans were in a hurry, but still maintained impeccable order. What kind of people were they? For those who had taken cover in the birch wood it seemed offensive even that their uniforms were so clean. And so damned uni-form.

Kempf observed the column through binoculars. First the wounded passed, carried on stretchers by men and women with a red cross on their sleeves. Then the supply convoy. Recollections struggled in Kempf, opening windows onto deposits of things he would prefer to suppress. For months he had felt that he was at a crossroads, but that he was incapable of reading the road signs. What he could read were the signs posted by the Red Army propaganda, and they were frequent. BERLIN and the distance in kilometres was written on many signposts.

"7.5 calibre guns," Kempf mumbled, more to himself, but Sergey nodded as though he had been waiting for just that. "Light artillery."

The planes came back. The pilots had evidently not seen the detachment in the young forest, or else, which was more likely, they had a different task: to oversee the withdrawal and protect it from Soviet bombers, and not to incur still greater harm by pursuing bandits. The Soviet squadrons were at the time somewhat further east, where the battle for an important town was taking place.

"Take a good look at them, lads," Alyosha said. "Tonight they'll be blown to smithereens."

They all knew that already, however. Scouts had announced that the division was on the move, and someone on the inside (someone like Ania, where was she?) had said that their rendez-vous point was the railway station, where wagons were ready to transport them.

They knew too that their unit's task was to blow up the railway line, if possible including the engine, at the point where the track left the station.

They returned to the village. They were told to rest until dark, but before that they had to carry out the trial of a certain Vladek, who had stolen a sausage from a peasant who was emphatically loyal to them, which complicated the affair. The atmosphere was full of tension, and their supporters were curious. The trial was brief, as always in war.

Commissar Sergey was, predictably, the main judge. He proposed the death penalty by hanging. In a sense, the whole village was jury. It heard the sentence in silence. Vladek muttered something, cursing the sausage, which was taken as a complaint. The court, which now functioned also as an appeal hearing, withdrew to consult. It consisted of Alyosha and Sergey from the Soviet side and Kempf to represent international public opinion. No Poles. The court modified its judgment: Vladek was ordered to report to every house in the village, wearing a skirt. The village was relieved, Vladek especially.

Kempf recalled how, after he had swallowed the raw potatoes, he had an apron tied round him. Aprons and skirts, that's what's accompanying me through this war.

When they reached the railway line, the moon had started to fade, as they had expected, for their work had to be carried out in the dark. Now they could clearly make out the station lights and the stop lights on red.

The previous day they had observed it well, albeit from a distance. They knew that the track was defended on both sides by bunkers, they could see the black barrels of heavy machine guns poking through their slits. Had anyone asked, Kempf would have replied like a shot: *Maschingewehr zweiundvierzig.*

And they could see guns buried in trenches above the bunkers. The station was well – expertly – fortified, and it was clear that the Germans would defend it as they had those Polish towns where they fought to the last man, in keeping with Hitler's command. It remains a historical puzzle why Hitler thought that dead Germans would not be defeated.

This station had been chosen because, despite the bunkers, it was not as well defended as other sections of the railway. The

Germans had counted on the substantial barracks in the town and its permanent personnel. They felt fairly secure so they had excluded an attack on the track just here as a scandalous outrage that not even the most hardened bandits would consider.

Kempf and the others could now clearly make out the rumble of the engine that was already well stoked.

Now the rail inspection, they all thought.

And, indeed, the rail inspection team emerged from the station, they had their own vehicles, which sounded like cars.

"Blue police," said someone, spitting. Polish flesh that could be blown to bits for their German masters.

"Now for the fireworks."

They were calm and collected. No-one dared utter another word.

The station, the track, the bunkers, the gun nests were illuminated by rockets and for a while it seemed to be broad daylight.

They all knew what they had to do. They had to wait until the inspection cars with the Poles had passed. Then they had to wait until the fireworks had burned out, however attractive they were. And then, once it was dark again, hurry down in total silence and attach a mine to a sleeper beside the track. They had very little time, just seconds. The space around the track had been cleared of any kind of undergrowth, so approaching the track was hazardous. They had to run, creep, crawl some hundred metres. This would be done by the Soviet saboteurs. It was like sport to them. They had clearly been carefully chosen. Built more like runners than boxers. They had practised this same action hundreds of times at training sites in the Russian backwoods. The others, including Kempf, were here to cover their retreat should they be discovered. Each had his own target.

But it seemed to Kempf, although he would not have said so,

that the saboteurs were equally exposed with or without them. It would take a lot of military luck. Every movement, every phase, had to be calculated in seconds.

Now the engine, its cyclopean eye bright, came into the foreground. The composition it was drawing was long. The saboteurs knew that it included tanks, which it was assumed the Germans were withdrawing to their borders. All the heavy armaments of the Waffen-S.S. division, they had been informed, had reached the station the previous day, but from quite a different direction.

They've had enough of blundering through the Polish mud, thought Kempf.

They heard the Germans joking. Was this how they dispelled their fear? Kempf had heard from Poles that when they were surrounded the Germans wept. In this war no-one took prisoners. Perhaps the German soldiers were simply glad to be going home. Kempf was the only one in this detachment, now crouching in the little wood beside the railway, to understand the calls in the night. One would have thought: a group of men on an outing who had already had more than enough of this strange country and its surprises.

Kempf wondered again: What do I have in common with them? A language.

I can hear them and understand them. Until recently I wore their uniform. And if I was with them, I would be looking forward to the venison stew their cooks are preparing for them. There's nothing wrong with venison stew. They're looking forward to leaving, that's clear. They mention the Polish women they've had to abandon to the Russians, and who will soon regret a good German hiding. As the male love muscle is called a tail in German (*Schwanz*), they are probably now, in the half-darkness, verbally wagging those tails more than the railway oil-lamps.

Along with the stories in which the soldiers' tails were twitched, the only other theme was that, as soon as the train set off, they would launch into a binge that wouldn't stop until they reached home.

Kempf had heard about parts of "his" division, the Waffen-S.S. Galicia division, being transferred to the "cursed country of the Balkans".* The Germans sent only "their own" divisions to the Oder. They were afraid of the Soviet offensive, but equally of Allied landings in the Balkans.

Had he stayed with his division, he too could have ended up in the Balkans. That could even have meant that he had returned home.

But what would he have done, as a soldier of the S.S., in the Balkans?

What would have happened would likely have been what his old man had, with foresight, saved him from by paying money from the sale of pig fat for his son not to remain "at home". More precisely, old Kempf had thought: pig fat was to thank for it all, and not his son's year of studying medicine.

Kempf recalled his arrival in Poland, the lamps of the Blue Police, like the ones he could see now, urinating beside the railway, the timid buck ... When had that been?

For a while the train stood calmly in the station, the engine

---

* Parts of the Waffen-S.S. Galicia division were transferred at the end of the war to Austria and Slovenia. The war journey of this division to the east included massacres of civilians: Huta Pieniacka, Podkamien, Palikrowy. The S.S. Prinz Eugen division, composed of "Danubian Schwabians" could "boast" similar achievements. For instance, it left terrible traces in the Cetina region. [Author's note]

trembling, as though gathering momentum before setting off. Then finally it moved.

After it had gone perhaps three hundred metres there was a terrible boom and the engine, after rearing up like a crazed horse, turned onto its side, in a cloud of fire and smoke, along with several wagons. But that was not all: derailed by the impulse of the rearing engine, the munitions wagon also went up. This took the majority of victims. The soldiers who died here were sent to the other world by "friendly fire".

The guards fired furiously from all the bunkers. Furiously and in vain.

Kempf's unit threw off the branches under which they had hidden in the wood and, at a forced march, almost a run, set off into the depths of the forest, friendly, young but at least up to a point protective.

All around them was daylight. Dozens of rockets illuminated their path, and them as well, but they were already too far away. To Kempf his group seemed ghostly, lit up as it was in their dash through the forest, and so motley, as though hurrying to a fancy-dress ball where enchanted beauties awaited them. They were retreating, almost fleeing, but this night in this war belonged to them. And when their pursuers gave up, this victory would be drunk to and no-one would sleep till morning, toasting the friendship under the arms of their nations, cheering their leaders.

They didn't go towards the village, not wanting to expose it to persecution and, without doubt, heavy reprisals. They went in the opposite direction, towards villages they were not yet familiar with.

Kempf had completely forgotten this event. In that sabotage he had not fired a single bullet. Nonetheless, it wasn't clear why he had forgotten the action because after all he had risked his life. It would have sounded well in his account of the commissar's *bumashka,** which he would receive as an important document on his return.

He only recalled all the details when he was told in Vinkovci about the way German soldiers had suffered heavy losses at Vinkovci station, that important railway hub, when the Americans had bombed their army, the remnants of Army Group E, as it retreated from Greece. There was brain spattered everywhere, over the sleepers and rails, and on all the platforms. Yes, people went to look. Even to steal some mementos.

He remembered that reports of this diversion by leaders of the Polish Home Army had mentioned scattered human brains everywhere around the station.

Had not his colleague Mordechai spoken exultantly about God's sparks, in a loud whisper under his hat in the slurry?

Many of those divine sparks had been lost in vain after the defeat of the Warsaw uprising when Stalin had halted his divisions on the bank of the Vistula and so abandoned the fighters of the Home Army to defeat, and the city of Warsaw to total destruction.

The Poles in the unit seemed to Kempf ever more thoughtful, even those who were true fighters and didn't know how to "think politically" or intend to learn. The seed of new personal tragedies was germinating.

How little I learned about Poland, thought Kempf: only what

---

* Russian for "paper, document". Here, something like a testimonial. [Translator's note] could be seen through a gun's sights. It is said that war is a good school. But in war, in a drastically curtailed procedure, one learns only simplified things. Nothing about people or between people is simple, especially what is imposed by force.

Frog

Tanned, thin, not having felt tired for months, she circulated among the brigade headquarters, and only once since she had emerged from the forests had she been in the headquarters of the XI division that fought as part of the First Army. There she was given a document, stating, in black ink and fine calligraphy, that she had freedom of movement between Šid and Sombor, that she worked in security and that she was called . . . Frog.

She remembered the Partisan who had given her that nickname: "You're as pretty as a little frog!" – and with a salvo of laughter, she was immediately rechristened and became secret agent

It's still not time. Jurek Kempf is still dragging himself through the Polish backwoods, waiting for the great victory in which he will be both victor and vanquished.

There is no prospect of Vera and Kempf meeting. From my point of view that is excellent.

The two are nevertheless approaching one another across the expanses of Europe.

If he were to meet Vera now, he would find her strange and foreign.

He would surely have then remembered the tale of the German who fought in the "cursed land of the Balkans", when, in Operation Weiss, the Nazis had "completely suppressed Tito's bandits", and they had then been resurrected in still larger numbers like the phoenix from its own ashes. In the official reports to the Supreme Command of the

Frog. "Little Frog" was out of the question, it wasn't serious enough, that's what one said to a child, and not to a young woman with a pistol at her side. So it was accepted: Frog.

Wehrmacht there is no mention of this, but they do say that the women Partisans were furies.

The artisan, who had seen in her face something of a (little) frog, was thin and slightly built, swarthy, but he had a penetrating gaze and there was something dark about him. He had fought in the XII border brigade. His entire family, and there had been many of them, had been killed in a single day, two years earlier. Everyone in the unit knew this though he had never mentioned it. Only, in his eyes there was something absent and dark. As if he had used them up, worn them out by staring at a cold well. You saw at once that he was in fact looking inward, as though his eyes were turned inside out.

"You're like a little frog!" he had barely muttered, and since he was a man of few words, everyone was amazed that he had said anything at all. And so the nickname stuck, and the skinny man with the absent gaze became her godfather. In the document it was recorded that Frog was born in Slavonski Brod, which was appropriate as there was a lot of water there, and where there was water there were frogs.

From the beginning of January 1945, north of the line along which she was permitted to move as a courier between the headquarters of units of various sizes, thousands of Germans had lain buried behind a few fortified defensive lines: the Srem front,* that expensive victory of Tito's. In the headquarters, everyone was surprised at the tenacity of the Germans because, from a military

---

* Sremski or Syrmian Front in English. [Translator's note]

standpoint, their cause was long since lost: Army Group F was in fact trapped between the Red Army and the Partisan army, which had had armed forces for a long time by now . . . and no fewer than fifty aircraft.

People were surprised as they calculated the enormous sacrifice in young blood spilled here, some thought needlessly, for a victory that was already won. The Germans had hardly any tanks, their Tigers and Jaguars, along with the T-34 best panzers in this war were being devoured by rust in the endless steppes around Kursk, where, in Russian territory, elite Waffen-S.S. divisions had also remained, having been despatched, often in complete formation, to the next world. In addition, while the Soviets could produce ever more tanks, the Germans no longer could. There were some similarities between the massacre at Kursk and the one along the battlefields of the Srem front: the Red Army had simply smelted the German iron spearhead made up of S.S. armoured divisions with thousands of tons of bombs and grenades, and then the Generalissimus had sent in a mass of infantry troops several times greater than those of Hitler's generals to finish the job, with complete disregard for their own losses. In other words, in all reckonings of this final German catastrophe in the East, there was a huge disproportion between the losses on each side, in which the Soviet losses, in manpower and materiel, were several times greater . . .

Was the breach of the Srem Front, carried out in April 1945, so essential that the losses were unimportant? A great many families were sent wooden coffins.

Here, in the brigade headquarters, such questions were not asked. Few historians have ever crouched in the trenches they later described.

The horizon was all pink, this time not with shells. It was quiet,

the red clouds promised fine weather. One could hear the whinnying of horses, the clinking of dishes, the army was preparing
to rest. For a moment, everything seemed idyllic, as though this
was a group of students on an outing. Frog leaned against a tree
in which there was still warmth from the spring sun, watching
her fellow fighters ... How young we all are, she thought ...
how unjust it would be to perish now when it's all over.

A frontiersman approached her, tall, burly, rugged.

"I hear you've never fired from what you've got in your holster!" he said, putting his arm round her waist, presumably
reaching for her pistol.

"Get lost!"

"I only wanted to fire it . . ."

In every military collective in the world this would have been
followed by laughter.

The frontiersman lifted the pistol up to a ray of sun and examined it with respect.

"D'you know that S.S. officers are given something like this?"

"Yes."

"Have you ever seen an S.S. soldier?"

"No."

"I've got them here on mine . . ." The man showed her six slits.

Will anyone ever believe, thought Frog, that for weeks I crept
between the lines, mostly at a time that was neither night nor
day, with a pistol in my holster I didn't know how to fire? When
I have children, will they believe me? Will anyone believe what
I saw in Stara Gradiška?

In the early dawn of that day which was now coming to an
end, she had left through the gate of a small farm after she had
been offered warm milk from a newly milked cow and eggs ...
The villagers had tried to look friendly, but that effort was too

obvious, not spontaneous. In the evening, when she had knocked on their door, they had taken her in at once, no questions asked, but they were and remained somewhat reserved. Frog was going to ask them where their children were. But that was the previous night; in the morning, as soon as she woke up, her curiosity woke as well.

"Tell me, they've taken everything from you except one cow. Did they also take your sons?"

There was no reply. She was offered a cup of warm milk. She noticed that the farmer, who was in his fifties, was looking at her holster. For them she was armed and therefore dangerous. And so young!

"Is it true that your people will take land from the peasants?" the farmer said as they were parting.

"On the contrary: the communists will give you land."

"But we've got enough land for the number of hands left in this house."

"Don't be afraid. There will be freedom and land for everyone."

Unfortunately, after the war the new government's distribution of land policy was not under Frog's jurisdiction.

On leaving the farm Frog set off through the forest. The secret agent had learned to pay attention to her own safety. She had learned to listen, she had learned to distinguish noises produced by the movement of animals from those of humans.

At headquarters they had told her that the German army had infiltrated small groups of soldiers specially trained in various horrors and that they were merciless. The name of the unit dispersed behind the front was the South-East Hunting Group. Many of them were battle-hardened S.S. soldiers with arms steeped in blood to the elbow. But they told her that their side would also have no mercy when they caught them. Although, as a rule, they no longer killed prisoners because now they could solve the problem of feeding them.

And so Frog, young, thoughtful, wandered between the lines, seeking – what? Whom did she wish to meet?

She was twenty years old. She had seen and been through a lot. She was filled with unease.

Sometimes she lay down on the ground that the spring sun had already dried out and warmed. She caught herself watching ants, not that they were the object of her scouting duties.

The ant wars seemed to be over. The workers dragged twigs and other matter, they were building a new anthill. The fertilised queens were producing a new nation. That nation emerged from their mucus well prepared and with a deep understanding of epoch-making changes. And it did not ask strange questions about what was essential.

Frog now felt that something was flowing out of the earth, infusing her completely, and that she was but a part of that general flowing and infusion. This was not yet the joy of victory, it was a different kind of joy that sent shivers up her spine. But it was the intimation of a great victory and of all those joys that are the privilege of youth.

The hero she was waiting for could definitely not have been a runaway S.S. soldier in rags, hiding like a persecuted wild animal in the background of decisive battles. Nor, of course, could it have been the bearded man who had embraced her insolently with the transparent excuse he just wanted to see the make of the pistol at her side.

She wanted slowly . . . slowly . . . because she felt all time was now hers, that up to now everything had been forcibly speeded up, and now even the days in the camp, however long they were, seemed like just one day. Now she wanted to slow everything down, and what she wanted was the opposite of all that was going on around her; because in all of it there was a kind of speeding-up. The anthill was waking after the catastrophe.

So, who was she waiting for?

Almost everyone she had worked with underground was dead. Some had succeeded in joining the Partisans, but nothing was known of them. She knew of one, who had been her superior; he had lost a leg. So, alive, but on crutches. Another had thrown himself onto a grenade when he was surrounded and blown himself up.

In a few months, however, the S.S. soldier who had fled the flag would find himself here, not far away, on the opposite bank of the Drava river, if he survived hundreds of possible unwanted encounters.

It was absolutely certain that she was not waiting for him.

Moreover, according to the rules of her unit, which did not need to be written, and still more according to the rules she had acquired through her own experience, if there had been such a meeting, Frog would have taken out her pistol and fired, even if she didn't know how to.

Many women who had joined the movement had done it. Some, like Frog, were virtually still young girls. Not only in the battles coded Operation Weiss in the reports of the Supreme Command of the Wehrmacht.

Victory

Sergey Abramovich was a Jew, born in Smolensk. The other Jews in the unit were Poles, from Warsaw. In addition to their Jewish origin, they were connected by a sense that they were more enlightened than the Orthodox community. Kempf used to go with them to the shtetls scattered all over Galicia east of Kraków, and everywhere they were burned to the ground. These Jews dreamed of new towns, with broad avenues, modern traffic, without synagogues or ritual baths.

Hence the men judged those ruins with a purely military lack of sentiment: could a machine gun be dug in here and concealed, did this ruin offer a good prospect of concentrated fire and was there protection from air attack? The wretched fate of the shtetl didn't particularly motivate them. They had plentiful supplies of hatred.

The Warsaw men were all the sons of doctors or lawyers for whom in the independent Poland of Marshal Piłsudski life had not necessarily been bad. The Jews of their fathers' generation were veterans of World War I; many were proud of the days when Poland celebrated its independence (especially the day of the "Miracle on the Vistula" when, in 1920, the Poles had sent the Red Army packing) and brought out into the light of day the highest military decorations of the Polish state. When the Polish fascist Falangists began beating up Jews in Warsaw, the well-integrated Jews, just like those in the Reich, considered it a passing epidemic. They thought of popular antisemitism as something like mange or an itch and themselves circulated antisemitic jokes. No people are better at laughing at themselves than the Jews. By the time the laughter died down, it was already too late.

Sergey Abramovich was sent from the U.S.S.R. through secret channels behind the German lines. Kempf could not imagine that ungainly gangling man doing a parachute jump. But the Warsaw Jews had a wide choice: they could, with a little luck, join one of the units composed of Jews, overseen by the Jewish Military Union (ZZW),* but they wanted to see themselves as part of a wider movement and so they sought contact either with the Home Army or directly with the Soviets. They believed in the alloy that would consist of a lot of different "human material". These young Jewish men wanted to forge a new community in which every specific affiliation would be more a matter of folklore than anything else.

But now that new community was making itself known with tanks. Love and tanks didn't go together, thought Kempf, and later events proved him right.

Kempf thought a lot about the unusually colourful composition of the unit with which he had spent nearly a year behind the Waffen-S.S. divisions that were still fighting. Why, in that patchwork he himself was just one patch of a strange colour it would be hard to name. Just as he had once tried to imagine himself as a tiny dot getting lost in the vast green of the geographical map over which was written U.S.S.R., so he now endeavoured to get some distance and properly understand the place of his own little dot in all of this.

---

* Żydowski Związek Wojskowy.

On one occasion there was a dangerous conversation.

In one of their breaks, in a hiding place that was so close to the German lines that when a north wind blew they could hear the Germans swearing, Commissar Sergey looked closely at Kempf for no particular reason and pierced him with the question: "And how did you, Comrade Kempf, end up in Poland? And why Poland, and why near Kraków?"

In a moment of awkward silence, the always collegial, smiling Alyosha leaped to Kempf's defence: "A woman, Sergey! *Kobiet!** Comrade Kempf came to us in Poland on an amorous excursion."

"In 1943?"

"Love conquers all!"

In truth, Kempf had told Alyosha, to whom he had grown close, about those few nights he had spent with Sadowska. But he had not said that it was in an S.S. field hospital. In principle, he had not spoken about his real wound, nor of his other, symbolic wounds. He had once begun to tell Commissar Sergey about coming across Jews dancing in the forest, and then "falling" into a ritual of theirs, but Commissar Abramovich was listening with less than half an ear.

"And that was after Stalingrad?" Sergey went on digging.

Give it a rest, thought Kempf to himself.

"Love, Sergey, love!" Alyosha insisted, a good lad and an excellent soldier, whose fate would be so cruel.

So, he had once talked to Alyosha about Sadowska; shamelessly, the way a man talks about a woman who is very good in bed. Both he and Alyosha were fairly aroused by just talking about it.

In essence, he had said nothing. And they had become friends.

---

* Polish for "woman". [Author's note]

Kempf realised there would always be things he had lived through that he wouldn't be able to talk about. With time he arrived at a technique for producing half-truths. For instance, after the liberation he used to say, and even write in his official biography: "I spent the war in camps." At the level of the mere words this was true. The German word for a military bivouac and a concentration camp was the same. But anyone in the late 1940s who had an opportunity or an official need to read such a biography would have thought that Kempf had been in one of the German extermination camps in the East. That the same word was used for a "military camp" at that time would not have occurred to many. Or Kempf, already back in Yugoslavia, would write: "By force of circumstance, I fought in a unit of Soviet-Polish partisans." What extraordinary force of circumstance that was, no-one asked. In the middle of the war that was raging, a powerful hand had borne him away from Nuštar (neither town nor village), where the only object of interest was the ruin of a Benedictine monastery, and tossed him more than a thousand miles away to the east, just a month after Paulus had surrendered at Stalingrad.

Out of the war, sewn into his British major's jacket, Kempf brought a document: the commissar's redeeming confirmation that would save his life, otherwise worth less than a pipe of tobacco.

But for the time being he was still trailing along behind German lines, with that small Soviet-Polish-Jewish unit. He rarely fired his *vierundvierzig* rifle because shooting was not their main job. They were concerned with things on a far bigger scale.

That spring of 1945 was a strange time in the Polish lands. Wind, slush, sudden snow, abrupt warmth, south wind; all the seasons in one. There were no more Germans in Poland. Talk began of demobilising the Polish partisans. Many of them didn't know what to do with themselves, overcome by a feeling that they were suddenly redundant. For them, the terrible war had been better.

Former Sturmmann Kempf was experiencing perhaps the most testing times in this war. The unit over whose ideological purity Commissar Sergey Abramovich watched, and which had been led through hell, with few losses, by Commander Alyosha, was now engaged in consolidating conditions, whatever that meant.

In the first instance, that consolidation actually meant settling accounts with the remnants of the Home Army.

Prisons, abandoned bunkers, barracks in a pitiful condition, all those cursed places that the Germans had used for "isolating" Polish patriots, were now again filled with people who considered themselves patriots. Kempf was always astonished anew at their youth. The war in Europe had been waged, lost or won, by his generation.

Once again trains filled up going in the same direction as those that had just the day before taken people to German extermination camps. The trains were now making far longer journeys.

Transylvania = Transiberia.

The leaders of the Underground would be tricked into being taken to Moscow so that the Home Army was left leaderless. Sergey Abramovich may have received a radiogram about that; Alyosha was not informed, still less Kempf.

A normal state of affairs, thought Kempf, like a yawning soldier on guard duty trying to shorten the time of his watch with all kinds of thoughts. And not knowing whether he was right.

In the end all history is reduced to one simple equation: power prevails. Whoever is stronger wins. Everything else, but everything, is just embellishment of that ugly truth.

Kempf went for a brief rest after he had stood on guard for two hours.

He fell into a first sleep, the sweetest, helped by the vodka he had drunk with his friend Alyosha. He hadn't told him anything.

Infernal firing from all manner of guns began. In the dark, Kempf reached for his rifle, he thought it must be a large-scale attack. Perhaps bandits, perhaps Ukrainian nationalists? The supply of enemies was still great. The sky was glowing, washed with every possible colour.

On all fours, Kempf crawled out from under a roof, which had probably been the roof of a stable. In what direction should he fire? Where were the others? Why hadn't anyone woken him?

The scene that he now saw was unbelievable: in the middle of the shooting – poorly orchestrated, but powerful, the bass of field guns, the soprano of attack rifles, the chattering alto of machine guns – in an open clearing, soldiers from his unit were dancing ... the *kazachok*. And a "babushka" was casting off layers of several uniforms that must have belonged to various armies, including a scorched tent flap and some civilian clothes, like a butterfly emerging from a chrysalis. The woman who a moment before had seemed like a plump and unattractive Amazon now suddenly shone with femininity. In the luxurious light a white, shapely woman's leg gleamed ...

To Kempf, a famished male, this seemed like a supernatural revelation.

victory loves garish colours

Berlin had fallen

Alyosha danced danced danced
with the alluring Russian girl who had until now
hidden in the "babushka".

Would all that had been hidden in the war now emerge and would it be lovely even from close to?

Alyosha was not a man of questions, but of answers.

Sergey Abramovich had left before dawn. As many times before, he had gone to do theoretical work. He was the only one who understood how difficult it was to ensure that victory did not vanquish the victors. The Red Army was victorious. It had freed Poland, but for the majority of Poles this was just another episode in their enslavement. Sergey Abramovich felt the hatred of many Poles that seemed to be growing out of the soil. He had definitely not sown it, but it was his task to deal with it. Where necessary stifle it. But only if it could not be done any other way. The iron law of necessity did its job, but, here and there, it needed a little help; the machine of history had now and again to be greased, part of it rejected and replaced with something new.

Kempf had no feelings of triumph, just overwhelming weariness, but he couldn't fall asleep. For the first time he thought how much he hated gunfire. And that would remain with him until the end of his life. From day one, Kempf had a problem with his victory. The victors did not make it easier for him. On the contrary.

Essentially, Kempf's joy was a little subdued compared to his fellow fighters. And he felt that he was now beginning to understand them better, especially those who made up the Polish component in his Soviet-Polish unit. But Poland had many components.

Some of these men had fought with insane courage. Many had fallen. Many of the survivors now wanted swift demobilisation. But some didn't want that. They didn't know what awaited them in their villages. Many were joining the new government, often as its executive. There were also true believers, authentic communists. Things were easier for them now; later it would become more difficult.

The Swallowed Railway

Alyosha's unit was falling apart. The Polish communists were going off to new tasks. The Jews, by no means all, joined the NKVD. Leather coats were now a prerequisite. For the time being they remained with the unit which accompanied them on searches and arrests. Kempf had had more than enough of war. He wanted to go home. Everyone throughout displaced, dispersed Europe wanted to go home, even those who did not know where home was. Even those who knew that their homes were no more.

Everything was moving.

In the unit, there was a departure every day. They drank as never before. Kempf

Now everyone, including Kempf, could see where Ania Sadowska's heroic resistance had led her. Soon her leaders would be invited to Moscow, where they would be immediately imprisoned. There was no Canossa that could at that moment satisfy the steel Generalissimus.

Ania Sadowska had taken care of wounded men who were criminals and the deadly enemies of Poland. She had signed up to the cause of Polish nationalism, that is: fascism. She was an enemy of the Soviet Union, a bourgeoise, a German whore. In France those like her were shaved to the skull and hung on posts, sometimes stoned.

That is roughly what Commissar Sergey Abramovich told Kempf about Ania Sadowska, more in gestures than words.

What had Kempf wanted

held his own in competition with the Russians and Poles. Commissar Sergey, remarkably, drank just as much. He even maintained that good ideas came to him when drunk. What kind of ideas, he didn't say.

Searches and arrests at dawn sickened Kempf. What had he to do with them? Why, they were civilians. If the war was over, why was the army arresting civilians, what was the army doing now that the war was over? The Home Army, their deadly enemy, had announced its demobilisation. Germany had signed a declaration of defeat. What was happening here? Should not a terrible war that had so tormented Poland come to an end in Poland first of all? Did the Soviets not wish to go to their homes and their wives? What were they still doing in Poland?

What was he, former Sturmmann Georg Kempf, still doing in Poland? Searching

to say to him and fortunately not been able to summon the courage? At times it's sensible to be a coward.

He had wanted to tell him that this woman had got him out of the Waffen-S.S.

And then what?

He wanted to say that she had wished to connect him with the Polish Underground, but then he bit his tongue.

And the contact might have worked.

I know, but Kempf doesn't know, and Sadowska was unable to call to him from behind the bars of the cattle truck, that just a dozen kilometres from the hamlet where he had asked for a cup of milk as a password, a unit of the Home Army was coming into being, which was supposed to be named after the old Polish regiments from earlier wars. More precisely the regiment that participated in halting the invasion by the Red Army of Warsaw in 1920, which event is considered in Poland a miraculous deliverance by order of Heaven.

Kempf didn't utter a word of this.

Then Alyosha began scampering beside him, a plucky fighter, who had learned the and arresting. That was not heroic.

With such thoughts, he was marching with his unit towards the railway station they were to protect for a time from bandits who had a base in the nearby forest. The bandits were young men from the Underground army who refused to give up their weapons. They had attacked the station the previous day; there had been dead and wounded.

The headquarters of the National Army, in an agreement with the Soviets, had now despatched Alyosha's unit to that station. Only the day before, that same unit had attacked stations such as this one, successfully capturing them from the Germans. And

craft of war well and frequently put his head on the line.

Now he was looking around him dejectedly, afraid of his own shadow as he walked alongside the train carrying Sadowska to Western Siberia.

Alyosha and I, the Unborn, know what Kempf could not have known: that a whole division of the NKVD was operating in that territory.

Kempf would remember Ania's gaze through the bars of the cattle truck that had begun to move, the gaze of a cow being taken to slaughter, aware of it with animal instinct.

Now the Petrarchans of all countries will leap up: how could Kempf dare compare a woman he had loved to a cow? Wait, gentlemen Petrarchans: the ancient Greeks called their heavenly patron Hera "the ox-eyed".

now the sabotage unit was to defend the position along the railway, just as the Germans had done until the previous day.

Kempf recognised the station instantly. It was, and still is today, on the line Warsaw–Białystok. It is the line that at one point turns right, looking from the perspective of the engine driver, and leads to Treblinka. His colleague Leon Mordechai knew all about that.

At the station, a composition of badly rusted cattle trucks was waiting. There was just the occasional opening in the trucks, covered with barbed wire.

Beside the train there was an armed guard, Red Army soldiers. The men were complaining, urinating by the track, trudging up and down. From his post, Kempf couldn't see who was being protected by so many guns.

The train wasn't moving, the noonday spring sun blazed as in the middle of summer.

It must be hellishly hot in the trucks, thought Kempf. As soon as his replacement guard arrived, he hurried towards the trucks.

That isn't her, it can't be. It mustn't be.

Behind one of the openings covered in wire was a face framed in short hair, almost boyish.

Kempf thought for a moment. His days in the forest had sharpened his sense of risk, of danger, in this case not for himself but for the woman sitting in the cattle truck. Perhaps it would be better to try something neutral, without emotion, with Sergey?

There was an expression of indescribable disappointment on the woman's face when Kempf hurried away. On either side of the train, there were now only guards with machine guns.

Commissar Sergey had a table in the station master's office. There were telephones on the table, several of them. Kempf looked alternately at the train, fearful that it would start to move, and at the telephones that kept ringing. He saluted the commissar, who didn't raise his head. In front of him was an ashtray and empty packet of Kazbeka. He's really been smoking today, thought Kempf.

Five minutes passed before Sergey told him to sit down. Then Alyosha came in with a problem. Kempf was drenched from head to foot. He no longer knew what he had intended to say to the commissar.

He took his leave, touching his cap with his fingers, and followed Alyosha. He felt that he might understand him better. After all, he had told him several times about his amorous adventure, only of course he hadn't mentioned that it took place in an S.S. field hospital. And he didn't mention that now either, how could he explain to Alyosha that he wanted to save a nurse who had tended the wounds of Nazis? How could he explain that he wanted to save a brave woman who had worked for the Underground? Officially, of course, she had tended the wounds of German fascists, but through her organisation she had belonged to the Polish fascists.

Kempf was stuttering about Sadowska when Alyosha suddenly turned pale.

"Keep your nose out of others' business!" he whispered. "No-one can help her, and definitely not Sergey if he is the NKVD. It's good that you didn't say anything to him today. You were lucky. And, in general, Yuri, it's good that you never told him anything. He knows, but pretends not to because it's easier for him that way. Your love story is naive. A child would understand how you ended up in this Polish stew. We were watching you from the start. When you proved yourself, Sergey sent a favourable report on you."

"Where did he send it?"

"Where he had to. That's all you need to know, don't make waves."

Appalled, Kempf realised that Alyosha, this young man who had destroyed bridges, who had blown up trains, looked death in the eye innumerable times, was now trembling like a leaf at the very mention of the NKVD.

"Come on, my boy, pull yourself together. Use your head!"

Kempf realised that Alyosha was suppressing fear, more his

own than Kempf's.

The composition of cattle trucks, crammed with men and women designated for deportation, begging for water from anyone who walked by the track, began to move.

For a while Kempf ran beside the track waving. The worst thing was that he could not be sure Ania had seen him.

"Distance is swallowing the train . . ." Kempf was mortified that he hadn't thought of anything other than one Croatian classic line of verse.* Such ornamentation does not suit our times, he thought.

He was to report to Commissar Abramovich the next morning. Late the night before an utterly exhausted Sergey had come to his bedside and in a subdued tone had said to him: "Forget reporting, man. Come to my office in the morning, we'll have a coffee. Your *bumashka*† is ready, it's in my drawer."

For no particular reason, he laughed. "Remind me to sign it."

The commissar had recently taken to laughing for no reason. Who laughs without a reason? Children and madmen.

Kempf woke up with a terrible headache although he had drunk virtually nothing the night before.

"I betrayed her! I'm heading to one end of the Earth, Ania to the opposite end. Transylvania. Transiberia."

When dawn finally came, Sergey, freshly shaved and evidently in a good mood, was waiting in the doorway of the station master's office. For some reason, he wanted them to go in together and, until they parted, to erase the difference between subordinate and higher ranked. They shook hands like friends, and

---

* From the Croatian poet Matoš's poem "Nokturno". [Author's note]

† Russian: paper, document, identification paper. [Author's note]

Kempf embraced Alyosha as though he were his brother.

They all went off for a plate of barley porridge fried with bacon that the Polish cook had made in Jurek's honour.

"I've got something for you," said Alyosha, as Kempf was getting onto the bicycle they had "requisitioned" at the station for him, and he pushed a packet of Kazbek cigarettes into the pocket of the famous jacket.

That day marked the beginning of the anabasis of Đuka Georg Jurek Battle Yuri Kempf.

The Doll's House

They spent the whole night in a field, and it was one of the longest in their lives. Everything around them had turned the luxurious green of May, but the sky was clear so they had been chilly. While shots still echoed from the direction of the town, couriers brought news that the resistance was waning. Although there were still uncleared points, informers confirmed that the enemy had evacuated Zagreb and that quite a number of civilians had left with them.

Estimates of how many succeeded one another, each different from the last. Some maintained that the town was empty, others that only those with something to fear had fled with the army. But then, no-one could say for certain how many of those there were. The main ratcatcher had certainly wanted to empty the town completely, but he hadn't succeeded.

That thinking was a stop-gap solution: Pavelić's army, and those who had served his state along with those who had simply been swept along, hurried to give themselves up to the Anglo-Saxons. Horse-drawn carts were filled with all kinds of things, crammed trucks blared their horns at places where the traffic was blocked. The only things they couldn't take with them were their houses and apartments. A small number still believed the main ratcatcher and they set off stylishly, with one suitcase of jewellery or cash. They were convinced that the Anglo-Saxons would not want to see a Soviet republic in the Balkans.

Then the order came to move and the Partisan army set off at a brisk march. The limbs of the soldiers, who included quite a number of women, seemed numbed by the cold and night damp, but now the sun promised a fine day.

After crossing the bridge, which by some miracle was still whole, the column in which Frog was marching came out onto Savska Street. A song was ordered, so they sang. To start with, just after the bridge, there were very few civilians; they stood to one side, some waved. But that's alright, the town's still asleep, thought Frog.

As they entered the town, more and more buildings rose from the ground, and the shanties disappeared; it seemed to Frog that the houses were stretching after sleep and taking a bit of exercise in the morning mist. Very rarely did they hear a shot or even a round of machine-gun fire. Strange, thought Frog: there are still people here who don't realise the war is over and their cause lost.

There were more people on the pavements. Frog endeavoured to look straight ahead, at the back of a comrade walking in front of her with a machine gun over his shoulder. But she still saw the occasional pair of eyes watching fearfully from the pavement.

From the avenue of people that was becoming ever more dense, a little girl ran out and gave her a bunch of flowers.

Frog tried to recall how it had been when the Wehrmacht entered Zagreb: she had seen footage in the cinema. All her people had then waved wildly. But later it was officially affirmed that the joy of the citizens of Zagreb was fake, that it was all a Gestapo frame-up.

As they came closer to the town centre and main square, even more people waved and threw flowers to them.

A little worm of doubt crept into Frog: was this organised? But then she managed to catch someone's eye in which there was joy, unfeigned, real.

People are always either this or that, thought Frog. That was life.

Beside her a woman, who had until then been trying to march and keep up with them as best she could, collapsed. The column stopped, a man in the crowd shouted: "Water! Give her air!" No-one had known until then that she was epileptic.

The column settled and carried on.

Out of a side street, a fighter ran up waving as though he had gone mad. "Take cover!"

And indeed a bullet hissed after him, but missed. More bullets began hissing over their heads, a sound that they knew all too well.

The man who had run up pointed to a window: there, between the open panes, peered a black gun barrel.

Holding onto their caps, several soldiers, hugging the facade, hurried into the building from which the shots continued to come, but randomly. The street emptied in a moment.

A plump woman, with curlers in her hair, rushed out of the entrance shouting: "Don't, don't shoot! That's my son, my boy Oliver! He's crazy!"

There was a moment of ominous silence.

"Get away, everyone," the woman went on, "he's got a grenade!"

Which immediately afterwards bloomed an intense red, shattering glass, pieces of which fell onto the pavement like hail.

"Sweet Jesus!" sobbed the woman. "He's done it, he's killed himself! He threw himself onto the grenade."

A fire started in the room, so a few men stayed to put it out. They tried to comfort the sobbing woman.

"And who are you? Who sent you here? Are you Russians?"

The company, including Frog, continued on their way. It appeared that Savska Street ended here and poured, like a river, into the lake of a large square.

On the square was a large yellow building: the Croatian State Theatre.

There did not seem to be anyone in the yellow building. On its facade, above a little angel trumpeting, a flag with a star was fluttering cheerfully in the spring breeze.

This was the building, thought Frog, where the glass woman lived before she came to us in the forest. She had the whole building to herself, just as in the forest she had her own tent, where her dinner and no doubt breakfast were served to her in bed. Here people like her lived and for days on end, dancing and singing. These were a better class of people. Now they were perhaps hiding, crouching in the cellar because they didn't know what was going to happen and whether anyone else would need their art. It was a doll's house. Just like those sold at fairs, on church feast days, by wandering Jews.

Frog remembered the little silk slippers and ribbons wrapped round their ankles, the little skirts made of gauze, of which there was never enough: the eternal wail of the medical corps. But the glass woman had as much of that gauze as she wanted. She remembered the little ballet shoes, looking down at her legs, swollen from marching, in their white woollen socks that disappeared into boots, fit for marching but not for dancing. Male legs, full of lumps, swellings and blisters.

Inside the building was a large stage surrounded by boxes. Frog had never peered into it in her life. She had only been in Zagreb once before now, but then she and her mother had no time for the theatre. They had been visiting her brother, who was being treated for tubercular open cavities in the Brestovac sanitorium. Between arriving by the morning train and leaving in the evening – they couldn't afford to stay overnight – there was no time for the theatre. But Frog clearly remembered that one day of hers in Zagreb, in the late afternoon when they had come down from Sljeme hill but it was too early for the train, she had walked around the yellow building that had seemed to her a hermetically sealed box.

But from inside had come the voices of singing rehearsals; a woman had shrieked, almost sobbing, returning always to the same place, and then starting all over again, it must have been a death, or some other great sorrow, which had to be drummed into the head of someone else, while a man buzzed like a bumble-bee flying round a room unable to find the way out, probably from jealousy. Vera wished a giant would come and lift the roof off the yellow building, so that beneath it little men and women could be seen practising assiduously, apparently forever calling for help, and then the jealous bumblebee would presumably fly out.

Vera noticed that the large door at the northern entrance to the theatre was being opened: so, someone was in there. Perhaps someone had slept through the war in there?

A small man in a black frock coat, fairly threadbare, came out and peered at the column, where it had stopped, adjusting his top hat. He peered at the sun as though he had been asleep for a thousand years.

The man stretched and disappeared, closing the door behind him.

Just like a cuckoo that pops out of a clock on the hour, thought Vera. What had he come to announce? What time was it here?

Then she waved her hand to bring her thought to some kind of conclusion:

Well, let it be as it is! Although all this is strange, and maybe not right, and though the burden of struggle and suffering, in which there is a lot of injustice, is not always evenly distributed, the woman who danced in the middle of the forest was nonetheless a higher being from the other side of reality, which could not possibly have been more terrible. The laws that apply to us who covered ourselves with the sky do not apply to her. Why, even last night, preparing to enter the city, we polished our boots with wheel grease, washed in barrels brought to us by peasants, ate in haste what we always ate, no luxury, no relaxation in victory, and we did all that in order, as the commander put it, to "enter our capital city as an organised army that guarantees order and peace, and justice for all who have not transgressed against justice . . . to enter that city as citizens and not peasants . . ."

In the glow of victory, the man had forgotten that Tito's army was composed largely of the sons and daughters of peasants.

So what, Frog forgave him in her thoughts: now we must stand on tiptoe, look higher than ourselves . . .

Vera recalled that this was exactly what the porcelain woman had done then, dancing on logs in the middle of the forest. She had been able to stand upright on her toes, which ordinary mortal women couldn't do. That must hurt, but some things are worth enduring for the sake of beauty.

Later in her life, Vera was unable to recall the function of the man who saw her in his office that same afternoon when the liberators had marched into Zagreb. It was obvious that the office had been quickly evacuated by those who had fled. Everywhere were piles of papers they had not succeeded in burning. The man in uniform was sitting over a heap of documents and told her to sit down.

"So, Frog, how does victory feel? Would you like some coffee?"

Vera declined. It was only later that she came to love coffee to the extent that she could not begin her day properly without it.

"You'll take courses now. You need to complete your secondary education. You'll do that in Vinkovci. It'll be quick and painless. I'm told you're hardworking, that you know how to study and you cotton on quickly. What are you thinking of doing with your life? Come on, tell me, what's your heart's desire?"

She was grateful that he had made things easy for her. But Vera well knew, because others had passed on the contents of conversations like this, that in the end the Party would tell her what she would do in life.

"I'd like to do something in the arts. Literature, but only the greatest. Sometimes I think I would like to study acting."

"Sometimes this, sometimes that."

"I think I'm too old for ballet."

"What do you mean, too old? You have to want, you have to dare!"

"So, I'd like to study something, only in the arts."

"Alright, I get it. Tell me, Frog, how about this: last week when we set off towards Zagreb and passed through all those many villages, what did you see there of the comforts enjoyed by the civilised world? Think, Frog! I don't mean cultured, just civilised. To put it simply! Let's be modest, let's not aim too high! You say nothing. Let me tell you. You saw windows without lights. Broken electricity cables if there were any at all. Burnt telegraph poles if there were any. And you saw villages where there had never been cables or telegraph poles. Right?"

Vera nodded.

"Do you know, Comrade Frog, what a plug is?"

"Yes."

"And what about a fuse?"

"Yes."

"Have you ever in your life replaced a burnt-out fuse?"

"My brother always did that."

"There you are. You need to learn. We have to bring electricity to every home. We need to e-lec-tri-fy our whole long-suffering country."

"How long will that take?"

"Electricity runs at a speed of 300,000 kilometres a second. Did you know that? No. A fine speed, you'll agree. Good for those of us who are now in a hurry. But that only applies when you have electricity. And in order to have it, you need to build dams and weirs, make batteries . . . that's all current, even if it's water; you have to have turbines; then wires, poles, and, finally, you have to have fuses and plugs. You'll study electrical engineering."

Her world went dark, as though the power had gone off.

She registered to study electrical engineering because she was a disciplined member of the Party and because it was the only way she could get coupons for food in a canteen.

In the office, Vera placed her trophy pistol Frommer 7.65 mm, which she had never fired and did not know how to fire, and got a receipt for it. Not long afterwards she registered for a degree in electrical engineering although she had never changed a fuse. She was given a student card.

She had the impression that the moment she laid the holster with her weapon down on the desk in front of the unknown Party comrade, a little frog, a tree frog, hopped out of her military jacket onto it.

And in truth, at university and in her later life, no-one ever addressed her as Frog again.

Georg Kempf's Anabasis

I can go no further today, thought Kempf, getting off his bicycle. This Rosinanta of mine may fall to bits under me.

There was a stream with tidy banks ahead so he walked over and lay down on the embankment.

It was silent, everything was settling down, waiting for dusk and the beginning of the nocturnal hunt. He disturbed an owl in a thicket which moved soundlessly to another tree. It had never occurred to him that owls fly soundlessly. How do they manage it? How good it would be to travel through the world soundlessly, invisible. Even the owl's prey perish in a nicer way, they vanish without warning. The creator did a good job, if one had to perish.

Like the Greek mercenary and writer Xenophon, Kempf now set off towards the south and the warm sea. Admittedly he would not cry "*Thalassa, Thalassa!*" like the Greek. But at the end of his anabasis he would wash in the waves of the Drava river, shave and enter Tito's country like a young bridegroom. Before that he would see Central Europe in flames.

And a great deal more that, in later life, he would most gladly forget. He had been away a long time, and he would have to present himself as one who had returned from the dead.

His first impressions were not promising. In addition, his birth certificate aroused suspicion.

That was why it was sensible that he kept his *bumashka*. That was now his "birth certificate",

It would be like dying in your sleep.

But maybe the dreams of those who die in their sleep do herald it? What are such fateful dreams like?

He had heard innumerable times a story that was part of his family's lore: one evening his ancestor Kempf had stoked the fire well and, instead of sitting beside it and smoking his pipe, he had said: "Children, I'm not feeling too good, my heart is thumping, I'm going to doze a little." In the morning his eyes were wide open. The Kempfs die in their beds. That ancestor Kempf had had his fill of travelling and died in Nuštar. He was the ancestor who had suddenly stood up, thumped his hand on the table and shouted: "I'm leaving!"

That wasn't easy. What could his ancestor Kempf have known about Transylvania? Only what the Empress' envoys had declaimed to him. And none of them, those envoys, had ever been to Transylvania.

he could show everyone that he had been born again (what luck!), this time as a co-fighter with the Red Army.

By this time, Vera had already been demobilised. This boded well for their future meeting, on the Vinkovci corso, their mutual recognition, disclosing and concealing, and, finally, my conception.

The danger that they could have met too soon has passed. There is now no need for them to kill each other, which is a big thing, if one considers that the opposite could easily have happened. Some Volksdeutsche had been camp guards during the war and carried out their work under the sign of a death's head. As a communist, Vera could easily have been sent to a German concentration camp.

But Kempf had joined the army and gone to the battlefield. He could have returned to Tito's country sooner and been captured by the retreating Germans or now be wandering in no-man's land. Then it could easily have happened that Vera, with her people and a revolver in a holster at her side, came across him as he wandered. His people would not have made him take down his trousers in front of Vera. But the mark on

That was why they were able to paint that distant land in the finest colours, without feeling they were deceiving anyone. People who advertise industrial products don't use them themselves, just in case. This goes for ideas as well. Those who endorse them most loudly are far from trying them out on their own skin. For that there are herds of people in the world, kept in experimental conditions. Under fascism they are called "the nation". In Russia they are called "the workers".

the inside of his left upper arm would hardly have been a recommendation.

All that is now receding into the past and fading in importance.

But has that past really passed?

Meanwhile, Kempf still has to travel; he will keep pressing the pedals of his bicycle and covering himself with the open sky for some time yet. He will drink rainwater, dreaming of champagne, constantly catching the sound of distant music. A lot of good music was composed in Europe.

Now I, if not a particularly successful descendant of my ancestor Kempf, am following the same path by which he arrived. He had it easy: he spent most of the journey dozing in the corner of the raft, watching villages and towns pass by, and at night counting the stars. I push pedals until I can't see anything anymore. In the old days, those people were fleeing from hunger; I am fleeing to save my life. My ancestor Kempf was a child of good fortune, he died in his bed, initiating the legend that the Kempfs die in their beds.

Let anyone believe that who can! The only person who could be sure of that would be one who dragged his bed everywhere with him. That's impractical. Let's be modest. Let's pray for death in our sleep, and a place to lie down where possible.

This is what the owl communicated to him, after moving soundlessly again onto a lower branch: What a shame you've grown so big: you would have been a delicious morsel and we would both have been happy.

"It's a pity you don't understand where your happiness lies," said Ilonka, the "easy Hungarian woman" he had paid for one night, "we'd have made a fine couple."

In fact, the family legend was meagre: Our ancestor stood up, said something or other, set off, arrived. His wife came later, in a flock of marriageable women. There's not much more than that. That's why Kempf occasionally felt a strange need to fill in the family legend with his own inventions. He had been living for such a long time skimpily, in both the emotional and material sense, that he simply couldn't bear a similar meagreness in his memories, so he augmented them with kilometre-long thoughts in every breathing space.

Hence his Novi Sad lover had come into his mind.

In Polish love is *miłość*. He has an even better understanding of *śmierć*, death.

His British jacket was still in one piece. It's in a better state than me, thought Kempf. The buttons were hidden, you couldn't see that every second one had fallen off. I'll have to find a female person to put me in order, he thought. His pockets, so big that they covered almost his whole chest, were full of all sorts of odds and ends. A little piece of bread, a hip flask without a drop of vodka in it, a penknife, a small piece of bandage . . . it was a long list. Kempf had sewn his *bumashka* into the inside of the jacket. From time to time, he would feel it, to make sure it was still there. Here I am, don't worry.

How long is it since I slept with a woman, wondered Kempf, recalling the Volksdeutsche recruits, who had greeted enslaved

Poland with their semen. He remembered the buck, hoping that he and the dog they had pulled out of Swan Lake were both still alive. That dog will have a good opinion of me, dogs understand and remember everything, they are more grateful than humans.

Suddenly he heard voices and made out German words. He hadn't imagined that he might come across Germans on this route at this time, particularly not armed Germans, although they had travelled this way two centuries earlier. After Goebbels' total war, Germany was now totally *kaput*.

Kempf had heard here and there – the Russians had talked about it among themselves, as had the Polish partisans – that there were now units of "vampires" who intended to continue the lost war by guerrilla, partisan means, and that these "vampires" were the last remnants of German pride, and they would have no mercy, no *milost*,* for anyone.

That is why Kempf decided to slip further down the embankment and not raise his head. The question he had addressed to the owl on her lookout post remained unanswered. The soundless lady was sleeping peacefully, like a person of independent means who was above human foolishness.

When Kempf heard the sound of women's voices, and even children among the men's, he finally peered over the top of the embankment.

And he saw a lengthy snake-like procession of men, women and children, some of whom were tiny, carried in their parents' arms, moving who knows where. There were no uniforms, they were all civilians. They called to one another in Polish and German, hurrying each other along. There were trucks waiting for them, open, for bulk freight, or closed, for livestock.

---

* *Milost* in Croatian: mercy. [Translator's note]

From time to time, fortune would smile on him: he would be picked up by a lorry, more often by a horse-drawn cart, if they were going in the right direction. He spent one night on a lorry, with his bicycle chained to his leg. He was tied to that bicycle, which he thought of tenderly, by many other, invisible chains.

The roads were filled with columns. Everything was pressing on to the west and the Anglo-Saxons; he was hurrying south.

The smell of burning. Everything here was in ashes.

Kempf prowled through ruins, pushing his bicycle. His practised eye assessed what had been destroyed and how. Tanks had passed through here, a lot of them, and not long ago.

It seemed to him that someone was stirring in one of the wrecked houses. Kempf judged that it would be wisest to conceal himself and crouched down behind a wall.

At the window of the burnt house a white rag appeared. Someone has survived and now wants to surrender to him. Kempf called to the person to come out.

Waving his white rag, a child of ten or so emerged from the ruin.

"Is there anyone else there?" asked Kempf.

The boy shook his head.

"Where are your parents?"

The child pointed to a large building at the end of the street.

"Let's go and find them," Kempf said. "Take me to your home."

And the two of them set off towards the house at the end of the street.

The boy stopped in front of it. On the window was a notice printed in black letters: A POLE LIVES HERE.

"So where's that Pole?"

"He went off with the Reds to chase us Germans."

"But where are your mum and dad?"

"They're a bit further on. At least I hope so."

"And what about these black rags on the windows, what are they for?"

"My uncle hung this one up as a warning: typhoid!"

"Was he German?"

"There were only Germans in this whole street. My whole class lived here."

"And the typhus idea didn't work?"

"No. We tried white flags to start with, but then the S.S. came and killed all the Germans in the houses with those flags."

"But you were waving a white rag?"

"Because the S.S. have run away to Germany. Where are you going?"

"South. Let's walk along the railway track and see what happens."

They were at a railway station, small, just two parallel tracks. There was nowhere here to manoeuvre, thought Kempf. You could only come and go. Which means: some came and others had to go.

He took the boy's hand and the two of them walked round what had been a station until perhaps only a few days before, when fire had turned it to ash.

On the benches, and even more underneath them, were several bodies. Men and women. As a rule, the women's stockings were pulled down to their ankles. Some were old. But some the same age as this boy.

"Did you know them?"

"Of course. Everyone knew everyone here."

"Every Pole knew every German?"

"How could they not?"

The Red Army came through here, on its march to Berlin, concluded Kempf. He had gone too far west.

He should hand the boy over to the Red Cross.

His parents weren't among the bodies. The boy said they had run away, but he would find them and save them.

It was out of the question to drag this child with him south, to "Transylvania".

The boy showed him a storeroom behind a shop that the Red Army had not looted. Kempf stuffed the British major's jacket with tins of meat, sugar cubes, tea and prunes. He calculated that the child could live for a month on the remaining supplies, if nothing went wrong.

The boy and Kempf parted like war comrades.

Kempf pushed the pedals of his bicycle until it got dark. The smell of burning everywhere. Central Europe was in ashes. This was presumably Slovakia?

Kempf did not travel by night. He usually huddled down under a tree, mostly covering himself with sky, rarely finding a roof. Now he could satisfy his passion for observing the sky to his heart's content. He lay on his back, munching prunes and babbling to Europe, the old whore, who had once again miscalculated. It had set off after the wrong ratcatcher, stood beside the wrong commissar . . . In the Europe of Bach's fugues, Kant's Europe, the advocates of the dream of "world peace", precisely those to whom it had surrendered, had built barbed-wire fences and crematoria. And so was Europe complicit in a passive way, a submissive female?

Or were things different: was Hitler as much "Europe" as

Johann Sebastian Bach? The fact that this thought is so appalling is not sufficient testimony against it.

If a beautiful maiden was carried off by a divine bull, how could she have defended herself? Was she raped, or did she acquiesce? One excludes the other. Europe, voluntarily forced!

Freiwilliges gezwungenes Europa!

Are any of those Jews who stifled their baby in the dugout, above which they danced and sang about saving the world, still alive?

The god who transforms himself into a white bull now travels in a tank, while Europe the old whore strews the tank with flowers. That's the way it always was.

Leaning on a tree, half-asleep, Kempf thought that he heard sounds – music, laughter . . . In the distance there were lighted windows.

He decided to creep up.

Before him he saw a large stone palace. It was a warm night, light was coming out through the windows. But these were no longer the openings in tank turrets. A terrace in front of the palace was full of people, everything was clearly lit by flaming torches.

Servants in livery stood to one side, waiting for their masters' signal to bring chilled champagne.

And they were even more concerned to catch the eye of the powerful ruler, sitting on a throne at the end of the terrace, high enough for everyone to see her and the other way round.

Although she had successfully survived her times, it was clear that she was very old. She was certainly rooted to her throne by the new charm of the waltz. The noble presence of the Empress bore witness to the widespread power of the mummy. A later examplar was dozing on the Red Square in the form of a wax doll.

The servants noted the Empress' thoughts and commands; while here and there in the night a coach hurried by. Thus it was by the swiftest coach in the land that the order went out that the subjugated peoples should not learn to count beyond ten or to write anything other than their own signature.

In front of the palace were large numbers of tailcoats and long white dresses. A small orchestra on a podium played waltzes. The rhythm was provided by "Liszt" from Zimmerman's Tavern, whose face emphatically suggested a maestro entirely dedicated to his ecstasy.

So he's found a better engagement at last, Kempf concluded. But where was his lady who was served on a table?

The tailcoats and dresses were dancing a waltz.

No sign of an army. Here invisible power was dancing. The popping was cultured: just champagne corks. People had disguised themselves in the costumes of a previous age. Invisible power, the power of money for instance, is stronger than the visible. Disguised like this, these phantoms nevertheless come from the future, thought Kempf. There are better ways of enslaving the world than through war. The one who understands that will be the victor in tomorrow's world. Should one forget everything and start from scratch?

But what would these people here need to forget? The news of some kind of war has evidently not reached this castle. Here everything is as it was before, and that will always be the case.

They danced. Ever faster, crazily now. The tailcoats were cast off, shawls and other items of clothing flew ... The orchestra was playing in honour of the blue Danube; three-four time crackled, but now it sounded like a march. Kempf could no longer distinguish the male and female dancers in this masked ball, it was now just one single pulsating globe, stretching and contracting, flinging far and wide the reflections of its past and future triumphs. It sparkled in the completeness of its civilisational, political, social and erotic fulfilment. Only victories were sexy. That globe reminded Kempf irresistibly of *krupnik* – a drink drunk in Poland and served like a huge flaming vase.

At the bottom of the Danube, in glass jars like those in which fruit is preserved, languish the souls of the drowned, listening to three-four time whirring through the air above the waters like a proclamation.

Kempf woke drenched with the morning dew.

His Rosinanta groaned, whinnied, neighed . . . For the time being it was nevertheless bearing him well through Europe.

Kempf heard voices once again. He heard Yiddish, for sure, and he heard German; one on one side, the other on the other.

The road led out of the town like an extended tongue. Out of this town came a procession of the kind Kempf was already used to as he travelled through the burnt land: women, old men, dragging themselves like ants, but less successfully and with more effort, trunks, bundles, small children, parrots in cages, cats, they carried with them their joys, their customs and their fear. They all wore white ribbons. The stronger propped up the weaker, some were simply pulled along, exhausted.

He asked them: Where are you going, people?

They were following a hunch, they had no leader. There was no ratcatcher to be seen.

They would like to go home, but their homes were what they had just left.

It is said that the Leader came down from the column of his glory, that he spent some time in his underground Reich office and that he then fired his revolver so he would be incinerated on a petrol pyre of his own choosing. The Generalissimus captured his skull, which showed up treacherously white in the ash. Others laughed at that, maintaining that the Leader's exit strategy was quite different, that he had been resurrected, that this was the first in a series of resurrections in South America where he was studying the collapse of ancient cities he came across as he moved through the jungles. They say he was trying to find where he went wrong.

On the other side, a procession similar in many ways: here there was murmuring in Yiddish, all the rest was just the same. This procession too was carrying its former life and present fear. They all wore yellow ribbons on their sleeves, they were weary and thin. The stronger dragged the weaker, sometimes carrying them on their backs.

Kempf asked: Where are you going, Jews?

They were going to Jerusalem. For them that was "Transylvania". Besides, a good part of their route followed the map of the decent Alexis Hubert Jaillot, the French king's cartographer, and Kempf's anabasis was going in the same direction:

Ruska ziemia . . . Palatinat Luwow . . . Hongrie . . . Valaqui que d'autres nomment Moldavie . . . Transylvanie . . .

This procession was led by Leon Mordechai, his colleague, who had revealed himself to his people, and now dared to wear the clothes of a rabbi from the age of Babylonian enslavement. Although he was skin and bones, he strode briskly, encouraging the procession he was leading, fanning himself with his hat. That was understandable. The more distant the destination, the faster the movement towards it must be. In May 1945 all destinations were a long way off.

The two processions met on the road, which was the extended tongue of the town in ruins.

And they passed each other, without ever touching. White ribbons, yellow ribbons.

They were not a means of exchange. They did not negate each other. They were merely statements.

Kempf was ever further from Poland. This was presumably Slovakia.

What was Poland to him? A fantasy.

He had learned a bit about Poland. He would make an effort to forget it. What he would later call "his little Polish war" was over.

Everything passes.

What was coming?

Kempf finally plucked up the courage to leave the dense undergrowth beside the embankment and emerge onto the shore of the Drava. Its calm flow, which on these first days of June had forgotten the alpine snows, reminded him at once of the Bosut. There, beyond the Drava, was his homeland, whatever that was. In the green Bosut, he had swum with otters. Who was that young man, Đuka Kempf, who had swum with otters, and who was Georg Kempf now?

He glanced at himself in the water's mirror and backed away. It was too dark for him to shave, so he postponed that ritual to the morning. Like a bridegroom approaching his bride, that is how he intended to return to his homeland: shaved, with clean cheeks, and not like a satyr, a wild man.

The greeting was not nice.

A corpse was floating along the central current. In a few hours, the Drava would hand it on to the Danube, and then, in a few more days, to the Black Sea. A lot had floated along this route in the war. Probably only the Sava had more travellers. As it slipped by, Kempf also noticed that the dead man was wearing the remains of a uniform. Whose could no longer be made out.

He found a rowing boat, old, black, but it would do. Kempf got in: it would be his bed for the night. I could describe this whole odyssey of mine, he thought, simply by listing all the places where and how I've slept . . . and how muckheaps engender the best ideas of how to save the world. The world would get by, but the saviour would stink, perhaps forever.

In truth, he went on thinking, where have I not slept, recalling that night in the train before they entered Poland, when he was leafing through his Baedeker guide. It's a pity I didn't see that hotel in Auschwitz. Then came the Ulan barracks, Stockerau; that barracks was the last place in the war that Kempf had slept in a clean bed under a solid roof; then S.S. tents, the bed in the field hospital . . . where was Ania Sadowska now? Then he had spent the night in muckheaps, barns, in the crowns of trees, in dugouts gouged by Red Army soldiers who had escaped from German camps, and then with Alyosha and his men increasingly often in the houses of the mostly terrified population . . . The only place I haven't yet spent the night is in someone's grave. Amazingly, not even my own.

He really should have slept in the hotel in Auschwitz. And even signed the guest book: "First-class service. Thanks to the staff, especially the chambermaids. The greatest fucker of this war, I,

Georg Kempf, Sturmmann of the Waffen-S.S. Galicia division, escapee."

He wriggled in the boat, covering himself with the remains of his military jacket, endeavouring to sleep. But there was little chance of that, so he turned onto his back, intending, like the prophet Mohammed who had travelled over the sky by night, also to travel across the magnificent arc of the Milky Way. That arc must be visible even to a floating corpse, even if it was face down. Why, the stars shone everywhere, even in bushes, even in dark water, it was hard to make out what was up and what was down.

On this night, on the eve of his return to his homeland, *Deus sive natura* arranged a magnificent firework display for him: pilgrims' trudging feet had swept clouds of dust into the air, freeing a multitude of burning desires. It was strange: something like this shower of shooting stars only occurred in August. The galaxy looked like a hat adorned with yellow stars on the head of a fairground magician. In form, not in colour, it resembled the hat under whose brim Leon Mordechai had hidden his face.

It's far nicer, thought Kempf, to ride into one's native town on a white horse, and safest in a tank. How good it must have been to kiss the girls of Paris as liberators on a tank or a horse.

That is what he would have liked.

It was pitiful to arrive like this, a thief, a ragamuffin, and let oneself be arrested by Tito's border guards. Kempf's intuition, thoroughly honed by the costly method of his own skin, told him, correctly, that it was better for him to enter Tito's country as a lost individual than in some formation of the defeated armies. It was better the victors should find him like an item of livestock that had strayed, than to give himself up as a soldier. And that was particularly valid for livestock whose owner had branded it.

Kempf stroked Sergey's *bumashka*: thank God, it was still in the inner pocket of his jacket.

Kempf inhaled deep breaths of acacia blossom: his mother used to put the flowers in pancakes.

But another scent came to him as well: Sofija's. All the aromas of a young, vigorous female body. He wanted Sofija badly. In fact, for the first time in a very long time he felt like a man again. At least like a soldier or a prisoner, far from a woman.

He didn't know how long he had slept but surprisingly, when dawn came, he was no more tired than he had been in recent days when he had pedalled his bicycle to the point of exhaustion.

He took out his small knife and a piece of soap and leaned over the mirror of the river.

His face was a white mask when he noticed that he was the target of a gun barrel calmly observing him from the bushes. He put his hands up at once.

"Finish the job, lad!" a large soldier called to him, apparently pleasantly, but at the same time pointing his gun at Kempf as he knelt on the pebbles.

Excellent position for liquidation in the nape.

"Got any tobacco?" asked another soldier.

"Not even a potato leaf!"

That evidently went down well. As though for a moment a little flame of solidarity had flared between men, soldiers, suffering deprivation.

When Kempf had finished shaving, he wiped his knife and washed in the clear Drava water (the corpse had long since floated away); the two men with red stars on their caps ordered him to get going. Kempf took his bicycle and walked between them. They had their own large rowing boat in the undergrowth, the three of them got into it and, luckily, there was room for the bicycle as well. Kempf would not have parted from it for anything in the world after it had served him so well.

Besides, he would need it, if he survived this arrest, that is. Because it was an arrest.

The fact that he could understand what the soldiers said to him, and even respond with quite complicated phrases, did not give these soldiers confidence; on the contrary. He abandoned the idea of selling them the story that he was in fact a fisherman who was in the way of spending the night in a boat. The soldiers had immediately realised that they had to take him to headquarters, that is, that the "next steps" exceeded their competence. It was very likely that he was an enemy of the people, so not a deserter or a smuggler, but their superiors would deal with it.

After crossing the Drava, they walked for another half-hour, Kempf always in the middle, pushing his bicycle.

The headquarters was in a house that, for any purpose other than serving as headquarters, was obviously abandoned. A man whose rank on his shoulder Kempf recognised as that of captain asked him who he was.

That was the most difficult question.

Kempf replied that he had, by chance, ended up in Poland and spent the war in camps, and that he had fought in a Soviet-Polish partisan unit.

That was the construction which he had devised and turned over in his head a thousand times, pedalling his bicycle from Babia Gora through Slovakia, Austria, Hungary, to the Drava, and even more as he rested wherever the night found him.

It was true. More exactly, it sounded like a convincing truth. Kempf thought that a formula that was, from a linguistic perspective, true would be more convincing than if he simply lied. He had admitted where and how he had spent the war. He said that he came from Slavonia, that he was born in 1919 in Nuštar, which was also the plain truth. He said that he wanted to go to Nuštar, and that then he intended to look for a job in Vinkovci where he knew some people, although he didn't know whether they were still alive.

The captain wanted to be cunning. The fact that Kempf understood and spoke to him in comprehensible language aroused his suspicion. The captain asked: "What's the name of the river at Vinkovci?"

Kempf replied promptly, in the manner of a prize pupil: "That river, captain sir, has always been called the Bosut."

"You fought with the Soviets?" asked the captain, suddenly frowning.

"Of course." That was again the simple truth. He had fought with the Soviets, in the sense of against them, and also in the sense of together. Kempf hated lies, and language itself, with its ambiguities, enabled him not to tell the truth without lying.

"And you don't know that you have to say: 'Comrade captain'!"

"I've been travelling for a long time, comrade captain."

"How long?"

Now Kempf hesitated, he concluded that the interrogation had reached a critical point and took the document out of his jacket lining.

The captain took the *bumashka*, looking at it for a long time, as though doubting it. He held it up to the light, to his nose, sniffed it, turned it around. Kempf clearly saw his eyes widen.

In a moment he'll stand up and salute, he thought, with satisfaction.

But none of that. The captain and his men had the task of hunting down people who looked just like him, even if they were disguised in civilian rags. To hunt them down and hand them over to the people's courts, and sometimes without a trial to the fury of the people, that is to a lynching.

But this case had suddenly grown complicated.

Not because of the mark of Cain, the captain and his men barely knew anything about that. They didn't ask Kempf to raise his left arm. They were hunting for the Quisling army, about which he had heard here and there when he had by chance found himself beside a radio. For the Germans they were allies, for everyone else traitors. Kempf wasn't well up on this. He compared them to the Polish underground army, the Home Army. But this army had been forever redeemed in Kempf's eyes by Ania Sadowska. Her Poles had fought against the Germans and had never been their allies. Besides, given that Kempf was recruited into the army in March 1943, by then he had time to hear something about the Croatian Ustasha movement. He knew that some of his schoolmates had joined them, including some he would not have dreamed would do so. Others, meanwhile, had flown off into the forest, to the Partisans, which was often more surprising.

Generally, Kempf barely read newspapers. At their home, only his father read them, though he would sometimes underline something in the paper for his son. When Sofija was captured, he had shown him an article, maintaining that while Jasenovac was not a hotel, neither was it a place of torture.

But Kempf had his own ideas. What was whispered under the roofs didn't hold out much hope. The terror was growing, and as the war went on, that terror increasingly affected the Croatian population as well. The hunting of Jews and Orthodox Serbs was of course continuous.

When Sofija was taken away, Đuka Kempf sought out some of

Nuštar's influential Germans. He was prepared to pay for their intervention because his father, no matter how often they quarrelled, had taken a liking to Sofija and he would have given him money. The trade in pig fat was going extremely well.

Kempf's influential Germans laughed at him.

When mobilisation began, it did not at first occur to Kempf that he could have been sent to one of the camps as a guard. In the Polish camps there were Croatian Volksdeutsche who in no way lagged behind the Ukrainians in their cruelty. Dr Schlauss' son would certainly have been one of them. It had not yet crossed his mind that his military journey and Sofija's fate could have become intertwined in the worst possible way.

At a sign from the captain, the soldiers who had nabbed him while he was shaving led him to a bunker. The tradition carries on, he thought. He had spent his first night with the Bolsheviks in a bunker. He would likewise spend his first night in Tito's state on concrete.

Around midnight Georg Kempf acquired a companion. A man who had clearly been beaten almost to death was thrown onto the concrete. The poor man stammered, asking for water, which Kempf didn't have. It was a moonless night, but the beacon of the Milky Way sufficed for him, with his year of medical studies in Belgrade, to see what was wrong: gangrene throughout the man's body. He said they had been beating him for days; that he was a Volksdeutscher from Osijek.

The beaten man begged Kempf to kill him. Kempf did not have the means. Victors learn the craft of the secret police with astonishing speed; presumably talent also plays a part. So, when they searched Kempf before taking him to the bunker, they had removed the laces from his shoes, although the word "shoes" only approximately described what he had on his feet; they had naturally also removed his "cold weaponry", in the form of his penknife.

Having carried so many different weapons during the war, Kempf now had nothing with which to kill the man begging him to do it out of compassion. He could have suffocated him with his jacket or something else; it was unthinkable to do it with his bare hands. Perhaps the way the Jews had killed their baby in order for their group to survive?

But, essentially, for Kempf killing him was unthinkable.

There, he thought in that night, which was one of the longest in his life, all I really wanted was to get through all this as a civilian. And now what?

The man groaned, neither he nor Kempf could close their eyes.

He learned that the man had been forcibly recruited into the Waffen-S.S., that his division had been named after the unfortunate Prince Eugene, whom the beaten man began to curse with all his remaining strength, it had been crushed, it no longer existed, Hitler was *kaput*, and he himself had fired into the air and not killed anyone in the whole war. In a way, the man was his companion in arms, until he had changed flags. Kempf could have suffered the same fate, but he had avoided the ill-fated Prince Eugene and fallen into the Galician mud.

I don't know, thought Kempf, whether I killed anyone in the war. To start with I didn't shoot into the air, I fired along with everyone else.

He was tormented by the fact that they had taken away Sergey's *bumashka*, in which he had placed all his hopes. If they started beating him up like this, he too would want to die. How much cleverer the S.S. were. Kempf's master from whom he had escaped and who had before that branded his signature into his skin, the second man in Hitler's empire, had killed himself with cyanide after he was captured by the Allies. He had carried a fatal dose sewn into his uniform. Clever.

The beaten man, "dressed" from head to foot in gangrene, stopped groaning, and Kempf hoped that he had died.

At dawn the door of the bunker opened. To his surprise, totally drained by lack of sleep, Kempf saw that it was not the captain who stood outside, but an officer of evidently higher rank. Kempf thought, that's it, the judgment has been made.

The commissar, for that's who he was, a well-built Montenegrin, with a short thick moustache, like Stalin's, said briefly: "Comrade Georg Kempf?"

"Yes."

The commissar gave him back his *bumashka*. He remained upright, solid as he was, as though he had been sculpted from stone by Meštrović, but there was something in his gesture that was similar to a bow, although invisible; the moustached Montenegrin resembled someone opening wide a door through which a guest worthy of respect could enter the city, state, empire.

"Here you are, welcome. How do you intend to get to Vinkovci?"

Kempf could hardly believe his ears, but he had no others. "Bicycle."

"Towards evening I can let you have a place on a truck."

"I'd like to see my family as soon as possible."

"Of course. You deserve it. Would you like to borrow a revolver? There are still vermin crawling around here."

Kempf declined.

And the commissar thought to himself: What does he need with a gun, when he has that *bumashka*?

Because for him that was a relic which, to preserve it, is not taken out into the light of day. A Catholic would show it only at a monstrance.

"Not long now, comrade, and you'll be with your people."

Kempf had correctly concluded that he could have also been a guard in a concentration camp. Sofija could have been driven on a transport to Auschwitz. He could also have met, either as a pursuer or the pursued, the woman in whose womb I place all my hopes. If he had made a bit more haste leaving Poland, their paths, here at the entrance to Tito's state, might have crossed.

No-one knows the horror of possibly not being born suffered by those who wait. Not long now!

III

Revolution in the Brass Age

Conversations of the Dead

At the beginning of June Georg set out on the well-known path towards the graveyard. His first visit, after a lengthy absence, would be to the dead, he thought. They are the only ones who still exist; there are no more living.

For instance, in the house where he was born no-one lived anymore. Nor could they, given that it no longer had a roof. A young birch was growing in the middle of the kitchen. There were caked turds everywhere, except in the toilet. The house was uninhabitable. That was why there were no new people living there. It barely crossed Kempf's mind that he was the owner of this ruin.

Here Kempf was fantasising again. As he was no longer in his first youth, he was ashamed to tell his parents that he had fallen head over heels for Vera when he had seen her a couple of days before, strolling on the corso in Vinkovci. He imagined that he knew her from before the war, which was not true. Of their meeting he said: It was written. And what is written, should presumably be read.

In any case, their paths, going in opposite directions up to now, had joined and they would soon start making plans for the next stage. As I am part of those plans, I formally approve this connection and observe its blossoming with empathy. Many of the unborn congratulate me. There is no envy among us, so I believe the congratulations are sincere. Envy is among the privileges of the already born.

At the end of the war, the house had been occupied as a position. No-one was able to tell him whose. The same thing had happened with the building that had been the public library before the war. The fact that the buildings were now ruins was put down to military reasons, so it wasn't necessary to say who exactly had destroyed them.

Walking now towards the cemetery, he noticed that the earth was already dry, wild apple trees along the path were already stretching their little sour fruit towards him. The poplars were where they had always been. They had barely grown any taller. A large flock of crows were carefully monitoring his every step. They're waiting, thought Kempf, they're always on the alert. This is where they spent the war. And they will certainly have had their feasts here too. They never have enough.

The Srem Front was near here. One of the last massacres, perhaps senseless? Or not? Had the Partisans left that job to the Soviets, a more experienced and better-equipped force, perhaps a Poland would have reprised here? The Partisans wanted a military operation on a grand scale; the kind that only established states could successfully carry out. Or had it been conceived as a sacrifice of cleansing, a kind of punishment for the fact that the Partisans in Serbia had often been left alone? Just like the Polish partisans? Why had it been so important to cut the line of the German armies' retreat from Greece, when the Germans had already been defeated?

Kempf had asked here and there about one or other of the lads he had known, often real wasters. Many had fallen or disappeared in this last episode of the war under the heavy guns of German soldiers who fought well, although it was pointless.

The cemetery gate was barely attached to its post. This should be fixed, thought Kempf. I'll fix it.

Now, in June, all the headstones were covered in grass that had grown waist high.

This should be scythed, he thought. No-one has set foot here for a long time. I'll cut it.

Making his way through the wild weeds, Kempf finally found himself beside his family graves. "Look who's come," the ancestor Kempf said, straightening into a sitting position.

Although his grave was to one side, next to the fence, he had the best view. "But it's been two years since he disappeared."

"He didn't disappear," said Ferdo Kempf, Georg's father. "He went off to the German army."

Kempf's father had died in his own home, which was then still whole, in his own bed, in his sleep. A fortunate man. As was to be expected: heart failure.

"That was never good," the ancestor Kempf observed. "A peasant will never get on with a gun."

"My son stopped being a peasant a long time ago," his mother said. "If he had wanted, he could have gone into commerce."

"He's very thin," the ancestor's wife said.

"Thin! He was never fat," replied Kempf's mother, who had died only the previous winter. "Just let my eyes take a good look at you!"

She had died in a horse-drawn cart in which she was travelling in the middle of the winter of 1944 towards Zagreb, with the intention of reaching Passau in Germany. According to a directive from Berlin: "Germans outside the Reich" should return to its then borders in order to defend them. Kempf's mother didn't manage to defend the Reich, she died on the journey, nearer to Vinkovci than Zagreb, a very long way from the town of Passau on the Danube.

In 1944, Maria Theresa's colonists were supposed to return to

Germany in the same way they had reached their "Transylvania", on Slavonian soil, nearly two centuries earlier. As then, in 1770, many had perished on the way.

Kempf's mother, they said, had frozen to death, but Kempf knew that she had died of sorrow. The desolate long to die.

"Now our son's almost a man," Ferdo Kempf said. It seemed that he had been permitted to stay here. The Reds had nothing serious against him.

The Kempfs sat up in their graves while Georg pulled up the weeds around their grave markers.

"It's time he got married."

"Let him settle down by the autumn."

"He's been roaming for a long time."

"I just hope he hasn't done anything bad."

"A German soldier does nothing bad!"

"All soldiers do!"

"Whatever, that's all over now."

Kempf sat down on the gravestone of an unknown relative, thinking: These new crosses won't last long. They should be replaced by stone. But that's expensive. My father and mother must have memorials. Otherwise, these graves will fall apart, just like the house.

He tried to remember where the man who cut gravestones had his workshop, but in vain. That kind of workshop was usually near the cemetery.

He sat until it grew completely dark. The dead go to rest early, and it is perhaps surprising that, although in principle they have time, their conversations are brief.

It wasn't long before Kempf persuaded his future wife to go with him to visit the dead, who could hardly wait. The daughter-in-law seemed healthy, a little too thin, but otherwise alright. Her breasts suggested she would nurse well. She had brought a container of water and started cleaning the headstones with a rag. The Kempfs approved of this. By the time Vera spread the rag out in the sun to dry, she had completely won them over.

"This is Vera, my future wife. I've known her since before the war. I saw her on the corso, in Vinkovci, and realised at once that this was it. If there's such a thing as love at first sight, this is that kind of love."

"That kind of love can pass at a second look!" said a *tante* from a grave over by the fence in a rather hoarse voice.

"Mind your tongue, Rezika."

"How refined she is."

"And how clean!"

"She seems a decent girl to me."

"She'll be a good daughter-in-law," her mother-in-law said.

"If she knows how to obey," her father-in-law, Kempf's father, added.

"Just let her give us a grandchild as soon as possible," her mother-in-law sighed. "What's nicer than a grandchild?"

"A great-grandchild," said the patriarch, the ancestor Kempf, and his laugh drove a fat crow into the air.

Everyone in the graves was in a good mood.

The ancestor Kempf even sang a German song so ancient that the younger dead could not recall anyone ever singing such wanton foolishness, not even at "Schwabian carnival" when the Germans were allowed free rein at the farms.

I, Kempf's son, whose mother is called Vera, visited that graveyard in the middle of the 1990s. Too late. I had neglected the dead. I had been a bad son and a bad descendant. I'm a bad Kempf.

The graveyard was where it had always been. The poplars now cover the entire horizon.

The descendants of the former crows still settle in their branches. With that German graveyard, things are as follows:

As early as the autumn of 1945, the new authorities wanted to plough up the German graves. Why should there be graves when the living were no longer here? Who would care for them, who would pay for them? As though the Germans who had made it to Germany cared about those graves. Why, they had even abandoned their houses.

The original idea was ... a sub-station. A useful thing in itself. It was a nice idea to bring electricity into everyone's home. Socialism came up with nice ideas, some of which it succeeded in implementing.

They sketched the sub-station, pegged it out in the middle of the German graveyard.

Then someone remembered that this was a flood plain and it happened that a coffin would simply be lowered into the water in the bottom of a grave when it had been dug.

Water and electricity don't mix. And so the graveyard remained.

Until 1991 there was a graveyard, where the first Georg Kempf and then his wife had been buried – she next to him – two hundred and fifty years earlier.

But in that year, 1991, the German cemetery near the little town of Nuštar (which in the meantime, under socialism, had grown quite a lot) was designated a war position.

Across from it, five hundred metres south, the opposing side had dug itself into something that it decreed was its hill. They fired day and night. After two weeks, the side that had dug itself into the graves broke through to the south, capturing the enemy's hill. At the same time, the enemy started skirting round the advancing company, came round behind it and occupied its former position. There was firing again by day and night. When it all stopped, the graves were ploughed up by shells, the headstones knocked over, the crosses burned. Even the crows had moved away.

Then there was a big flood. It poured with rain, day and night.

The dead were washed along by small tributaries which flowed into the big river and set off towards the Black Sea.

Their despair was indescribable. They had not been allowed to disintegrate fully in the land where they were born. It was so hard, so wearisome, to wait for resurrection in an unfamiliar place, and not, as Schiller put it in *The Robbers*, in one's own native land. In Slavonia.

Black Bone

On midsummer's day, Kempf shoved his *bumashka* into the back pocket of his trousers and set off to the administrative headquarters in Nuštar. He had decided to go and look for Comrade Kosta whom he knew superficially from his secondary school days in Vinkovci. Comrade Kosta was now the big chief in the Second Department of OZNA, the State Security Police, founded while the war was still raging. The Second Department had jurisdiction over the liberated areas, and, as since June 1945 all areas were liberated, its jurisdiction now covered the entire territory of the former kingdom, while Comrade Kosta was responsible for Nuštar and the surrounding villages in which there could still be found some "doubting Thomases", for whom the casualties lost for freedom were not sufficiently convincing. The Second Department had its own ways of convincing such people.

Kempf was received with open arms, as they say, by a tall man with a pince-nez.

Kosta had always been the tallest boy in the class, but, surprisingly, his coordination in ball games had been poor, his kick hopeless. Kosta was weak in sport, but strong in history.

Later Kosta had joined the black shadows that had slunk off to secret meetings, particularly in summer, while others were taking it easy, fishing, and chasing girls through the vineyards. Immediately after the April war, Kosta had sunk into the

Underground and Kempf had not heard anything more about him. Now he was standing in front of him, like a pupil afraid of being examined on material he had not prepared, on botany, for example, when he had revised trigonometry.

"Where've you been, old man?" Comrade Kosta spread his arms wide as though surprised that he was only just seeing him. "And a lot of water has flowed through the Bosut and the Sava, hasn't it? We've been through a lot. If at all possible, we ought to begin to forget. We have to look forward. Now we're going to build our country. And we'll do that with everyone who wants to build it with us. But you see, old man, it's easy to say that but hard to bring it about. People muddy things up wherever they can, the reactionaries stir things up. Tell me, what can I do for you?"

Kempf thought Kosta could easily have organised a sack of flour, ham and tobacco for him. And Kosta would have been glad to do that, if only Kempf didn't ask him about the Germans.

But Đuka Kempf *had* asked him about the Germans. "Isn't the mill now a camp . . . ?"

"Temporary accommodation, Comrade Kempf, let's be precise. A camp is something else. You know what a camp is."

"But there were camps here too through which people just passed."

"How do you mean?"

"Before the war that mill belonged to Kiršbaum. Kiršbaum was taken away as soon as Jews began to be rounded up."

"And so?"

"He didn't come back."

"No."

"Before he was taken away, in despair, trying to find a way out, Kiršbaum sold the mill to a respectable Croat for one kuna."

"The mill was Aryanised, as they called it then!" Kosta exclaimed and spat.

"Whose is it now?"

"It's ours, a national mill."

"Whose would it be if, by some miracle, Kiršbaum came back?"

"That mill is too big and too important to be owned by an individual."

"So you would take his mill from him?"

"The mill would be expropriated."

"For one kuna?"

"Listen, man, don't fuck about. Didn't your Russians *up there* tell you how it's done? And how quickly!"

"Alright, it's now a national mill. So why, instead of being a camp, is that mill not grinding wheat?"

"Because there is no wheat. When the Germans retreated, they burned everything the people had sown."

Kempf fell silent. Kosta meant that it was alright that Germans, "our Germans", who had sided with "Hitler's Germans" and approved all kinds of atrocities, should now be imprisoned in the mill. He didn't say anything about the crimes committed by "our Germans" in the Waffen-S.S. Prinz Eugen division. Comrade Kosta wanted to be considerate to his old acquaintance. But nor did he mention the fact that in the Partisan formation there had been a unit of "our Germans" who had joined Tito's movement.

"I've heard that those Germans 'of ours' are going hungry and that they're dying in large numbers."

"Sorry to hear it! Where were those Germans 'of ours' when things were going well for Hitler? They're hungry, so what? The whole country is hungry."

"There are a lot of children behind the wires there."

"Unfortunately, there are quite a few children. We're not wild beasts and we aren't thinking of taking their children away. What would we do with the children?"

"Those children will remember and when they grow up they'll be our enemies."

"Oh, people forget. What do you remember about your childhood?"

Kempf didn't want to say that he remembered virtually everything.

He had now realised that he wouldn't get anywhere with Kosta, that there was no point in showing him the document from the Soviet commissar, although it was a relic and Kosta a believer. He got up to say goodbye.

But then Kosta suddenly cut across him.

"Come now, old man! You were in Poland. So you saw. You saw what the Poles did with 'their' Germans. Onto trains, into cattle trucks, to the west. Just like 'our Germans' here, they had to leave the Polish people everything apart from what they could carry on their backs and in their hands."

"And memories in their heads!"

"That's up to them. So, up there, houses, land, factories, even their churches are all now the property of Poland and the Poles. I think that's quite O.K. In Silesia they played the wrong card. Like these people here. And the forfeit in that game was very great. They played for all or nothing, and they lost. Very simply: that's how it is in life, and especially in history."

Kempf was already on his way out when Kosta, still with a pleasant mask on his face, of the kind one keeps for acquaintances from one's youth, observed: "If the Waffen-S.S. had won, we'd be the ones in the mill today."

Kempf stopped, as though hit with a hammer.

"If you were to listen to me, for instance," said Kosta, with feigned casualness, "you would work on founding a public library. The old one was burned to the ground. There, we're building something from nothing, renewing something from the ashes. We need everyone. We need something of what we've lost, along with completely new things. I tell my people, let's not rush, let's not be foolish. Not everything old was bad. For instance: a public library.

"Think of our movement like a very long train that has now slowed down. And do you know why? It has slowed down so everyone can get on board. And there's nothing wrong with that. We still need to do a bit of cleaning up, we can't be sentimental. But then, after all, we will be magnanimous. The revolution is for the people, what else, or isn't it? It's all for the people."

As he left the O.Z.N.A. official's office, Kempf was almost dazed by the hot air filled with dust: a column was passing along the road, herded by soldiers. It was a new contingent of Germans from the Bačka region. They too were being driven towards the mill.

Kempf sat down on the bank of a stream that he knew well: long ago he had fished there for chub, which his mother had later fried. Fine little fish, only they have a lot of bones.

Captain or Major Kosta knew everything about him, that was clear. And he could blackmail him with that knowledge whenever he felt like it. Kempf realised that, despite the *bumashka* he felt for in his back pocket just in case, he could end up in the mill. Particularly if he went on asking questions about "his" Germans.

He had originally thought that, after his conversation with Comrade Kosta, he would go to the mill to have a chat with the prisoners. But now that seemed senseless. He was afraid of their questions, and even of their gaze.

He found a patch of shade thrown by an acacia bush, lay down on his stomach and thrust his head into the turf, wishing not to be. And more: he wished that he had never been. Not to be so completely that, by descending through time, he would eliminate all those from whom he was descended. Because they left a trace, and he now wanted to vanish without a trace. He wished that his ancestor Kempf had never uttered: "I'm going to Transylvania!", because the count's servants had cleaved the head of the imperial envoy, the piper of Hamelin near Hannover, Germany.

The sun had long passed its zenith when he set off after all to the mill.

Several people were standing in front of the mill, it was easy to see they were colonists, new colonists. They were carrying bundles, cardboard boxes with chicks peeping in them, and beside them a herd of pigs was grazing. The first trains without a timetable were beginning to arrive.

There were a lot of small children among the arrivals. The children looked dirty and neglected, but that had to be put down to misery and poverty. They were all, every one of them, very thin.

Now the children behind the wire fence, in the space in front of the mill, were also in great distress. But they were washed, their hair was brushed and they were relatively well dressed. The German sense of order and cleanliness was still maintained by what they had been allowed to take with them from their property and home; their property and houses had already been allotted to the colonists. On some of the houses there was already an inscription in whitewash: THIS HOUSE IS OCCUPIED.

Kempf saw something similar much later, in the 1990s, when his son drove him to the sea through the hinterland behind Zadar. On one house was written: CROAT, DON'T TOUCH. But before that he had seen something similar in Poland: A POLE LIVES HERE.

Through the wire, two worlds looked at one another. The children were particularly inquisitive.

"What have they done to be in a cage?" asked a little girl among those who had just got off the train. As no-one answered, she added: "They must've been very naughty."

Suddenly, Kempf started to see images from his childhood: in a large courtyard a group of children was playing a game they called "black bone". In his head, sitting on a milestone in front of the mill, he ran through the whole game from beginning to end.

One little girl was the Mother, another was the Black Bone. We others were simply children. We approach the Mother and say: "We're hungry, we want to eat."

"Go to the cellar, children."

In the cellar the girl assigned the role of Black Bone was waiting for us.

"Boo-boooo!" the Bone shouted.

We ran to Mother. "Mama, there's something in the cellar shouting: 'Boo-boooo,' we're very frightened, Mama. So frightened, we've shat our pants."

Mother took us by the hand and we all went to the cellar.

"Who are you?" asked the Mother, while we all trembled with terror around her.

"I'm Black Bone."

To which Mother replied: "And whose children's blood are you drinking?"

"Yours."

Within a month Đuka Kempf had restored the public library in Vinkovci.

Long before that numerous trains, trucks and even horse-drawn carts had taken "our" Germans back to where the invisible but powerful hand of Maria Theresa had collected them, in the eighteenth century, as colonists, and sown them through the then empty lands of Slavonia.

Now one circle was closed.

The piper of Hamelin's flute was not heard this time, nor were there drums, instruments that in the 1930s, on the wave of a "modernist" mass movement, replaced the outmoded flute.

All that was heard was the clanging of the iron wheels over the joins in the track, the coughing of old trucks and the sad whinnying of horses that probably realised they had been driven out of their stables and pasture. The same scenes could be seen, the same sounds heard, in Silesia, in the Sudetenland and in Yugoslavia. In the whole country and in the one that fell apart in the 1990s.

At the Whim of the Wind

Summer was at an end, all that would continue to bloom were asters that held on longer than the first frosts. The Bosut was waking up. The first early autumn rain had increased its flow and it looked like a real river again, and a real one flows from its source to its mouth. Before long the birds, whose destiny it was, would set off for the south; the flocks were already gathering.

The two of them were thinking of moving west, into the main city of the Croatian Republic, in the opposite direction to the birds. It's true that there was also a metropolis to the east, the capital of the whole country, where Đuka had spent a year studying medicine, he had known a lot of fun places there, but what had become of it during the war he knew only vaguely. On the other hand, Vera had never been to Belgrade. They calculated that there, given that the city had been liberated the previous year, everything was already consolidated, which properly translated would mean that it would be hard to find a "liberated" apartment. Belgrade was swarming with Soviet allies, some of whom were experts, and others spies and layabouts. There were some of those in Zagreb too, but most were probably keeping an eye on Tito, and he ruled from Belgrade.

That decision, to move closer to the centre of new events, took Kempf a lot of persuasion, and the months passed. But he had a strange sense of everything speeding up, while Vera wanted to take everything more slowly, step by step.

In truth, Vera quickly understood what Đuka said: that she, as a former Partisan, would easily find in Zagreb accommodation more appropriate than a hotel by the station. His own war story was perhaps far less convincing, but the *bumashka* would surely play its part, Vera consoled him.

Perhaps Kempf was in a hurry to go to Zagreb also because in his native town and in Vinkovci things were altogether more complicated. There were people who remembered that he had been recruited into the German army. They knew that there had been among the Germans those who went off singing, but also others who had endeavoured somehow to "redeem" themselves or had performed dissembling dramas in front of commissions. Those people knew that his late father had grown rich through his trade in pig fat, including with the German army; an army should always be greased. So why had his father not greased the palms of the Waffen-S.S. and tucked his only child away in the security of a featherbed? Some had been understandably surprised at his return, because between the lines of Nazi propaganda they had nevertheless been able to get an idea of how the German soldiers had fared in the East. While the Führer was counting his last days in Berlin, the only Germans on the front to have escaped with their lives were those whose commanders were disinclined to follow their insane orders. And those who had escaped had fallen into Russian captivity and who knew whether they would ever return? The Germans who had ended up in the Prinz Eugen division here, in Yugoslavia, had even less chance of survival. They were still being rounded up in large numbers then, in September 1945.

All in all, those who now saw Đuka on the Vinkovci corso,

on the banks of the Bosut, in taverns, with his arm round the shoulders of a young woman, had two question marks in their eyes: What did you do over there in the East? How come you survived?

If you did what your people did in the "home" Waffen-S.S. Prinz Eugen division, you're just one of them. If you didn't, how did you get away, in the first instance from them, from the S.S., which, without asking many questions, shot their deserters at the first opportunity? And in any case, how was it that you weren't mobilised into the Waffen-S.S. Prinz Eugen division, into which our lads were recruited, our own Krauts* from here and from the Banat?

There was hatred in the eyes of the few Germans who had not yet been driven out; but their expression also contained an occasional question mark. However, there were no questions in the eyes of those who had lost someone close to them, either in the Forest, or on the opposite side . . . Only hate. Kempf had disappeared, like so many German boys . . . But he must be the only one to have returned from the east. And see how he's returned. He went off with those who were convinced of their total victory even in 1943. So, Kempf went off loyally, with his own people, in the sense that when the going gets tough, every bird flies to its own flock, and then everything fell apart for the Germans, they got what they had sought, but he came back – as a victor. What was defeat in this case, and what victory?

Kempf went less and less into town, and never to taverns. Vera brought him alcohol, mostly brandy, Vera's mother cooked for

---

* The derogatory term used in the original, *bubašvaba*, is colourful: *švaba* (from Schwabe, Shvabian), is a colloquial term for German; while *bubašvaba* means "cockroach". [Translator's note]

him, they lived with her in a rented flat in which this mother of Vera's had awaited the end of the war and the news that her only son, Vera's brother, had been killed. By an American bomb in Mauthausen, just before the Americans entered the camp: May 1945. The news had caused the old lady virtually to stop speaking.

No-one interrogated Kempf, apart from the questioning when he arrived in Tito's state. At that time a lot of people were brought in, the slightest insinuation was enough, many of those, taken in at night or early dawn, simply disappeared. Many personal hatreds and human jealousies came into their own. Once again, as in 1941, it became dangerous to own something: a mill, land, a house . . .

All those malicious or questioning glances on the corso could be uncomfortable for Kempf, but he never felt in danger. Like a saint's halo, the Soviet commissar's *bumashka* floated over Kempf's head, with its first early traces of grey. The young, whose consciousness and intelligence were not so burdened with the experience of evil, saw him as a hero who "with the Soviets had liberated our Polish brothers . . ." Some even maintained that he had been to Moscow and shared a drink with Marshal Stalin. Others, that he had saved many lives, that he had killed a whole host of Germans and "local traitors", although they didn't know what these last were called in Poland because there were a great many candidates. Idiocy, thought Kempf. I may possibly have saved one Polish dog. And maybe that little boy who luckily had not swallowed a lot of water when he fell into the fishpond. The Poles I didn't want to shoot were killed by men just like me then, without mercy. But the dog was mine. Just mine.

Still, he thought, in one of the long sleepless nights that beset him recently, no-one here has interrogated me under a police light, they haven't arrested me, they haven't tortured me. No-one has asked me to take my trousers down. They believe in – my *bumashka*.

Nevertheless, with every day the decision was growing firmer that the two of them should go to the city and try their luck again where no-one knew them. Kempf had reasons for not wanting to meet anyone from his "old" life. Vera had fewer.

For his Vera indisputably belonged to the winning side. It was known that she had been despatched to the Stara Gradiška camp after someone in her group had "sung", it was known that she had fallen into a trap, through no fault of her own, and been captured, it wasn't known whether she had been tortured (she hadn't), she was exchanged for Germans as soon as her brother had been caught. It was known that this brother of hers had always been a communist (which was true), that he was a true son of ours, an excellent student, that he had always been engaged in the movement, but that he had been captured, in Zagreb where he had gone to hide, thinking that no-one there knew him and also to be treated for the tuberculosis that was ravaging Vinkovci, that he had survived the camp at Jasenovac, only to perish in Mauthausen (tragically at the beginning of May 1945). And, imagine this: he had been sent to take refuge there by the "inner party" of the Jasenovac camp, because it was believed that their camp would be liquidated to the last inmate as soon as Tito's guns reached the Bosnian side of the Sava river; so Vera's brother was "shoved" into the Mauthausen contingent, at the very last moment – in order to survive – and there a bomb got him.

All in all, Vera's star had not been sullied in any way. Her sleeve was tugged whenever it was necessary to "intervene" for this or that person, although she didn't figure very highly in the new hierarchy. As though the authentic Partisans were already beginning to be pushed aside by the "new bureaucrats" . . . In truth, some folk, who had spent the war snoring under their quilts, began to crawl out of the woodwork and thrust their way into power, beating their chests with tales of their non-existent heroisms and priceless services.

Although Vera had no "administrative" power, nor any kind of function, nor had she sought it for herself, it quickly emerged that she was an excellent activist. That was easily explained by the fact that Vera, in her youthful, pure way, was a devoted believer in the revolution. In that phase, the revolution was a wrathful and discriminating deity, but human trash had already begun to collect around its feet.

Since she was an excellent activist, the comrades sent her into the villages around Vinkovci.

Everywhere she went, she organised circles of "antifascist women"; made speeches, brought new flyers, just as before, only now nothing had to be hidden. She also passed on meagre knowledge about infections, about parenting for "new women", about hygiene . . . about increasing yields, about better varieties of fruit trees, not necessarily the most common figs . . . She prepared for those lectures in the backwoods the way a star pupil prepares for exams: she leafed through the scorched pages of the encyclopaedias from the burnt public library . . . Of course, she talked (or rather preached) also about the "first country of workers and peasants", like our own long-suffering country, soaked in the blood of enemies, and Vera did so as vividly as though she had grown up in the lands of the Soviets . . . In some mental sense, perhaps she had. Had Vera been born in the age of Saint Francis, she would have founded the women's Franciscan order of Clarissas, and not by force, but through the triumphant power of conviction. She was accompanied into villages deeper in the forests by armed members of the State Security Police. That didn't please her. She was convinced of the power of her words; so convinced that she considered she was capable of turning around even the most obdurate enemy. However, she never talked about her battle in the Forest, or her "camp residency", she didn't even want to go to children in schools.

Some did. But some didn't. However monolithic a "grouping" the Partisans had seemed, they differed among themselves.

But immediately after the war, while the ashes were still smouldering, those were nuances noticed by few. What prevailed at that time was a general joy, partly prescribed, partly spontaneous. Kempf wasn't entirely sure about the extent of these two kinds of joy, that is, how much of each there was in the actual mix. He thought that at the source, in the metropolis, he would be able to study the question better. Perhaps it was precisely on that proportion – organised delight versus joy for its own sake – that everything depended: would the communists succeed in mobilising the people, or would the revolution stifle itself, the way the Bosut came to a halt with all that grew from its bed? Would it remain pure, or be suffocated in the general hypocrisy?

So, Kempf didn't feel persecuted by his past, at least, not officially, although he did feel some unease. To be on the safe side, he had participated in the renovation of the Vinkovci public library. It had been badly damaged, the collection scattered by the wind through the alleys, Croatian, Serbian and world classics had fluttered in the crowns of chestnuts and limes. Couples in love, in pauses between embraces on the benches in their shade, read the pages of individual books at the whim of the wind. Some took it as a kind of fortune-telling, the voice of destiny: poems were generally welcome, Tolstoy even more so. He had written lengthy novels, and the young concluded that their relationship would also be a long romance. That in those novels the heroines threw themselves under trains because of their unhappy loves was of no consequence.

Various theories were circulating about who was in fact responsible for the burning of the library, that pride of the pre-war municipality. The most probable was that it had been burned by the Macedonian Partisans liberating the town, because some remaining Germans and "local" traitors had holed themselves up in the library building. Some maintained that it was burned by the Germans as they withdrew. The former could be explained by military necessity. But the latter fitted better with the history coming into being.*

In general, it was a time when only simple explanations prevailed. That some superstitious mysticism (revolutionary?) had to be mixed in was understood only later, in other words, too late.

The pages of the library's collection that had fluttered away were gone forever . . . Taken by migrating birds. That could have been the first and last opportunity for someone in Africa, riding a camel, to have read something by the poet Silvije Strahimir Kranjčević. The few books that had not burned were protected from the damp under a new roof. Comrade Kempf was partly responsible. And what he had succeeded in doing for books, he wished for himself and the young couple: a roof over their heads. In the end, everyone has the right to their own little hole, even animals. They intended to register in Zagreb. As a "new woman", Vera had no time for such formalities, for petty-bourgeois nonsense. Remarkably, Kempf was more practical in this matter: he thought that as a couple intending to "register" they stood a

---

* It is known, however, that the shell which destroyed the library to its foundations on the night of September 16, 1991 came from the east. [Author's note]

better chance of getting their own roof. Their own home. Was that because for two years he had covered himself with sky? Not that Vera had fared better.

Among other things, however, Đuka wanted "working conditions". For years things had been in a state of feverish movement, it had all been frenetic and that was becoming unhealthy, even pointless. He needed to stay still for a while.

Never mind Kranjčević. Đuka Kempf had been reading more of his own poetry to his beloved. Contemporary, revolutionary poets must go among the people, certainly, but those people didn't live in pigsties or sleep in the open air, they were all trying to find their own little corner of privacy. It was high time to settle down. Poets are people too. It's all very well for nightingales, especially when nightingales are the emperors.

Vera was comfortable in her little town, she felt strong, everyone wanted her, everyone respected her. Only rarely, on the corso, was there an occasional glance with a trace of animosity or mockery . . .

It bothered her for a moment, and that was that. They were leaving for Zagreb early so that she could begin her studies. She wasn't especially interested in poetry, but she did want to study, in truth not electrical engineering. Literature, yes, the great novels, great stories about real life, which is always a battle . . . Of poetry, she held that it was something that came into being quickly, and she didn't value that. Poetry was something like drunkenness, and some people had told her that her boyfriend had always been a drinker. On the contrary: work, work and only work! She wanted to be more active, at least in the villages. The news that the Party was sending her to study electrical engineering pleased her, that is, she was talking herself into it. It was a powerful cause because it concerned the powerful force of electricity. She didn't know how to change a plug, but she would learn far more difficult things: had not the great Lenin said: "The Soviets + electrification = socialism"? How clear it was, how simple! Simple because it was clear! Clear because it was simple! How often in recent days had Vera carried out her activist work by the light of an oil-lamp. With the setting of the sun, the villages all around Vinkovci were plunged into darkness, as though we were still in the days of Turkish Slavonia. There were to be no oil-lamps in socialism!

Kempf too was pleased at the news because now he was sure his Vera would accompany him to Zagreb. This was, then, a new beginning. And that was normal for the times. They were full of beginnings.

Those whose properties had been burned, the persecuted, the refugees, the displaced (as in the camps for displaced persons in destroyed Germany) – all had just one thing in mind: to settle down, to live a bit . . . and Kempf was no exception. The war had scattered human splinters far and wide, in all directions into the swirling winds: people, like dandelion seeds, were blown about at the whim of the wind. Many were only now beginning to grasp that life was the only fortune: a planted corpse would not bear fruit.

In "old Europe", the young talked about a beginning, the older people about continuing. But continuing in an entirely altered world looked more like a new beginning. And that was why everything, in all directions, was crackling with new beginnings. It was a mythic time.

Execution

Why had he suddenly remembered the hanging of Tolj, the Vinkovci chief of police who had Vera brought in and then let her go, astonished at her boldness? As he had at the same time ordered her to be closely followed, he probably hoped that she would lead them to something. Or had she simply seemed to him too young to be a real threat to the state he served? That same man had ordered that a trap be set for her, one she avoided thanks to a police informer (called Bartol, she knew him well), but they set another one for her, into which she unfortunately fell . . . That was after a raid.

At the interrogation, Tolj threatened her violently. He wanted her to reveal her brother's whereabouts. Then he gave up, knowing that Vera was too far down the hierarchy of the Movement to know where a true illegal and dangerous communist was hiding, even if he was her brother. They sent her to the camp at Stara Gradiška.

Tolj was captured, that is to say he gave himself up as soon as the liberating forces, a Macedonian brigade, arrived in Vinkovci. At his hearing, he said he was too old for a new beginning, and too young to kill himself. Also, he wasn't a coward like all those who had run away.

He had made Vera a persecuted person. Tolj and decency?

"You're from a decent Croatian family, my girl. I knew your

grandpa, he was a drinker, but his own man. Your mother Marija is a model of civic modesty and decency . . . the poor widow of a railway man who supported the Croatian Peasant Party; politically, therefore, a right-minded Croat. What drives you into that rabble, when you come from quite different stock . . . ?"

That's what Tolj had said, looking across the desk on which there was a chess board with the pieces set out on it.

This Tolj didn't play cards with drunks, he didn't like hunting and its cruelty, he didn't chase women, people said he was incorruptible, for a policeman he was dangerously irreproachable. Only the chess. Where did they find him, thought Vera then, not at all afraid, which was certainly foolish. Because at that time he was all-powerful.

But what had brought about this onrush of memories of a creep, who had to an extent settled his accounts after he was arrested immediately following the liberation? What was this dwarf to him, a man whose eyes shone with a sickly brilliance, like a cat that wanted to gather with its pupils whatever remaining light there was in the cellar, in the street? In fact, Tolj looked like someone for whom the waking day was actually night and who saw better in the dark than in daylight.

Tolj was arrested immediately after Vinkovci was liberated. There was just one hearing. A man whose official duty had been to defend him brought a list of people whom Tolj had protected. But the list of those he had sentenced to death and the few he had himself tortured in the most unimaginable ways was far longer. The hearing was attended by a crowd of women in black who shrieked . . . Like the Furies, their hair stood on end. Tolj sat in the courtroom, completely absent. In the end, even his own lawyer said that he was impressed by the number of executions attributed to his client. To the question of whether he felt guilty,

Tolj declined to answer. When he was taken out of the courtroom, only a strong contingent of police prevented the women from lynching him. Their rage, despair and sorrow would have torn him to pieces.

Then Tolj disappeared for a while. Many asked what had become of him. The news spread that he had made a deal and bought his life by denouncing some of those from the top of the state he had served so devotedly. It was true that he had been taken to Zagreb, and that the new authorities did indeed expect him to give them important information about people who had been caught or were being pursued.

Then Tolj was returned to Vinkovci.

It isn't clear who in the government decided that the execution should be public as that had only been the practice immediately after the war. The condemned were now usually liquidated in the cellars of prisons or hanged in their inner courtyards.

It's easy to put up a good scaffold if you have good wood.

So a scaffold appeared on the square. The days when people were hanged from trees were over.

That afternoon, probably everybody in Vinkovci able to walk, even if on only one leg, gathered on the square, which was of course now named Freedom Square. The corso looked empty, unreal. In later times, a similar effect was achieved only by football matches when Yugoslavia was playing, and by popular music festivals.

Tolj was already standing on a stool, his hands tied behind his back, the noose swinging in the light breeze. There was a smell of ripe fruit and before long picking would begin in the vineyards ... People would go back to their work, just get this done, put a full stop to the damned war.

Tolj appeared entirely absent. He was guarded by a detachment of police. The sentence was read out in silence.

Then, Kempf stepped into the front row and shouted at the top of his voice:

"Checkmate, Tolj!"

There were people there who had seen Tolj at the height of his power, playing chess in his office. So no-one took Kempf's exclamation as a random wisecrack.

Kempf himself was surprised at the volume of his voice. If anything surprised the better-informed among those present, it was the vehemence in the voice of the returnee from the east: no-one, that is, guessed that Kempf had any issues of his own with the condemned man. Because that is how it appeared.

As soon as Kempf had spoken, it seemed that something moved on the condemned man's face, that his eyes shifted around looking for whoever had called him by name. He looked as though he was going to say something – or it could have been a desperate gesture to take in with a last effort the air that would soon be denied him. Tolj stared at Kempf, or at least that's how it appeared; but immediately afterwards he realised that the condemned man was looking through him at an unusual figure shoving its way towards the scaffold. Kempf moved aside to give way to a huge woman whose black uniform was bursting at the seams and threatening to spill in all directions. Kempf recognised the uniform of a member of a tank crew of the German army. He had come across it frequently, particularly when the Nazis had begun to pile up machinery before the clash at Kursk. The tank crews would leap onto the backs of their Tigers like black exclamation marks and slide into their innards . . . Everything about them was smooth, with no folds or buttons. The elegance of German military fashion was well matched with the need for a man to be part of the machine and for it to function without friction.

But this woman was large, it wasn't clear how she had stuffed herself into the uniform. Her boots weighed her down, they were Soviet-made and had probably never been cleaned. No-one would have accepted her into a tank crew.

And now she was fighting for her space and time, and immediately succeeded: whenever Kempf thought of this event at a later date, it was combined with the impression that everything had stopped, and that several people, not just he, had shifted to let her pass.

It was this woman, not the person who had called to him, that Tolj's eyes were following as he stood on his stool. The woman had brown hair, long, now waving in the breeze. An absurd thought occurred to Kempf.

German tank crews wore helmets, those ordinary black chamber pots . . .

That this woman was a Fury, Kempf added later, rummaging through his cultural treasury, his education. There had been no time then for any kind of associations, time had stopped, and in his memory this remained like a slowed-down film.

In reality, it was all quick: as soon as the executioner moved the stool, the Giantess put her arms round Tolj's legs that were kicking through the air, looking for the support that was no longer there . . . and she pulled down on the body of the once all-powerful master of Vinkovci. The last movements of the condemned man soon stopped, the full length of his tongue jumped from his mouth, looking larger than his head.

People began to disperse before his last movements had ceased. Only the children remained. Why the children? Because they had nothing else to do, there was no school that day.

Kempf put his arm round Vera's shoulders and the two of them set off along the corso to the bank of the Bosut, where

they intended, as often in recent times, to find a bench and have
a bit of a cuddle. But they usually did this later in the afternoon,
closer to the protective darkness. Now they could have a chat
about what they had just witnessed. Vera knew very well who
Tolj was; Kempf knew virtually nothing about him. As the chief
of UNS˙ for Vinkovci, so presumably also for Kempf's native town
of Nuštar, Tolj was not responsible for the Volksdeutsche. They
were a state within a state. Why her boyfriend had behaved like
that at the execution, Vera had no idea. A slightly murky light on
the whole event was cast by the fact that he himself didn't know
what had come over him; he had simply shouted.

Vera didn't ask him anything about the chess. Then he said:
"Do you know the woman in the black uniform?"

Vera shook her head. No subsequent enquiries led any further.
No-one could say where the woman had disappeared to after
the execution.

"You saw how she behaved?"

Vera said nothing.

"She had something against him."

"There wasn't a woman in the square of whom you couldn't
say the same."

"Maybe she wanted to make his death easier?"

"How do you mean?"

"Immediate fracture of the cervical vertebra. I'm a medic after
all."

"But why ever would she want to make anything easier for
him, especially his death? That was a just punishment."

Kempf agreed. But where on earth had she found that uniform?

Then this thought occurred to him: perhaps she was taking

---

* Ustaška nadzorna služba: Ustasha Surveillance Service. [Translator's note]

revenge for the massacre of Tito's nurses by the tank crews of the Waffen-S.S. There was no proof. And it was a long way from the Bosnian gorges to the plains of Slavonia.

"Could you have done anything like that, I mean, tug him by the legs?"

"No."

"They say that at a certain moment the hanged ejaculate."

"Don't be crude."

That's how it was left. This event remained unmentioned to the end of their relationship.

Never again did Kempf raise his voice, in the street or in public.

Within Four Walls

Less than a week had passed since they rented a room in the hotel opposite the station in Zagreb. The hotel was not yet heated and the damp of autumn rains had found its way into the sheets and covers. The toilet was shared by all the rooms in the corridor. At night they slept badly because of the shouting of the railway workers manoeuvring trains ... which arrived night and day, from all directions. The town was seriously hungry, fuel and everything else was scarce, but people were arriving in large numbers. This meant that problems with supplies would get worse. Many of the new arrivals would become its new inhabitants. The town was entering a new heroic era, a time of "renewal and construction". Nocturnal roundups were coming to an end or were rare. Although denunciations still poured in: the revolution was continuing. But the city streets were swept, the street lights fixed, the trams running. Every morning peasant women arrived from the surrounding villages with baskets of their produce carried on their heads, on a folded scarf. On Sundays, the parks and squares were full. On the Zrinjevac small, linked parks, there was music again. In the hospitals, the last liberators of Zagreb were dying. They gathered again in the cemetery of Mirogoj, they had a communal grave there.* There were

---

* Today it is somewhat hidden, away from the main cemetery paths. [Author's note]

numerous people with wooden legs on the promenades. On the day of their arrival in Zagreb, Vera and Kempf read in the newspaper about children without parents roaming the streets and living from crime and prostitution. Trains with no timetable had Zagreb as their transit point on their way to Slavonia and Vojvodina. But the city too was changing. Its blood is being renewed, some said. The town was being taken over by illiterate and arrogant barbarians, said others. These primitives shove others out of their way, they maintained. They'll be dancing peasant ring dances on the main Jelačić Square. History has witnessed this often, said a third group: the countryfolk come into the city, take it over, and then the process of civilising them begins. In the end, the city will conquer them and, just as that has happened, new savages will come and take it over.

For a week they walked through the city streets, absorbing impressions, waiting for their appeal to be decided. They wanted to have a permanent address before they stepped in front of the registrar. The only park they saw was the Botanical Garden, but the benches no longer appealed to them. In their imaginations they saw images that they could only properly realise under their own roof, hidden from the gaze of others. True love is for two people. They were tired of always waiting for darkness.

On the fifth day, as every day, Vera went to the council offices to enquire. Kempf waited for her in the canteen for which they had been given vouchers. He didn't eat, just waited, mostly because he was tense. When she appeared in the doorway, he couldn't immediately make out what was happening; he was even more doubtful about the two men in leather coats who accompanied her. He thought for a moment that they had come to take Sturmmann Kempf away, something he often experienced as a nightmare. But a smile on Vera's face dispersed all doubts. "The comrades don't have much time. Let's go straight to the apartment. We'll eat later."

It turned out that the guys in the leather coats were to play the role of witnesses. They removed the lead seal from the door of a flat on the first floor on a long street that ended at the beginning of a wooded park. That huge park was named after Bishop Maksimilijan Vrhovec, who was the one to have it laid out in the eighteenth century. Vera signed the register of transfer. In this world, her signature was more powerful than his. Between Vinkovci and Zagreb, his *bumashka* had lost something of its shine. There were very many people here advertising their association with the Soviets. The comrades took their leave, wishing them well, winking impishly, and vanished.

Both Vera and Đuka were grateful for that.

Kempf embraced Vera firmly with the idea of taking her to bed. But changed his mind.

The bed was not only made up, but the corner of the cover was turned neatly down, as though someone was just getting ready to lie down, and next to it, on the floor, were corduroy slippers. Instead of desire, something drove them to satisfy their curiosity. And their unease grew. Whose apartment it had been they didn't know, and the council hadn't told them. That was how things went. The apartment was secure in the sense that no-one could return to claim it. Because that person either couldn't or didn't wish to return. *Nomen nescio*, name unknown. Perhaps he had perished, perhaps he was still alive. In either case, if he came back, he would be a ghost. Ghosts, as every child knew, could not come in through a door, but potentially through walls. There was nothing to be done about that, but for securely based people who knew their place that shouldn't be a problem. Indeed, it was banned from being a problem. The apartment had two rooms, in the bathroom there was a copper boiler for heating water, with wood stacked beside it. There were a few towels in the cupboards. The toilet gleamed, as though it had been cleaned the day before.

In the kitchen, in a light-green cabinet with a multitude of drawers, there was some crockery. All modest, but functional. There was no luxury, but the apartment was fully equipped.

They looked for signs of earlier presences. They opened drawers, sniffed: there was a smell of lavender everywhere. In each drawer there was some trace of the people who had lived here until recently. Who knows how long they had been here? Was it their own apartment, or rented? Who had been ill here, who had died? In one cupboard, decorated with an unusual carving – the Sun and Moon, like a bridegroom and bride – they found Christmas tree ornaments.

In another box they found a heap of children's toys. Some were traditional, like those played with by children from the surroundings of Zagreb and they were as colourful as they could possibly be. They were made of wood; but there was a small metal tank, evidently cast in a mould. A Kampfwagen V, Panther. A Panther! Kempf couldn't resist, admitting to the fact that he was capable of recognising almost every model that had been firing until the previous day. Vera put the little tank down on the floor and started to move it. "It's not realistic enough," Kempf complained, "the caterpillar tracks don't move."

"Were you ever in something like this in Poland?" Vera said.

Kempf remembered this moment forever because it was the first time she had asked him anything about his "little Polish war".

"I was in the infantry," Kempf said drily and that was the end of it.

Kempf tried to cheer up the woman with whom he was to set up a household here: "Let's go and look at our surroundings. It's like when you are staying in a hotel in a big city, you leave your luggage and go to look around . . ."

They set off to Maksimir park.

On the open space at the entrance to Bishop Maksimilijan's park, the first post-war funfair had set up its attractions. There were a lot of young people and children. And, of course, a lot of soldiers. It seemed to both Vera and Đuka that the whole world had become infantilised. Everywhere screams, merry-go-rounds . . . people shot at little rag dolls that fell over when they were hit, winning a prize. There had been dolls like that in that box. Hasn't there been enough of this, thought Kempf, watching the soldiers firing, showing off in front of the girls. But then he felt ashamed. Where would we be if we measured everything by an absolute yardstick? Only God can do that.

God had been the occasion for a little argument with Vera. They had been discussing whether they would opt for a church wedding too. "Opt for" because Vera considered marriage, sec-ular or any other kind, to be an agreement between free people. It was something that had to be stipulated. To that he responded, half joking, that it wasn't bad to have everything tidily confirmed in heaven as well as at the council. Vera took him seriously and said, almost like a slogan: "You know what excuses God? Only the fact that he doesn't exist!"

They strolled, watching people enjoying themselves. That enjoyment wasn't deep, it wasn't a revolutionary manifestation of the vitality of the masses, but it was spontaneous. Otherwise, there was marching every day in the city, military parades were common . . . From time to time on the squares the city authorities roasted an ox. The theatre began to function, the cinemas had never stopped. The first children were born in freedom. And of course the first liberated people died.

The continuity of birth and death does not fit a revolutionary calendar.

The parades provoked universal delight. The masses often paused on the edge of pavements, the enthusiasm was still great enough that children didn't need to be trained to wave at black limousines. As ever, Kempf wondered how big a part was played in this by real spontaneity, and how much was organised joy.

But who could measure that with absolute accuracy? How much among us all is absolutely pure, how much is completely shabby?

What is cynical about people is perhaps the fact that this last could be named. Much that had been done in the war was an absolute abomination. But where was absolute good? Where would it get us if we, humans, were judged as though we were gods? You will be like gods, God promised humans. Preferably not. Besides, that promise is ambiguous.

Perhaps not even God himself imagined all this as a promise of happiness. You will be like gods! That would mean there would be a lot of gods. As many gods as people. A contradiction.

He Himself couldn't bear any other kinds of gods . . . so perhaps that was why He permitted everything that happened to mankind, or was perpetrated by mankind? Especially by those who proclaimed themselves gods, taking that promise of God's at face value. While He was probably joking. Afterwards He simply looked in the opposite direction. So when things started burning here, because flames were being lit on all sides, He looked upwards, and there was no longer anything to see. Poor God. But He wants to be One.

So, they had just entered the apartment of some former people. They were on the threshold of a new beginning. Just as those former people were. By an absolute standard, they too ought to be former. Two lots of former lives that would probably never meet. And if they were to meet, how would they greet each other? Certainly not with bread and salt.

They climbed onto brightly coloured wooden horses and spun on the carousel until Vera felt queasy.

Completely exhausted, they went back to the apartment. They unlocked the door carefully as though they didn't believe the apartment was empty. Then, below them, on the stairs, they caught sight of the caretaker bowing to them. He was dressed in a blue uniform, with a screwdriver poking out of his pocket.

"If anything needs fixing, please let me know," he said.

Kempf thought he ought to give him a tip, and then remembered that they weren't in the hotel any longer.

Conversations in Bed

In trams, in bars, at the market, out walking, in funfairs, in the theatre, two Zagrebs met. One was left over from the war, the other just coming into being. There were still "liberated" apartments. The courts still made judgments hastily and according to the law of war. But just as the city had endeavoured to retain some appearance of normality even in the worst years of the war, even when the Allies were bombing it, even when there were raids and shooting somewhere every night, even when the Jews were disappearing, so now too all would seem normal to a superficial eye: the city was renewing its blood. It really did appear younger. It's worth knowing that the average age of those who joined Tito was under twenty. Now the Marshal, with gilded epaulettes and his dog, revealed himself to the masses, who cheered.

As during the war, one segment of the citizens decided to observe but to participate only minimally. Perhaps the whole thing was provisional. Perhaps nothing was yet decided. There were few among them who wished for the return of the Ustasha. But the people who had now "landed on the city" didn't know how to behave. The Germans say that good is not always new, and that new is not always good. But there were no more Germans. There were no Jews either. The citizens saw that as some kind of balance, almost justice.

When the Jews, their neighbours, were being rounded up on

staircases, they peered through the spyholes in their doors. When the sirens warned of American aircraft, they climbed up Sljeme mountain, with thermoses and provisions. When the Ustashas were fleeing the city, they photographed them secretly with their Kodak cameras through half-open blinds. They went to the opera, applauded or grumbled because of a badly sung aria. Along with the archbishop, they were afraid that the Allies, who didn't understand the concept of holiness, might bomb the Cathedral. On the terrace of the Esplanade hotel, beside the main railway station, they licked ice creams. Some had even managed to see Heinrich Himmler, the all-powerful master of the Waffen-S.S., on the main street, Ilica, when he flew into Agram* one May to check whether the situation *in Kroatien* was really as bad as it was described in the reports of Hitler's plenipotentiary in Croatia, Edmund Glaise von Horstenau. They had seen Hitler's plump general, the highly decorated Esterajher, at masses and operas. Secretly, along with reports to Hitler and the Supreme Command of the Wehrmacht, he wrote music reviews. It annoyed him greatly that Archbishop Stepinac sang his masses better than his Viennese colleague Innizer. Otherwise, in his diary he wrote of the archbishop: "He's no great intellect." When he had to flee Zagreb towards the end of the war, he was sorry to leave its panoramas, but most of all the fine villa, today the Hunting Museum, where stuffed wild boar and birds reside.

Zagreb was, and remained, a town of Mitteleuropa.

But look at it now. Many indoor baths were home to grunting pigs. Cockerels crowed from balconies, leaped on hens, chicks peeped. Only a few days earlier, the new authorities banned goats from being kept and pigs fattened in the central urban area. The

---

* The historic Austrian-German name for Zagreb. [Translator's note]

country women behaved oddly, they didn't shave their legs. Apart from that, they were all tanned by the sun, which was not a sign of good taste.

That Zagreb of ours truly had no luck. Just look, another wedding. But it wasn't a Saturday. Why these folk mate like rabbits, muttered an elderly gentleman at the sight of a procession, with wide banners, following an accordion player. All that was missing was a Gypsy with a bear on a chain! The Balkans have prevailed in every way, my friend.

But that was not Vera and Kempf's wedding procession, although they also married on a day that was not a Saturday. When their turn came, this is how it went.

The registrar had just seen off a wedding party that had occupied all the seats and several of whose guests had spent the brief procedure in the corridors. The bridegroom was a young lad who had obviously borrowed a suit that was too big for him, with a large medal on its lapel. The bride, evidently unused to high heels, stumbled as she reached the desk. She was of a similar age to the groom, sturdily built, but clearly timid . . . not used to ceremonials. There were a lot of soldiers in the hall, probably war companions of the young groom. Then, as the climax of the ceremony, after the newly married comrades had signed a document stating that they were joining in a matrimonial association in the name of the people, a soldier in the street outside the office fired a volley of shots. That coincided with the midday bells of Saint Stephen, that is to say the Cathedral, and the experience was complete, regardless of whether the ceremony was being observed as a secular or holy event.

Singing at the top of their voices, the guests stood up and began to line up behind the accordion-player . . . The evacuation of the hall took some time, but it was carried out smoothly. One group inside, the other outside: marriages, in the name of the people, were conducted as on a conveyor belt. The new wedding party entered the hall unnoticed.

The registrar studied their papers, they sat down in the front row.

Without looking up, the registrar uttered the formula that he had repeated countless times in recent days: Let the bride and groom and their witnesses sit in the first row and the others . . .

Only then did he raise his head. He looked relieved that, in the hall, in the front row, sat only the bride and groom and their two witnesses. That was the entire team. Kempf had asked a drunk, whom he had "bought" for two brandies to be his witness; Vera's witness was one of the antifascist women from the local organisation. The man had kept his promise of arriving sober and clean-shaven. On his face, smoothly shaved, his nose stood out even more prominently, dappled with red and blue veins. Vera's witness conducted herself seriously. There were no rings. Vera considered the custom of exchanging rings outdated.

They all signed and went to lunch in the canteen. A table had been assigned to them some way away from the door, and on that table was a carnation in a glass.

That red carnation had to perform the entire ceremony: it alone was something out of the ordinary.

Well, alright, they did have potential witnesses in their comrades from the Party.

But they had decided to carry out the little petty-bourgeois ceremony almost in secret. There was no-one who could have been offended. Kempf's parents were dead, and the newly-weds sent a telegram to Vera's mother Marija.

They consummated their marriage, as the petty-bourgeois put it, and there was no blood. So there would be no display of a bloodied sheet to the wedding guests in the morning, as was the custom in the villages, proof of purity that would guarantee their marriage vows in the future. After their first love-making, three months earlier, Kempf understood that Vera was not without experience. Well, it was wartime, people lived fast, Kempf had thought then, and he was not troubled by the fact that she was not a virgin.

Except momentarily, like a short, sharp prick in the area of his consciousness where he otherwise relegated unwanted memories: for an instant he was aware of the patriarchal male concerned with the purity of his possession.

The two of them lay, after an embrace that turned out too brief, each on their own side of the double bed, under a picture showing a recently ploughed field and a peasant scattering seed by hand. Vera said it was a poor effort bought at some country fair. Surprising, because there were other traces of the previous occupants that bore witness to their attention to detail and good taste.

They were both awake, which might have seemed strange, given the excitement of the day. For instance, in the canteen, people had kept coming up to them, in fairness more to Vera than to him, and there was no end to the toasts. So many good wishes were expressed that they would have filled even the thickest album.

"In Gradiška," Kempf began suddenly, "was there any violence against women?"

To be honest, he had long been thinking about asking something along these lines. What he really wanted to know was whether the guards had been involved in mass rape, and then through her response to possibly learn something of her own situation before she had been exchanged. And he chose precisely this moment to ask.

Vera said nothing.

"People drank there, didn't they?"

"You know what an army does as soon as there's an opportunity."

"So, was there mass rape?"

"Did you ever take part in something like that?"

"No," he said, and it was true.

He waited for Vera to go on, but she was silent.

"How did you get by?" he asked, after five long, painful minutes, and immediately regretted it.

"Croatian women were less threatened. There were plenty of young Jewish and Serbian girls behind the wire. To choose from. But when they drank, we'd retreat into the hut, and the more appealing of us would hide under beds or somewhere. When they started drinking, all we could do was pray to our God: just don't let them beat us!

"Once there was a little Jewish girl in our hut, about seven years old, no more. She was covered in bites. If you're asking about your Sofija, I don't know."

Kempf realised for the first time that she knew about Sofija. How much did Vera in fact know about him? She had never, but never, asked about his recruitment, about Poland, about the S.S. Now she had brought Sofija up; those were probably women's preferences.

She thought that her newly inaugurated husband was asking not about her but about Sofija.

Kempf felt desire again, she woke and responded. Nevertheless, the sower above the bed sowed nothing that night.

In the morning, they got up refreshed and cheerful: it was a sunny day, clear, with a north wind blowing. It was cold outside, but the stove warmed them well, it was still warm from the night before. Kempf knew that Vera would not be bringing him slippers and he would have to make the coffee. Vera had a particular aversion to irons. Kempf had two shirts he had been wearing unironed. But that was in keeping with the image of an incipient poet, a Socialist bohemian who understood that there were shortages, of almost everything, including irons . . . Besides, Vera had easily come by vouchers for the canteen, where meat was served at least twice a week; it would have been hard for him to have been so well fed in the prevailing circumstances, overseen by deserving and orthodox purists, while bohemians were just a bit of a luxury, a kind of iron for bumpy reality.

Bohemians, poets and similar eccentrics were the grasshoppers from Aesop's fable of the ant and the grasshopper: the ant was the proletarian who worked, the shock-worker ant, while the grasshopper was the crazy bohemian who didn't know that summer fun is followed by the woes of an icy winter. This was not the time for grasshoppers, this was ant time. The broken anthill had to be rebuilt. The proletarian would understand that surpluses, a very provisional expression for what was left over after the satisfaction of modestly assessed basic needs, had to be invested in heavy industry . . . The poet would simply squander those surpluses on sprees and orgies with his muses. There was talk in the town of a spree at the Society of Authors at which Muses had ridden on writers and galloped "round the table". People are not equally serious in times which are, however, equally serious for everyone.

There was no doubt that Vera managed better in the new times. One had constantly to look upwards, and everyone had to know his true measure, determined by those on top of the rostrum. That had a soothing effect and was a good antidote to the doubts of the poisoned; of course, it was also the best cure for one's own doubts. Eros himself had to become serious, disciplined. All sorts of things were said, officially, but what was emerging was a new puritanism.

The First Five-Year Plan

Kempf's drinking was finally noticed by the Party. In no way was it the kind of drunkenness that the Party would consider desirable. Comrade Kempf was criticised increasingly often in the local organisation.

Vera went to the clinic for an examination, everything was fine with her.

Đuka Kempf went for an examination, everything was fine with him. Alcohol "provokes the desire but takes away the performance" it says in *Macbeth*. But Kempf had sober days.

I'll have to take action, thought Vera Kempf. And half a year of the five-year plan flew past.

Just let things stay as they are, thought Đuka Kempf.

I believe that I have reason to be tense, impatient. The whole country is making plans, short- and long-term. I am not in the plan. Heavy industry is flourishing, the crops have been sown, hunger is receding.

The Kremlin is an ever-growing enigma, but faith in togetherness still endures. Tuberculosis and many other troubles are retreating, more and more light bulbs are shining. There's talk that Yugoslavia will soon manufacture its own car.

But, although a lot of creches are being opened, there is no mention of me. The frequent allusions of Vera and Kempf's friends to a new generation, to an heir (of what?) – sighs along the lines of: Everything will be better when there are children, and so on – all fall on deaf ears. My father is completely unmoved, but my future

Vera Kempf was determined. I'll take action.

One could say that a light bulb had lit up for her.

She didn't like people mentioning light bulbs. She had learned where the fuse box in the apartment was. But her studies weren't going well. With considerable effort, she passed some minor exams. After a while, she was revolted by powerful currents. As a devoted Party member, she realised that she had missed the mark. That she had failed the exam set by the deity called Heavy Industry.

A little pre-history is required here so as to see what Vera Kempf dreamed up.

When they had entered the apartment allocated them by the local council as a still unmarried couple, they had been accompanied by two men from the local council as witnesses of the transaction. But the inventory was

mother, on the other hand, does finally decide that something must be done. We'll see.

After all, they've been under their own roof, in favourable conditions for love, for two years already. And nothing.

What a dissipation of national energy. If Kempf were truly a man, he would see me already peering out from Vera's eyes. Instead of giving free rein to the laws of the flesh, they argue about the laws of iron necessity and other historical questions that they want to solve in bed. Is there a worse place for something like that?

The unborn gather around me. Like me, they all know that a woman can achieve a lot. Nature, itself a wise female, has its ways. The unborn believe that I shall soon be leaving them. I've had a lot of congratulations in advance. "There, you see! And you doubted it," say some. "With very good reason," I reply. Which is true.

With birth, we lose the privilege of being informed about past events. I'll miss that. For the most part, I won't dare ask. Whatever I'm told, I'll remember.

We who have not yet been born must forget.

No-one is born as an already

minimal: on that day another dozen apartments were occupied that in May 1945 had been liberated from class and all other kinds of enemies. And these two men had acted

written page. I believe that is the wisdom of existence itself. It would be terrible if there was no such wisdom.

as transaction witnesses for all of them, which required speed, that is a minimal procedure.

That was why nothing of the contents of the apartment was listed, apart from the furniture. The boxes, what was hanging in the wardrobes, slippers under the bed, towels in the bathroom – none of that was included in the inventory lodged with the council. Those things were left officially unnoticed, as though they didn't exist.

The Kempfs opened the trunks and cupboards without much curiosity. And whenever they found some object, an article of clothing, a toy, something that suggested in a more vivid and concrete way the presence of former people (because they had been erased from the new order by the mere fact of having fled), they felt an onrush of unease.

Not even a week of their living in the allocated apartment had passed when the Kempfs called the Red Cross, having first wrapped all the clothing they found, all the towels and toys, and above all the corduroy slippers in sheets. The Red Cross responded quickly.

The Kempfs were greatly relieved.

At the council, they reported their needs: the flat was fine, but it was empty; they had found it empty, not only of people but also of possessions. Their real home-making began. Friends contributed this and that; they received something from the Red Cross. The Army added some things. It was a bit soon for toys.

Among other things requisitioned from the possessions of class enemies, they received a wall clock with an inscription saying it had been made in Werkstatt, Vienna.

Not a thing belonging to the previous residents was left in the apartment, as the young couple had agreed.

Nevertheless, Vera had secretly retained two items belonging to the previous lady of this house: a petticoat, pink, thin, almost transparent, trimmed with black lace, and a pair of red high-heeled lacquered shoes, from which only the dust had to be blown off.

I'm taking action, thought Vera Kempf.

But perhaps that unfortunate petticoat would not be sufficiently effective? Who knew what Kempf might have seen in Poland. Another kind of calculation was required, a clever plan. That plan should be scientifically based. Children are not born like chicks, from every egg on which the mother hen sits. It was necessary to carefully plan, for example, what was to happen in the first, second and third year of the five-year plan. Very intelligent people had come up with the idea of a five-year plan. Why should women lag behind the prudence of good managers? Why should they not manage their bodies, like productive machines? In the same way? In the name of the people?

Vera picked up the leaflet entitled *Sex Life, What and How,* printed with the approval of the national government and supported by the thinking of the Antifascist Women's Front. Vera took that leaflet with her to women in the Slavonian backwoods, beyond the ancient oak forests ("Transylvania"), which exist only in Slavonia, and possibly in Lika, where she later also went. How often had she explained to the village women how to calculate their fertile days, how to avoid something unwanted (an erotic predicament, a baby "out of wedlock", which was social death in the villages), and how to induce the men to give them what they wanted. So, if she had helped some of them, and she was sure she had, why not help herself?

Following the procedure of the brochure, step by step, she easily calculated her fertile days.

I'm making good progress in this venture, she thought with satisfaction. The following day was in fact D-Day.

Kempf came home late as usual, a little less tipsy than often. Instead of waiting for him at the door with a rolling pin in her hand, Vera, dressed only in the pink, almost transparent petticoat, her legs crossed in their high heels, was sitting on the bed smoking. She smoked rarely and almost always ended up coughing like a child. Her breasts were prominent, as if swollen. And Vera was well endowed, she was beyond reproach in that department. Her body may have been rather delicate for peasant taste, but in Slavonia she would have been eyed up as a good prospect. Her egg was ready.

She sat there, watching her husband put down his coat and go to the toilet to pee (she hated the sound of pee hitting the bowl, she had told him a million times, but he took no notice, only this time there was no sound), then he came and stood in front of her, dumbfounded.

Had his Polish prostitutes looked like this, wondered Vera, endeavouring to produce the smile of a seductress, a woman on a mission, just that parting of the lips that she had seen in the local cinema, in a schmaltzy Mexican movie.

No doubt those prostitutes jumped onto tables. This was after all something different.

Vera felt a little like what she imagined the ballerina in the forest must have felt, dancing to the plaintive notes of a violin on the tips of her toes, floating, as though she had lost all contact with the boards under her pumps, and as though the whole world was spread out beneath those pumps; Comrade Vera remembered every detail of that fantastic little show which had ended with a general washing of underwear and uniforms in a Partisan barrel against lice. Even the most obdurate soldiers, including the officers, had devoured the ballerina with their eyes. Even our girls and women: it was as though that nymph had descended down a silken ladder from heaven.

It seemed to her that all she had undertaken was good and in keeping with expectations. She felt an onrush of pride, believing herself suddenly powerful and strong: as though she was sitting on a throne ruling over a current of intense emotions.

Kempf, feeling a different kind of onrush, knelt in front of her, aware of wild arousal, but at the same time a kind of incapacity, which was not unappealing, as he waited for her further initiative; she grasped him firmly with her legs, which she had shaved that morning, for the first time in a while, and which glowed in the half-darkness, without the slightest need of a powerful current, just as they were, the smooth, firm, seductive legs of a young woman who had walked for miles through forests; she pulled him onto her and I would be conceived. That was now a distant, nine-month past, or somewhat longer, because I was overdue.

In the third year of the five-year plan, I would emerge from my mother, in hospital, as ordained by the new age of progress, rather than in a shack. I was greeted by a powerful electric light, rather than an oil-lamp. My umbilical cord, I was told when I was old enough to understand, was wound round my neck. I was born with difficulty, by caesarean section.

Children born with their cords round their necks can sometimes go a bit berserk. My mother considers this a superstition she suppresses in the process of enlightening the people.

But that's a long way off. I am still a distant, very small comrade.

Ernst Thälmann, a Distant Comrade

The mutual attraction of the young couple was slowly dissolving, love was vanishing like soap in a sink. Like two animals which sometimes reveal their needle-like claws and growl, they began, at first under their breath, for the time being, and only in allusions, to mention divorce.

Vera now slept in a different room, with the excuse that his snoring bothered her.

Kempf didn't know that he snored. Vera maintained that during the night he sawed several cords of wood. Ania had never told him that. But of course Ania could never spend the night with him on his camp bed, and after their embraces she would disappear until morning. He remembered

The intimation of my arrival not only did not strengthen the relationship between my mother and father, it heralded storms. Kempf suddenly announced that he "was not yet ready to be a father". Vera responded that fatherhood was easy to bear, but that she was no longer a very young mother. Slavonian women of her age had usually had all the children they intended to have. While they just kept going over historical questions. If everything was now full of new beginnings, why would children not be part of it? I am not impressed by Kempf's feeble excuse that the general circumstances were improving very slowly and that he would not be in a position to feed a growing family. Vera's entirely justified response is that she was the one who fed the family, and let us see what tomorrow brings.

that Ania had sometimes liked to be on top for a long time, to simply sit on him, but the conditions in the field hospital had been more like a bustling crowd in a railway station than a love nest.

Vera and Đuka did not leave their shared table because they had never really established one. Vera saw the meaning of emancipation in cooking when she felt like it, which was rarely. Besides, it was far harder and more expensive to come by groceries than to eat in the canteens. The food there was increasingly good, and what is more neither of them had to wash the dishes. So meals when it was just the two of them were reduced to breakfast, on the hoof. Vera never had supper, so Kempf had then to fend for himself.

Nevertheless, they did have good days when it seemed to them that everything had settled down. Vera knew that other couples had problems. Perhaps her pregnancy was making her over-sensitive? She read in her textbooks that a pregnant woman could change a lot.

More than their arguments, she was upset by the fact that Kempf came home increasingly often blind drunk.

One day comrades from the council were eating with them at their table – someone from the political police service, a Montenegrin and a Partisan captain – when the conversation turned in the most unfortunate direction: Germans, yesterday, today, tomorrow. Vera was the only woman there. The waiter had kindly pushed two tables together for them. Kempf ordered a litre of wine and everything began jovially. The Montenegrin complained that Zagreb women were unapproachable, to which the captain said it depended, and Vera snapped that women here didn't get up when a man came into the room.

How they got onto Germans, Kempf couldn't say, however

often he mulled over a conversation that hadn't pleased him at all.

Of course, as soon as Germans were mentioned, it was as though everyone, at a hidden signal, looked at him and there was an uncomfortable pause to assess whether to continue with the topic or move on to something more cheerful. Because at that table Germans were accused of all the evils of the world, and particularly of responsibility for the war that had just ended.

The conversation happened to be overheard by a Russian, one of the economic advisers sent by Stalin to help Tito with "the collectivisation of the villages" on the Soviet model. Hearing that they were talking about the war, the Russian raised his glass and they all had to drink a toast to Stalin and Soviet weaponry because, after all, that was what had won the war. Then they drank to Comrade Tito, and then to the liberation of Poland.

They all looked at Kempf again.

"Not all Germans are equally guilty," the Montenegrin said.

"Germans are good fighters. When we went to fight the Italians, we sang. When we had to fight the Germans, we said goodbye to our wives," the captain said.

Kempf would most have liked the ground to swallow him up. Worst of all was that Vera too was looking at him in a hitherto unknown way. Not so much hostile, as full of curiosity.

"Of course," the captain said, "a German, properly directed, can achieve wonders. But, badly directed, he can do great harm. The fact is that a German, regardless of the direction, will always go to the end."

"But we still rubbed their noses in it," the Russian said finally. And they all toasted Josif Visarionovich again. Kempf drank as well, that wasn't hard for him. Vera, on the other hand, was drinking lemonade. They all laughed at her, offering her wine.

There was some charm, Kempf noticed unexpectedly, in her refusal.

Pregnancy had made her more beautiful. But nothing showed as yet. A woman becomes interesting if she knows how to refuse. It seemed to him that the Russian was flirting with her, and that the Montenegrin was not indifferent either. What about the captain? He too seemed to be waiting for a chance to compliment her. And it was the captain who now began to speak.

"Take Thälmann's men. Worthy lads. They are proof that the Germans are also capable of good."

It was just a few days earlier that Kempf had heard about a German detachment that had fled to the Partisans. It had been a chance conversation in which an agreeable man with a large moustache had asked him about a German from the town of Nuštar who had fought in that company and disappeared ... and he had logically expected Kempf to know something about him, either because he had shared a native town or because he was German like the vanished man.

Kempf had no idea about the man in question, nor about that company. He barely knew who Ernst Thälmann was, other than that he was a big noise in the German Communist Party. But he had no clue about the German company that had crossed over to Tito's Partisans.

"Those Germans of ours fought well, particularly against their own side. That's how it goes. And we were particularly pleased about the victories over the Ustasha."

Kempf was sure that all of them, if furtively in some cases, were looking at him. Or was that just paranoia?

"The company named Ernst Thälmann after the head of the German Party was formed in August 1943," Vera said.

"What's that got to do with anything?"

"It's good to know."

Kempf glanced at her gratefully.

Vera was evidently referring to the fact that Kempf was recruited into the Waffen-S.S. in the spring of 1943. He could not therefore have joined the Thälmann company because it did not yet exist.

But no-one, apart from the two of them, understood why she had mentioned that. It was a surprise to Kempf. Why had she not mentioned this Thälmann before?

Besides, he was quite sure that he'd never told her when he was mobilised. He knew he had sometimes talked about the medical examination and how he'd endeavoured to use his haemorrhoids and inflamed joints to outwit the doctor, the Volksdeutscher Schlauss from Osijek, but mostly in a tone reserved for unimportant anecdotes. Kempf suddenly realised that she must have made enquiries, and the fact that he couldn't have joined a company that had not yet been formed when he was mobilised had pleased her. It seemed that, thanks to that sequence of events, the conclusion, that is, that some things had been possible and others not, Vera had satisfied her curiosity. When the company of German defectors was formed, in August 1943, he was already scampering over the clearings and forests of Poland like a frightened rabbit.

But why had she gone to enquire? Because she wanted the father of her child to be an upstanding and courageous man? Why had she not asked him? Granted, he had known nothing about the Thälmann contingent, but he knew so many other things that she would do better to ask him rather than research them herself. One doesn't lie to a woman in bed. Women in German beds knew about the mass liquidations of Jews behind the front line that the Wehrmacht had been pushing ever further east since 1939; they knew all about the concentration camps. They knew about Zyklon B, about the murder of captured Russians, and

Polish civilians, especially children. Women knew everything, without asking.

And Vera had not asked either. But as he was on the whole silent, or just told anecdotes, with details that were bizarre as well as incidental, she had begun to dig around herself. Since when? While they were still "down there" in Vinkovci, when it seemed that she was still making up her mind, and wasn't quite certain that she wanted to go with him to the metropolis, nearer to the authorities? She was making up her mind, but she belonged to the deserving, the right-minded, the faithful of the new church. Despite that, she hadn't wanted to go to "her people" in Zagreb. Because that would have been a final decision in favour of a shared life with him.

Kempf felt humiliated. Although, in this conversation, she had defended him. In truth, only the two of them knew that. How often had she been able to see the letter "A", the designation of his blood group, tattooed under his upper arm, which was the way the Waffen-S.S. had "branded" their soldiers like livestock.

"I don't know whether you know, but of those Germans of ours only one in ten returned from the war."

"Good for them," the Montenegrin said.

"Do you know something else interesting?" the captain went on. "Most of them were killed in Slavonia."

"Let's drink to our Germans!" The Russian stood up and they all drank the toast.

Kempf's glass was empty, so he ordered another litre. Vera glanced at him reproachfully. But the Russian, who thought (mistakenly) that he had understood the problem, interrupted: "No problem at all, this round is on Comrade Stalin. And we have to drink with him. Whoever doesn't is against the international proletariat. Whoever doesn't drink with us is against us. Did you know that Generalissimus Tito isn't a great drinker? He doesn't know how to drink. We'll drink for him. Long live Marshal Tito, who doesn't know how to drink, long live our fraternal Yugoslav nation!"

The Russian was drunk, and in the wine that he knocked back the truth foamed. The Soviets had started to doubt the loyalty of the Yugoslav leadership, Tito above all. In the great love that was projected to last forever, cracks had begun to appear.

The comrade from the political police service was largely silent, not showing his cards. The Russian kept offering him wine, but he excused himself saying he had a weak stomach.

"Tito has a weak stomach as well. Two or three vodkas and the marshal is out of it. And then the state starts to shake too."

The captain stood up, red in the face as a crab and shouted that this wasn't true.

The comrade sat him down again with a light touch to his shoulder. Things were bubbling at the table, but they didn't boil over.

Swan Lake Without a Dog

Vera and Kempf were sitting in front of a café overlooking the theatre. He had considered wearing his British army jacket this evening, the best item of clothing he possessed. Thinking better of it, he put on a jacket he had bought in a second-hand shop. Maybe it belonged to a dead man. Today for the first time Kempf regretted that they had given all the previous occupants' clothes to the Red Cross. Who knows, perhaps this evening they would see some items out of their predecessors' wardrobe: suits walking, shaking hands, bowing to suits just like theirs . . . A Red Cross fancy-dress ball. There is an Istrian folk tale according to which all the people who wander through the next world are hollow. Presumably not naked. In that world it is eternally dawn and through its landscapes roam hollow people. Former people. That's why it's possible to slip into their clothes. They don't resist.

That was how it all looked to Kempf as he sat with his wife watching the audience arrive: empty clothes. Only the uniforms were filled. They were taut, ironed, with sharp creases, puffed up. The army was everywhere in the town, even in the theatre. The army played in the bandstand in Zrinjevac park and other promenades. An army band even played on the terrace of the Esplanade hotel. The war was not far off: the army still determined fashion and set the beat. Everything else was hollow, hiding, possibly waiting for some spectacular change, or maybe it was just resigned.

This didn't of course include the "new audience", "the new men". But they too looked like a kind of army. A rickety bus, painted dark green, a double-decker, requisitioned from who knows where, brought a group of proletarians for their cultural edification. After leaving the bus, they arranged themselves in a column to enter the theatre. They weren't in uniform, but they might well have been.

The students didn't get in line. They would stand in the balcony through all four acts of Tchaikovsky's ballet. Officially, the revolution makes a special effort for them; they are the hope for better times, the mainstay of the people. Nothing is as much a concern for the authorities as the young; not even the subversion of the "class enemy" in the backwoods.

Vera was trying to give up her electrical engineering course. She was being helped by a Partisan whom she had known in the forest and who had now risen high, as dean of the Electrical Engineering faculty. He had some connection with the profession before the war, he originated from what was now called the local bourgeoisie. Despite this, he was a good comrade. It was harder with those who were now advertising their merits and seeking this or that in recognition. The problem was that their merits were in principle impossible to reward. They were greater than any possible recognition: for instance, one of the more modest of them wished to be made into a doctor . . . believing that becoming a doctor was just like being promoted to captain because in an action he had proved himself a worthy fighter. He couldn't understand that to be a doctor one had to study. Doctors had always impressed him and since he thought that he too, in a similar way, impressed all those who weren't enemies, he had concluded that he too could be a doctor.

Kempf felt that the stranger's jacket was too tight for him, and the thought that it might have been worn by someone who was now lying in Mirogoj cemetery made him still more uncomfortable. For this occasion, Vera had simply put on what she had brought from her former life. She had nothing else, nor had she acquired anything. The bun of her hair had been wound in a broad ribbon. And she had brought that ribbon from her mother's home. She didn't wear make-up, not even lipstick. Kempf ordered a black coffee with lemon. The waiter leaned towards him, saying he had not heard properly. Had the gentleman perhaps intended to order tea?

In Poland Kempf had drunk black coffee with lemon whenever possible. He believed that coffee served in this way not only kept one awake but also soothed a headache. But in his "little Polish war" Kempf had hardly been in a position to sip real black coffee. The Germans had swallowed substitutes. The most elite S.S. divisions were the first to acquire the latest panzers, rifles, uniforms, but few took coffee into account. On the morning of the Normandy landings, Hitler had been sleeping soundly and no-one dared disturb him.

"That's why the Germans lost the war," remarked Kempf suddenly. "They slept through D-Day!"

Taxis were arriving at the theatre. These were the most prominent of the contingent of hollow people who arrived at the last minute. They were so important that the curtain could not be raised until they had taken their places in their boxes: the ones above the middle of the stalls. In the centre box sat a woman in violet. Everyone turned to her. She looked out over the front line of the "ideological struggle".

The auditorium was full, there was a murmur of joyful expectation. Here all national groupings were represented, a far better reflection than in the national parliament.

When the curtain rose, a sigh of wonder spread through the auditorium, acknowledging the stage designer. It was impossible to imagine a sight more remote from what could be seen outside: a castle with a mass of towers on a high rock, partially in the clouds.

Three and a half hours of forgetting everything apart from what existed in this non-existent castle or beside the non-existent lake where enchanted beauties danced, led by the swan Odette, who then became Odile, the Sorcerer's daughter. The beauties gleamed in short white skirts, the Sorcerer was black, like a chimney sweep . . . with black wings reminiscent of a bat. In this world it was good to win.

Kempf didn't have the patience to study the programme: the aims of the dancers didn't interest him. He didn't belong to the theatre world, he knew nothing of power struggles or intrigue that were a true copy of relations in the "real" world. He worked in the superstructure, as did Vera, a propaganda activist. In the sector of the poetry of "renewal and rebuilding". That sector regarded itself as the avantgarde at the forefront of the "ideological struggle".

He abandoned himself to Tchaikovsky's music. It was music that commemorated an irretrievably former world. Kempf had heard that officers of the executed tsar, listening to Russian music as émigrés, shot themselves in the head, in Odesa for instance.

All at once the lake in the Polish backwoods came back to him, frozen, smooth as a mirror, he saw the swans, thought that they should not be there, marvelled at the play of the sun's rays and frost on the branches; he was no longer looking at the dancing of the fragile, unreal, enchanted young women, but suddenly saw the dog whose longing for the wild ducks had nearly killed it . . .

He remembered that he had been entranced by the landscape,

for an instant believing that he had somehow dropped out of the "little Polish war" and woken in a world of pure beauty, which he dared observe without any interest but itself. It was not a landscape that had to be conquered, crossed in a marching column, "sanitised" after a battle, which meant collect and bury the dead ... nor was it something that had to be sold, they were not forests that had to be cut down, it was not a region through which a railway line had to be built ... This place was better suited to a prehistoric mammoth than a tank. Why not a stag? If people were permitted at all, they would be indicated by smoke from houses huddled at its foot, lights that flickered behind sooty windows. This was not a world in which Good vanquishes Evil, this was a world before good and evil. From the mythic tree, about which the Bible preaches, nothing had yet been picked.

Hollow people staggering around in an eternal dawn. That's something quite different, coming after everything. That's on the other side, that world, a reflection, an image of eternity. Here, it's this world that's being put in order.

He was jolted out of this reverie by the theme of the little swans, the enchanted, white, slender-legged girls, heard in varied rhythms throughout the performance. When the tempo speeded up, some of the charm was lost. Its real rhythm was *maestoso*, slow: that was the absolute triumph of Good. Hooray for Tchaikovsky! The main credit for this triumph was Prince Siegfried. What a strange name. The real Siegfried had not, fortunately, triumphed anywhere, even if there is a suspicion that victory over him is not definitive. In the background of the libretto is a Russian fairy tale rather than Germanic mythology in which Siegfried rules the roost.

Kempf cast a glance at Vera. She too seemed to him somehow

unreal, remote . . . Had she too been bewitched by the evil sorcerer, or had the music carried her away?

Kitsch, undoubtedly, but magnificent. Kempf suddenly came to and raised his eyes towards the central box where the violet woman was sitting, inspecting the scene through her opera glasses.

That kitsch certainly had an effect. It was even dangerous, thought Kempf. We must seek new forms in everything. Intoxication with old schemes and models is dangerous. But nevertheless, this music is a masterly work. It's hard to resist. People would have to cover their ears. It was even harder to resist a degree of erotic arousal. So, white ballet does have a purpose . . . In warming the hearts of older gentlemen.

That's why you hear people in the street singing a bawdy verse, thought Kempf:

Ballerinas on your pegs, wave high your slender legs

This crude couplet ended with a rhyming line about a sausage that had to be shoved deep.

It was interesting that the worst crude insult today, after the revolution, was directed at two groups of women in particular: ballerinas and nuns. The first are priestesses of art who glorify the beauty of a non-existent world, the others sacrifice themselves to a non-existent god . . . Is that what provokes our people so violently? The people want gods that let you see them, at least from time to time.

That was why Tito too was in a hurry, and as early as the end of May 1945, from the box which had first hosted the emperor of the Dual Monarchy, he had applauded a propaganda playlet.

He was taking account of the needs of the masses. At that time, Kempf was still pushing the pedals of his bicycle through the ashes of Europe.

Here the whole of Europe is singing and dancing, thought

Kempf, when the scene changed to a ballroom: flamenco, czardas, mazurka . . . It was good that "Katyusha" also made an appearance.

Pyotr Ilich Tchaikovsky was a gentleman, not a soldier.

In the interval, the two of them listened in to what was being said in the audience, which evidently included Soviet advisers: there was one highly decorated Russian who was served with champagne on a tray; Kempf interpreted his stripes as those of a colonel. All the others had to wait in line. The violet woman was not there, she had remained in her box, perhaps she was holding an urgent meeting.

"It's good, it's good, a high standard," one man said in Croatian. "But nothing compared to the Kirov or the Bolshoi."

"The Bolshoi will come, you'll see our ballet in Zagreb," the colonel said.

Only not on a T-34, thought Kempf. He fancied a drink, Vera ordered lemonade but did not get back in time from the ladies' toilet, where there was also a queue, and that wasn't the Russian colonel's fault. They returned to their seats in the stalls at the sound of a bell. That bell's just like at Mass, Kempf thought.

Without realising it, the two of them had been seeing two quite different performances. As soon as the enchanted women appeared, Vera thought that she recognised the ballerina from the Forest. And that whole event came back to her unusually clearly: the stage of unhewn wood, the thin devotee of white ballet in her little pumps, and the almost crazed gaze of the men who until that moment had firmly believed that nothing else in the world could confuse them, who had watched countless times as those closest to them died in terrible pain, who had seen a fellow fighter crawling, leaning on his arms because he had been left without legs . . . Vera remembered their rapture over the glass woman. It could not have been called lust, it was enchantment . . . intoxication. To the point of tears above their beards, an incredible phenomenon, incongruous . . . but still, that's how it was. Besides, precisely in order to feel the delight of such bewitchment, the privileged in feudal and bourgeois societies would exempt a small percentage of women, withdraw them from the obligation of heavier means of material production, or the shackles of marital discipline, to make them devotees of beauty in their perfumed rubbish heaps, to turn them, that is, into icons of their onanistic adoration . . . What other purpose was there for those short little skirts, as though made of crepe paper, hiding nothing? It was the theatre of masters: they had the right to see everything.

Here all of a sudden the activist in Vera bristled. We communists don't need swans, we need new women, and not enchanted beauties . . . We're solving the problem of the hungry masses, and at the same time hunger in the sense of physical deprivation, and hunger for culture in the sense that it must become accessible to all, as essential as our daily bread. That is our programme. Art cannot, must not, be a means of stimulating lust and other smutty passions.

This temple is a church of sorts, only in this church Man and not God resides. But then the Sylph from the forest appeared before her eyes, and she wanted, as always, to be true to what she had experienced, and Vera recalled the way she had then looked at her knotted, swollen, red fingers, hands that were hardly a woman's, they could have been the hands of a manual labourer, a miner who dug for coal, for instance . . . when she had run that hand through her greasy hair, which she had not been able to wash for days . . . the colony of lice that considered her body their home . . . the Partisan barrel in which she had ended that enthralling evening . . . then, wanting to be truthful, Vera confessed to herself that then, in the forest, she had wanted at least for a moment to be like that Sylph, and that she had thought about that woman, who had seemed to her then, briefly, but not now, more fortunate than her, when she entered Zagreb in the column that had stopped right in front of the theatre.

Flea

At the end there was prolonged applause, but not as vehement as the applause that had erupted when the wooden silhouettes of life-size swans glided over the stage. As the Kempfs were sitting a little to one side, they could see a man drawing the swans towards him, believing he could not be seen from the auditorium. Perhaps the young women in their little skirts were not sufficiently bewitching? Perhaps the women in the audience thought they were indecently arousing raw passions? Perhaps for most of the audience it was only the swans that were . . . art? They reminded one of a fairground – like those silhouettes soldiers aim at with airguns at fairs for a little packet of acid drops that improve the breath. Art vanquishes the scepticism of a primitive mind through illusion. And the audience craved art. Also, with all their hearts, they longed for the triumph of Good. Tchaikovsky, on the other hand, had written his music for a different kind of audience. Unlike the Sun King, Russian tsars did not themselves dance, but they nurtured their theatres, and especially white ballet. What was the meaning of Tchaikovsky's victory this evening? It was a triumph of his magnificent kitsch. And there were no more Romanovs. Who was replacing them?

Various people.

Ante Pavelić didn't like the theatre. Josip Broz Tito had hurried to occupy the state box. Franz Josef, who had opened this theatre, had died long ago and in time not to see the disintegration of the Dual Monarchy. Broz too would die in time. He had inherited, to a lesser degree, the emperor's problems in that both were ultimately linked to a similar failure. Death in this world is sometimes merciful to those who die without believing in another one.

They strolled for a while before getting their tram. Each preoccupied with their own thoughts. In Vera's mind that evening Kempf had not yet come onto the stage; and he was thinking about his "Polish war". They strolled, unhurried, it was a warm evening.

In an old text about the "social life" of the citizens of Zagreb, Kempf had found the following: "The audience hurries home, so that the husbands can as soon as possible enjoy their rights!" The two of them took their time.

Her husband noticed that Vera had acquired a little bulge and her breasts were larger. She's carrying her child well, he thought. He was convinced that it was a little boy, and said so to Vera who not only wasn't sure but didn't want it to be. After wars, Kempf reflected, more male babies are born to make up for the loss of men who had perished or disappeared. Nature was clever.

"It'll be what it is," Vera said. "Just as long as it's healthy."

That evening she gave herself to him for the last time. He had been sober because they could not get spirits at the theatre, and the enchanting young women had helped: he was a better lover. But from then on she thought about the child she was carrying, afraid something could happen to it if he was too violent. That it was their last time, they may have suspected.

In the middle of the night Kempf woke and discovered that she had gone to her room. After lovemaking, she usually stayed, otherwise they slept apart. I must have snored, Kempf thought.

An absurd question occurred to him: he was trying to remember whether on that lake, before he had gone with the Polish peasants to save the dog, he had actually seen swans and a castle on a cliff? He remembered only red clouds, an intimation of fine weather and cold, and numb hands . . .

But had any enchanted young women danced on that lake?

He tiptoed up to the slightly open door of her room: Vera was sitting up in bed, reading by the light of a small torch. So, she wasn't asleep either.

"I've been meaning to ask you something for a long time," Kempf said, sitting on the edge of her bed. He sat down slowly, as though fearful she might send him away.

"Go ahead."

"I'd like to ask whether there are questions you'd like to ask me, but for some reason you're reluctant, or you simply don't want to ask."

"No."

"How would it be if you replied with more than one word?"

"There's nothing."

Kempf went to get cigarettes; they both lit up and sat in silence; Vera had switched off the torch – "economising", thought Kempf.

"Do you realise that, if I had met you while I was in the German army, the regulations of my unit would have required me to shoot you on sight?"

"That could only have been possible if you had stayed in Yugoslavia," she replied at once. "In the division named after that baroque count."

Kempf was astounded. He had expected at least a little thoughtful hesitation. Perhaps even that his question would be left unanswered again. Because it was rhetorical. Of course an S.S. soldier would have had to kill a communist on sight.

"So, Mr Sturmmann Kempf, would you have killed me?" Vera broke the silence, and it was like a gunshot.

"You can think all kinds of things about me, both what you know and what you think you know, but I wouldn't have shot civilians."

"Ever since they let me out of Gradiška, until the breakthrough in Srijem, I was armed."

She stayed seated, but she seemed to straighten up; as though she had suddenly, defiantly puffed out her chest, exposing it to the rifles of a platoon that was meant to shoot her; suddenly she was resisting with her whole body, with every cell.

She's bristling, thought Kempf. Better not to touch on these things: time heals all. "If I'd met you then, and if you'd had your S.S. insignia on your collar, I would have fired on the spot." She patted her side, as though she had an invisible holster there. "I would not have fired only in one situation: if you had been in the Thälmann unit!"

"But I couldn't have been."

"I know."

"Did I have any other option?"

"Not really."

"Of the hundreds of thousands of Volksdeutsche, only ninety joined the Thälmann unit. Only every tenth one survived. Almost all the other Germans were driven out in 1945, often brutally, including women and children."

"I'm aware of that."

"If I had stayed in Yugoslavia, in the Prinz Eugen S.S. division and somehow survived the war, your people would have killed me."

"That was only just."

"So, let's drink to my good fortune that landed me in my 'little Polish war', so that I managed to escape."

"You've got the commissar's *bumashka*. That's all true!"

Vera felt that she shouldn't have said that, not now. This conversation had taken a bad turn.

"I need to rest, I've got a demanding day tomorrow."

"I've got a flea!" Vera exclaimed suddenly, jumping out of bed. "Pesky creature!"

She began to hunt. Kempf watched her from a stool

> My parents are becoming enemies, which in fact they have always been.

beside the window lit by occasional headlights. The morning hubbub was beginning, the town was waking, a tram screeched on its tracks.

"Damned creature, a hundred times damned, get your fill of my blood and die! Do you know what a partisan barrel is? We would gather round a steaming barrel with a fire lit under it and soak articles of our clothing in it – all of us, men and women – and one man even brought the ballerina's outfit, not, to be fair, her shamefully short little skirt, and we dunked it all in that barrel, to kill lice, fleas, every possible creature that drank our blood, unceasingly ... because the circumstances that allowed us to drag up our partisan barrel and make a decent fire under it were rare, given that we were almost constantly on the move."

Lice aren't racists, thought Kempf. He knew very well what a plague they were. One of the things that, as a civilian, he wanted to forget forever.

These parasites, he went on thinking, made no distinction between a swastika and a star, nor were they exclusive in terms of blood groups. But Germans set great store by cleanliness, many S.S. soldiers dragged a bottle of cologne around with them in their rucksack; but conditions were such that the question of hygiene in wartime, constantly on the move, as Vera put it, had to be suspended – "until the final victory", in a world that was completely cleansed of Jews, communists, Slavs, Gypsies, homosexuals, freemasons, fleas and lice.

Me, I whisper in the dark, but no-one hears me, which no longer bothers me.

This is my last comment.

I have just one more appearance, but that's in Kempf's sleep. Over to him. Thanks for your attention.

Vera went back to bed, after showing him triumphantly on her palm a black dot mixed with a drop of blood. Kempf looked at Vera as at a total stranger. She was half-naked, she had a little bulge, the lines of her face could pass for beautiful as they were regular, her nose looked a little squashed, like a boxer's – which Kempf noticed for the first time – her hair greasy. This woman was exulting over a tiny black creature that had just paid with its life for its greed – for blood – and the woman was scratching herself everywhere as in some low dive. As though she was still in a war camp. Well, mentally, she had never left it.

What have I to do with this woman, he thought.

"Bumashka"

Was this paranoia, wondered Kempf, staring at the ceiling lit by occasional headlights. Day was breaking: nightbirds returning home and proletarians on their way to work met on the recently washed streets.

Was it paranoia, did those people at the table in the canteen that stank of everything ever cooked in it, really, as though by agreement, pass over the provocation directed at me by that Russian saying: "Why, you're one of us, you've got our *bumashka*, you liberated Poland with us!" And he had gone on: "If Tito slides under the table after his second glass, that's not yet a reason for parting, that is for leaving the table. No offence meant, I didn't mean anything bad. Simply, we Russians wouldn't do that, it would be dishonourable! We Russians drink to the end with those who drink with us. You can't leave just like that."

Kempf didn't carry that *bumashka* of his on his forehead. But it turned out that everyone knew about it, even those he thought had joined their table by chance, in passing. Nothing was accidental.

"Today chance has been dialectically eliminated and surpassed. The law of iron necessity doesn't acknowledge the category of chance. If gentlemen poets don't accept that, it's their business; if they wish to be, say, surrealists, let them, but they have to know that no-one is above reality, however freely he flies . . . This is not the time for loose cannon."

This was what he had been told a few days earlier, in a perfectly friendly manner, by the editor of a journal to whom he had taken his poems.

"Write, comrade, about what you see, and not how things appear to you. Write freely, but responsibly. Remember Goethe: *Freedom consists in recognising limits.* Go among the people, be the responsible poet of an epoch being inscribed by the millions . . . Read the Russians, that's your world. If you really want to write poems about the universal soul, be its engineer; because engineers build, they don't lament. If you must have your 'spleen', then go and get it cured, brother, it can be cured nowadays. Shake off that 'spleen', and imagine, I beg you, your ideal reader. Someone who will swallow your poetry by the heat of a Siemens-Martin furnace. That's how you should write, that's how we all write. As though we were standing beside a great furnace and enduring its heat in solidarity. It's not as difficult as it may at first seem. Just between ourselves: writing poetry is after all easier than standing by a Siemens-Martin furnace. Believe me, writing poetry is easier than living it."

And before shaking hands:

"Go and be our Mayakovsky, you have talent, only be sure" – here the editor began to smirk – "to avoid his fate. Not everyone should play with fire. If you really want fire, go to the railway, spend time with the young people of this country, write about cubic metres of earth, about metres of track, about roads; and in the evening, sit with them by the campfire . . . recite your poems to them . . . Write about them, about those young people. No-one wants to hear endless droning on about someone else's merits."

What had the editor meant?

Once, at the district council, he had been asked to write his biography, in a couple of lines, only what was essential.

For the "before the war" part, Kempf had written that he had worked for a time in a brickworks, which was true, and there he had come into contact with workers. True, for how else could he have worked there: the contact consisted in lifting a prepared brick and handing it to a proletarian man, or, increasingly often, a proletarian woman, who was the first in a chain of human hands that led to the truck. For "the war" he wrote that he had, *by force of circumstance*, spent it in Poland. Was that not true? Yes, it was true. In his mobilisation itself what was at work was chance arising from iron necessity. From the standpoint of the Waffen-S.S. it was necessary and could not be avoided. From his, Kempf's, standpoint, it was chance that could have been avoided, let's say, by him hanging himself.

"Come on, man, let your pulse beat like the pulse in the breast of the national masses who are now beating on the door of history; who want finally to be the subject of that history, and not splinters it throws to them, and indeed often wastes in vain. Because the new man can find himself only by merging with the collective. Find himself by losing himself."

He could have been told that, in the same words, by Commissar Seryozha. It's what the Waffen-S.S. officer told him: "Germany expects a little more enthusiasm from you!" Kempf was beginning to see himself as a man who could serve as an example of total failure.

In the Soviet Union, commissars lived dynamically. Particularly those who had served in Poland. Many of the Russians who had been captured by Germans and then freed by the Red Army at the end of the war were ordered by Stalin to be shot like rabbits; because, from the Kremlin's perspective, once they had let themselves be captured, they *were* rabbits. Besides, Seryozha and Jurek Kempf had the impression when they parted that they would never see each other again.

How, otherwise, to explain that neither Alyosha nor the commissar had mentioned the possibility of ever meeting again?

Kempf did not lie in any way in describing his life as the very truncated theme of an unwritten novel. Although he hated lies, he hadn't told the whole truth. Besides, the whole truth was almost always unbearable. What good was truth that could not be borne? He took out his *bumashka* only in situations of extreme need. But he had it, as it was written, provided with a seal and signed. As soon as he had crossed the Drava, on the last stop in his anabasis, he had survived with its help, returning as an obsolete phantom to a country where everything had changed. And in the local council, in Zagreb, they had turned that document over in their hands, held it up to the light, sniffed it. Perhaps a poet with a commissar's certificate wasn't a great recommendation for poetry. But, alright, it did nonetheless suggest a right-minded person. Mind you, everyone had become right-minded now. To be right-minded was not enough. Now they wanted upright people. That was achieved by a man bowing down before the energy of the nation that was waking, to bend in keeping with the ordinances of *diamat*, that is, to acknowledge the canons of dialectical materialism. One had to stoop in order to stand straight.

Good intuition advised Kempf to use the *bumashka* judiciously.

That was not in any way his own, personal paranoia, certainly not. This entire age was paranoid.

As soon as he had made sure that Vera was breathing regularly, Kempf found the keys to the store cupboard and went down the steps to the cellar. It smelled of cabbage and rotting potatoes, the walls were green with mould, one could have spread bread with penicillin, like pâté.

A rat, sitting in front of the store cupboard, the length of its half-metre tail away, refused to move. Kempf was overcome by unease. It seemed to him that the rat was intending to tell him something. It was so big that it would have overwhelmed any cat, it was evidently sure of itself, more sure than Kempf had ever been.

As though at a command, from all corners of the cellar came rats just as big.

Kempf considered the situation unequal, then tried to convince himself that these were just rats. But there were so many, they were the majority residents here, he thought, vainly feeling over the damp wall for a light switch. It's said of rats that they would survive a nuclear catastrophe.

"You see how many we are," said one of them simply through its presence, its dimensions. "We're all spoiling for a fight. The next time it will be to the end. Nothing is as yet over. Nothing will ever be over. Even when we get to the end. For that end is in fact endlessness. You will always have it in for us, or we for you . . . But we reproduce more quickly than you do, and more quickly refill the regiments of our incalculable black armies . . . Our banner will once again be unfurled over the Earth's Globe!"

At last, by chance, Kempf found the light switch and the cellar was illuminated with a yellow, flickering light. The shadows vanished into holes. Were those rats, with their leader leaning on half a metre of tail, just an illusion?

He must remind the caretaker tomorrow to set traps. Presumably we are the masters at least in this building, in this cellar? Presumably we won't be driving the rats away with tanks!

Finally, Kempf opened the store cupboard that belonged to their apartment. When they had invited people from the Red Cross to hand over the traces of former lives in the apartment allocated to them, they had also asked that the store cupboard be emptied.

There had been some old pieces of furniture in it, old newspapers, some calendars, a bicycle wheel ... one could hardly imagine anything more superfluous, anything that could have been rubbish in a more absolute sense.

They put everything out with the trash, and they had nothing of their own to put in ... people moving into a house don't bring their rubbish with them. You have to live a bit to have rubbish. Refugees become people only once they begin to produce rubbish.

Consequently, there was almost nothing in the cupboard. As a prospective couple, they had been given vouchers for a metre of wood and some cabbage. On no account did Vera want to tread that cabbage with her bare feet, as was traditionally done. Kempf tried to persuade her, but without success. It would have been better to give the cabbage to the Red Cross as well, it could only rot in this cupboard. There are on the planet women who have nothing against treading cabbage with their bare feet. There are even some who iron their husbands' shirts.

In the cupboard was a wooden box to which Kempf had entrusted his document.

Now he held it up to the light bulb that was spreading its subdued yellowish luxury.

The *bumashka* was changing. He tried to remember when he had last opened the box: two weeks ago. It evidently had its own life. Or, on the contrary, it lived the way time changed around us. Kempf had the impression that it had grown thinner ... the seal was already quite pale, the five-pointed star was barely visible, as though it only had three points ... the others were left to the imagination; the signature had been illegible from day one. Like the portrait of Dorian Gray, the document had broken away and become independent. Kempf thought it might be best to destroy it. But again, who knows, perhaps that would not be entirely sensible.

Silent Comrade

It was already the fifth day that Đuka had been visiting the huts of the youth brigades building the railway. At the evening poetry readings he was introduced as Comrade Kempf who had fought in Poland against the Nazis and local, Polish traitors, and had been wounded in the shoulder, so he could not himself lift a pick.

Only once, in the brigade's headquarters, after plum brandy had loosened his tongue, had he told them how he had helped blow up a section of track at a bend, at the mouth of a tunnel, and that the landscape was astonishingly similar to this very section where now compressors were thundering, mines cracking and stone flying into the air – just as his Polish partisan unit had made happen in that late summer of 1944. Comrade Kempf didn't of course mention that the track had been destroyed by Soviet saboteurs, who were the only ones who knew how to do it as they had been trained for that purpose in the U.S.S.R., and then dropped by parachute behind the lines that were then still being held by the decimated S.S. divisions.

"We destroyed, you're building!" Kempf concluded his story. And then they all drank themselves senseless.

Virtually everything in that story was true. The similarity of the landscapes, along with the brandy, had loosened Kempf's tongue. He hated lies. Perhaps because he was forced into them so often.

However, he had retained sufficient self-control – indeed, over time, Kempf had become a grandmaster at it – and he had not expressed aloud the comparison that had been bothering him a bit since he had set off to visit the building site and huts. He had the opportunity to watch – and after all watching was the reason for his journey – young men and women whom the war had spared on the basis of what was later, in Adenauer's Germany, called the mercy of late birth. Now they had come of age for a new war, whose most important front line was here, on the railway. Strolling idly among the huts, between the benches where those on duty served meals, to the improvised open-air showers, Kempf saw the same cheerfulness that is probably everywhere in the world characteristic of young people gathered together. Then, when with the sunrise the hunt had begun for cubic metres of earth and quotas, Kempf saw frowning, serious faces, as there had been in the heat of a difficult battle. He was struck by the comparison with his first Polish experiences, acquired as a forced volunteer of the Waffen-S.S. Young men there, young men here. Before the S.S. soldiers set off to kill, they behaved like wild puppies, exactly like these brigades. Admittedly, there were no women in the German military camp, or else they could be counted on the fingers of one hand. Here in the brigade camp there were a lot of girls. That's the difference, Kempf concluded, almost happily. The girls boldly emphasised the outline of their breasts, they were suntanned, like the boys, they were working towards their quota, like the men, and they demanded that the jobs of cleaning the huts and toilets and work in the kitchen should be equally shared between the sexes. They did the same work as the men, without being at all masculine. Were they the younger sisters of those nurses whom the S.S. officers had called bitches and feared more than their male fellow fighters? Truly, those girls were not at all rough, many were desirable, just because they were so free.

Everywhere in the world, young people are similar, more similar than old people crushed by life. Everywhere in the world, the young are an unwritten sheet of paper. It seems that everything depends on the pied piper of Hamelin whom the young follow, for good or ill ... They will set off, like a procession of rats, to drown in the first stream, or, like children, often tiny, in a children's crusade, in the Mediterranean Sea. The young follow their shepherd, the pipe of a piper in a colourful uniform, and the difference between Good and Evil is so indecently fine that anything is possible. Why is the piper's uniform brightly coloured? Because it is patched together from all the banners under which people on Earth have ever killed. But the piper is cunning: he does not summon his flock to kill, he summons them to "Transylvania", to a better future. That is always a straight line, regardless of the expense in human material. The piper is shrewd, a great seducer. He always knows how to pull out of the shreds he has wrapped himself in a rag of a currently opportune colour as his new flag. History is perverse.

But I am a cynic, Kempf continued his self-tormenting soliloquy. His colleague Mordechai was right. But I too was right when I confessed to him that I had always been more interested in the riddle that a dark-skinned girl, the Jewish Sulamith, bears between her legs. I shall certainly never solve the riddle of history. For that one would need a life several times as long and a mindset that was capable of suppressing cynicism. And then to resist the cold gaze of the bronze serpent. Who can do that today? Only a cynic. And so the circle is closed. A cynic will never achieve anything great. For instance, if he is a scribbler, he will become a *poeta minor*. Because for him all raptures are suspect and because he is poisoned by that doubt.

Endeavouring to catch his reflection in a mountain stream, Kempf had refused all kinds of indulgence, wanting to be merciless to himself. But still, as soon as he could, he had chosen the side which at a certain moment there, in Poland, had seemed to him the right one. Kempf forgot that he had not had any choice, there by Swan Lake. But he did not feel any guilt that his contact with the Polish underground army had failed. From what he had seen, his Soviet-Polish unit fought the right battle. He had had incredible luck that, after he ran away from the flag, he had not been dug out again by the Waffen-S.S. Or he would no longer be alive.

But there, yet another similarity came into his mind, another comparison knocked on its door: all young people, along with external similarities that can be counted, also have their commissars. The S.S. had theirs, that is the only reason they shot Soviet soldiers as soon as they came upon them. Here too, among the huts, new commissars were watching, often no older than the brigade members. Because young souls are unruly, it's hard to shove awakening instinct under a puritan greatcoat.

Where am I in all of this?

Have I not remained a small scrap that has had somewhat better luck than those who ended up in pits? By what right am I still alive? Am I, no matter what kind, nevertheless a poet? Am I not an invalid (that is to say, worthless), incapable of lifting a pick over my head? Of course I lied, but that lie is innocent. I don't feel like getting into harness, I worked out my serfdom in Poland for all time.

The red sky in the west brought news that the next day would be fine.

Must that redness on the horizon, transformed into verse, necessarily suggest the spilt blood of the killed and the suffering? Must the thought of the new dawn necessarily be associated with the liberation of the international proletariat? Was it not permissible for a landscape to be simply beautiful, with no particular purpose? Might not nature please disinterestedly? Like that time, in his "Polish war", when, carried away by the beauty around him, charmed by the world as it was – he had saved a dog from certain white death? The saving of the dog had sprung from rapture of an aesthetic nature.

Farewell Immanuel Kant. You are only an old dog baying at the moon, as I am. You cannot be saved by anyone like me, and those who could do that haven't heard of you.

Kant grows pale, and the old moon comes out, as though at a sign from an invisible stage illuminator. The whole landscape dedicates itself to silver. The black tracks, laid this morning on their sleepers, are equally silvered.

Here, on that stone, barely making out his own handwriting, Kempf wrote these lines:

> Listen to the roads growing and say:
> isn't the loveliest glow of the Moon
> in the lap of just laid tracks.

From the distance, already darkened now, Kempf heard the sounds of the Last Post and the song accompanying the curtain being lowered.

Tomorrow he would be moving on. That's why he had to order his thoughts. Before long he would have to read. Not talk about his "little Polish war". *The moon in the lap of the tracks*, thought Kempf, maybe that wasn't so bad. He decided to read that poem to the brigade workers. But first he joined them in a ring dance round the pole with the slack flag at its top.

He would later include that poem in his collection *Sweat for Steel*, which in his later life he erased from his bibliography.

One Has to Believe

Vera was still struggling with electricity. She rummaged through handouts, notebooks, hefty tomes . . . Before exams she put handouts under her pillow as she used to do at school.

Formulas went into her head but didn't stick. She sat some exams but not others. There were ever more frowning faces round her. In her life up to now she had always known who were her enemies. She had known how to take a stand. At her interrogation by the police after the break-up of the kingdom she had even been defiant. They had let her go, but under surveillance. Someone from the police, with whom she had been a bit involved as a very young girl, had warned her that she might be arrested again. She kept changing addresses, but she'd been denounced: they'd lay a trap for her. Vera hadn't managed to discover what happened to him after the war. The chief, however, Mr Tolj, had been hanged. On that occasion, Kempf had shouted something. Now that event had paled. Now it seemed to her inconceivable that her husband would have made any such public display. When he got very drunk, he would whine and weep. There was nothing violent in his drunkenness.

Vera didn't dare tell anyone what a torment electricity was for her. The fact that she failed the harder exams was not because she was lazy or careless. She simply had no understanding of electricity.

Everything drew her to literature. She just wanted to spend time with beautiful things, they muttered in the organisation. She wanted to sit in comfort rather than trudge round sites in boots, installing power lines. She stuck her nose up like a bourgeoise. She wanted to be a lady.

Vera, who didn't wear lipstick because it was too bourgeois?

Our villages are languishing in darkness, the Voice of the Party went on. The Soviets + electrification = socialism! If Lenin was right about anything, that was it. Lenin was right about everything, but our new Technical Faculty – department of electricity – ought to display that inscription from the treasure trove of wisdom of the classics of Marxism and revolution. Why was it so hard for her to get that into her head? Comrade Vera was taking the line of least resistance. Her behaviour was self-serving.

"I want to change subjects. I'm no worse than the average student," she wrote to the Party. That was unacceptably little. The Party wasn't a club for the average and idle.

Who could she tell about her misery, who could she confide in?

In the churches of her childhood, there had been a cupboard with a little window, in them priests sat, and through the little window you could see their ear. Believers had at least that ear. Once Vera confessed that she had stolen her brother's fountain pen. It was so beautiful that she simply had to steal it. Her mother and brother turned the whole house upside down. Vera was terrified and ran to the church, where she confessed all to the cupboard with the ear.

"Have you got a boyfriend, do you think about men?" asked a nasal voice from the cupboard and Vera immediately recognised the local priest who liked to touch young women.

"No, father, I think only of Jesus."

"That's good, my child. God will hear your prayers."

She said a few Hail Marys after returning the pen and it was not mentioned again.

Where could she now find a shoulder to cry on and that so necessary ear?

With Kempf, in bed? Why, he was locked up like a strongroom of secrets it wasn't safe to mention.

Besides, he would be unlikely to encourage her to go against the Party, which had proclaimed: "Electricity!" – because she was needed by the people. But how was it that the one she had thought was the man of her life couldn't see how much she was suffering?

I'm not a bad person, she thought, how is it that I'm so alone with my troubles?

The shadow behind her lengthened. She had noticed several times that comrades lowered their voices as she approached their table, or abruptly changed the subject.

So she and Kempf, although for different reasons, became people with a shadow.

Those shadows dragged behind them even on cloudy days. They belonged only to them, at a time when everything was supposed to be communal. Both would gladly have renounced that ownership. That they dragged shadows with them didn't yet mean that they had become a "case". But it was better to eliminate that possibility in advance.

In short, the believer found herself in her first serious crisis. In the camp and the war there had been no time for that. In a sense, the war had been better.

Before the war, Vera had a friend who became a nun. The order was very strict. Her friend parted from the world. She saw her only once, they talked through bars. The convent burned down in the war. Vera didn't know what had become of the Carmelite nun.

Had she had any crises?

Probably. She had once been a saucy girl. Everyone knew that she had rolled around with boys in the vineyards. Hence her decision so astounded everyone. The priest spoke about her at Mass, praising God for her having opted for God. How had she explained her decision to him, as he sat in that cupboard behind the grille, what had that ear said to her at her last worldly Confiteor?

She imagined her friend barefoot, washing the floors, and, before she slept, beating herself to draw blood. But Vera knew nothing about her life in the confines of the convent. Why, she could have joined us, in our church, we're a kind of church too, thought Vera.

In any case, it would never have occurred to the Carmelite to blame her troubles on God, the Almighty, for not understanding her. But she, Vera, was blaming the Party, which didn't understand her.

She was so far below the Carmelite.

Vera began to compose her self-criticism. That was just what the Party expected of her. The Party could not be blamed for her not liking electricity.

Young Kempf found his mother's self-criticism, with which she hoped to cleanse herself before the Party, among her papers.

It could have been signed by every nun of the strictest Christian orders. Vera wrote:

> *I have come to the conclusion that not all members of the Party are communists, but the Party educates them and makes them communists. There are some who are incorrigible, who have also found their way into the Party. The Party is cleansing itself of unhealthy elements.*

In view of the above, I ask that my case be considered.

I am an unhealthily proud and stubborn person. At a given moment I came to the following conclusion: "Either I am not a good person, or else there are bad people in the Party." To acknowledge that there are bad people in the Party means to abandon the idealisation of superior people in that Party. But then, who am I to weigh up what I think and feel on the one hand, and our Party on the other side of the scale? I fear that I am terribly arrogant and should be punished. With all of this, my concentration when I try to do something has lately lapsed. I know this should not be happening and that torments me with each day. Put simply, I often conclude that I am not worthy of the Party, that I am not the communist I ought to be because I know that I ought to be doing more ... that I am, for instance, despite all this quite a good public speaker. Although there are moments when I lose faith in myself, I feel that I am approaching a time of madness, that my nerves are increasingly taut and that one day I shall either kill myself or go mad. At such moments I see no point in my being on the Earth. I ought to get through this crisis, to become a communist such as is needed or be expelled from the Party.

Fundamentally: one must be strong and believe in people. I am not sufficiently strong. I understand that it is essential to love people, to seek what is good in them, and not to constantly look for their human weaknesses.

The Party read Vera's Confiteor, but then the discussion turned to the external political situation, which was difficult. The comrades dispersed with anxious expressions. Vera remained alone in the meeting room and wept.

After Vera, it occurred to Kempf too that it might not be unwise to write something like his own self-criticism. Besides, everyone was doing it, including the most honourable, according to the standards of the age, as well as those who were, according to the standards of all ages, scoundrels. It was a kind of political fashion: confessions were worn on the sleeve, like the insignia of rank.

Some confessions were even praised in literary circles. After all, was not Jean-Jacques Rousseau's famous book called simply *Confessions*?

It was popular, it was well thought of, to give the Party an insight into one's intimate being.

Why, even Jean-Jacques Rousseau didn't do anything different, and his book, however intimate in places, provoked a revolution of emotions, and in the end led to the guillotine . . . Did not a woman somewhere say to the "natural man" Rousseau, after he could not get it up: "Monsieur Rousseau, give up women and stick to mathematics"?

So Kempf joked, taking a piece of paper, and began to write:

My impatience on the path to fame has got out of hand. At times it occurs to me to abandon myself entirely to my Muse and let her lead me, to stop counting piles of dug earth and metres of new railway line; simply, to be alone with my Muse, in some deep Underground, to do to her and with her whatever I fancy, regardless of any protocol.

I am pursued by other temptations as well. I don't know why or how, but from time to time I may drown in a glass or two. What I want to drown in it is of no interest to this Confiteor of mine. But I dare not hide anything from the

Party, I write what is truly important. So I move on to what is most important:

Allow us to create freely.

The slogan "May a thousand flowers bloom!" is no good, for we are not flowers. Let poetry be ugly as the great Baudelaire wanted . . . it will never be as ugly as this reality of ours is capable of being. Only then will poetry not be outside our reality.

By commandeering poetry, you want it to be ABOVE reality. But that is precisely what you accuse us poets of being: that we live in a reality of our own, beyond or even in opposition to the spirit of the age of renewal and building.

I confess my greatest sin: I am isolating myself. I am increasingly alone. I know that is unhealthy. I would so gladly be part of a collective, a true collective, I would so gladly feel a sense of belonging, without that having to be an effort. If I have to make an effort, my doubts will always surpass my sense of belonging. But, on the other hand, it is clear to me that solitary witnesses of great events and profound social transformations will always arouse the suspicion of those who know better. Isolation is a form of sickness.

Nevertheless, imagine what it was like for Gulliver and the Lilliputians. Be considerate, the Gullivers are in the minority, while you want revolution in the name of the majority. Do not blame us for not all fitting the template of the New Man. That takes time. If the Lilliputians were the size of Gullivers, neither would exist.

Please, help me! I am for the revolution with my whole being, but it seems, judging by many signs, that I do not know how to fit into its formation. That formation is

marching, holding firmly to the designated direction, while I
keep swerving. Lately I have taken to swerving chronically.
I stand out, but please, don't cut me back.
Đuka Kempf, by his own hand.

To Vera, who was going out, Kempf said he had just finished
a new poem.

When he was sure that his wife had gone – briefly, to buy
bread while the little one was sleeping – he took his lighter and
burned the sheet of paper. He left the little door on the stove
open. The paper flared with a stronger flame than it would have
been reasonable to expect.

"Something must be burning!" he heard Vera say when she
came back.

"Some heretic."

"Are you burning your poems?"

Incompatible Characters

Was the revolution losing its impetus?

It had ceased manoeuvring, had stopped in a siding.

The empire of necessity just was not becoming the empire of freedom.

In a situation in which everyone has to be served, but there is not enough for everyone, more and more people appear who want to be served before others. Some remembered that this was how it had been in the forest: leaders of all kinds and ranks were served more lavishly, even in the midst of the most terrible shortages, than ordinary fighters. What was considered the slander of class and every other kind of enemy seemed now to be confirmed. On the other hand, there were those who had borne witness to moral rigour without precedent; to shootings because of a stolen potato, to the fact that in the forest the communists had shared good and ill to the last crumb, in every detail. Who knows? The silence of the original Partisans was deepening.

The high command of the Party began to think – it was a collective intellectual, so one could think for all, just as all thought for one – that, since the people were dissatisfied, they were in fact ungrateful. The communists could not be held responsible for the fact that the currents of social wealth could not flow more abundantly. But it was hard to conceal another fact: that many of them did not wish to be patient, that they did not intend to deny themselves. There had been enough self-denial. Too much. "Diplomatic stores" were opened. A caste of managers came into being at the top of the working class. Those who had exposed themselves to danger were increasingly loud. Some among them thought that their heroism could not be repaid. The best of them thought the same, but declined to be recompensed. Others became insatiable. The former poured silence, like a kind of alcohol, over themselves. They saw that the revolution was in a moral crisis. Some suffered at the hands of the political police because they firmly believed in loyalty to the revolutionary ideals, embodied until the day before by Stalin, but it was also possible to suffer for a joke that would have sounded benign in normal circumstances. Or because of who knows what old grudge. In a word, the witch-hunting season was open.

One way or another, the ice had begun to spread. The working class was given a Christmas gift called self-management. But the working class appeared not to take it seriously. Individual people were ungrateful, and a whole class, which after all consisted of people, could also be ungrateful. However, it appeared that the classics of Marxism had not anticipated this. News of the first strikes had to be suppressed out of sheer logic: it was illogical for a class to strike against itself. For purely doctrinal reasons, those strikes ought to have been foreseen. Marx had confirmed some things in his theoretical writings. About many things, however, he had said nothing. One had to steer a middle course through all those rapids. Not to mention the international situation. Here, in the country, everyone wanted everything and at once. But for the time being that was impossible. The revolution had won, but it had not yet produced anything much. How easy it had been, and in its way agreeable, in the forest.

So, the communists had problems explaining that the laws of

iron necessity were not equally valid for everyone. Those who thought more intensely about the general good had a greater right to satisfy their needs. The masses were expected to respond with disciplined enthusiasm and, particularly and above all, discipline in their needs and desires. Must everyone really have both a left and a right shoe? Must one really indulge in meat three times a week?

Kempf couldn't see how it was possible that the organised joy appeared so spontaneous: what did the anthill really think? Was it really so united, was the brotherhood of different kinds of ant really so firm, even eternal? It should be protected like the apple of one's eye with great care, just because it was so exposed, so vulnerable. Was that not the strangest slogan? When was the euphoria genuine, and how far was it artificially produced? But what most astonished him was that he sometimes felt that he was caught up in it, elated – for instance, on the First of May when the tanks of Tito's army began to rumble down the street, the Soviet T-34, almost an in-law to Kempf.

All in all, Kempf could see the first cracks in the new system – the corsets of some imposed truths were starting to burst open – but on no account did he dare confide his impressions in conversations with colleagues, even in the fairly relaxed atmosphere of the Writers' Union.

Tonight he was trying to guess the way to his flat after leaving a drinking bout at the Writers' Union at which a poet had been celebrating his birthday, and in the course of which they had all fallen under the table, together with some ladies of the night. To be on the safe side – they had had that much presence of mind – they had dragged with them under the large conference table their commissar who otherwise observed them constantly, in a perfectly open, friendly and warm way. Under the table, in a completely alcoholised state, they really were all equal, and brothers, and, perhaps for the first time they had exchanged kisses, more with their commissar-tutor, on whose cheeks they planted wet kisses, than with the ladies of the night, and why should they have kissed them when, at that moment, the whole world was theirs?

Kempf was barely able to find the entrance to his block, and was already at the end of his strength because he had staggered home on foot, the trams having long since stopped running. He found his key in his coat pocket, he even aimed at the lock. But there was a key on the other side of the lock. He rang and banged on the door.

Vera was not one of those women who greet their drunken married partner at the door with a rolling pin and a hand on their hip, waving that piece of wood over their head. As the ringing didn't at first succeed, and neither did his blows on the door, and when the tenants of the flats on their floor had already begun peering through their spyholes (Kempf could hear those petty-bourgeois people breathing, thinking that someone was being arrested again), he thought he would have to spend the night in front of the door like a dog, and that suddenly defeated him. He fell onto his knees and began to whine. "You can't do this, open the damned door . . ." That was, in his drunken sprees, his true self.

The door opened and Vera let him in with her finger on her mouth, for the baby was sleeping.

Kempf felt an attack of fury, a flame that seemed to run right through him from his toes and emerged over his head in his raised fist.

"Never, Kempf, but never, try anything like that!"

Kempf, himself afraid of a gesture that was not really his,

now faced a mutinous being, sizzling with every cell of her body, bristling, contorted in an attitude of defence that could at any moment have turned into attack, ferocity, total, annihilating . . .

Kempf thought the woman was touching her hip on which there was the invisible holster of an invisible gun.

However, his appearance, crumpled, soiled, with traces of vomit, could not have looked like a real threat. The blusterer tripped in the doorway and entered the flat on all fours.

"Go to the bathroom. I'll make you coffee."

The following week proceedings for divorce began on the basis of incompatibility of character. They went on living in the same flat for a while because it was difficult to find accommodation. In addition, the Party did not like communists to divorce.

The First of May was approaching again, in barracks boots were being polished and the guns of tanks and howitzers oiled. The army still slept on straw mattresses and the cavalry was still important. So the straw mattresses were aired and the horses groomed. The infantry stamped out its marching step, still in the manner of armies from the East.

Stands were erected in the larger towns of the republic, the anthill rehearsed its formal procession. Beneath these stands, the people would raise their eyes towards the political leaders of the country, and those leaders would look down at the people. There was happiness in this. There was balm against doubt in this, as God explained to Moses when he ordered him to make a bronze serpent.

Is it better to live in sanctioned love, or to admit that this love has not succeeded, in both cases regardless of the cost in "human material", that is, seen in some pure, ideal assessment? Let that be for future generations to put to the test. Dilemmas that can be decided at once are not real ones.

Divorce

The revolution was beginning to creak. Some people, not many, thought that submission to iron necessity had to be carried out as free compliance; only the intellectually more inquisitive saw a contradiction in this. A great deal of store was set by extracting that compliance from the people; that was the task of a system of joy and directed enthusiasm. But the immense moral capital brought out of the forest was gradually being used up. There was no sign of any other capital, however. The majority waited in vain for the milk and honey of Canaan. The streams of that milk and honey were not only not abundant, to some they seemed more scarce than they had been in the kingdom. That was of course reactionary propaganda. Could land you in prison. People couldn't see that they were fed and happy. They didn't want to see . . . How much more grateful plants are than people. Unfed, unwatered, a plant will wilt, but it will not complain. The people want to have their cake and eat it. People are, in general, impatient beings, they have to have everything now or never.

The connection with the Soviets ruptured. It did not happen overnight, there had been indications before. But nevertheless, it was abrupt. No conciliatory talks were arranged.

Kempf had just returned from the youth railway when the

famous Resolution was proclaimed.* It seemed that the whole country was going to divide in half and shatter. It would not have been the first time. Some checked every morning whether day would dawn at all in the east, or would the east deny us the sun? There were alerts in the barracks, with no-one knowing whether they were just exercises or whether the state really was under threat. Tanks were started in the dead of night.

What began then was ... differentiation. From Olympus, where the political gods waged their wars, to the last marital bed, loyalty was tested to the new general line, which was in fact an about-face so sharp that many would fall out of the speeding train. The Party, and the homeland, could be difficult lovers.

After lunch, the daily runs, from one editor to the next, carrying his new poems about "renewal and rebuilding", quite worn out, Kempf remembered that he had meant that morning to check whether his *bumashka* was where he had hidden it. Heads had fallen for less. People were being arrested at dawn again, beginning to disappear, often those who had been doing the arresting the day before.

At meetings, in the local councils and elsewhere, people sat under photographs of Tito and insisted on the purity of their line, and the value of Partisan recollections suddenly rose.

Why? Because the Partisans had fought for their own thing, alone. In the East that was denied of course. Now everything was in dispute.

---

* The Resolution of the Informbiro was proclaimed in June 1948, including serious accusations, in fact slander, against the Yugoslav leadership, which was said to have set off in the direction of breaking away from the International Front of Socialism and towards imperialism. For Tito's Yugoslavia, until then economically and politically dependent on the Eastern bloc, it was a heavy blow. [Author's note]

Of course, no-one summoned Kempf. Poland was far away, and now it was clear that Stalin's boot had enslaved it. With each day, the difference between Stalin, the Cossack knout and imperial autocracy was diminished, and ultimately it endured only in a theoretical sense. And as far as theory went, the engine drivers of the Yugoslav revolution continued to lay all their cards on dialectical materialism, which Stalin had abandoned. It was not easy: uprooting Stalin from one's head meant sacrificing a part of oneself. It was necessary to adapt swiftly and to lobotomise the brains of revolution. It was necessary, even among the best, to take account of phantom pain.

Vera was in demand, they wanted her everywhere. She was no longer promoting hygiene (sexual or any other kind), freedom of marriage, the socialist upbringing of children, and the fight against the darkness spread by people of the Church; she was now working as an activist in preaching, hundreds of times, in various auditoria, the history of her Forest. After all, Vera had gone to the forest of her own free will, she spoke about her fight for freedom as her fight for her own emancipation, which in a narrower sense was called women's liberation. She spoke now more about those who had fallen, and how they were the best . . . she spoke in the name of those she had known, and she knew where and how they had died. She would usually leave a cheerful anecdote for the end, afraid that the pathos of her stories would eventually tire her audience. But they were equally taken with her cheerful stories, such as the anecdote about the Partisan barrel. Besides, the fascists had been driven out of the country, but not also the lice or the fleas, the parasites that sucked the blood of the working people.

Was Kempf jealous of Vera's political success?

Not as much as one might have thought. He too had his early, poetic, successes.

Kempf recited in front of young people who listened to him with enthusiasm. Those above were now convinced that the new socialist man could not manage without his verses, and gave him vouchers for the canteen, for wood, for apples and cabbage.

There was a difference, however: it is true that he recited his poems, but they were not about himself, particularly not about his "little Polish war", apart from distant allusions. But Vera spoke about herself. Quite directly. She was the subject of the revolution. He was only the object of many revolutions from Mussolini and Hitler's to Lenin's, Stalin's and Tito's. That was the difference between splinters scattered by the winds and a person exercising her will, even in a camp.

Kempf had never told Vera how much all that tormented him. Meanwhile Vera was too taken up with her propaganda in a new form. She was working on notes about the war.

Carried along by the new flourishing of Partisan epic poetry on the theme of shoring up the so necessary but now threatened self-awareness of revolution, Kempf initiated a conversation with Vera.

"There's something I've been meaning to ask you for a while."

"Better not, last time it ended very badly."

"Did your nurses kill the wounded if your formation was surrounded and the military situation hopeless?"

"What brought that on?"

"I heard that they didn't."

"Who told you?"

"A German."

"?"

"He had no reason to lie. It seems that in one of their offensives in Bosnia the women caring for the wounded were a military problem for the Germans."

"Which offensive?"

"The ones the Germans called Operation Weiss."

"We call that the Fourth Offensive."

"So did they kill the wounded if there was no other way out?"

"No. But they sometimes left them weapons so they could kill themselves."

"That means they left them to the Germans?"

"No."

"So, they died alongside them?"

"That's right."

"How do you explain that?"

"It doesn't need explaining."

Kempf said nothing. In truth there was a lot that didn't need explaining; it seemed those were the only things one remembered.

"In Poland they killed the wounded if the Germans were closing in."

"We didn't. Full stop, a new order!"

Kempf retired to bed. This time there was no major clash between the two of them. Kempf remembered that on that occasion, in Poland, an event from his "Polish war", hearing the S.S. soldier talk about the Partisan nurses, he had felt admiration. Why deny that to himself now? If he had been an object in the wider events and stronger forces that had caused such havoc in that turbulence without precedent, he could allow himself to be objective, could he not?

He no longer needed the protection of that distant commissar. Was it not time to start to live by standing on his own two feet? Finally to breathe with full lungs? He didn't need Vera. He didn't need someone who would constantly remind him that up to now he hadn't lived as an independent person, except in very rare circumstances that could be considered incidents. He could carry out this self-inflicted torment on his own.

Politically, not the slightest reproach had been held against him. It's true that, as he walked through the streets of Zagreb, he would notice here and there a pair of inquisitive eyes boring through him as they endeavoured to catch his eye to ask: "So, how do you feel now? You have your Russians, take them home!" It was similar to the first months, on the Vinkovci corso, after his anabasis out of Poland. Or was that paranoia again? But people were disappearing, there was a new paranoia now. The patterns of those disappearances were not very different from those this city had lived through, in 1941 and 1945.

As soon as he judged that his tired wife was breathing steadily, he went down to the cellar to check his *bumashka* again.

It lived its own life. More exactly, it had lived out its life. It was so thin that he thought it would crumble at the least touch and vanish like dust. The star could no longer be made out at all.

That same night, Kempf burned the *bumashka* in the stove. No regrets.

The following day a second meeting had been arranged in the marriage-divorce case of the legal couple, Vera and Đuka Kempf, for the time being conciliatory, with no witnesses. The comrades did their best to smooth over the unfortunate affair.

They were not reconciled, they left the court at 11.30 and each hurried off in their own direction: Kempf to a printer and Vera to a meeting at the local council.

Now the time had come, at five to twelve, for the comrades, first through the witnesses, to see whether anything could be changed. It turned out that the address of Kempf's witness could not be found. This was followed by visits with a mission: the Kempfs received their visitors separately. The Party comrades invested their best knowledge and experience in their endeavour to talk them out of divorce. A lot of literature was cited, several stories with better endings were told. It was not the time for divorce, the external political situation was unstable, there was trouble also in the country itself.

The parties would not be moved. The statistics were against a better ending. A lot of marriages were breaking down, especially those forged in the forest, and those ruptures had various causes. Those who had loved each other fervently until the day before were now drawing knives against each other (with the arrival of peace, the non-political disaster pages of newspapers revived), or they separated in silence. Those who had been closest until the day before became total strangers. It appeared that many hopes, just like those in the rapid changes that the revolution was supposed to bring about, had been set too high. Many "wartime loves" fell apart. That expression began to resemble the phrase "summer love" used for a passing affair. Some marriages were destroyed by the Party. The married partners were asked to inform against each other. Because of the external political situation and the turmoil in the country.

In addition, it was easy to dissolve a marriage. To a great extent, the Party resembled the Church, but a civil marriage could be dissolved with a few court appearances and some stamps. There was a widespread view that it was better to part than to live a lie.

That is what people thought about the break with Moscow as well. It turned out that the enthusiasm of the masses, the real, unfeigned component, had not been entirely extinguished. Indeed, the conflict with Stalin homogenised the communist elite, and the very fact that Yugoslavia had provoked such a terrible opponent, until the day before its friend and most important ally, filled many with pride and generally stimulated self-respect, admittedly with a touch of trepidation.

Of course both Kempf and Vera presented their Confiteor to the Party "court", and did so some time before the whole problem was sent lower down to the level of civil court. When all means, legal and collegial, had been exhausted, that same court declared the annulment of their marriage. To the surprise of the judge and jury, not only did Vera not ask for alimony, which everyone in the courtroom, Kempf included, would have considered normal, but expressly rejected it. There began a long period of silence on Vera's part that was an expression of her refusal that Kempf should in any way participate in the upbringing of the child. That could not, of course, be achieved as fully as Vera wanted, so that I, at the age of around nine, was taken by tram to meet a man in a hat, who waved to me from the tram stop, and who I was told was my father. For many years afterwards I drew that hat and that man in hundreds of versions.

For now, the judge had pronounced his judgment. They both signed it in front of witnesses, and, at the door of the court, at Kempf's initiative, they shook hands and each set off on their own way, which is to say they went off to eat in their own canteens. So all that great distress ended with divorce from their table, divorce from their bed having taken place earlier.

Snoring had not been mentioned in the divorce proceedings.

Vera spent time after the divorce at a friend's apartment, until she found one of her own. And Kempf too had to leave what had been allocated to a promising couple of communists, after it was abandoned by a "class enemy". Vera was one of the deserving, but still not "in the top division of the revolution"; Kempf was an "honourable intellectual".

Because there were others. It would not have occurred to anyone at that time to divide the working people, the nation of workers, into the honourable and dishonourable. The apartments the divorced individuals now moved into were smaller and in less agreeable locations. In a sense, that fact was the external expression of their shared failure in the eyes of the Party.

Some friends stayed in contact with Vera, some, more rarely, with Kempf. Like everything else, friendships were divided. Only the child could not be cut in half.

In the end, why did that marriage fall apart?

The court, of course, could not be in any way cleverer than their closest friends, especially not the Party. At the meeting where the case of the divorce of two communists was on the agenda under Any Other Business, the Party had meticulously noted each oral Confiteor, and then asked them to leave the room. The two of them sat outside, not looking at each other. The Party clergy approved their divorce with regret. It would not help the proletarian revolution in any way. In their submissions, both partners had emphasised that their parting was necessary. The Party greeted this somewhat critically. Communists are expected to behave better in all aspects of iron necessity.

As the cause of the break-up, the court had confirmed differences in character. There was no mention of Kempf's alcoholism, nor, as in the cases of divorce of many members of the Informbiro, whose marriages were falling apart on a grand scale in those historic days, the political differences of the married comrades.

Both Kempf and Vera, before their initial encounters, had been through a lot. Many important events were behind them. They were not children whose characters were just forming. They had both brought their characters to their first assignations.

However it was, I had just become the child of divorced parents.

The revolution had wanted to abolish many differences, and it succeeded, but not this "difference of character".

Drang nach Westen

My mother placed me on the windowsill, firmly holding me with both hands. I saw women at other windows had brought their children out, just as in spring pots of flowers are placed on the windowsills.

Beneath us paraded soldiers. At that moment I couldn't have known much, and if anyone had told me, I wouldn't have understood: Tito's army was going to Trieste. That fine, rich city had to be liberated, and there was an army for that very purpose, the one that had grown out of the "national liberation" army. Liberating was its job.

Like the other women, my mother waved her handkerchief. On the news film I saw that the soldiers waved back to the women and even blew them kisses. Instead of hanging laundry out to dry as on every sunny day, the women hung out tricolour flags with a star. The crowd lining the street watched the armed force, which was then said to be the fourth in Europe in strength. The crowd was on the whole silent. That was because there was no "organised spontaneity", there were no schoolchildren, students, trade unions, workers, it was not the First of May. These men were going to war. And everyone had had their fill of war.

The tanks thundered. And they did arouse the crowd's applause, but it could hardly be heard over the noise of the caterpillar tracks ploughing the asphalt.

"Now you'll see our field guns!" I heard my mother say. "There they are! Our own! Local!"

The newspapers announced "our field guns", the work of the hands of "our working class" and the "national intelligentsia", that is "our" engineers.

"Those guns are recoilless," said my mother, but I hadn't the faintest idea what that meant. The crowd clapped.

Was my father in that crowd?

He had disappeared from our lives, slamming the door. My parents had quarrelled until he had taken from the flat the last item he possessed. And he was not there anymore. There were a lot of people with hats on in the street.

The tanks, and later "our field guns" made little impression on me. I did actually have a small gun, which fired peas. I couldn't say whether it was recoilless. I couldn't wait for them to pass and the supply train to come again. Never mind tanks and guns. What I most clearly remembered were the field kitchens. They were dragged by well-groomed horses; the cauldrons gleamed, just like the cupolas of the tanks. On each cauldron, there was a black pipe that later reminded me of a submarine periscope, which was foolish. I was fascinated by the field kitchens.

The soldiers didn't wave to the women at the windows, that was probably forbidden. They were likely thinking how stupid it was that they were the ones, as they rendered unto Caesar what was his, that is, performed their military service, who had stumbled into . . . war. Without doubt, they looked just like soldiers who were going to war. It seemed to me that they weren't very cheerful, but all my love and attention was lavished on the field kitchens.

After the crowd had greeted our guns, our local guns, and as the last field kitchens had passed, and the infantry arrived, I looked at my mother's face. It was joyful. I even thought that she might go downstairs, mingle with the soldiers and go off to war. So I would be left without a mother, without her glowing face, which would have to become serious because war is, generally speaking, something more serious than a military parade. Who would then be my mother?

The helmets, which were so serious, so warlike, reminded me of the little black tin containers my mother had given me as part of a kitchen; in that little kitchen everything was miniature. That gift was in keeping with her views on the upbringing of children in which one had to pay great attention to the equality of the sexes. So the soldiers wore on their heads the little containers in which I made pastry, except that my containers did not have a five-pointed star painted on them.

Would war begin with the dark, somewhere over there in the west?

The West listened to Tito's sabre-rattling. In Trieste there was fear, even panic. Rumour had it that Bosnians were coming with knives unsheathed. What would the Americans do with those knives, and what about the Russians? Would the Italian partisans – for the fascists were no longer in play – support Tito's? Would Europe finally calm down, would war finally end?

If my father Kempf was standing under one of those hats, perhaps he could have seen me?

I couldn't have seen his face, because of the brim of that unfortunate hat. But now I know that it wouldn't have been glowing. The two of them, Vera and Kempf, watched the same event from completely opposed viewpoints. This demonstration of force did not appeal to the poet, although he was himself sometimes inclined to excitement at parades. But my mother's surname was still Kempf. She had not sought to change it after the divorce, to go back to her maiden name. I suspect that was so that I wouldn't have a different name. The patriarchate, the power of the father, could not be as quickly demolished as the previous state had been.

Vera did not ask for anything from her former husband. Against the advice of her lawyer, and the comrades from the local council and those from the Party, she was too proud to sign a demand for alimony. She became a self-supporting mother.

She went through life entirely alone, like those self-propelled weapons that now thundered past our windows, a last greeting on the eve of war, immediately after the cavalry had passed, leaving behind them masses of large droppings on the asphalt.

There they were, Pullman howitzers, American, therefore. After the Russian tanks. The crowd watched them with awe but didn't applaud: we've been left on our own, we're self-supporting, we have to have our own, local field guns. There was even something sensual in that! You accept a bitter truth, you take a deep breath and manage.

Anything was better than rotten compromise.

My mother at the window, the elated true believer, devoted with every cell of her physical being to the general course on which the country was sailing, and the man with the hat in the crowd, were two worlds with their hackles up.

Who am I to reproach them? I am both of them. Who should I side with?

My mother took me down from the window when I was already half-asleep. I dreamed of bowler hats hiding the heads of serious men, and a multitude of field kitchens, stretching their periscopes, that is their chimneys, upwards towards our windows.

Tito's threat of war was an empty gun.

A Yellow Mercedes

The travelling group of poets "of rebuilding and renewal" were to hold a literary evening at the Vinkovci library. On that occasion, Comrade Kempf was to be given a plaque in memory of his co-founding of it after the war. His poems, particularly those connected with his birthplace, were anticipated with great impatience. There would certainly be a lot of inquisitive people.

After a night spent in the renovated hotel, which even had a swimming pool, the group were sitting in front of the inn. Local people who had come to greet the poets were also sitting at some of the tables. A man from the Lika area sat down beside Kempf. He seemed to Kempf to have been completely "domesticated". He was even wearing a Slavonian waistcoat in which red and blue dominated. That he was from the Lika, Kempf knew because he had introduced himself. Jozo had come with the first unscheduled train from the backwoods of Lika and ended up here immediately after the war.

"But why come here?" asked the poets.

Ah, poets, thought the man from Lika. They scamper around and chirrup, but they don't understand anything.

"Because there was no-one here."

"How do you mean no-one?"

"There were houses with no-one in them. There were empty villages, soil untouched for years."

Maria Theresa's colonists built their own houses, Kempf thought.

At that moment a Mercedes scattered dust down the road. The car turned right and disappeared.

"Not for me. Thank God," the man from Lika said. They ordered another round and the story began. This was the story of Jozo from Lika.

So Jozo had come here by train with his wife, they had no children yet.

"There were two kinds of German here:

"The first type, A, had left Slavonia in 1944, before the end of the war in other words. In response to Hitler's *Befehl** that all Germans should retreat within the then borders of the Reich. That was Passau, the upper Danube, God knows where. Their houses had on the whole been demolished. Do you have any idea how many villages in the Lika were wiped out, destroyed, burned? The type B Germans stayed to the end; to their end.

"They were driven out of their houses. Those houses were still standing. We had spotted some of those houses from the train.

"At the local council, my wife and I were given the address of a house some way away.

"I had never set eyes on it before, and now it's the house that I'll be carried out of feet first . . ."

Jozo scratched his head, wondering at his destiny.

"Believe me when I say I felt very uncomfortable . . . The two of us go into the house, and I remember the old customs, and I say to my wife, wait, I'll carry you over the threshold . . . and I do. The house is in good order, you can see at once, you could eat off the floor. The beds stripped. I lay my wife down on a bed.

---

* German for "command". [Author's note]

"In the hall, there are boots, cleaned, shoes arranged . . . cupboards full of clothes.

"Wood tidily piled beside the stove. The house is like a chemist's. There's not a living soul in it; apart from bats fluttering in the attic. I swear to God, they're the only witnesses."

"They're blind," Kempf says.

Jozo stops and looks at each of those present in turn.

"When, at the end of the fifties, all of a sudden a yellow Merc stops outside the house. German registration, German car, German driver. I think, he's going to ask for directions.

"'Could I have a glass of water?' asks the German in our language.

"'We drink brandy here, plum brandy!'

"'Do you make your own?'

"'Like every other house in Slavonia, this one makes its own.'

"The German who speaks our language takes a swig and compliments it: 'Fine, soft, it slips down as it should. I can see, you're keeping the place well.'

"'I do my best, sir.'

"'And where have you come from?'"

Before it occurred to Jozo that it was no business of this German where he had come from, he said: "From Lika."

"Did a lot of you come from Lika?"

"And where have you come from?"

"Germany."

"Do you make brandy there?"

"I sell textiles."

"We don't buy anything."

"Nice house, isn't it?" says the German.

"Yes, I give thanks to whoever built it."

"With good reason."

Our people are hospitable, but also gullible. Jozo led the German into the house. He was on the point of offering him bread and salt. With the assurance of a sleepwalker, the German set off up the stairs. That's it, the stranger was sleepwalking, he seemed to be shaking. Jozo didn't dare disturb him because he was afraid the man might collapse.

That's all he needed: for the stranger to die in his house.

"You see, sir, this was my house."

Need one say that Jozo's jaw dropped to the floor?

The German took a brick out of the wall on the upper floor. In all these years, there had been nothing to suggest to Jozo that this damned brick concealed anything. The man took a box out of a hole behind the brick, opened it and immediately closed its lid. Behind the stove, Jozo kept a stick that he had used when he sprained his ankle in the summer. The stick had a knot at the top, which was a good handle, but it could have served as a mallet. Jozo thought: I'll crush his head, fuck his thieving German rat's head, that's what I should do now.

The German went downstairs, but this time calmly and confidently. Good God, he's under his own roof!

"But I'm under my own roof too!" Jozo said to himself.

The German took his leave with a slight motion of his head, got into his pumpkin-yellow Mercedes and disappeared.

Jozo went upstairs and started tapping on the bricks and pushing them with his hand.

Were there any more secrets here? The German had got away with jewels, for sure. What else could have been in that box? They had left everything in this house, including silver cutlery. They had left in a hurry. Fear's good.

"I tap, examine, sniff around for hours. And then a brick gives. It had been in front of my nose for years as I pissed into the

toilet. It was downstairs. It would never have occurred to me . . .
In the hole behind it was a folded flag. Red, like blood, like our
flags. But in the centre – a swastika; black on white. I took the
swastika to the police. A file was opened about that flag. I don't
know where it disappeared to, just as I don't know where that
German disappeared to."

There was silence at the table at the inn. They were all quiet,
but Kempf was the quietest of all.

Jozo's story had been intended for him, although he was the
only one who could understand that.

Who had been in the yellow Mercedes? The waggon-maker
Ferk or his son Ferdo Ferk, Đuka's schoolmate from Nuštar? How
come Kempf had never wondered what happened to Ferdo Ferk,
whether he'd survived. Old Ferk had been clever, and prescient.
A fabrication that belonged to the world of Gothic novels worked
here. It's true that no-one actually knew what kept our people
here together, what metaphysical angst connected to this had his
son wrestled with? A dark force, a black hole?

At a certain moment, it occurred to him to ask the man from
Lika to describe more precisely the man from the Mercedes, as
best he could from memory. But people change, don't they?

Sons look increasingly like their fathers. One or other of the
Ferks had come to that house.

Fortunately, the waiter saved him from such foolishness by
inviting them to come to the table inside, now ready for them.
Even had the two of them met and succeeded in recognising
each other, what would they have had to convey to one another?
Would Kempf have invited his friend from those distant days to
this evening's event?

The literary evening was a quite routine performance. That

wasn't fair given the expectations of these people, thought Kempf. We're hoodwinking them, we're not in form.

Surprisingly, his verses about the sweat being shed, a lot of sweat, increasing amounts of sweat for increasing amounts of steel, were the ones that received most applause. That was the advantage of being on his home ground. For some time already, Kempf had known that he would always be a *poeta minor*. The thought was painful, although, on the other hand, even that recognition was a big thing and bore witness to a man with a fair amount of character. Although he was already in the process of freeing himself from socialist-realist models, he was beginning to realise that the impetus with which he had set out was too weak and that he wouldn't be able to overcome the vast abyss in which his experiences inimical to poetry lay drowned.

Kempf slept badly that night. There was a north wind, he couldn't get warm in bed.

He remembered that as an S.S. soldier he had never had more than one cover.

That wasn't much help. He felt cold, somehow from the inside. When you build a fire in a stove, you light it at the bottom. If you try the other way round, there'll be no fire or warmth. So now Kempf's head was burning feverishly, while his feet were as cold as though frozen.

How often in the course of his "Polish war" had he dreamed about these plains, about the vineyards bathed in sunshine scattered over the slopes of the low-lying hills, about the plum orchards stretching as far as you could see, about the wood known as Spačva like the stream that ran through it, about the lazy, dark-green Bosut, where otters swam?

In Poland I was more Slavonian than ever in Slavonia, Kempf thought.

Slavonian, Šokac, yes; German, no way.

We Germans arrived in the reign of Maria Theresia. In this part of the world people kept arriving, and, when possible, also fleeing. For instance, when Slavonia was part of the Ottoman Empire. Wars are always the same, all armies have always behaved in the same way, for thousands of years . . . A drunken rabble assaults women, there are rapes in every chicken coop . . . Men who try to fight are taken as slaves. The Turks settle Wallachians here, sowing the seed of new wars. Some Christians go over to the Prophet, some dare remain Christian but Calvinist. Then the eighteenth-century wars against the Ottomans . . . Prince Eugene unfurls his banners and attacks the Crescent. Christians, of all denominations, flee again. The Orthodox Wallachians, *martolos* paid by the Turks, are afraid of revenge.

Many flee with the Turks. The Šokci arrive – from Bosnia. Some Christians live in the marshes, or under the protection of the forest for up to twenty years, they are born, grow up and die as refugees. Here refugee is the key image of existence.

That someone entered someone else's house as its owner, a house in which the stove was still glowing and the bed still warm, happened in this part of the world no fewer than a million times. But for those affected, or for the beneficiaries, it was always just once.

The original Kempf evidently chose a more difficult solution: the Kempfs erected a new house, in which they were helped by the Viennese Chamber, that is, the Empress.

But who had been living in the apartment into which he and Vera had moved in the autumn of the first year of peace?

He got up early. The north wind had died down, clearing the horizon.

Kempf and a poet colleague were sitting by the hotel pool, smoking. They were dressed in identical suits that made a theatrical impression: as though they had escaped from the Grand Guignol. The hotel was still asleep.

Two weeks earlier, in Varaždin, the textile works had made it possible for them to buy, in fact virtually as a gift, suits that had been made there, roughly for the price of the thread used. The suits had not been made to measure, but the two poets, at least physically, were up to the "Yugoslav standard". The working class had dressed its poets, comrades who were a bit distant, but who tried to come closer to them, to them and to the benches where the women workers sat in rows like schoolgirls, cutting and sewing.

All the poets had "performed" the previous evening in those suits.

In his childhood Đuka Kempf had known how to get many games going. His reputation was such that often games wouldn't start until he gave the signal. Had the S.S. sniffed out a leader in him? Unlikely. His rank in their formation, admittedly the lowest possible, had been decided by the banal fact that he had done his military service in the old Yugoslav army and was allocated by chance to Nuštar.

But now, beside this pool filled with clean, warm water, he again felt like a leader, although he had only one colleague to take with him.

There was no other explanation for the fact that both of them, dressed in those grotesque suits of pre-war design, suddenly found themselves in the pool and swam from the end where their shoes still reached the bottom towards the deep end, where the water was up to their necks . . .

With them the sun's rays also swam: as though the Almighty had sprinkled those little sparks about which Leon Mordechai had spoken (sung?).

The poets swam.

Food Supplement

One question troubled Kempf in connection with Terezija (known to everyone as Rezika), Franja's mother, who had died, at a great age, the week before: who had been paying for her nursing home? The nurses caring for the old people said that Mrs Lauber had had her own room, and that was considerably more expensive. Kempf went to see the room, it was modestly arranged. Old age has reduced needs. But it costs money to have a room of one's own.

On the late resident's birthday, Kempf went to the home with a cake in a plastic container. They were delighted, the nurses and the old men and women in the home clapped. On her birthday, Mrs Lauber had always treated everyone to a cake just like this, in a plastic container. Now it had been brought by her son's friend, because she could no longer organise it and it had been her wish.

The cake would be cut after the midday meal.

Kempf sat in a small room, lined with plywood, where the nurses spent their "peaceful moments", where they drank coffee.

"She was a lovely person," a nurse said. "And strong, given her age. She never fell. She washed herself and loved cleanliness in everything."

"Even on the day she died, she sat in the park, sunning herself."

"Who paid for her room?"

"She had an account in the bank where she received German marks. She said that she had relatives in Germany."

"She didn't have relatives in Germany."

"Well, she was called Lauber, her husband was German."

"He died before the war."

"No-one is alone on this earth, Mr Kempf. But one can be forgotten. We have many here who have been completely forgotten. Even though they have relatives, even children. Someone in Germany took care of Mrs Lauber."

"Franja Lauber was her only son. And he disappeared in Russia."

"You're right," one of the nurses said after a while. "Rezika didn't have any relatives in Germany. We were quite close."

"So who paid for her place here?"

"Germany."

"Why would Germany pay for anything?"

"It's a strange country, Germany."

The nurse told him, thinking that perhaps he didn't know: "Her son fell in Russia. Or he disappeared. His mother tried to find him through the Red Cross."

Kempf began to take his leave. He had discovered what he wanted to know. One could say he got what he wanted.

The nurses wanted him to stay for their modest meal, so that he could cut the cake and distribute it to everyone in the name of Mrs Lauber, of good memory, as, in a sense, her representative. But Kempf declined the invitation, wanting to leave this place as soon as possible.

"A fine, well-preserved older gentleman," said one of the nurses, as soon as Kempf had quietly closed the front door after him. "With manners!"

"There are few like that in this town now!"

"There are only peasants and barbarians here now."

Kempf was furious, and he hadn't wanted the women with whom he had no connection to see it.

Germany had supplemented Mrs Terezija Lauber's food.

By way of compensation for the life of the son of Volksdeutscher Lauber, forester, whose son had volunteered for the Waffen-S.S. (that was recorded in a document from Germany) and who had then disappeared in the expanses of the Soviet Union (that was recorded in the German documents as well).

It didn't take long for Kempf to get confirmation. There was a legal organisation in Germany concerned with supplementing the income of former soldiers. The Third Reich remained a grateful partner to the end, and even after its end.

I'm old and over-sensitive, thought Kempf. That was nothing but evidence of an irrevocable reality. The Red Cross had searched. Franja had been recruited six months before me. He could have gone to Stalingrad. By a miracle I avoided Kursk and Brodsky.* I too could easily have disappeared in Russia. The old fox Adenauer had managed to bring some back. Many had disappeared forever.

Now that the old lady had died, Kempf felt ashamed that he had not visited her more often. They had sat together on a bench in the park two or three times, talking about the old days. He had never been into the home before, he didn't know the conditions she was living in.

Now it was too late. Ageing was in fact the accumulation of such immutabilities. A man had to be careful: his every dream could be his last, every word, even those uttered by chance, could be his last wish.

Another reason he hadn't gone more often to visit the old

---

* The S.S. Galicia division was massacred at Brodsky. [Author's note]

lady was a feeling of something like guilt. That was of course absurd. But it was impossible, on those visits, that the old lady would not have thought something along the lines of: "Now my Franja would have grey hair too." The way she looked at him, and she was still perfectly lucid, could sometimes make Kempf uncomfortable.

It was somehow after that visit to the home, the first since the death of his friend Franja Lauber's mother, that old Kempf virtually stopped going out. As though he had somehow shrunk, shrivelled. As though he had given up. Not even for bread and milk, so a little arrangement was made with his closest neighbours. He could walk, he hadn't declined physically to that extent. But he lacked the will. They'll find me, he thought. A matter of days.

We began to wonder about putting him too into a home. His second wife, my would-be stepmother, had taken ill and was virtually immobile. Kempf's vision was deteriorating. What troubled him most was that it was increasingly difficult to read for long, if at all. Throughout his life Kempf had always read whatever came to hand, he had devoured books.

I came to his flat to read to him.

He admired Sienkiewicz, and we quarrelled, because I thought that writer old-fashioned, slow-moving. He said he liked him because of Poland. I read mostly *Quo vadis?* There was no trace of Poland in that huge book.

He would often snooze over Tostoy's *War and Peace*.

I quite understand that. It is hard to conceive of anything more tedious.

"You see," said my father, "Sienkiewicz wrote about ancient Rome as though he had grown up there."

"Immanuel Kant wrote about universal peace as a citizen of the world and he never left Königsberg."

"Well, you're not exactly a traveller yourself," my father said. "Get yourself a Baedeker, go to Poland."

Something had broken in Kempf after his visit to the home. He was no longer the old man he had been, my father, of whom I had wrongly thought that I knew him at least up to a point.

He too had disparaged his father. We Kempfs have problems with our fathers.

Hungry Years

There was a crowd in the station restaurant. All the tables were occupied, and people were sitting in the corners on suitcases. They were mainly dozing. Kempf sat down at the counter.

How miserable, he thought. In Poland there was always food to go with drink. Caviar with onion and oil, for instance. Maybe herring? Rabbit with cranberries . . .

To be fair, Kempf had only read about this. In Poland he had eaten whatever he could and had never encountered caviar or herring. Although that goulash on their patrol, in Zimmerman's Tavern – traditional Polish cuisine for gentlefolk – hadn't been bad. And as for the new Poland, he knew that his poet colleagues there didn't leap into pools in new suits.

"Who are these people?" Kempf asked the woman behind the counter, a girl whose nipples could be seen under her blouse. She told him they were going to Deutschland.

"At midnight? But there aren't any trains."

"In an hour's time."

Kempf was relieved to hear this. He felt suddenly sorry for these sleepy people, and had been thinking that they were homeless and had nowhere to sleep so had come to the station to get warm.

He looked at their suitcases: wooden, cardboard, often just ordinary boxes tied with string. Then he looked at them individually: on the whole young people, all of them men. Some were almost still children. Youngsters, at the height of their strength, thought Kempf.

Let them travel, who can stop them these days? A bottle was going round the room.

"Give some to the gentleman as well," called the men sitting on their suitcases. The bottle reached him, Kempf took a swig. Good old Slavonian plums.

More than a hundred young men were travelling, leaving ... They were just waiting for their train to get on board and turn their backs on us. The women would follow in some future contingent.

Deutschland! Precisely the country that Germans such as his ancestor had once left ... and they had come here, to that "Transylvania" these young men were now fleeing. Back then, Germany had been hungry. These people were now going in the opposite direction. They would not be floating along the Danube, which would have been upstream this time, and in the eighteenth century that was only possible pulled by horses. They didn't face the threat of rapids or crags where their raft could have been crushed. They had to face customs officers, but they had existed in the time of the Empress' reign as well. They could be managed.

How long would it take for waves of colonists, "guest-workers" this time, to settle in a new stream bed, put down roots, make themselves at home, become naturalised, assimilated? How long would it take for them to stop being identified as foreign? For my Germans almost two hundred years hadn't been enough. That is ten generations. And then they became foreign again.

These lads here have decided to look for something better. Are they going of their own free will? Poor prospects, if not also pangs of hunger, are hardly conducive to free will. These are new *frei-willige Gezwungene*, forced volunteers. They are going, in their prime, to be *Gastarbeiter*, as they will be called in Germany. That Germany is foreign. In other countries guests are not expected to work. The old inhabitants of Slavonia called those they couldn't understand dumb, *nijem*, people without a language.*

That the special train to Munich was waiting on who knows which platform was announced over the loudspeaker by a woman desperate for sleep.

A multitude of bodies suddenly seethed like a mass of single-cell paramecia under a microscope, they all woke at the same instant, they were all on their feet.

Immediately after this announcement, Kempf heard a sharp whistle. A hundred men rushed for the door, there was a jam, they almost came to blows.

On the platform a man was waving his arms, like a traffic policeman at a crossroads, from time to time blowing hard on his whistle. The multitude formed an orderly procession, following the commands of his arms as they cut through the air. The drilling of these young men had begun.

The column marched off with an almost military step, at the rhythm set by the man in a crumpled uniform that had once been dark and could have been worn by an undertaker.

His shoes were yellow and muddy, they had high soles, as though he had wanted to increase his slight stature.

Kempf watched the polyphemus eye of the beast that first began, panting, to crawl and then speeded up. The eye dwindled, now it was just a red dot that finally dissolved into the darkness.

---

* The Croatian for "German" is Nijemac. [Translator's note]

In his lifetime nothing connected with trains had been cheerful.

In the same way, the darkness had also swallowed the train in which, behind bars, Ania Sadowska had disappeared.

Strange the way the ratcatcher's pipe had been reduced to a guard's whistle. What a culturological comedown.

Meeting with the Young

Ever since the cardiologist confirmed *angina pectoris*, Kempf had
begun to think that he ought to put at least some things in order
before his final departure. Buy a graveyard plot, for example.
That was like a full stop in a sentence. Those who died with
an exclamation mark did not have to worry about a grave, they
would get one gratis. While those who died under a question
mark had to worry not only about a grave but often also about
the graveyard. When an ordinary mortal died, it was problematic,
you couldn't die just like that at today's prices.

That was why Kempf had recently taken to walking round
Mirogoj, a cemetery renowned for its beauty. Mirogoj was most
beautiful in the early autumn when the totalitarian green was
transformed into a symphony of all shades of yellow and brown.
Kempf's walks now took a long time, so long that they became
real little expeditions. He always carried in his pocket the locations of the grave plots that had not yet been occupied, and which
were available. Of course, those locations were a long way from
Bollé's arcades, where the immortal lay in their eternity. But the
whole of Mirogoj in those days was the prime address for the
dead, and therefore expensive.

The graves on offer were shown in marble, because it was
worth spending a lot on their location. Their geometry was
severe, they were arranged like soldiers on parade.

Standing in front of one of them, Kempf wondered, was this the one? Two square metres, with a cover and a square gravestone. For the moment without any emblem of religious or any other allegiance, they really reminded one of apartments on the doors of which the new occupants had yet to put their names. Perhaps also their occupation: dentist, stationmaster, actor, teacher, opera diva, writer, pilot ... None read: good-for-nothing, murderer, street sweeper, housemaid ... immigrant ...

On the whole, the peace of the dead was respected. That respect was preserved in the name of this place along the paths of which Kempf was now looking for his grave.

The way I looked for Franja's grave in the East, he thought.

Kempf's walks often went on so long that the setting sun would find him sitting on a bench beside a stranger's grave. The Kempfs did not yet reside in Mirogoj, he was to be the first. This cemetery was on a hill, the Sava river could not flood it. Likewise, it was not interesting from a strategic point of view, it would be hard for any army to occupy it, as had happened to the graveyard in Nuštar. Apart from passing cars, a person could count on finding peace here.

He was already fairly worn out when he became aware of his heart, which had again begun dancing in his rib cage. What if it were to stop right here? At this time of day, before the cemetery gates were closed, Mirogoj was virtually empty of the living.

How would you say that in German? The way this or that town was described as *Judenfrei*, free from Jews? Free from the living?

Kempf hurried along the path leading north, knowing that at a certain point he would have to turn right, towards the main cross, where on the Day of the Dead candles were lit for those whose graves were unknown. Kempf himself had lit such candles on that day, or more exactly in the evening of the Day of the Dead, remembering all those whose graves he had sought in vain, Franja's above all, and then those of his people, the Kempfs, his remote and close forebears, whose graves had been shattered by mines and grenades, so now their occupants wandered the world like the homeless. The path from the main cross led along the arcades of the deserving. Those arcades of ours offered more secure residence than the Paris Panthéon, where the traffic of the deserving could be fairly lively.

Kempf followed this route because he knew the way, but also because he heard voices, although he wasn't sure that it wasn't his senses deceiving him, now when the shadows were growing longer and every rustle aroused nameless dread in the solitary walker. What he had heard, or thought he had, was like a group of voices, a prayer. If it was a whisper, then it was very loud, louder than ordinary speech, but nevertheless a whisper. It was too late for funerals, besides the bell at the main entrance had not sounded as a signal of any last send-off. People are not buried in the twilight, there had been enough for the day, the shop was closed.

Nevertheless, one place here was visited exceptionally often.

Kempf slowed his pace and turned abruptly off the path between the graves. What he could now observe, unseen he hoped, was the following:

Some twenty young men, strongly built, dressed from head to foot in black, were circling round a monument that Kempf had not yet come across in all his wanderings. And had he done so, he would have considered it a relic of past ages; a splinter fallen out of history and its mosaics that no-one could ever include in a new (old? renewed?) whole.

But these people thought the opposite.

All at once, Kempf remembered, word for word, the Führer's

oath that he had made as a forced volunteer in the barracks, after drilling under the supervision of S.S. officers in the town of Stockerau. What's more, he could declaim the whole oath, whispering in the half-darkness. And he had forgotten so much of what he wished to remember. And remembered so much he wished to forget. He noticed that he had hidden behind an unfinished stone and calculated from the inscription that the occupant of the grave was virtually a child. Admittedly, the graves of adults were also rarely palaces. Eternity doesn't need much more than a basic dwelling.

No, thought Kempf. These people round the monument are not children. Nor was the one who was now speaking, energetically cutting through the air full of the emanations of the dead (how strongly and sweetly flowers in a graveyard smell) – he was no child.

The dead seemed to have suppressed their moaning the better to hear the sermon of the man in black whose outfit didn't differ from those of the men standing round him in a semicircle. His outfit was not yet a uniform, but nor was it the clothing of a civilian: he was a larva that had not yet completed its transformation, but was well on its way.

This new marriage broker was wearing a leather waistcoat, the task of which was to emphasise his muscles. No bright colours, no pipes. And his voice wasn't up to much, here in the open air and without the support of a microphone. So what was it that made it possible for this black cockerel to lead and transport his audience? Had the black companies of Florian Geyer returned?

He was now going to thrust into the ground in front of him an enormous sword, a new Excalibur.

That sword would transform what was in itself neutral ground, by staining it with the blood of the enemy, for the time being only in spirit, and transmute it into the homeland. The only way for it to become a homeland.

Partially concealed behind the gravestones and trees, Kempf noticed a stranger in a dark suit, feeling at once an onrush of disquiet. The stranger took off his hat and wiped his brow. Kempf was particularly struck by the shape of his skull: part of it seemed to be missing. His head was distorted. One could easily imagine him on a stretcher, somewhere near Kursk for instance. But he evidently possessed so much life that he could easily have enjoyed some kind of immortality.

The stranger did not join in the dramatic scene with the sword and singing. The broken skull was waiting for *the spirit of the troop* to form. That was the task of his envoy. Like the cat Carabas from the fairy tale, he went up to his master, praising all that he had, all that he was and all that he brought with him. When the envoy announced what was decreed for him, the stranger would lead these young men into a new thousand-year empire. It was so easy. He had only to blow into his pipe and its irresistible sound would draw the troop off after him. Stockerau, the Ulan barracks: it had no function apart from raising the spirit of the troop. And then in Galicia, when his unit . . . proved itself. That was when the holy spirit of the troop descended into it. The irresistible effect of the piper would be enhanced precisely by the spirit of the troop, well-tuned to the always renewed playing of the Hamelin piper. But this time he was not many-coloured like a bunch of field flowers and didn't wear different coloured shoes as he is portrayed in children's picture books, he was no Struwwelpeter or Till Eulenspiegel, his stories were not lullabies. He was dressed entirely in the fashion of the day, for formal occasions. Part of his skull was missing, but otherwise he had everything necessary for the revolutionary transformation of the world. He was a ghost from the future.

Kempf was appalled. Why, if he could see the stranger, he could himself be seen.

For a moment it seemed to Kempf that everything around him had begun to spin. My time has passed. They are here again.

He lowered himself onto a bench and from the bench onto the grass beside a grave. By the time he had recovered a little, it was already getting dark. He had never stayed so long. Now he hoped that Mirogoj was not locked like the entrances to better houses.

Kempf felt that his shirt was soaked in sweat.

He should have called for help, but his Super-Ego would not permit it. That Super-Ego was all that remained to him of the Superman.

Once his heart had calmed down and he had begun to breathe normally, he got to his feet, leaning on the bench. There was no-one here anymore. They had come out of the earth and vanished into it. Had it all in the end been just an illusion?

His life seemed again to be a terrible muddle. How to connect that epic, which could have had the title *The Little Polish War of Volksdeutscher Kempf* into a whole which he would have dared relate to anyone, including his son? That could be the criterion for a life that might be considered virtuous: that it could be related to anyone, and that anyone would shrug his shoulders and say: "It was all for people!" But the lives of most people are terrible shreds of all manner of things.

Having established that his legs were obeying him again, and his dizziness had passed, Kempf strictly forbade himself from succumbing to any self-pity.

What, for instance, would Vera have said, if she had seen that gathering of a while ago?

She would have said that she was capable of winning over the indifferent and turning around the most recalcitrant enemy if she was able to talk with them alone.

The young men who had just been here, in front of the monument, mumbling their oath (or was it a curse?) would not have bothered with conversations.

Kempf turned up his coat collar because the autumn evening was chilly and made his way to the tram stop at the bottom of the hill.

I still haven't found my grave! How careless is that. Above all, it's impolite to those who are left. But these walks aren't good for me. I'll look for a grave in the small ads.

How he ended up in the morning on a bench in the park not far from the two-storey building where he lived, Kempf could not explain. Maybe I've become a sleepwalker? That wouldn't be surprising.

He was sitting on the bench in a dressing gown, blue, that he had bought in case he was taken to hospital or a home. He was warming himself in the sun. He felt warm. However, the new cycle of the renewal of nature was far away and Kempf didn't believe that he would participate in it.

His gaze fell on a column of ants: in a great hurry the sexless workers, the ant proletariat, were dragging pieces of something that their state needed. Evidently the anthill's supplies were not well stocked . . . What the proletarians were dragging with their forelegs looked like building material.

There were many fierce ant wars and they were waged constantly. Perhaps this anthill was being rebuilt after it had been destroyed?

Kempf looked around him. There was no-one. The dogs had

already been walked. He knelt on the edge of the lawn and laid his hand on the anthill.

Through his hand he received a message from the ants' state: a trembling, a shivering that he didn't find disagreeable. The harmonious effort of the millions. Constant general mobilisation.

Kempf closed his eyes, without moving his hand. But he spread his fingers, like feelers, trying to draw into himself as much as he could of that humming.

Were they happy?

They seemed happy and were sending him that message. Was it feigned? You'd have to be an ant yourself to know for certain.

And as the ants tickled the palm he had laid on the soil, Kempf decided, his eyes still closed, to draw, at least provisionally, a certain line.

But what if those enthusiasms are not feigned but real, if they are a reflection of real happiness, and I am the only one who spoils the games, not knowing how to fit in because my scepticism is septic, and that sepsis is fatal? Would it not be wise for the whole of me to be ... amputated? What if Vera and her people are right and I am the one who doesn't wish to acknowledge their success, given that the world has become at least a little better thanks to their efforts and their courage, while I keep reviling them as do-gooders who squandered the immense capital they had brought with them from the forest in 1945?

The raft of communism had in fact become worm-eaten and disintegrated, in the torrent of awakened hatreds.

The piper with the deformed skull was absolutely counting on them, those hatreds. No prayers could have prevented the catastrophe, whether despatched to the gods in the sky or to those who hold court at the world's markets. Iron Necessity, in which people had so blindly believed, above all those fervent believers who were holding the tiller, had been eliminated. And it was still possible on that raft, the Medusa's, which was now floating on a turbulent sea, just as in Géricault's famous painting, to make out a thoughtful individual, his arms leaning on his knees, asking "Why?" while others waved the remaining rags of their hope.

That outcome seemed inadequate. But Kempf knew that Vera would never come to the same conclusion. He would die, of that he was now certain, as soon as it became a matter of complete indifference to him.

He would die the way someone shrugs his shoulders.

Germany Calling

Since his eyesight had deteriorated, old Kempf listened more and more to the radio. He often fell asleep in his armchair. In the real sense of the word, Kempf didn't communicate with anyone. He only listened to "serious music". The former card-playing clubs had folded. Those who had appreciated his four little collections of verses had long since died. His name meant nothing to the younger generation. Politics didn't interest him. He didn't share the enthusiasms of some old colleagues, or former friends, for the "new ways" that now dictated life in their country. The fact that he had seen many such upheavals in his lifetime armed him with cynicism. But he did not, so to speak, put that cynicism into circulation. There was no bitterness in him, because for something like that one had to be in better condition. Hatred takes strength and he had none. The troubles of old age pressed on him from all directions. His heart often wandered off according to its own crazy rhythm, he imagined he could see it in front of him expanding and contracting. He was constantly anxious about his liver. The worst was that he could hardly see anything.

Fortunately, he was not hard of hearing.

Not to be hard of hearing was sometimes not a blessing.

If there was something he genuinely hated, it was shooting in honour of some holiday or another. That he hated it was to put it mildly. Like his neighbour's dog, he felt like hiding under the table; and he would have crawled under the table, had it not aroused the suspicion of those around him who were in any case looking for signs of dementia to send him to an old people's home.

Just as in the war he had almost always been able to make out what weapon was being fired, now he felt compelled to name what was playing in that holiday orchestra: Kalashnikovs, ancient rifles, carbines, *parabellums*, flags . . .

No-one who knows as much about weapons as you do can be senile, my not-fated-to-be stepmother consoled him.

Simply, he greeted the new year under the table, like the neighbour's dog, which had to be given tranquillisers.

So old Kempf lived, from day to day, in uncertain silence. At any moment a shot could shatter it.

That is how things were with Georg Kempf, poet of four little volumes of verse, which some people considered not at all bad.

But he himself knew that he had fallen out of history. There was no justice in history. There were only the weak and the strong; the once weak, now strong. There were also the righteous who were weak even when they were strong. But they are not the ones who "make" history. Kempf certainly didn't. Why did people require him to take responsibility for it?

When, at this age, he thought about the failure of his marriage, he no longer attributed it to their different "war journeys", his and Vera's. Now he thought that the judge's formulation of "incompatibility of character" was about right. It was a matter of the chemistry between two people, which initially misleads, and then dissolves, with no apology. That is simply how it is. But a doubt was still niggling that this was a rationalisation of the irrational. How to introduce some minimal coherence into that nightmare?

A telephone.

"Herr Georg Kempf?" said a voice at the other end of the line.

"Yes."

"Jahrgang 1919?"

Yes, that was his birth year.

"I have in front of me the list of your formation. Can you hear me, Herr Kempf?"

"Yes, I hear you clearly."

"From April 11, 1943 to . . ."

"Who would remember? It was a long time ago."

"Herr Kempf," and here the voice paused, "we have you down . . ." another pause, "as *verschollen*."

So, thought Kempf, not as "one who ran away from the flag", a deserter, but one who disappeared. A fighter who vanished in battle. Indeed, as a volunteer, whom an orderly and prosperous state was intending to reward for his goodwill.

"What do you live on, Herr Kempf?"

Kempf put the receiver down. The telephone rang twice more, and then stopped. My father, Georg Kempf, died that night, in his sleep.

First Love

After her divorce from my father, my mother Vera wrote men off as an inferior subspecies of the human race. I know nothing about my mother's erotic life. So I didn't have anyone to kill because he had slept with her. The Oedipus in me was stunted. Was that why, in the absence of the man with the hat whom I sketched for years on every blank piece of paper, I had sought some external authority, quite outside the framework of my family novel, so I could destroy them and finally grow up? Without that, there is no growing up.

On one occasion I plucked up my courage and asked her about any possible friends, but that provoked an attack of moodiness.

"People who don't live as couples have their ways."

After her death, I found some letters with demure indications of possible relationships. I never met the men who sent her those letters.

To this day I don't know what drew my father to my mother if it was not a game of pure opposites. They say that every man looks for his mother in his wife. In some, sepia, photographs of the Kempf family, I saw my father's mother. A broad, serious face, curly blond hair. All very regular. She seemed to me a person without an excess of qualities. Solidity in everything. Of course, that assessment could have been unjust. It was natural that I should take my mother's side, particularly in the battle she lost against a third person, my un-destined stepmother. But who could make a competent judgment? It's better for me to keep silent. Chemistry between two people functions, and it either lasts or it doesn't.

In fact, what I said about a lost battle was only half-true. She had not, as they say, fought for her man, at all. She simply wrote him off, even as an economic being by refusing alimony, to her Party comrades' astonishment. The two of them went to court several times and that was the worst aspect of the whole thing. I was the cause. The case was always initiated by Kempf. Those court appearances were a real torment for her, psychologically. And what was strange about it all was that Kempf remained to the end the man of her life. She simply knew how to come to terms with the greatest disappointments. This was true also of her wider battle, for a "better society".

Having written Georg off, Vera found herself in a different kind of struggle: for the rights of the world's women, and those rights were always in the firm grasp of the Father. The revolution had promised a lot, but it was led by fathers. At parades, images of classical and contemporary leaders; on platforms – always the fathers of the revolution. No mothers. The revolution had been born in the head, a virgin conception that men carried out among themselves. Women were only exceptionally allowed into government.

Once, while they were still married, Vera was given tickets for a production on the theme of the Partisan struggle. On that occasion, in the ceremonial box, sat a woman in violet of whom those in the stalls knew that she was "responsible for culture".

In the middle of the performance, the violet woman had stood up in her box and shouted:

"That is not who we were!"

The performance stopped for a moment, the people who were seated remained seated, those who were moving stopped moving. Everyone in the stalls waited for the curtain to be lowered.

The lights came on in the auditorium. Nobody moved.

For roughly half a minute things could have gone either way. In the early days of theatre, that would have been called a "tableau".

The violet woman left the theatre, slamming the door of her box. That echoed like a shot.

The applause at the end was half-hearted. The actors didn't come out to bow. Everyone in the theatre felt as though they had survived a shock. As the audience collected their coats, they congratulated each other on being alive.

Nothing happened, the play continued to be performed.

That evening Vera and her husband had a shrill argument about freedom of expression in art. Vera was in favour of responsible freedom. Kempf railed against the "glaring interference of politics in art". This time plates didn't fly, but there was no agreement in this area either. The violet woman had not recognised herself on the stage, believing that her right to be portrayed the way she saw herself had been attacked. Kempf found that comical, Vera didn't.

How had the two of them ever come together? Had Vera had any love life before Kempf?

I was sitting on the balcony, looking through old photographs, when someone called me, introducing himself as Bartol never-mind-the-surname.

Bartol never-mind-the-surname told me that he would like to talk to me about something very important in connection with Mrs Vera Kempf, whom he admired greatly, indeed more than admired.

I asked Bartol how he had come by my number. I learned that he got it from Mr Kempf.

"So why didn't you talk to him about Vera, he was her husband?"

"I would like to talk to you if at all possible. Mr Kempf declared that he had no competence with regard to his former wife."

The very next day, for, he said, he was just passing through, he appeared at my door. What could I do, besides, I admit, I was interested. I was putting my mosaic together, every little piece of stone was valuable, particularly if individual stones were in conflict.

Bartol was tall and thin. He dragged one leg, I asked him whether that was a problem from his birth, he said it was a shell and he had got off lightly.

In the course of the conversation, it turned out that this Bartol was the man from the Ustasha police who informed Vera about Tolj's ambush.

The war was knocking on the door again.

"So you worked for Tolj in the police?"

"That's right."

"He was hanged?"

"He let himself be caught, that was the right thing to do."

"People say he was despicable."

"Things look different in wartime."

"I heard something about women screaming . . . Was he the one who sent Vera to Stara Gradiška?"

"Of course, who else?"

"How did you escape from it all?"

I was expecting something from the Bleiburg epic, I didn't want to encourage him to let rip, believing that there could be no agreement about that question.

It turned out that Bartol had taken his rescue into his own

hands. He had simply set off towards the west, in civilian clothes, with some provisions, unarmed . . . and let come what may. He knew that he had to keep going west.

"I'd have some tales to tell you, my son."

What a strange way to address me.

I realised that he had done what had worked for Georg Kempf. Like my father, he too had dragged himself over scorched earth, through half of Central Europe, only, from some point in Slovakia, he had gone in the opposite direction. Both had sought a lair they could crawl into if necessary. Perhaps their paths had crossed somewhere?

"I sometimes got a lift in a car, but mostly I tottered along on foot. I'm alive. Until recently I worked, for Opel, I didn't do badly, I've got a good pension. Did Vera never talk about me? I was her first love. You know, youngsters. You don't forget that, my son. In the war, she went off with her own people. I didn't know how to persuade her. She was too intelligent for me. I was always somehow too slight for her."

He asked me where Vera was now. In a home, I said. He wanted the address, I didn't want to give it to him.

"She wouldn't recognise you, Bartol, she doesn't recognise me any longer and I'm her son."

"If it hadn't been for the war, I would have been your father."

That sentence contained sadness, sympathy and a curse. Had I not been the offspring of a forced volunteer of the Waffen-S.S., I would be the offspring of an agent of Pavelić's. Was there a third option?

Bartol limped off down the road.

The sirens summon people to go underground. The media affirm that we should expect attacks from Yugoslav Army MiGs. I watched passers-by scurrying to shelters.

Bartol would not be distracted in his dejection, he continued to drag that leg in the direction in which he had intended to disappear.

He was now tiny, around him scuttled Gullivers carrying cushions and blankets, as he was diminishing then slipping under the pavement. I could no longer see him.

I took a book and candle and went down to the cellar.

Our building has a shelter, which it is said will protect us even in the case of an atomic bomb attack. When the end of the alarm was sounded, the civil defence team dragged pipes connected to a hydrant and washed the toilets. They were containers for faeces; the shelter is not connected to the sewers, it's a large concrete box with no connection with the outside world.

The amount of shit is beyond description. It is in fact the amount of expelled fear.

But Otherwise Life Goes On . . .

What kind of damage to one's shoulder makes it impossible to raise one's arm? I ask acquaintances who know more about it than I do. I'd like to understand. A doctor friend says it could be this or that. Bring your father so I can examine him. That was of course impossible. How could I say to the old man: "Let's go to my friend who's a good doctor, so I can find out something that interests me too?" He would certainly have refused. And given that he had recently become very sensitive, he might have been deeply offended. But let's allow old people the right to be sensitive.

In a picture book about World War II, the kind that always sell well – because pictures say more than a thousand words – I see an American soldier inspecting an S.S. prisoner. The soldier is black, and the German is a prisoner, so there was no scope for revulsion that he had been captured by a primate. The German was big, like a walking image from the cover of an S.S. promotional brochure, fair-haired. Evidently very young, probably from the last call-up, not to say the last scything.

In the photograph the young S.S. soldier had raised his left arm, and the black soldier was running his fingers over his skin.

Who knows how often I had thought of it, but now I decided: I was going to check. We were sitting in my father's flat, smoking.

I noticed that he was getting smaller. I saw a lot of brownish spots on his arms. He was evidently not in a talkative mood, but that was almost always the case. A picture of nameless guilt. As though he was waiting for his death sentence. That thought made me very uncomfortable.

"Read this! I have to go to the toilet," said my old man, taking an envelope out of his bureau. "It came yesterday, it might interest you. From Johann Kempf, if you know who that is."

Here is the letter from Herr Johann Kempf, the brother of my grandfather Ferdinand from Germany, written in blue biro, in handwriting that could be said to be illiterate:

Reutern, 7.9.

Dear nephew Đuro and everyone take a little time to read a few words in this Letter we're still alive and our health's like that of all old people and we hope the same all good to you dear relatives today we got your letter that you wrote and we understand what you wrote and need I can't do anything about it I don't know the date of my fathers birth or when he died you have to go to nuštar to the priest hes got all that in the register of births and when granddad and granma died and we had to send from our three children who had died 120 marks to the priest everyones doing allright here and theyve got married children weve got seven and 17 grandchildren only we are old im 86 and your aunt is 82 and getting near the end but still we get by somehow weve got a nice garden where we have to work but otherwise we manage lifes good weve got all we need my pensions 1,250 marks the house is big its got 13 rooms and so on until it all comes to an end there are 20 cars in the family your son can take statsangerhajt because he comes from his uncles family I worked in stuttgart and munchen till I was 65 then I got my pension and now lifes peaceful now theres war over there again and things are bad if you need food or anything let us know here theres talk that theyre taking on people at opel again so im letting you know for your son I don't know if he has a trade he doesn't need one just to be healthy if hes literate it will be easy for him you've got my address and phone number I do what I can in the garden we grow allsorts at home I had a garden like you neversaw do you go to nuštar nephew Đuro ifyou need to pay for a grave I'll send what you need

I didn't notice that Kempf had come back from the toilet and had been sitting beside me for some time, smoking like a Turk, watching me.

There was another piece of paper in the envelope, on the same squared, "commercial" paper as the letter.

On it was written, in the same handwriting, in larger letters:

My father was born in nuštar
I and your father and uncle Tonča
and your sisters we were all born in nuštar
and our greatgrandfather georg came to nuštar when marijaterezia was in power

As literature, this letter can only be compared to the prose of James Joyce.

"Have you ever considered taking *Staatsangehörigkeit?*"* asked my father.

"Now and again."

My father's death confused my daily schedule. I didn't immediately call the number in the letter from Johannes Kempf.

When I did remember to do it, a voice told me in German that Herr Johannes had died.

I thought of asking whether he had died in his bed, but I didn't.

Slavonia, our homeland, now existed only in bones swept away by spring torrents, without direction, without aim. The man I spoke to no longer understood Croatian.

But he could still recognise what language it was. A circle completely closed.

Probably only my grandfather's brother, Herr Johannes, communing with his pumpkins and beans, in a small town near Passau, had prattled to them in Croatian.

---

* German citizenship. [Author's note]

The Mark of Cain

When I found myself outside the door of my father's apartment, the clock on the tower had struck ten. It was ajar. I knew that his next-door neighbour had a key in case anything happened.

His neighbour was sitting at the table, knitting. A ball of green wool was thumping wilfully between her slippers. That must be how Kempf's heart had thumped the night before. Her husband had settled beside the stove and was sipping brandy. "We came," they said, "to sit here for a while because when someone dies, they shouldn't be alone." A candle was flickering on the bedside table.

"Mr Kempf didn't open the door as usual to take his bread and milk. We came in, he didn't reply. And his mouth was wide open. But the mirror didn't mist over."

I had known about my father's arrangement with his next-door neighbours. It had included the newspaper, but Kempf had stopped it about a year before. I no longer remembered the reason for that decision, but I could imagine many. When Kempf decided to go out, which had happened increasingly rarely, and get his own provisions, he would knock on these people's door, as though it was the reception desk at a hotel.

I asked them to leave me alone with my father, which they immediately understood.

"The police have been informed," the woman said. I thanked her.

So, "the fact of death" had set the relevant services in motion.

"They'll bring Mrs Kempf from the home only after the midday meal."

I wasn't displeased to hear this. I would be alone with my father for a time. I would not have to share him with my undestined stepmother.

"Have you called anyone else?"

They shook their heads. The old man had given instructions *in case anything happened.* There were just two telephone numbers on the little note.

"It would be good to announce it in the paper, sir."

"Of course."

"In this mad world, there's no time even for death," the woman said as they left. "Death snatched your respected father. Poor man, he didn't even have time for confession. He was a good man. But still, no-one ever came here. That's why it would be good to sit by the phone and call a few people. Because otherwise his funeral procession could be shorter than the coffin."

That my father was a good man I heard repeated many times over the following days. There was always something unfinished about it, in the rising intonation: "He was a good man, but . . ."

The neighbours had opened all the windows, the flat had got cold. I put a beech log that was not completely dry into the stove, but the embers were warm so a new flame licked it at once.

Now I was standing in front of him, alone. His expression was peaceful, as though he was sleeping a dreamless sleep; healthy, restorative. I don't know. Who knows what there is in the dreams of even the truly righteous. His chin had been tied up, as though he had toothache, his arms crossed on his chest. Those who build a whole science by studying our movements affirm that this is the stance of someone defending himself. Stupid, of course. His neighbour had crossed his arms and tied his chin. Kempf had died in his sleep, peacefully, in his own bed. In life, he hadn't had even a 5 per cent chance of achieving that.

On the shelves that were bent with the weight of printed paper I tried to find one of his collections of poems. In vain. Was it possible that old Kempf had burned his poetry?

That man, my biological father, had once walked out of my life, slamming the door, to come back into it at a time when I needed him less. Hence the two of us had always talked like two intellectuals, rarely like father and son.

About his childhood and youth, and then about his "little Polish war" I knew almost nothing. At times, and at some periods every day, he had put on the mask of a mythical drinker and bohemian. He had drunk a lot, but was never bohemian.

He would return from those bouts of his, they told me, dirty, covered in spittle and pitiful, but he came back; not admittedly to my mother, but to his second wife. He was one of those drunks who became sentimental, who wept and whined, never rough. I could imagine that he had drunk a lot in Poland as well. But those drunken bouts didn't at all fit with the image of an S.S. superman. Not in the slightest. Even when doctor friends warned him that this multiplied the risks of sudden departure to the other world, he didn't stop drinking.

But he hadn't needed alcohol for writing his poems, he hadn't learned his craft from Rimbaud or Tin Ujević. His Muse was a bit cold, sober, but never unfeeling. She had abandoned him after being fairly patient with him for a long time. So, he would have considered writing in the emanations of alcohol deceitful. Something like doping in sport. Occasionally he found in himself a source of real poetry. He remained a *poeta minor*, and you have to be able to deal with that. His stature was in knowing his measure. That can be said of very few. I consider some of his poems magnificent.

I know that in the 1990s he became reclusive, driving himself into what was to me an invisible inner world. Even his card-playing with acquaintances who weren't involved in intellectual pursuits had ceased. There's no more tedious company than writers, he used to say. From the nineties on, Kempf decided that he had no public duties anymore. He no longer did public readings of his poems, for instance. For him, those 1990s were yet again . . . a new age. And when people, some of whom he had known well, began to totter down the streets wrapped in flags, Kempf, sinking into the dark of blindness, whispered his *semper idem*. "As long as they were just boozing, they were tolerable," he used to say. "Now they've impaled themselves on ideas and history, and that's far worse."

Many of those who had known him now crossed to the other side of the street as soon as they caught sight of him. For them he was an individual who had once again run away from the flag. Kempf buttoned up his ego, growing old in good-humoured seclusion, once again a *freiwillige Gezwungene*, a forced volunteer. His social death came much sooner than his biological one.

He had followed the strike in Gdansk, and the journey of *Solidarność*. When the Wall fell, he told me he had always thought that its destruction was a matter of time because the very idea of the Wall had no inner coherence, other than physical, and that it would fall of its own accord.

Did he ever think about that phantasmagorical experience from his pre-war student days? Often. He told me in detail all that had occurred in Sremska Kamenica, from moment to moment – "The inn had been put out, now it's on fire again!" was how he ended his account.

He never recounted any of his experiences from his "little Polish war" in such detail. Once he said something like: "I saw Auschwitz from outside, it smoked day and night, don't think it didn't."

That sentence was one of a rare few.

I knew what had been burning. At the time when he was retreating around Kraków with the Soviets and the Polish Home Army, Hungarian Jews were burning.

When all is said and done, I wasn't a good son, and he wasn't a good father. Simply, he never opened up to me. Maybe that's better. He never told me why he had given up on his marriage. I know as little about that as about his Polish episode.

But now I wanted to read his poems. I couldn't find them anywhere in his apartment. I had some of his collections myself, not others. Later I bought them second-hand.

I had the stupid idea of taking off his pyjama top to see whether he still had the mark of Cain: the Gothic tattoo of his blood group, which was the same as mine, the one letter A. The sign which made him first invent the notion that he couldn't lift his left arm because of the wound sustained in Poland. He was afraid that the two of us, father and son, might once again go swimming together. However, intellectuals are not in the habit of swimming together.

I supposed that he had kept that mark, although he could easily have had it removed. That was not out of loyalty to the army he ran away from, which, had they managed to get hold of him, would have killed him on the spot. Rather, he may have wanted to bear part of the guilt, although he could not have been responsible for it because he was never truly free. There's no responsibility without freedom.

In Nürnberg, the S.S. was proclaimed an army of criminals.

It may sound paradoxical, but Kempf may have kept that seal of belonging just because in his case there could be no question of real belonging.

Some paradoxes may be resolved, some not. Some may even endure till death in one's own bed.

I sat in my father's small flat waiting for the doorbell that would pierce me like a needle. The flat looked like an antique shop. He had lived surrounded by books. Had he gone on living, books would probably have filled the entire space, and he would have been squeezed into the armchair in which he read as long as his eyes served him. Kempf had lived a turbulent life but he was a man of books. And wasn't he recognised as having restored the library in Vinkovci?

What else was left for someone who had been recruited into the German army in 1943 other than, immediately on his return, unbelievably fortunate, to renew a public library?

Kempf had always read a lot. What had he found in those books? What had he been looking for? Had he read the wrong books? A young man easily grows into some allegiance. Had books after all helped him at least in not letting him be misled? Did they arm him with scepticism against being carried away, especially by mass euphoria? Did my mother Vera read different kinds of books, or the same ones in a different way, so that she remained dedicated to what she considered her path, up until her present darkening?

The fact that towards the end of his life he had not been able to read had affected him badly.

I took one of the volumes of *War and Peace* down from the shelf and leafed through it randomly. In many places old Kempf had left his mark in the sense of: I read this! Like those who write "I was here!" on monuments.

I read an underlined passage:

"It is now clear to us what brought about the defeat of the French army in 1812. No-one will deny that the collapse of Napoleon's army was on the one hand caused by the fact that it went deep into the Russian interior late in the year, and that it was not prepared for winter fighting [. . .]. On the other hand, the meaning that the war acquired because of the burning of Russian towns and hatred for the enemy that was aroused in the Russian people [. . .]. From the French perspective, despite all their experience and Napoleon's so-called war genius, all their efforts went into reaching Moscow by the end of summer, that is to do exactly what had to be their downfall."

I know what he was actually looking for: balm that would forever put an end to the horror of immediate experience. That would neutralise the poison of its sting. He had wanted somehow to objectivise it in his poetry, but had not succeeded. His poetic voice was subdued, except in the first post-war years when everyone shouted. In Tolstoy he found a credible analysis of the German defeat.

He gave up when he realised that he couldn't escape from those experiences of his, other than by complete loss of awareness. And he didn't dare give himself over entirely to the Muse. She had retaliated by being increasingly cold to him.

That's no excuse for his soaking himself in alcohol. He had drunk also as a young man, young, happy and strong, chasing girls through the vineyards round Nuštar.

But I'm not the one who has to provide his alibis and grant him forgiveness. Who am I to judge? Am I interrogating my father?

I was startled by the bell. I led the coroner to Kempf's bed. He was in a hurry, he was irritable. An official in civilian dress, with no hint of the demonic.

"Please, put the fire in the stove out at once. Why do you think dead bodies are kept refrigerated?"

He had shamed me.

"Forgive me for being direct," the man said, pulling on thin gloves. "This is my third visit today."

The man carried out his routine examination, cast a quick glance over old medical records. I tried to mutter something about my late father's heart.

"Yes, but his liver, sir . . ." the coroner said, frowning as he read the records. "Still, nothing but good about the dead. That presumably includes the liver."

"That man drank all the rivers mentioned in the Croatian anthem. He paid his due in full."

The coroner looked at me in surprise. "Your father has just died, sir."

The doctor in civilian dress confirmed the "fact of death" and signed the piece of paper he had brought with him.

"Find an undertaker, there are plenty of them. They're all the same. There's not much philosophy here, everything has been prescribed by the state. The undertaker will transfer your father to the Mirogoj morgue. It says he was married? Usually it's the wives who wash the deceased."

"His wife's in a home, immobile."

"It doesn't have to be the wife. It could be the son. Wash your father, dress him, put his shoes on. Or leave that to the undertakers. And for heaven's sake, start telephoning around. Last night the temperature was at a record low. They say the world is warming. These days people don't like to leave their warm rooms. Do a bit of work on the final farewell! I must go. Forget fine ideas for the time being. You've got a few practical problems to solve."

However, I couldn't imagine being the one to wash him. I remember my mother washing my grandmother's dead body in our old house, white, enormous, streaked with blue and red veins. Did the generation that gave birth to us at times have something superhuman about them?

So, he had to be dressed for his "final journey". I stood in front of the open wardrobe: there stood Kempf, hanging, upright, in all his suits. There was his blue dressing gown that he had bought in anticipation of a hospital stay. On the upper shelf were hats. What should I dress him in? All those suits looked the same to me. I don't wear suits. I realised that I couldn't and didn't know how to prepare him for his "final journey". Where would that be for him – Transylvania?

I leaned over the deceased with the intention of taking the left sleeve of his pyjamas off; I wouldn't need courage for that. But maybe a dose of sneakiness? What would be changed, after all, if I saw that mark?

A ring at the door this time came as a relief.

I pressed a kiss onto my father's forehead. While he was alive I never attempted anything like that.

I had not checked the mark. Besides, did not Cain bear his mark on his brow? There were those who believed they had seen it.

I had not seen it on Kempf's forehead.

Just So Long as They Don't Fight!

The home into which I had tossed my mother like debris (I never forgave myself for that) was in the same state as the one in which Franja's mother had lived towards the end of her life. The sign at the entrance said visits were from 6 a.m. to 11 p.m. There is no other public institution where you can turn up at any time, apart from the dead of night. Few take advantage of this privilege. These people no longer remember that there is anyone out there who would be able to visit them. Nevertheless, I confess that my heart used to contract whenever I went up the steps to the door with that "6–23" inscription.

After my father's death, I visited my mother more often.

I wasn't sure whether my mother already belonged to the group of the only partially aware, that is, whether she still recognised me. Her consciousness was being slowly extinguished. She would suddenly begin to describe the way the women in the camp had lured a duck that they then roasted, and that the fat they had collected was knocked over by a clumsy movement by one of them and they had all cried out: "There goes the fat!" I had heard about that duck often. It was an anecdote that was in no way typical of camp life. I hardly heard anything about the true horror of her internment in Stara Gradiška apart from a sentence about the women who were herded to the Sava river. After the famous duck, I heard something about their radio that stopped working. I knew that the Kempfs had bought that radio, which was a triumph of socialist production, "goods for widespread use"; seamless pipes, cauldrons, turbines were less a cause for delight among the ordinary people. The radio was the real star in her memory. But the story never related what happened to the radio. Later my mother started reminding me that I had to pay for the gas in her apartment. She had been in the home for two years, there was no-one in her apartment, the gas was turned off, the bills had all been settled long ago. She often mentioned her mother, Marija, maintaining that she had been here the day before and brought plums. In her time Marija, my grandmother, had told fantastic tales about those plums of her youth, when God had walked the earth and everything in the world was plentiful, but especially plums.

So, everything in my mother's head had become muddled up in one NOW. Through that now processed everyone who had entered her life, in any way, tapping politely or bursting in violently. And of course the story also contained all who had left it. Like the bowing of the whole cast of an opera at its end.

With one exception: Kempf. It was as though he had never even entered her life.

It had nothing to do with the fact that he had died, because most of my mother's visitors were long since dead. He didn't come because he was the only one to whom that inscription about visits from 6 to 23 did not apply. Alive or dead, he had been written off.

I told her a bit about what was happening outside. And it was a turbulent time, something like a revolution, admittedly conservative. It would have been hard for her to applaud it enthusiastically.

"The reaction's muddying everything for us," Vera concluded. "How come they're not fed up? Don't they understand that their time . . . came and went? The Voice of America is what they listen to. And you see, even their Kennedy climbed down when Khrushchev banged his shoe on the lectern. When a butterfly takes off in the Kremlin, they think at once that it's an atomic warhead. When it's neither a butterfly nor a rocket but a sputnik. That's what bothers them: how come it was the Russians who sent the first satellite into space?

"And since then in Europe all they see are Russian satellites, day and night."

Vera moved into her past at a precise moment. Her time machine was set to preventative suppression. This now was her NOW. I wasn't sure that she understood anything. Was it possible that she remembered the Cuban crisis and the missiles the Russians had set up all over Cuba so they could reach New York? Did she remember the story about the red telephone?

When I told her that there could still be all sorts of trouble in this part of the world, that a lot of people had gone astray, many heads had been turned, that a lot of people had already been killed, that tiny children had come to Zagreb from Vukovar with grey hair, that there could be a third world war, that everything here was falling apart, she suddenly stared at me as though that was the first time she saw me properly, and asked: "Why doesn't Tito talk to the people?"

I thought of telling her that Tito was hunting, that is, in the eternal hunting grounds, but decided against it.

"I'd like to go among the people, to the villages, but you see how I am, my legs are weak. But I used to know how to speak. I'm sure that I could put everyone back on the right path, with the right values, and that I would turn every meeting in the remotest backwoods into a collective of decent people. They always send me where things are most difficult."

One day I told her that there were more and more T.B. patients in the country because there was more and more poverty, to which she immediately responded that her brother had visited her the day before and that his cavities were still open ... "I asked him when he was going to come back from the camp, and my brother replied never. That is, not exactly never, that's not what he said, but: 'Expect me when you see me.'"

I didn't tell her that the memorial plaque with the name of her brother and my uncle had been smashed and that the school in Vinkovci was no longer called after my father.

Even if I had carefully informed her that Tito was dead, she might have said, "Then there's nothing to be done," and in the next sentence perhaps told me that she had seen him the evening before on television and that he looked well, despite those problems with his leg "which makes us all fearful and that leg hurts all of us day and night". She might even have said that he had been to see her the previous day and that they had sat together in the dining room discussing T.V. and his speech to the masses.

Vera was getting lost, and those processes that were erasing parts of her memory were preventative. However, I saw no significance in the fact that she could no longer name individual fruits but lumped several together as "fruit". I brought her various fruits, oranges, apples, figs. She called sweets "little squares", etc. Here Alzheimer triumphed. In other aspects of her NOW she was still a sovereign being. She herself chose and erased, preserving the core of what she felt was the meaning of her life. Somehow, she remained the subject despite the defeat of the project she considered the meaning of her existence.

Alright, never mind the fruit. What I found hard was that I wasn't always certain my mother knew who I was. On the other hand, did I know who she, Vera, was? What can we really know about other people even when they are half of us? Had not Vera got lost because she was completely focused only on truly useful knowledge? What things had been like in the Forest, where her brother was and when he would come back, what the opposition was doing, which had to be constantly watched and kept in one's sights. The Soviets against the West and the other way round, activism in the countryside, cultural enlightenment, the liberation of women from the chains of the patriarchy, habits of hygiene, hybrid kinds of maize, how to increase the productivity of fruit trees, the general harm of sweets to the teeth . . .

But again, there were moments when Vera would surface from her confused, but in its own way lucid, darkness, and gaze at me as though in this NOW of mine she could see all the phases of my life: from the difficult birth, the umbilical cord that might have suffocated me, breast-feeding, my successes at school, to my first drinking bouts, which could never be compared with Kempf's; from whimpering whose cause was hard to discern, to my first waywardness and love pains that came with the first hairs on the chin; from my voice breaking to police searches in 1968. As though she could look through me and see what was going to happen. I admit that I found it uncomfortable: as though she was not looking at me but at a glass ball. Not the little one where it is always snowing, but a large one that really did hold all my own and her NOWs and there was room for everyone and everything . . . Because when I measure Vera and Kempf's shared life and my own, mine contained fewer fateful events, which could be a definition of moderate happiness. I had rarely met "history in action", and Napoleon on a horse like poor Hegel – never.

But now out there history was thundering again. Events were piling in on each other.

Mostly, that was no promise of happiness. Hegel maintained

that stable periods in a people's history were blank sheets. Here in this NOW, history is seething, and the cherry trees in suburban gardens do not blossom of their own accord but try to adapt to the blossoming of a nation.

As we sat in the dining room which was almost constantly aired, but in vain, Vera heard the shouts of a surging crowd passing down the street. She heard police sirens as well. She asked me whether something was burning again and if so where.

"People are passing," I said.

"People are passing. The question is: who's coming?" Suddenly she stared at me with that clear gaze that was capable of sending a chill through me: I saw that she knew where she was, that she understood everything, that she knew who I was, she knew who she was and how things were with her, that is, where we had despatched her – like junk. And, especially, she knew what was happening outside.

The demonstrations were now virtually across the road from the home. One could clearly make out what was being shouted and how, over it all, as though gasping for breath above turbulent water, a speaker was struggling to get the crowd's attention.

"Just as long as they don't fight," Vera said.

Vera died in her sleep, like my father, Kempf, whom she outlived. She would have been entirely indifferent had it been the other way round.

There is a popular belief that before death, particularly in sleep, people run through the film of their life, reminding the soul of what awaits it in the other world. What is contradictory here is that the dying person is expected to assess his or her life objectively. It's true that the dead are reluctant to lie. Nevertheless, all the sects that engage with such questions leave the question of the meaning of someone's life to another judge.

Working as an activist on the enlightenment of the broad masses, Vera had denied this prejudice like all other superstitions, for instance, the one about the child born with its umbilical cord round its neck: that it would have bad luck. The greatest idealist I had ever known, Vera was a materialist when it came to the first and last things.

Man is a material being, there is no such thing as the soul, God does not exist, after death all that remains is what a person has created in his lifetime, Vera read to the peasant women in her literacy class.

Vera Kempf's Dreams Before Her Death

She's clinging to a railing that could be a roller-coaster at a children's playground it's a sunny day although the sun's a pale disc everything around it is black as pitch a red ribbon is winding out of her womb from white helmets gleam miners' lamps in the shape of stars the soviets are trying to help her or perhaps rather something that is wriggling at the other end of the ribbon and waving its little feet their gestures show that the situation is critical they must be well practised but this is something else it's a matter of a child such a tiny cosmonaut had never been seen they don't know what to do it's also in a spacesuit short rapid movements someone who's trying to tear himself off the sea bed and reach the surface to breathe people are waving wildly from the platform of the ship wanting to encourage her you've given birth he's been born watch the ribbon I'm new to this help me we have to get him onto the ship I can't hold onto the ribbon any longer it's going to drag my womb out it hurts terribly people in white endeavour to catch the little spacesuit with a butterfly net without success the little spacesuit lifts a tiny hand the fingers are barely formed he's waving he's ever smaller now only a white dot in the immense blackness which is how the distant galaxy looks

like a tuft of silk

Vera sat up in bed and screamed. A nurse came and straightened her pillow. "You had a bad dream? I'll bring tea."

Vera said nothing.

That's not my dream, thought Vera. It's my mother's dream, it's about her son, my brother, and that business with space is a deception. I'm being deceived with a dream that isn't mine. The night before she heard about her son's death she dreamed that he, my brother, was waving from the distance, becoming ever smaller, until he completely disappeared into the earth, like a mouse in a field.

Give me my own dream! Why do I have to fight tooth and nail for everything in life? Giving birth to a baby with its umbilical cord round his neck is not a subject for Party criticism, and to believe that this is ominous is plain stupid. And the Russians have no connection with it whatsoever.

celebration I don't know what's being celebrated we're holding hands as we step singing round a table that's entirely covered in sandwiches cakes drinks I know for sure that some of these men and some women had fallen when we were still in the forest the man next to me died last year I spoke at his funeral I'm not so old that I couldn't remember that I've seen many of them off I'm good at that I don't get nervous speaking to a crowd I'll find the time to prepare I read the biography I'm on close terms with sorrow maybe he's come to thank everyone we're all so old old-age is a terrible thing we only see others like us

young people don't believe us why are we so old what's the point of old-age we sing through the woods and mountains how often the same song on my right is a man who didn't come back from goli* I knew his wife as well she's no longer alive either their marriage was annulled there she is at the other end of the table how primitive we were now that's all forgotten we all hold each other's hands we've no reason to be ashamed of our youth

isn't that it – that we have nothing to be ashamed of – isn't that the reason we're so alone those who have something to be ashamed of always doll themselves up and shove themselves into groups while we're always alone we keep harassing those young people do something pull yourselves together it'll be too late it's already too late those of us here are all almost dead

you can already see some of their bones through their skin that's terrible still the song must not be interrupted the column must go on even in a circle there aren't any more of us but we go on

we hold each other's hands tightly if only as sacks full of dry bones over there then we had a good time we didn't believe in the other world so there was nothing left for us apart from being immortal and we are as proved by this danse macabre death is only a temporary discharge from the battle then there is always an event like this there are lots of celebrations then we all get together somehow people hear about it we have our methods everyone answers the invite

the young watch this they don't believe us they can't share our ancient enthusiasms

you can't teach anyone anything it's not worth even trying they're so cynical while we are just simply dead we don't count

---

* Goli otok, a barren, uninhabited island that was the site of a political prison in use when Croatia was part of Yugoslavia, between 1949 and 1989. [Translator's note]

and the young don't believe in immortality they want to live now and immediately I don't blame them that's what I wanted too and I don't believe in immortality

I still want that we still want we want

> Through the woods and mountains
> Of our proud land
> March bands of Partisans
> Bearing victory's glory

here are the young they are our new manpower mainly in new suits they're bored standing by the window watching the crowd on the square they won't join our ring dance which they may despise today they dance differently they're waiting for us to stop our braying and move away from the table full of sandwiches so that they can come

there's still something we want

and that's why they bring the partisan cauldron into the clearing we take our clothes off as we are old drooping men with bellies and huge chests that hang like the tits of old women old-age is clever but ugly pieces of wood under the cauldron of water crackle merrily it's already steaming we stand in line modestly covering our hair and genitals here's the ballerina too an old woman now dry as a twig with her accompanist he is a skeleton who draws wonders out of his violin even now he too wants to be young again I think everyone deserves that we deserve to be young again just because we have no reason to be ashamed of our youth that's why one by one we climb onto the tree trunk and jump into the cauldron

we come out after splashing cheerfully about to the loud encouragement of all those waiting in line with military discipline young as we were beautiful healthy and full of hope

I run I am that little girl running from the room to the well I see my coal-black eyes in it

I wash them with soap bartol who I can't see in the shadow says or whispers those are the loveliest eyes and here is my son the three of us are the same age and we go down the roller-coaster the day is a gift fine spring

The nurse related to the morning shift that Vera, before she died, had laughed in her sleep.

"We thought that her whole life was running through her head then and that it would go on for a bit longer. When we turned her onto her side, all the tension in her face was gone. She seemed somehow to glow. Your mother has gone to heaven."

I think that's true. Although the question of faith has nothing to do with heaven. They hand me the last medical records. On one is written T.P.

She would have died of a tumour on the pancreas, in pain, if she had not escaped into death first.

I sat on the edge of her bed. Vera was already prepared, that's the routine here.

She lay, bathed, lightly perfumed with a scent she liked, in a new nightdress that she had assigned in writing to her "final journey". It seemed to me that she had shrunk still further, and she was very thin. Her face looked completely tranquil. They had tied her chin up with a handkerchief, but something of her smile still remained on her face. I lit a candle and secured it with its wax to a saucer, moving aside the tea from the night before that she had not touched.

I kissed my mother's lips that seemed to me had not yet grown cold.

In the course of the day, I resolved the "outstanding duties".

It turned out to be exceptionally difficult to agree that there be a star on the death notice. I had to argue in the undertakers' office. There was everything in their computer: you could get crosses in any configuration. And other sects, including Jewish, could easily be satisfied in this last requirement. But there was no star. They told me no-one asked for it anymore. In the end the undertakers' employee said he would draw it himself. "Anything's possible nowadays," he went on explaining, "are you this or that – and it can all be decided with a couple of moves of the mouse."

Things went more smoothly at the stonemason's, in a workshop next to the cemetery. Although it took longer to engrave a star than a cross, the price was the same. How much would it cost to engrave nothing?

For her, however, the star was her due: she died under a star.

I paid for her to be seen off with a song. A small male choir sang. Nothing bellicose. In the end it was a song of thanks, "For your every word . . ."

Vera had lived in harmony with her decisions and her choices.

My father could have permitted himself, probably in a last wish, unknown to me in detail, that there should be nothing beside his name. He lay in my stepmother's family grave, was he resting? In that grave he was as much a stranger as he had always been.

Once he said to me: "As long as your mother is alive, I can't tell you why I left her." But his calculation was wrong since he died before her.

Who would be able to relate his pre-death dream?

Only the unborn, the shadows that hover in the abyss. They know, but that knowledge is useless, just as a shadow is not real if there is no body between it and the sun.

Georg Kempf's Exit Strategy

Sofija your name means wisdom and in constantinople it would
be a church I'd like to see your tits oh no you can't why not
because I say so I'll buy you ducats I've got ducats have you got
enough to cover your tits I've got as many as I need well you
need a lot don't be crude I'm not being crude I'm glad you exist
I'm glad I exist as well just as you are that's just how I am and
I'm happy with that

I'd like to see your breasts
    when the time comes then I'll see everything
    you'll see everything when the time comes
    who knows when that will be
    it'll be when it is don't force me stay on your side
    I'm itching
    what's itching
    something's creeping up my back
    you've lain down on an anthill
    I'll move
you don't even know how buttons work have you had a woman
yet you bungler women's buttons do up on the inside get off me
you bungler
    what do you think you're doing on me
    her nipples are violet with a mass of little red veins

that form a flower round it
I was almost startled
under her neck a line drawn as if by a ruler she scratched
herself picking blackberries
I was startled
by the unexpected colours of those nipples
I think you were startled
why you're as innocent as I am
we're both innocent
but we're not exactly pure lambs
they're calling me home
you haven't picked blackberries
help me pick blackberries
come on you know at least that buttons do up on the inside
it's so complicated
you'll learn
I'll learn everything
and who's going to teach you
you will
I don't know how to
you know I feel you know some are born knowing
hungarian girls do you go to the hungarian girls the jews
I went once
and what did you learn
to drink
you don't say
I drank plum brandy it was no good
come and try my old man's we make real brandy
I thought you sold textiles
a real slavonian house has to make its own brandy
but you're serbs

but you like me, don't you
yes
so what if we're serbs
no problem
you're a švabo your folk came from far away
that's right
when will you show me your poems
one day
go on you must have some in your pocket
no I carry them in my head
go on tell me one
marvellous maiden may I nibble you a bit
that's no poem
what is it
impudence
just a bit go on let me
it's late the shop's shut up for today
look what lovely blackberries
let's get away from the road dogs have peed on these
come on no-one can see us here let me see your tits again
god you're pushy
just a bit
go on beg me I like it when you beg especially in vain time's
up for today
little hunter.

No doubt it's a monastery now. Franja explained to me that he'd been thick as thieves with the Father Superior and that he'd been thick as thieves with the custodian of the monastery. And she would take us to the cells where the nuns lived. She wouldn't be able to take us further than one little room with a grille. But they wanted to see Franja's girlfriend, who was now a nun. Behind the grille stood a masked woman, like a veiled Turkish woman.

But it wasn't Franja's love. It was Sofija behind the grille. I knew her by her voice, but I couldn't see her. Now she was dead too. It was her voice, but not her thoughts. Someone had borrowed her voice, whether her body, her breasts, nipples as well I couldn't say, she was completely covered and in that habit there may have been nothing other than dried flowers and dust.

Some people I had never seen before came up to me. They asked me to take down my trousers. I felt terribly uncomfortable. They looked at my underpants, at my cock which they turned left and right with a stick . . . Who are you? We are those whose hearts have been circumcised, and not . . . They let me go with a kick in the backside . . . you're not even a Jew. Who are you? Donau-Schwabe, what kind of animal is that? Get lost.

Oh, how many times have I had to take my trousers down.

Ania who was now bobbing on top of my humiliated penis and asking me to come inside her.

What if you conceive?

Don't worry, I've counted the days. My child won't be born while the world is the way it is now. It's all been calculated, both defeat and victory!

Ania who had won only to lose everything.

I betrayed Ania. For the *bumashka*, a piece of paper. I betrayed all the women whose paths crossed with mine.

Here I am among my own kind. I'm standing in the middle of a yelling crowd. On top of a column sits a huge rat whose tail is wrapped round the pedestal on top of it; it's a snake's tail. Thousands of tails respond to him, rising into the air, above all their voices, towards the seducer under the heavens. He is becoming a monument, his movements are increasingly slow until they stop altogether and that pose characteristic of him, with his right paw raised ... his tail is now turning yellow like brass and now it's more a snake than a tail.

The millions below the column raise their right paws, stiffened in a Roman greeting.

It now seems to me that the hideous snout from the top of the column is looking only at me ... and that all the millions of them are looking only at me as though I were suddenly completely naked in the middle of a vast square or theatre ... For I had not raised my paw which still seems like a hand to me I ought to have cut my fingernails I omitted to do that last week because I was busy we live at a crazy tempo but now we're all frozen here standing in a living tableau

Everything hurts, my heart leaps out, circumcised, and looks at me. It has already left my body.

I can no longer maintain my proportions. I am shrinking, I see that I'm now only up to others' waists ... now I'm barely higher than the heel of their boots.

Must I now think of those who gave birth to me and those who didn't? For years I've been waiting for my son to ask me: "What did you do in the war, Dad?" I told him to go and see for himself, and recommended Baedeker.

> I didn't ask. I waited for you to tell me yourself. There's nothing in Baedeker about your little Polish war.

From the distance, in the shape of a field mouse, hidden in the rushes on the bank of the Danube, I watch an enormous ship on which the crew has gone berserk and they're all beating each other up. Prayers can be heard, of all possible kinds, and each one is trying to outshout the prayer of his rival. It's that kind of age:

fellow-sufferers are transformed into opponents. They crush and tread on each other in the vestibule of God's rooms. The ship has no commander, he died long ago and it is being carried along by the will of the current. It will crash into the Djerdap cliffs . . . it will be a shipwreck on a grand scale which will drag many into the depths. God changes with time, unfortunately. Kempf knows that this view is blasphemous, but he learns from experience. A political God no longer likes prayers in too many languages, he will punish the Babel confusion again. The log raft once had a better chance, at least fifty-fifty.

Are they there, in the depths, the glass palaces and in the glass palaces the souls of the already drowned?

Can one sail this river to reach the infinite forests, already cleared, meadows full of flowers, nectar, scents, is this the way to Transylvania?

Unlikely.

The fish are surprised. But there's never a clever one.

Off you all go, however many you are. I forbid sympathy.

Ich, Georg Kempf, am vanishing, and I'm glad of that.

nihil

Send-Off and Greeting

My father Kempf's funeral was held on a Friday afternoon, when people are reluctant to leave their homes even for more important reasons. He would be buried in the town known as Agram in German, but my father would never have called it that. Zagreb is a town whose finest asset is its cemetery. For instance: Bollé's arcades.

On the morning of the funeral the telephone rang:

"Mr Kempf, this afternoon is the funeral of your father, a very honourable man."

"With whom do I have the pleasure?"

"We would like to provide a guard of honour for Comrade Kempf."

I say nothing.

"There'd be nothing to pay, sir."

"Where did you get my number?"

"You're not in the Underground. Not yet."

On that January day the cold was Siberian, frozen birds fell off the ridge of the mortuary roof.

Hardly anyone came to my father's final send-off. The Union of Croatian Writers participated in the form of a wreath. Since there was no official writer to lay it on the coffin, that duty was assumed by a neighbour. Another wreath bore the inscription: *Society of National Readiness*. As no-one came forward, the undertaker put it on the coffin.

A few pensioners from his building were the only audience. Fewer people than the books Kempf had published.

The priest had no clue about the person he was seeing off. He read from the Bible about the Crucifixion and the barbarians on the other two crosses. The Pharisees, that is, writers, come off badly in the Bible, worse than robbers. The priest was very thin, and the thin are even less able to withstand the cold, so he kept hopping.

All at once, with a crack, a branch broke off and all those standing round the open grave felt uneasy.

The silver hoar frost that the branch scattered turned their coats white. For a moment we looked like a wedding party sprinkled with confetti. Enough of the macabre! Let's brush off this paraphernalia!

As though it had been waiting for the crack of that unfortunate branch, suddenly on the road beside the graveyard where we were burying my father, a Mercedes drew up with a terrible screech of its brakes.

A man got out of the car, elegantly dressed, evidently elderly, and everyone afterwards affirmed that what was unusual about him was that he lacked part of his skull. They could all see this as soon as he took off his hat.

The man dragged a black cross from the car, with HIAG written on it in white letters, he shuffled up to the grave and threw it onto the coffin in the grave. He returned equally quickly to the car and sped away, pressing the accelerator so hard that the tyres screeched again.

Of the few people who were there, I was the only one who knew what HIAG meant.*

A funeral is a send-off from the point of view of those who remain, but it is at the same time a greeting to the new arrival from those who have already left. Perhaps there is a law whereby the fewer people at the send-off the more deceased people there are to greet him. But that could be a delusion to comfort beggars and foreigners.

Almost no-one had followed Kempf's coffin. The funeral procession was shorter than the coffin.

But there were many settled on the surrounding graves. So Terezija, my grandmother, was sitting in a family vault the iron gate of which had been unlocked for this occasion by the residents' kindness.

Ania Sadowska was hiding behind an angel carved from white stone. She had died in the late 1950s in her Siberian exile: one morning as cold as this one she had got out of bed, fallen backwards and was forever stilled: pulmonary embolism. That can kill you anywhere, but for "fascists" it was obligatory to die in Siberia. She built her political career long after her death.

"Liszt" and Katarzyna, the Polish artistic couple, were already casting angry glances around: there was no piano anywhere in the cemetery, nor a table. How come? The deceased had seemed to be a gentleman.

Poland was otherwise abundantly represented. Many of the Poles who had made their way here were not well liked in their lifetime.

---

* Hilfgemeinschaft auf Gegenseitigkeit der ehemaligen Waffen-S.S. (Society for mutuality and support for the former Waffen-S.S.). [Author's note]

Here was Kempf's master, the one who had sold him on for a pig. He was the victim of an accident, he had ended up under an Ursus tractor, but that was in the National Republic of Poland.

The funeral clearly lacked organisation in that it was not clear who had the right to approach the grave.

Here was S.S. Rottenführer of course, the drill sergeant, who had come to say farewell to his lad Sturmmann Kempf who had his foibles but was, from a purely military viewpoint, reliable and in terms of his physical efforts persistent. The sergeant had died of heart disease in the midst of the German economic miracle in which he had not succeeded. His attempts as a property dealer had failed.

Kempf's grandmother was seen sitting in a grave, but my grandfather had come as well, he had chosen to strut around. He had been, in his lifetime, very enterprising. In death he had barely calmed down. In Yugoslavia, only the state had been able to sell pig fat, in Germany the talk was about margarine. It was good that he had died in time so he stayed to rest in the graveyard at Nuštar. Kempf's parents' memories were important although they were not reliable. Everyone gives their children a certain leeway.

Franja didn't come. Like those two letters, the news of Kempf's death could not be conveyed to him as his address has remained unknown to this day.

Those who in their lifetime had not had to wear a uniform came in the best they could find. But fashion changes fast, and that was the only thing about this whole solemn occasion that was a little bit, permit me, ghostly.

We note Alyosha and Sergey Abramovich, commissar, together. They both fell in one of the last large-scale purges on the eve of Stalin's death.

All of this, hidden behind a weeping willow tree, was overseen by Dr Schlauss. He had made a good career after the war, he ran a private clinic, he had died at peace, respected and wealthy. His obituary was published on half a page of the *Frankfurter Allgemeine Zeitung*. That was a real success story.

All in all, those shreds of perspectives and recollections were roughly what Georg Kempf was, a dead man such as one could only wish for.

Leon Mordechai, his learned colleague, brought to Mirogoj all the sparks that had been allotted to him, the way the Almighty had placed them in people when the Box of Light itself had fallen to pieces. But he did not push himself into the foreground. Kempf was, he maintained, an interesting collocutor although too attached to his delusions.

There, in those memories, every little spark was counted, every shaving, every chance encounter. The memories of the living would evaporate far more quickly.

Branko Šalamun, who was taken to Auschwitz and ended up under the gas, sent his apologies. He expressed conventional condolences and a welcome.

Where were the lads who had burned in Sremska Kamenica? In the heat of their tussle, they hadn't heard the sad news.

Sending warm greetings to the deceased, Franja's mother also excused herself. He was her son's friend who had been granted a fortunate old age.

Today's Poland was represented by Ania Sadowska, posthumously rehabilitated and decorated, with the rank of colonel. Where were the Partisans?

History does not recognise the category of justice and does not suffer from mercy.

No matter what, Kempf's death was not a death of reconciliation. People were reconciled to it, but it reconciled no-one.

Kempf had not succeeded in anything apart from remaining a stranger. And there is nowhere one can be a more complete stranger than in one's homeland. Hence his "final send-off" was attended mostly by those who no longer existed and, even here, where all are equal, they kept to one side.

The dead reveal themselves reluctantly to the living because they are greatly saddened by the reactions of their descendants.

The participants in the burial went back to the town that had totally frozen, it seemed that no-one lived there anymore.

They had seen the stranger off. If they had composed an image of him made of the little stones of their recollections, that mosaic would have remained blurred. Roughly like an ancient mosaic sunk in the sea, so the rocking of the waves blur what could be discerned.

Beside the raised mound covered in flowers, among which the wreath from the Writers' Union stood out, there was no-one anymore. They had all hurried down the hill to catch the tram that would take them into town, where they would be able to warm their living bodies to their hearts' content.

I, the deceased's son, went down into town with them. I didn't want to stay in the cemetery alone. There was nothing more for me to do there.

Now that Mirogoj was emptied of all visitors, after the end of "working hours", the dead dared approach undisturbed to stand by the grave of the new arrival. Colleague Mordechai, however, judged that it was better for him to stay behind the tree.

They were all silent, sorting out their recollections. Kempf's image was becoming, from moment to moment, increasingly clear, while remaining a mosaic.

After a long eloquent silence of those present, Ferdinand Kempf, trader in pig fat and Kempf's respected father, stood at the edge of the open grave and spoke.

"My son! I'm glad you didn't do anything up there that would have made it hard for you to come back."

As he began his formal speech, the others present began to cough and look at one another. Ferdinand Kempf stopped talking. It felt incongruous for a long dead father to speak at his son's grave.

Kempf had left two widows, one of whom didn't want to wear black and the other no longer wore anything else. Vera didn't come because as far as she was concerned burials were not reconciliation hearings.

The other women in his life were there: Sofija and Ania Sadowska.

The Polish woman who had danced on the table at the Zimmerman tavern admitted to her rivals that of all the soldiers in the patrol she had liked Sturmmann Kempf best, because his tight S.S. uniform was very chic.

Ilonka, his Novi Sad "love" for the night, came to tell Kempf he had made a serious mistake in not marrying her.

Then she added:

"There's no use crying over spilt milk!"

"That's not true!"

That was spoken by a woman who had hidden behind a black marble gravestone, not pushing herself into the front line. Hardly anyone heard her. Sofija's truth remained a whisper.

Some of the victims left this send-off to the perpetrators.

Everyone knows that the first morning in a grave is the hardest.

The first morning found Kempf thinking about Sofija. He was the only one who had understood what she had meant and sorrow began to melt his stopped heart.

Among the figures crowding round his grave or, maintaining discretion, just observing what was happening, there was no sign of the dog he had saved from freezing in the lake ice.

Among the assets of his life, Kempf had counted on that dog.

Dogs whine at the graves of those who were close to them. But the canine genus knows that not one of them had deceived the cherubs guarding the gates of heaven, not even the most loyal bitch. Dogs remain on this side.

How ridiculous! Here I am, in the soil in which I was born. The dog could have found me.

I didn't go anywhere, not ever really.

Although old people often get lost. That's how Kempf was directed by the child of the Volksdeutsche who had found the inscription A POLE LIVES HERE on his family home. There are no secure addresses in this world.

I must remember the address of my new permanent residence: Section 99, grave 75.

It would be wise to sew it under the lining.

Zagreb – Ploča, 2012–15

Some Sources

My parents' written legacy, biographical sketches, letters

Baxter, Ian, *Hitler's Defeat on the Eastern Front, 1943–45,* Pen & Sword Military, Barnsley, 2009

Böddeker, Günter, *Die Flüchtlinge, die Vertreibung der Deutschen im Osten,* Ullstein, Munich–Berlin, 2000

Browning, Christopher R., *Reserve Police Battalion 101 and the Final Solution in Poland,* Harper Perennial, New York, 1993

Die Donau, katalog uz izložbu, Eigenverlag des Historischen Museums der Stadt, Vienna, 1996

Druždž Satanovska, Zofija, *Neutrte staze, iz partizanskih uspomena,* Prosvjeta, Zagreb, 1948

Engelking, Barbara und Helga Hirsch (eds), *Unbequeme Wahrheiten, Polen und sein Verhältnis zu den Juden,* Suhrkamp, Frankfurt am Main, 2008

Gross, Jan T., *Fear, Antisemitism in Poland After Auschwitz,* Random House Trade, New York, 2007

Hilberg, Raoul, *The Destruction of the European Jews,* Holmes & Meier, Teaneck, 1985

Jakovljević, Ilija, *Konclogor na Savi,* Konzor, Zagreb, 1999

Klecel, Marek (ed.), *Polen zwischen Ost und West, Polnische Essays des 20. Jahrhunderts,* Suhrkamp, Frankfurt am Main, 1995

Leidinger/Moritz/Chippler, *Schwarzbuch der Habsburger,* Deuticke, Vienna–Frankfurt am Main, 2003

Maeterlinck, Maurice, *La vie des fourmis*, 1930

Magris, Claudio, *Dunav*, Fraktura, Zaprešić, 2013

Maslarić, Božidar, *Moskva, Madrid, Moskva*, Prosvjeta, Zagreb, 1952

Piller, Matija i Ljudevit Mitterpacher, *Putovanje po Požeškoj županiji i Slavoniji, 1782, godine*, reprint, Osijek, 1993

Prica, Čedo, *Bilježnice namjernog sjećanja*, three volumes, Konzor, Zagreb, 1991, 2001, Profil multimedija, Zagreb, 2006

Schödl, Gunther, *Deutsche Geschichte im Osten Europas*, Siedler Verlag, Berlin, 1995

Šnajder, Đuro, *Ljubavnici u tuđim očima*, Naprijed, Zagreb, 1958

Šnajder, Đuro, Pet stoljeća hrvatske književnosti, knjiga 145, MH–Zora, Zagreb, 1977

Šnajder, Đuro, *Znoj za čelik*, Novo pokoljenje, Zagreb, 1950

Šnajder, Slobodan, "Iluminacije", Književna republika, Zagreb, 2014

Šnajder, Slobodan, "Umrijeti u Hrvatskoj", Književna republika, Zagreb, 2018

Wegner, Bernd, *Hitlers Politische Soldaten, Die Waffen–S.S. 1933–1945*, 9th edition, Ferdinand Schöningh, Padeborn–Munich–Vienna–Zürich, 2010

Werner, Harold, *Fighting Back, a Memoir of Jewish Resistance in WW2*, Columbia University Press, New York, 1992